Dear Reader

Welcome! There
second chance at
these two stories.
couple back toget
Mine. And in *You Were On My Mind*, Margot
Early reunites her heroine with a husband and
daughter she can't even remember.

Two wonderful stories in one volume, we hope
you enjoy them!

The Editors

All the characters in this book have no existence outside the imagination of the author, and have no relation whatsoever to anyone bearing the same name or names. They are not even distantly inspired by any individual known or unknown to the author, and all the incidents are pure invention.

Harlequin, Harlequin Duets and Colophon are trademarks used under licence.

First published in Great Britain 1999 by Harlequin Mills & Boon Limited, Eton House, 18-24 Paradise Road, Richmond, Surrey TW9 1SR

CHILD OF MINE © Lynn Erickson 1998
YOU WERE ON MY MIND © Margot Early 1998

ISBN 0 373 59726 6

20-9908

Printed and bound in Great Britain by Caledonian International Book Manufacturing Ltd, Glasgow

Child of Mine
LYNN ERICKSON

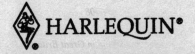
HARLEQUIN®

TORONTO • NEW YORK • LONDON
AMSTERDAM • PARIS • SYDNEY • HAMBURG
STOCKHOLM • ATHENS • TOKYO • MILAN • MADRID
PRAGUE • WARSAW • BUDAPEST • AUCKLAND

CHAPTER ONE

LENA PORTILLO RAN a tight ship at Al's Auto Body. She was secretary, mother, slave driver and psychologist all in one. In her cluttered office in front of the cavernous garage on Canoga Avenue in Canoga Park, California, she managed every facet of Al's business—everything except the actual repairs.

Al must have known he had a treasure; in the five years Lena had worked for him, he'd seen more profits and had more peace of mind than he'd ever had before. He paid her pretty darn well, too—for a *female,* he loved to joke. Lena's last raise made her salary thirty-two thousand dollars a year, more than she ever could have imagined, but increasingly less than she needed. Like everyone else, she guessed.

Lena hung up the phone and glanced at the grimy schoolroom clock on the wall. Four o'clock. Her mother, Gloria, would have picked Kimmy up at school by now. *Thank heavens for Mom,* Lena thought. She couldn't imagine how she'd hold down this job without Gloria's help.

Lena punched the last key to finish the weekly payroll, then pushed print, and the printer in the corner started whirring and spitting out payroll checks. Al's five employees, not to mention Lena, were waiting for them. They all lived paycheck to paycheck, working hard, raising families. Ordinary people.

Lena knew her co-workers well, and their wives and children. Their wives were mostly in the same boat as Lena was—working, harried, with never enough hours in the day, never enough money, just making ends meet, worried all the time.

She was just reaching for the phone to call Gloria and talk to Kimmy when it rang again. She picked it up and wedged it between her ear and shoulder. "Al's Auto Body," she said while tearing the paychecks apart, ready to hand out to the men.

"Is my car done?" asked a female voice. "The Mercedes?"

"Um, which one? Is this Mrs. Fairhaven?"

"No, no. I'm Lucy Hubbard. The blue 350SL."

"Oh, Mrs. Hubbard." Lena got up and looked through the window into the shop. "Just a second, let me check."

She put the woman on hold and pressed the intercom button. "Harry," she said, "is the blue Mercedes done?"

Harry's voice came back, tinny. "Nope. Waiting for the paint. Monday."

Back to the phone. "Mrs. Hubbard, your car will be ready Tuesday morning." She *always* gave the guys extra time.

"Tuesday? But I need it this weekend."

"I'm sorry, Mrs. Hubbard, but the paint color is a very unusual one," she improvised, "and we've had to order it from the manufacturer. You wouldn't want your car to have the wrong paint on one fender."

"Oh, God," the woman said petulantly. "I *need* it."

She probably had five other cars in her oversize garage, Lena thought, glancing at the woman's address on the invoice. Beverly Hills.

"It'll be ready first thing Tuesday morning. I think I told you Wednesday originally, Mrs. Hubbard, so this is actually early. I'm really sorry if we've inconvenienced you.''

"Oh, all right. Are you sure it'll be ready Tuesday?''

"Absolutely.''

"I'll send Rufio to pick it up.''

"Fine, Mrs. Hubbard. Should we bill you?''

"Send it to my husband's office. Do you have that address?''

"Let's see.'' Lena checked the work order. "Yes, I have it. Thanks, Mrs. Hubbard.''

She put the phone down and shook her head. These women—and men—with so much money that a two-thousand-dollar dented fender was no more serious to them than a broken fingernail. And the Hubbards' insurance would cover most of it anyway. Lena, of course, had to send her own bills to the insurance company. Someone, she supposed, took care of all Mrs. Hubbard's problems.

She reached for the phone again and dialed Gloria's number. She did this every day, an afternoon ritual, to talk to her daughter and reassure her mother she'd be there by five-thirty to pick Kimmy up so Gloria could get to her job as hostess at a popular steak house. She wished she could be at home all day for her six-year-old daughter, a regular *Leave It To Beaver* mother, but things didn't always work out the way you wanted them to. She had sure learned *that* the hard way.

Gloria's phone rang, once, twice, three, four times. Lena glanced at the clock again—four-fifteen—and a tiny stab of anxiety tickled her belly. Gloria was *always* home by now. And sometimes Kimmy would pick up the phone herself, her piping little voice, always excited, recounting to her mother the day's events. "And, Mommy, Mrs. Sherby let me *hold* the frog, and I got to read... There was a hard word, Mommy, but I sounded it out, and Tommy Daniels wanted to trade lunches, but I wouldn't, and..."

Kimmy. Kimberly Lee Portillo. With her big dark eyes and brown hair she could easily be Lena's natural daughter, but she wasn't. She was adopted, abandoned by her birth mother, a crack baby, a tiny screaming bundle left at a church six years ago. The minister had called the Los Angeles police, and a squad car had been sent to investigate. The two young cops on the call had been shocked, horrified, and they'd taken the infant to the nearest hospital.

Lena filed some invoices, stacked orders to go out tomorrow morning. Four thirty-five. She'd wait five minutes, then call Gloria again. Five minutes, she was thinking when one of the workers opened the door, came in and plunked himself down in the folding chair in front of her desk. He smelled of grease and paint thinner and was wiping his hands on an old rag.

"What now, Ken?" Lena asked, eyeing him.

"It's Stephanie. Got a minute?"

"God, Ken," she began, sighing. His wild relationship with his girlfriend was driving everyone nuts. And he never stopped asking for advice.

"She says last night was it. We had this fight, see, right after dinner at—"

"You want my opinion?" Lena broke in. "End it. Find some nice quiet woman. Stephanie's a neat lady, but you two mix like oil and water. It's never going to improve, either. Now, that'll be a hundred dollars for my services. Get out of here and let me finish the payroll, will you?"

Ken stood up reluctantly, pouting. "Hey, Lena," he

said, pausing, "what if, I mean, what if you and me went to that new rib place over on—"

"No way," she said, cutting him off. "I don't date fellow workers. In fact, I don't date, period."

"But it's not like—"

"Outta here, Ken. Shoo. I have work to finish."

The truth was that all the single men at work had hit on her over the years. At thirty-one, Lena was perhaps more attractive than she had been in her youth. There was a confidence and maturity in her bearing; she was tall, with shiny dark hair that she usually pulled back in a ponytail, a wide mouth with a deep indentation in her upper lip, a vaguely Indian look to her eyes and nose, and cheekbones from a Spanish ancestor's liaison with an Aztec.

After Ken finally left, she reached for the phone again, but it rang in her hand. She snatched it up. "Al's Auto Body."

"Lena?"

"Yes... Mom, is that you?" Her mother's voice sounded strange, tense.

"Did I forget... I mean, is Kimmy there with you? Did you pick her up?"

"No, Mom, I would have told you..." A hand of steel suddenly closed around her heart and tightened. "You mean Kimmy wasn't at school?"

"Oh, God," Gloria said. "No, no, she wasn't there. I asked her friends, every kid on the playground. I'm in the school office right now, Lena, and we can't find her!"

Lena closed her eyes, horrible scenarios racing through her head. Then she told herself to calm down. She put a hand to her forehead. "Mom, listen, she probably went home with one of her friends."

"She *never* goes home with anyone. You know that. She waits for me," Gloria said, distraught.

"Well, maybe she did today. Maybe she went…oh, I don't know, to the pet shop near the school. She loves the kittens."

"Lena, she wouldn't do that."

"Maybe one of her friends' mothers gave her a ride somewhere. To McDonalds' for a snack." Her mind whirled feverishly, thinking up safe venues for her child. "Or the library. Story hour. Or…"

"Lena, what should I do?" Gloria was near tears.

"I'll call her friends, Mom. I'm sure she's at someone's house."

"I'll stay here in case she shows up. The principal is very upset."

"I can imagine."

Gloria's voice was hesitant. "Should we call…the police?"

Lena's stomach clenched. "No!"

"But, honey…"

"I'm sure she'll turn up any second. I'll call her friends. Don't call the police, Mom." The police—that would make it official somehow that Kimmy was really missing, and she couldn't accept that. Not yet. This was all a big mistake. It had to be.

With difficulty, she dragged her mind back to her mother's voice.

"Will you phone me here if you find out anything? I'm half out of my mind. I'm calling in to the restaurant now. There's no way I could go to work. I'll be here. The number's—"

"I know it, Mom. I'll call you as soon as I can."

"Oh, God, I hope Kimmy's okay. There're such sick

people around these days. The poor innocent baby. Oh, Lena...''

"Mom, please, she's fine. She's got to be fine. We'll find her.''

When Lena hung up she noticed that her hands were shaking, her mouth was dry, her heart was racing. Kimmy, her baby. Gone?

Oh, I'll punish her when she shows up, Lena thought. *I'll paddle her backside. I'll ground her till she's twenty-one! I'll...*

What if someone really had taken Kimmy? Some crazy, demented child molester. You read about it every day. What if she'd been kidnapped? That was ridiculous, absurd. Lena wasn't rich enough to pay a ransom. She had nothing of value. She wasn't famous.

She had to calm herself and think of the names of Kimmy's friends, look up the numbers in the phone book. All cute little first graders. Benjamin Halloran, the boy Kimmy had a crush on. Ally Samson, her best friend. Mary Lue Shelton, Marty Figlio and that girl who'd had the birthday party last week. Ally's mother would know.

Her fingers shook, hit the wrong numbers on the phone, and she had to start over. Ally's mother had no idea where Kimmy was.

"When I picked Ally up she was at the school playing,'' Margy Samson said. "That was about, oh, just before four o'clock.''

"And she was okay?'' Lena asked.

"Sure, she was playing ball with another girl. I didn't even notice, you know. Oh, I wish I'd stayed there or something....''

"Why would you do that? I bet she's just gone off somewhere. Oh, is she going to get it when I find her.''

"Let me know, will you?" Ally's mother said. "Call me when you find her. Please."

Benjamin Halloran's mother didn't know anything, either—Ben had walked home. She asked him if he'd seen Kimmy, but he only shrugged, or so his mother told Lena.

A couple of numbers didn't answer, so Lena left messages. When she finally hung up, she knew nothing more than when she'd started: no one knew where Kimmy was.

She phoned the school, spoke to the principal, listened to her mother's frightened voice, and decided she couldn't stay at work another second. Where was her daughter? Was she okay? Had she wandered off or forgotten the time? Had she walked home by herself? Lena called home, in case Kimmy was there, but no one answered.

She took a deep breath and went out into the garage. She found Al working on a red Porsche, his skinny frame bent double as he polished the hood with a heavy machine. She had to tap him on the arm before he noticed her. He straightened, as always a stub of a swollen cigar butt held in his mouth. He switched the stub from one side of his mouth to the other, took off his protective glasses and earplugs and fixed his sharp blue eyes on Lena.

"Listen, Al, I've got to leave early today. Kimmy... Well, a little problem's come up. I have to get to her school. I put the phone on the machine and the checks are on my desk."

"Sure, go ahead. She's okay, your kid?"

"Oh, fine, yes," she replied vaguely.

"See you tomorrow morning," Al said. "Have a nice evening."

Have a nice evening. The words rang in her mind as

she headed for the parking lot. It was a beautiful, warm October day in Southern California, but Lena didn't notice. She got into her car blindly, her pride and joy, her one indulgence: a sleek black 1968 Pontiac GTO convertible. She'd had Al and the guys in the shop working on it little by little over the past five years, whenever she had some extra money, and it was restored to perfection now.

Today she didn't notice it, though, didn't pay the least bit of attention to its burnished gleam, the throaty roar of its engine or the smooth shifting of its four-on-the-floor gears as she drove toward Kimmy's school in Woodland Hills.

She told herself over and over that her daughter would show up. It was only a silly mistake, a little glitch in the usual routine. Kimmy had been missing for less than an hour—they'd find her any minute, and Lena would scold her daughter and maybe cry a little, then they'd all have a good laugh together and Gloria could go to work after all.

For goodness' sake, Lena had taught Kimmy never to talk to strangers, never to get into a car with anyone she didn't know. She knew about dialing 911, and she knew she should wait in the playground outside of her school until her grandmother picked her up. She'd been told and told those things, and she was a sweet, endearingly solemn, very responsible little girl.

Nothing could have happened to her. She'd probably be at school when Lena drove up. Sure she would.

Could you feel more responsible for an adopted child than a natural child? Lena wondered. She couldn't know what was in other people's heads, but she knew how she felt. Kimmy had gotten off to such a dismal start, abandoned, sick from her birth mother's drug habit, that Lena had an almost compulsive urge to make everything perfect in her child's life. One of the young policemen who'd originally found her had felt responsible, too; he'd gotten emotionally involved, checking on the baby every day, keeping track of her when she went to Social Services. He had a soft heart, the big, blond Los Angeles cop, even though he looked tough. Lena knew all about his soft heart—she'd been married to him then.

They'd decided to adopt the darling baby girl, and when the adoption agency finally located the birth mother, the woman had signed the papers relinquishing her rights so fast it made everyone's head spin. Signed the papers and disappeared.

Lena and her husband—Mike Quinn—had proudly brought the baby home. It was an occasion that had been covered by the papers. Sometimes Lena looked through her photo album and saw the grainy newspaper picture of her and Mike, so happy, so hopeful. Gloria was there, too, grinning. A grandmother at last.

Well, Lena was still a mother and Gloria was a grandmother, but the man in the picture hadn't been a father for five years now.

She pulled up in front of the school, shut the car off, drew a deep breath and went inside. Surely by now they'd found Kimmy. She'd be sitting in the office, contrite, with some excuse.

But she wasn't there. Gloria was waiting, looking slighter than usual, as if she'd shrunk since Kimmy had gone missing. Her usually neat hair, dark and glossy and pulled back into a bun, had strands falling around her face. Her small features were pinched, her olive skin sallow. Miss Trenholm, the principal, was with her, looking just as upset despite her usual professional calm.

"You haven't found her," Lena said.

"Oh, honey, I'm so worried!" Gloria cried.

"I'm so sorry about this, Mrs. Portillo," Miss Trenholm said. "I feel responsible. I don't know what could have happened."

Lena didn't correct the principal's misuse of her name. She wasn't Mrs. Portillo, as there was no Mr. Portillo— it was her mother's maiden name. People called her that all the time, and she didn't care, as long as no one ever called her Mrs. Quinn again. "I'm sure it wasn't your fault, Miss Trenholm."

"It *is* early in the school year, and first grade *is* a big step up from kindergarten," the principal said. "We've had several episodes over the years, and I assure you we've always found the children safe and sound."

"Do you have any suggestions as to what to do next?" Lena asked. "I've called all her friends."

Miss Trenholm hesitated. "Is there a…a person you're in a relationship with? Sometimes it happens that…"

"No," Lena said firmly, "there's no one."

"An ex-husband?"

Lena almost laughed. She shook her head. No, *he* wouldn't be interested enough to bother snatching Kimmy. And besides, he didn't even know where they lived.

"It's been nearly an hour and a half," Miss Trenholm said, checking the wall clock. "We'll need to call the police. There are procedures—"

"What if a child molester took her?" Gloria burst out.

"Mom."

"Oh, God," Gloria sobbed.

"She's fine. I know she's *fine,*" Lena said, but her throat ached, and she was suddenly terribly afraid. Her knees went weak and she sat down too quickly on an office chair. "Kimmy," she whispered.

"I think," Miss Trenholm said, "that we should call the police now and then you go home and wait."

Lena looked up quickly. "You really think…?"

"Yes, honey," Gloria said. "Call the police."

"Oh, my God," Lena said. "You both think something's happened to Kimmy."

"No, no, it's just a precaution," Miss Trenholm assured her.

Lena felt nausea rise in her chest and she could hardly breathe. It couldn't be happening, not to Kimmy, not to her precious little girl. She turned away.

"Let's go home," Gloria said. "We'll call the police from your house. I'll do it if you want."

Lena looked up again. "What if she comes back here? What…?"

"I'll be right here to watch for her." Miss Trenholm hesitated. "And then, of course, they'll send cars around to check the area."

They. The police.

Somehow Lena got out of the school and followed Gloria's car to her own house. The small stucco bungalow on the narrow lot, lined up on the street with others so similar. But it was *her* house; she'd bought it and fixed it up, and she paid the mortgage every month with a fiercely possessive satisfaction. She drove her car into the driveway. Gloria parked at the curb, and they both got out and stood there on the postage-stamp lawn in the gathering dusk and looked at each other.

"Come on," Gloria finally said. "Let's go in and make that call."

It was, oddly, as if they had switched roles—Gloria calm and in control now, while Lena could hardly move, her limbs leaden, her head thick, her heart beating so hard it sapped all the energy from the rest of her body. And her mind kept repeating the mantra: Kimmy, come back. Kimmy, be safe.

Gloria unlocked the door with her key. She lived in her own place a couple of miles away, but they were at each other's homes as often as at their own. She flicked the lights on.

"Do you want me to call or do you…?" Gloria began.

"Wait!" Lena said. "The answering machine. Maybe there's a message… Maybe…" She found the strength to move to her machine. Yes, the red light was blinking. She pushed the play button and waited, her breath trapped in her chest. Oh, there were messages, all right, four of them. The dentist's office, a friend who wanted to go bowling, a credit card company, a wrong number.

Lena sank onto the couch and put her head in her hands. Then she heard Gloria pick the phone up and start punching numbers.

Tiredly Lena lifted her head. "No, Mom, let me. It's my daughter."

Slowly Gloria held the phone out. Her eyes met Lena's with sadness and fear and understanding. "Okay, honey," she said.

The phone rang in Lena's ear. What was she going to say? Would they really do something to help find her daughter? It rang again, and Lena straightened her shoulders.

"Woodland Hills Police," said a bored masculine voice.

Lena took a long, quavering breath. "I want to report a—" she cleared her throat "—a missing child. Kimberly Lee Portillo, six years old, last seen at Jefferson Elementary School about four this afternoon."

"Your name, please."

And so she went through the whole rigmarole, the endless red tape, the questions.

"I'm sending a patrol car to your house, ma'am," the officer said at last. "It should be there soon. If you have a recent picture of the missing child, it will be helpful."

The missing child. "Yes," she said faintly, "I have one."

"You sit tight, ma'am. They'll be there soon."

"Okay, thanks," she said automatically, and she wasn't aware she was still holding the phone until her mother took it out of her hand.

Gloria hugged her tightly, then held her at arm's length and said carefully, "Call Mike, honey."

Somewhere inside Lena a flame of anger ignited and flickered. She welcomed it, a relief from the dread, a momentary respite from her suffering. "No," Lena said with finality. "Never."

CHAPTER TWO

THE WOODLAND HILLS police arrived twenty minutes later, two uniformed officers, an older one with a mustache and a younger one with fair hair and a nice face.

Lena let them in, and they stood, hats in hands, and introduced themselves: officers Krubsak and Mullin. They were polite and soft-spoken, and they were probably sympathetic, maybe had kids of their own, but Lena knew from being married to a cop what they were thinking. She knew all about the inside jokes, the foul things cops said, the black humor that kept them from going nuts when they saw the violence people could inflict upon one another. Oh, sure, she could just imagine what they'd say to each other when they left her house: "Probably got the kid locked up in the basement. Nah, hacked to pieces. Maybe some boyfriend got his hands on her. Hell, it's almost always the family." Cops saw those things and joked about them to stay sane.

And now it was Lena they'd joke about. And Kimmy. She couldn't bear it.

But she had to. She had to ask them to sit down, had to answer their questions and try to be calm because she needed their help. She had to sit there, her hands between her thighs to keep them from shaking, and watch them take out their notepads, and steel herself for their questions.

Gloria told them of her arrival at Jefferson Elementary.

"And it was your habit to pick Kimberly up after school?" Krubsak asked.

"Yes, unless she was going to a friend's house, but I always knew that ahead of time. She always waited for me. If it rained, I got there earlier."

"I called all her friends." Lena said wearily. "They last saw her at the playground just before four o'clock."

Mullin spoke up. "Would she have wandered off or gone with someone without telling you?"

Both women shook their heads emphatically.

"We'll need to go to her school and talk to the children, but we can't do that until tomorrow," Krubsak said.

"I can tell you some of their names, and I'm sure the principal will give you a list. She was very upset," Lena told him.

"Doesn't look good, does it?" Krubsak said. "For the school, I mean."

"It wasn't her fault," Lena protested.

"How do you know, Mrs. Portillo? We have to check out everything."

Mrs. Portillo again. "I'm *Miss* Portillo," she said. "I'm not married." Defiantly.

"Is there an ex-husband?" Mullin asked.

"I'm a single parent," Lena said firmly, ignoring the look Gloria flashed her.

"What about Kimberly's father?"

"Actually," Lena said, hating to have to explain it all, "my daughter is adopted. Her father was unknown."

"What about the real mother, then?" Krubsak asked. "We've had cases like that, you know, where the real mother wants the kid back."

"Not *this* real mother," Lena said. "She was a drug addict and she abandoned Kimmy. When they found her she couldn't sign the relinquishment papers fast enough.

Then she disappeared. Believe me, she never wanted the baby and she still doesn't—that is, if she's even alive."

"Still, we should check her out."

"I can't remember her name. I'd have to look in the adoption papers."

"Well, you might want to do that and let us know, Miss Portillo."

"Okay, sure, but what are you going to do about finding my daughter?"

"We've got patrol cars out looking. We'll get her picture faxed to everyone. You do have a picture?"

Lena went to the bookshelf behind the couch and picked up Kimmy's school picture from last year, slid the photograph out of the frame, held it, studied it for a moment—the wide smile with a front tooth missing, the big brown eyes, the soft tendrils of brown hair. Oh, God, Kimmy.

"Do you have a boyfriend?" Mullin asked.

"What?" She looked up, the picture in her hand. "A boyfriend. No. I don't have time. Are you kidding?"

"Sometimes it's a guy you're having a relationship with who takes a kid. Jealous or possessive. Whatever." Krubsak shrugged.

"No, there are no men in my life. I haven't even had a date in a year," Lena said, handing the photo to him.

"And your mother." He turned to Gloria. "Mrs. Torres, there's no one you can think of who would take your granddaughter?"

"No," she answered.

"An ex-husband, a boyfriend?"

Gloria gave a short laugh. "You flatter me, young man. I'm a widow, and I don't have *boyfriends* at my age."

"Sorry, but you know what I mean."

"No, there's nobody I'm having a relationship with."

"Enemies?" Mullin asked. "Someone who has a grudge against you, something like that?"

"God, no," Lena said.

"Okay, this is what we'll do," he went on. "We'll put a tap on your phone first thing. Anyone who calls, the number will automatically show up at the station. That is, of course, if there is a phone call."

"You mean for ransom?" Lena asked.

"Yeah."

"But what if it's not a kidnapping for ransom? What if it's someone…" Her voice trembled.

"We'll have patrols out all over the neighborhood. We'll start a door-to-door search around the school, then widen out. There'll be an APB out on her with the picture."

"Excuse me," Gloria put in. "Is there someone, some division, that specializes in this kind of crime? Should you call someone else in? The FBI?"

"The FBI can only be called in if we're sure it's a kidnapping," Krubsak said, "and then only after twenty-four hours."

Lena asked a question she knew was stupid, but the words came tumbling out of her mouth. "Do you think it's a child molester?"

"Well, now, ma'am, it's too soon to jump to conclusions, and there's nothing pointing to that at this time. Your daughter is most likely lost, probably somewhere not far away."

"I hope so," Lena whispered, "Oh, God, I hope so."

The phone tap was set up, and Krubsak spoke to his precinct on the phone, organizing the door-to-door search.

"I'm leaving Officer Mullin here until morning," he said. "Just in case."

"Just in case what?" Lena asked.

"It's procedure, ma'am. I'll take this picture down to the station, and we'll get it out. We're part of the new TRAK system—we can send it all over the country if we need to. Don't worry, we'll find your daughter."

At nine o'clock he left them with Officer Mullin. There hadn't been a phone call, not one, although Lena listened and waited minute after long minute.

"Try to get some sleep, honey," Gloria finally said.

"Oh, sure," Lena replied.

"I know."

"Can *you* sleep?"

"Probably not."

"You could go home," Lena said. "Maybe you'd sleep better there."

"Oh, sure," Gloria said, echoing her daughter's tone.

"I haven't eaten. Have you?"

"No." Gloria sighed.

"I can't."

"Neither can I."

"Where is she?" Lena asked. "Where is she?"

Gloria hugged her, and they stood like that for a long time.

THE PHONE RANG at seven in the morning, jerking Lena out of a fitful doze. She rushed into the living room to answer it, glanced wildly around for Officer Mullin, saw him nod at her. She picked the phone up.

"Hello?" She could barely recognize her own voice.

"Mullin, please," said a man's voice.

Lena stood there, her heart racing, her mind not quite comprehending who was on the phone.

"It's for you," she finally said, holding the receiver out, and he came over and took it from her.

Lena hadn't even bothered to undress the night before—she still wore jeans and a short-sleeved red blouse. She'd barely slept a wink, and now as she sank onto the sofa, she felt the weight of unending dread settle on her again. She listened to Mullin's conversation, but it wasn't news—they hadn't found Kimmy. Apparently it was only someone telling him who would relieve him.

"What is it?" asked Gloria from the hallway.

"Nothing, Mom. It's nothing."

"Oh, I thought…"

"I know."

"Did you sleep?"

"No, did you?"

Gloria didn't bother answering. She looked awful, her hair a mess, her face drawn, shadows under her eyes. Lena guessed she herself looked just as bad.

"All right," Gloria said. "They'll find her today. I know they will." She tried to smile. "I'm going to make some breakfast now. You have to eat, honey. And go take a shower, change your clothes. Go on now."

"Oh, Mom, I won't feel better until I've got Kimmy back."

"You have to stay healthy, keep up your strength. Do what I say."

Listlessly Lena took a shower and changed her clothes. She couldn't bear to look at herself in the mirror, because when she did she saw the black terror in her eyes, and it frightened her. She pulled her hair up in a careless twist and secured it with a clip.

When she emerged from her bedroom Gloria was feeding a tired-looking officer Mullin a plate of eggs and toast. She put one in front of her daughter, too, but Lena couldn't do more than sip some coffee and nibble a corner of toast.

Another policeman drove up and Mullin left, taking the police car back to his station. The new officer was heavy and dark haired. Fontaine, his name tag read.

"Is there any news?" Lena asked desperately.

"Nothing that I know of," Officer Fontaine said. "The door-to-door search broke off last night and will be resumed shortly. So far nothing's turned up."

After breakfast Lena decided she had to do something. The waiting was destroying her; she felt as if every nerve in her body was raw, twanging with agony. She was so used to being busy, working every minute of the day, that she couldn't just sit, tired as she was.

She drove around the neighborhood first, the convertible top down so Kimmy could see her. Several patrol cars were in evidence, some cruising, one parked, its occupants at the door of a house. The police were trying to help, Lena told herself, but it seemed so hopeless. If Kimmy had been in the neighborhood, she'd have come home, wouldn't she? Or perhaps the police were asking people if they'd seen anything suspicious. What? Some evil maniac stalking her daughter? Oh, God.

She saw the road ahead through a film of tears. Was Kimmy okay? Was she tired, cold, hungry? She got so hungry in the morning.

Lena reached the school, and there were police cars there, too. Children played on swings and jungle gyms in the school yard. She heard their high-pitched yells and stopped her car to watch. Kimmy should be there with them, with her friends, yelling and running and giggling, falling maybe and scraping a knee, bravely holding back tears.

It didn't seem right to Lena that life went on as usual

for these kids and their parents, that they could still run and laugh and play when her life was turned upside down and terror was her constant companion. She could barely recall what it felt like not to be afraid. She drove around the school, on every street that surrounded the school, block after block, searching the lawns and houses and stores and alleys and gas stations she passed, looking for her daughter single-mindedly, irrationally, compulsively.

She forgot to eat, felt sickness gnawing in her belly but ignored it. She drove and drove, and once she got lost and had to retrace her route, only to find herself on Ventura Boulevard again. She stopped several times to call home in case there was news, but there wasn't.

"Any news?" Lena asked wearily when she finally got home.

Gloria merely shook her head. "But the press found out somehow. We've had a few calls. Officer Fontaine handled them."

He nodded. "We can hold them off for only so long, you know. But if they get into a frenzy, we'll try to shield you from it."

"Thank you," Lena said. *Oh, God, the news media.*

The evening passed with agonizing slowness. There were a few phone calls, one from Miss Trenholm, another from Ally's mother, two more from local TV stations. Gloria fielded the calls—Lena sat, head in her hands, or paced like a caged tigress.

After trying to eat some of the food Gloria prepared for supper, Lena got up and went into the backyard. She wanted to scream, she wanted to weep and tear her hair, but none of those things would do Kimmy any good.

She heard the screen door slam, and her mother came out.

"You can't go on like this," Gloria said. "For God's

sake, call Mike. He'll get the whole LAPD in on the search. Lena, honey, he may not have been the best husband, but he was a damn good cop. He'll find Kimmy, you know. Call him, Lena.''

"You think he's magic, Mom? You think he can wave a magic wand and poof, she'll be home?''

"No, no, but he can help. If they know one of their own is in danger, the police will try harder. You know that.''

"Did it ever occur to you that he might not be interested in helping me?''

"No,'' Gloria said firmly.

"I haven't seen or heard from him in five years. I have sole custody of Kimmy. I refused any contact after the divorce, no visitation rights, no child support, nothing. He was an alcoholic who'd hit bottom, a danger to himself and everyone around him, and I cut him out of my life. Now you think I should go begging to him?'' She shook her head.

"Please, Lena, I know he'll help.''

"He probably drank himself to death by now.'' *No, not Mike.*

"He's not your father, Lena, if that's what this is all about,'' Gloria said quietly. "And he hasn't drunk himself to death.''

Lena gave her a sharp look. "How do you know?''

"I know,'' Gloria said, holding her daughter's gaze.

"No,'' Lena whispered, and she made a slashing motion with her hand, dismissing the subject, and went inside.

Her feet took her to her daughter's room, where she stood, staring unseeing into space. Then she sat on Kimmy's bed, smoothed the pink-and-blue plaid coverlet, patted the stuffed dog that lay on the pillow. She pulled

Kimmy's tattered old blanket out from under the pillow
and held it to her face, closing her eyes, drawing in her
child's scent, and then she cried, hot tears soaking into
the blanket, her body shaking, her mind reeling, lost, unable to think.

Where was Kimmy? Where was she?

THE KID WAS no problem at all. She lay curled up on the
back seat of the old station wagon and dozed most of the
time. Jane Cramm kept turning around and looking at her.

"It's too damn hot," Danny Hayden said.

"Do you want me to open my window some more?"
Jane asked.

"Nah, the dust blows in."

"We'll be out of the desert soon, Danny," she said.
She hated it when Danny got irritated, and she tried very
hard not to rub him the wrong way.

Fortuitously, Danny seemed to forget about his discomfort. He even craned his neck to take a quick look at
the kid. "She's cute, ain't she?" he asked in a pleasant
voice.

Jane turned again and studied the child. "She's real
cute. I can't believe I even had a kid that cute, you know,
Danny?"

"You're all right," he replied.

Jane couldn't help smiling. Sometimes Danny was nice
to her—as long as she didn't do something dumb to ag-
gravate him. That's why she'd gone along with this
caper—it'd been all his idea. But, Jane had to admit,
she'd been real curious to see the child she'd given up
for adoption; well, at least she had been once Danny
planted the idea in her head. "I'm sure glad you said I
could keep her, Danny."

He snorted, and Jane wasn't sure how to interpret that.

Sometimes Danny did things she couldn't figure out. She wasn't sure he'd meant what he said about her keeping Kimberly. You couldn't always believe him. Jane had a disquieting idea about why Danny had wanted the girl in the first place, but she tried not to think about it.

"Maybe we don't have to give her any more pills, huh?" Jane asked. They'd been feeding her Valium ever since they'd picked her up at the school yesterday. "She's awful good."

"That's *why* she's awful good," he said with heavy sarcasm. "Listen, the one thing we don't need is a screaming kid. Someone would notice. Or she could try to run away. Just do what I say." He shook his head in disgust and swore under his breath.

Dutifully, Jane said nothing. She fiddled with the radio knob, finally getting a station from Phoenix, Arizona, even though they were hundreds of miles north of Phoenix, heading east toward Flagstaff on Interstate 40. Around them the dry-as-dust desert was fading into dusk, the sky ahead blue-black, the sun's glow on the horizon behind them.

"I'm hungry," Danny said.

"Okay. You want to pick up some burgers or something?"

"Out here?"

"Well, I guess we could find a store, you know, a gas station store. I'll get us something. And she needs to eat, too. Kids need to eat a lot, you know, because they're growing. And milk, she needs to drink milk."

"Yeah, yeah, keep an eye out for someplace to stop."

Jane turned and knelt on the seat, leaning over to look at Kimmy. She was so pretty, with long, dark, shiny hair and huge brown eyes with long lashes and skin so smooth and creamy and untouched it made Jane's heart ache. Had she ever looked like this? She used to be pretty as a child; she recalled her mother saying so, and her aunt. She'd never known her own father, and she didn't know who Kimberly's father was, either. He must have been good-looking, though.

She'd gotten pregnant seven years ago, and she'd known right off she couldn't take care of a baby. To tell the truth, she hadn't minded being pregnant, because men had kind of liked the way she looked, but a baby? No way. She'd never regretted giving the baby up until Danny had started working on her, and now she wasn't sure whether the desire to keep Kimberly was hers or Danny's.

She put her hand on the little girl's head and stroked her hair back. "Wake up, Kimmy," she said softly. "Are you hungry? Want something to eat?"

The girl opened her eyes with effort; they were clouded and dull from the Valium.

"I want my mommy," she said plaintively.

I am your mommy, Jane wanted to say. "We're going to stop soon and get something to eat, okay?"

"I want to go home," Kimmy said.

"Want some ice cream?" Jane asked hopefully.

"I want my mommy," the child repeated, her eyes beseeching and scared.

Jane didn't know what to do. She was supposed to keep the kid quiet, but no matter what she said, Kimmy cried or asked for her mommy. Jane hadn't known a little kid could be so stubborn.

"You can't see your mother right now. We're going on a trip," Jane said. "Remember? I told you…"

"I want to go home."

Sighing, Jane turned around to face the darkening highway. Flagstaff Mountain loomed, barely visible in the dusk. It would be cooler in the mountains, she thought, and Danny wouldn't get irritated at the heat. The old station wagon had no air-conditioning, but it was big and comfortable, and Danny liked it.

She pulled down the visor and studied her face in the dusty mirror on the back of it. She tried very hard to see any resemblance between her face and her daughter's, but she couldn't. Maybe she'd looked like Kimmy once, but that must have been a long time ago. Now, at thirty-two, Jane was painfully thin, her dark hair dull and scraggly, her skin coarse, and she was missing a tooth.

She put her fingers on her cheek and met her own brown eyes in the mirror. It was so dark now that she could barely see herself, and she could imagine that there was something in her face that still resembled the pretty little girl she'd once been. An unaccountable sadness filled her, and she saw in her mind's eye the years behind her stretching back and back; she had a vague inkling that it had not, perhaps, been inevitable that she'd ended up here, in this car, with this man, driving through the desert with a child in the back seat.

"What the hell're you doing?" Danny demanded.

She sat straight up, snapped the visor back into place. "Nothing, honey, honest," she said, avoiding his eyes.

"I want my mommy," the child wailed.

CHAPTER THREE

MIKE QUINN BLEW a sharp blast on his whistle, then let it drop on its chain against his sweatshirt. "Front and center!" he yelled to the gangly black kids. "Get over here!"

All seven boys sauntered over to the sideline on the basketball court.

Mike put his hands on his hips and shook his head in disgust. "Marvin," he said, "how many times I gotta tell you? Follow the shot. You hear that? *Follow the shot.*"

Marvin shrugged wide, bony shoulders. "Sure, man, no prob." Then he grinned. "But when you gonna show me the money?"

Everyone laughed. Everyone but Mike. "Real funny, kid," he said. "But losers never see the bucks. Sure, they see the color of a welfare check once a month, but that's it. You wanna see the money? The real stuff? Then you work for it. You work till you ache all over. And for starters—and this goes for all you guys—you get those hands up and follow your shots in. You pay attention. To the ball. You never take your eyes off the board. You let the other guy get the rebounds and you're a loser, man, a big loser. Because that dude's going to get noticed. *He's* gonna make it to college. And then someday some scout'll spot him and make him an offer. The pros. The big time. The money. You guys get the picture?"

A few nods, a couple of "Yeah, mans."

"Okay, then." Mike clapped his hands. "Get on the court and run the drill. Marvin, you take the first shot and—"

"Follow the ball," Marvin finished for him. "Follow the ball," he began to chant, jabbing playfully at another player as he took to the court.

Mike watched the boys. They were quite a crew. All were from South Central Los Angeles, and all were on some sort of probation, either from school or from a judge. Two of the seventeen-year-olds were former gang members—one had been tossed out of school for pulling a switchblade on a math teacher. Two others had been serious addicts, still had track marks showing on their arms and behind their knees. They were clean now, or so Mike believed. For how long? No one knew.

They were all essentially troublemakers; that was fact. But Mike worked them out hard. Three nights a week. And at least on those nights he knew they'd stay clean. When he sent them home at nine they were too darn tired to do much except eat and sleep. Still, he worried about them. Sometimes at work one of their faces would pop into his mind and he'd think, *Is Billy going to make it? Or is he going to end up on the coroner's slab before his eighteenth birthday?*

With Mike on the court doing footwork drills alongside the team, they worked hard all evening. They were an odd-looking group, three of the boys under six feet in height, the others all taller than Mike's six-two. Whereas all the boys were still youthfully thin and gangly, Mike, at thirty-six, was built substantially. A big man. Lean but large boned, with Irish-pale skin, dark-blond hair that flopped to one side and a good, solid face that was some how handsome despite that slightly askew prizefighter's nose. For his size and his age he still moved well, keeping pace with the kids, never showing them any weakness.

Shortly before nine Mike whistled them over to the sideline. "Okay," he said, "good job. I saw lots of hands and arms in the air out there. You fellas work that hard tomorrow night and we'll beat the pants off the Westenders."

"Man, they are like already dead, dude," Ray intoned.

"Meat, they are meat," Marvin put in.

"You got it," Mike said, and he joined them in a round of high fives. "Now, keep clean till then. Think you *ladies* can handle that?"

Billy snorted. "Easy as pie, bro."

"Okay, then, go on home and get some rest. I'll see you all tomorrow."

"Ta ta, man," Ray said, and they all headed toward the locker room in the old neighborhood gymnasium. Mike hung out shooting baskets until the boys cleared the gym entirely, then he switched off the court lights, checked the locker room and left, crossing the cracked asphalt parking lot to his car.

It was a bad neighborhood, right in the heart of L.A.'s notorious South Central District. Some of the guys at work swore they'd have to be paid big bucks to get anywhere near the area, especially after dark. But Mike Quinn wasn't that concerned. As he often told Joe Carbone, his friend and mentor at police headquarters, "I have a better chance of getting killed on the freeway."

And Mike liked the kids. Liked coaching them and talking to them and simply being there if one of them needed an ear. He knew their brothers and sisters and parents, too. Knew where they were coming from. The hopes and dreams and the despair. Especially the despair. He'd been there.

He unlocked his car, got in and pulled out of the lot, driving toward Manchester Avenue as he tuned the radio to a talk show. Tonight's subject was apparently teenage daughters stealing their mothers' boyfriends. There was a lot of anger in the voice coming over the air, a shriek and the click of the phone. The talk show host took another call.

Mike turned north onto the 405 freeway and then west on 10, which took him straight into the Santa Monica beach district. Home. It sounded pretty good, but in reality his apartment was in one of those funky, two-blocks-off-the-beach old houses. Probably built in the late 1940s. The landlady was in her sixties. She'd renovated the place several years ago, and it now contained four small apartments. The building itself was painted salmon, with white trim at the doors and windows. The roof leaked, and the whole place stuck out like a sore thumb on the block.

The rent was nevertheless high—it was after all, the beach. Mike's apartment—two rooms and a bath—was at the rear of the house, stuffy in the summer and too cool and damp in the winter. But when the breeze was from the ocean, he could smell the salt in the air. And he heard the seagulls from dawn till dusk. The inflated rent was worth every cent.

When he was inside he eyed the shower, but that could wait. Right now he was starved. He pressed the button on his answering machine and went to the fridge, where he pulled open the door and peered inside. Ah, he thought, last night's leftover sub sandwich.

The machine spoke in the background. "Hey, Mike, Joe here. Nice job at that liquor store yesterday. You're catching on. Oh, and by the way, stop by my office first thing Monday. They want you over in Bakersfield to conduct a two-day training program. You're getting famous. See ya.'' *Click.*

There were a couple of other messages. One from a bank—soliciting—another from his mother, reminding him about the upcoming Halloween party at his brother's. The big, loud Quinn family at its best. Or worst.

Joe's message, though, was good news. Joe had taken Mike under his wing when Mike's life had been swirling straight down the drain. He'd lost his family. Damn near lost his job. He'd certainly lost his will to live. Mike sat on a stool at the Formica counter in his kitchen and munched the sandwich, gulping orange juice straight from the bottle in between bites, and his mind went back to that nightmare time.

Sure, he'd always liked a drink or two. His family drank—the men did, at least. A beer with supper, a few at the bars with buddies. And hey, cops drank like fish, so it had been easy to fall into the pattern. He'd told himself it was to ''let down.''

He'd loved the male bonding thing that came with his job; his partner back in the days when he'd been a young patrol cop in the San Fernando Valley area had been Jeff Davidoff. They'd been as close as brothers, closer. Davidoff drank only vodka, because he was Russian, and they'd always laughed like maniacs when he told someone that. God, they'd had good times. And they'd done good work, too, routine traffic stuff, domestic disputes, a few convenience-store robberies. Two tall young cops, Mike blond, Jeff dark. They'd perfected their swaggers and that slow, intimidating way of taking off their mirrored sunglasses when they stopped a speeder.

Jeff had been best man at Mike's wedding, and he'd hung out a lot at the Quinns' first small apartment. He'd adored Lena and offered to baby-sit Kimmy when they adopted her.

Life had been good. Mike had his wife, a new baby, a job he loved, a partner he trusted with his life.

Then fate had intervened. He remembered the day with absolute clarity. It had been in August, an inferno in the Los Angeles basin, the Santa Ana winds kicking up dust, driving people crazy. The air-conditioning in the patrol cruiser had been broken, of course. He and Jeff were bitching and sweltering and drinking cold sodas when the call came over the radio: officers under fire, suspected bank robbery.

They'd raced to the scene, siren wailing, as excited as kids. "Action!" Jeff had yelled exuberantly, driving like a madman.

The bank robbers were shooting it out with the police. They'd had machine guns, for God's sake. One officer had already been hit, the others were cowering behind their cars, and the bad guys were holed up in the bank, shooting out of the front door.

It had been a scene from hell with a pitiless sun baking the cops in their dark uniforms. Jeff and Mike were kneeling behind the open door of their cruiser, waiting for a clear shot, when Jeff told Mike he was going to get behind a concrete planter closer to the door. "Cover me, partner," he'd said, like in the old cowboy movies, and then he ran, crouched low, zigzagging, Mike laying down covering fire, but a stray bullet from one of the robbers' guns tore through Jeff's lungs and blew a hole out the other side.

He died there in Mike's arms, his blood leaking onto the sizzling concrete, and the last thing he said was, "Tell my mother...tell her...tell her..." And then he was gone.

Mike made something up to tell Mrs. Davidoff, and

that was the last coherent thing he did for a month. He started drinking seriously then, coming home late, hung-over in the mornings, sick as a dog, then drinking again to wash the memory from his soul.

Lena had tried talking to him, and so had his own mother. The guys at work hinted around. But Mike couldn't stop. If a day went by without booze, he shook and remembered Jeff's blood all over him, the way life had gone out of his eyes. He'd think of the funeral, the formal policeman's goodbye, with uniforms, a gun salute. Davidoff's parents and his sister. It hurt too much, and he couldn't handle it.

He was offered counseling at work, routine in cases like his, but he declined it. To talk about the event would be to relive it, and he couldn't face that—better to forget, to drown his memories.

It got worse and worse. He used up all his sick days. Lena cried a lot. His friends gave him a wide berth. He was either drunk or hungover or angry for months, but he could live with those feelings.

And then there was that final night with his family, with his beautiful young wife and his darling year-old baby girl. He and Lena had fought—he never recalled over what—and he'd had a few shots of vodka, which he'd started drinking when Davidoff died, and he'd felt so low, so sick, so utterly used up and worthless. In a moment of rare clarity he knew that Lena hated him, Kimmy was afraid of him, he wasn't doing his job any-more, and he knew he was unable to continue that way for another hour or minute or second.

That's when he'd gotten his police-issued .38 Special and cried and held it to his head, while Lena begged him to put it down, sobbed and stood in front of the baby's door, then called his father to come and get him.

Larry had come, taken the gun and led Mike away, out of the house, and Lena had told him never to come back, she couldn't go through this again.

He'd passed out in his dad's car on the way to his parents' house, and when he'd woken up the next day, he knew he had to change or die.

Well, he'd tried to die and failed, so change was the next step. Of course, it had been too late to save his marriage. Lena had disappeared, divorced him, taken a new name, and he didn't have the heart or right to fight her over anything. It was over.

Joe Carbone, a sober alcoholic Mike knew only casually from headquarters, had helped him pick up the pieces of his shattered life. Five years ago now. Joe had helped others, too, but he and Mike had become particularly close. And it was Joe who'd helped Mike get his present position with LAPD's prestigious Hostage Negotiations Team, which Joe headed.

Now Mike was making a name for himself within the police community. Not just in California, but in neighboring states, as well. He'd had a couple of breaks, he admitted. His first one had come shortly after being transferred to Hostage Negotiations; Mike had worked a situation in which a computer analyst had lost his job, been drinking heavily and had ultimately taken his ex-wife and children hostage. The man had been armed to the teeth.

Mike had gotten him to talk on the phone, and after four hours the man had surrendered. Mike knew he never would have been able to talk the guy down if he himself hadn't had some real-life experience with booze and guns and despair. It turned out the computer analyst was of some local renown, and the media made a big deal about it.

That had been two years ago. The next break in Mike's

career had come on the heels of the first, only this time it was a disgruntled postal worker holding a group of twenty fellow workers hostage with an automatic weapon. This dude had been sober, but the hopelessness was there just the same. It had taken two days to wear the man down, and Mike had been the one he wanted to talk to. The media coverage was impressive, and people on the street—a few, anyway—had recognized Mike's face.

It felt good to really help. Just as it felt good to work with his basketball group and the eight-year-old boy Mike saw on weekends as an Adopt-a-Buddy in L.A. It gave Mike's life purpose and direction. His one big regret was that he'd lost his own family on the route to self-discovery.

He finished the leftover sandwich and showered, then telephoned Jenn, Jennifer Hilty, a divorcée with two small children whom Mike had met several months ago. She was a down-to-earth woman, thirty-six—his age— who owned and operated an aerobics studio in Santa Monica. She had the body to prove it, too.

"Hope it's not too late to call," Mike said, stretching out on his couch, "but I wanted to see if you're free for lunch tomorrow. Can't do dinner—I've got that basketball game."

"Mmm, lunch," she said, hesitating, teasing. "Let me check my calendar."

"If it's a nice day, we could eat on the pier," Mike said. "Take the kids along."

"Bob's got the kids tomorrow. His weekend, you know." Bob was her ex. "So I'm free. I've got a nine-thirty class, but then I'm off till Monday."

"So it's yes?"

"Of course. But maybe we should just get takeout or something, eat at my place. And then who knows?"

Mike knew exactly what she meant. "Sounds good."

"Just good?"

"Sounds great," he said, and after he'd hung up he thought about that. Sex with Jennifer was as good as it got.

But then Mike frowned. That wasn't entirely true. With Lena it had been perfect.

Mike sat up and wiped the frown from his face. "Water under the bridge," he said out loud. He rose and turned off the lights and was heading toward the bedroom, when the phone rang. "Damn," he muttered, hoping it wasn't work.

It wasn't. But Mike couldn't have been more surprised when he realized who it was.

"Gloria," the woman said. "Mike, it's Gloria Torres."

He sat down in the darkened room, collecting himself. Lena's *mother*.

It all came rushing back, the checks and Christmas and birthday cards he'd sent to Kimmy through Gloria—all returned unopened. The calls he'd made to her, trying to locate Lena and the baby—Lena had changed her name, moved, done a real good job of disappearing. And all Gloria had ever said to him was, "You know I can't talk to you, Mike. I'll just tell you they're okay." Then she'd hang up.

But Mike was a cop. He'd pulled a couple of strings and found out Lena had taken her mother's maiden name, Portillo, and he'd located her only a few miles away in Woodland Hills. He'd kept tabs on her. Still did. But he'd never contacted her. Oh, he'd found out where Lena worked, where she lived, but he'd never invade her space, not after he'd put her through that living nightmare.

"Mike?"

"Ah, yeah, Gloria, I'm here," he said, rubbing his cheek absently.

"I...Mike, I need to see you."

Her voice sounded strange. "What is it?" Mike asked, the hair on his arms raising.

"It's...it's Kimmy."

He was struck numb for a long moment. "Gloria... Oh, God, don't tell me..."

"No, no, Mike, it's not what you're thinking. I mean, I just need to see you. There's a problem. I can't talk now."

"What the hell kind of a problem can there be with a six-year-old?" Mike demanded.

"Can you meet me in front of my house in thirty minutes?" she asked.

"Gloria."

"Please, Mike, not on the phone. Please. I... We need your help. Thirty minutes?"

And all he could say was of course he'd be there, and Gloria hung up.

WHEN GLORIA HUNG UP the bedroom telephone, she had a sudden sweeping moment of panic. She never should have called him. *Never.* But then the panic subsided, replaced again by common sense. If Lena were thinking rationally, she'd realize how much greater their chances were of finding Kimmy with the whole LAPD on the search. And only Mike could accomplish that. Not only was Mike a cop, but so was his father, his uncle and even his first cousin. All cops. Mike could call in the troops in a way no civilian ever could.

Gloria rose from the side of Lena's bed just as her daughter walked into the room.

"Who was that on the phone?" Lena asked wearily.

"Ah, work. I had to check in at work. I'm afraid I've got to run over there for a few minutes," she lied.

"At this hour?"

"They, ah, can't find the time-clock key or something," Gloria said, but already Lena was someplace else, sagging onto the side of the bed, her face in her hands.

"Oh, Mom," she said, her voice breaking. "I just don't understand any of this. Who would take her? *Why?* I don't have a dime to my name. And if it's some sicko... Oh, my God, we'll never get her back. Never."

Gloria eased down next to her daughter and gently brought her head to her breast, stroking her long brown hair. "We'll get her back, honey, I swear to God we will."

"You can't *know* that, Mom," Lena sobbed.

"It's a gut feeling. I have a gut feeling she's okay."

Lena's head came up. "Are you sure? I mean..."

"Shh," Gloria said, smiling, "shh. You know my intuition's always been pretty darn good. And I do have a feeling, sweetie. Now, try to lie down and close your eyes. You're exhausted. There's nothing you can do right now, and you need to rest. Please, honey."

Lena did lie down on top of her bedspread, an arm flung over her eyes, her chest rising and falling unevenly. Gloria touched her reassuringly, then rose.

"I'll only be a few minutes," she said quietly. "The policeman's in the living room, and he'll get you if there's a call. Try to sleep."

She left the bedroom reluctantly, wanting to be with her child every moment of this terrible ordeal. But more than ever she was convinced that Mike Quinn had to be brought in. If they were ever going to see Kimmy again, they needed all the help they could muster. Despite everything, Mike was a good man deep down where it counted. Surely Lena, if she ever allowed herself to think about it, knew this.

She told the policeman monitoring the phone the same lie, even though she knew her call to Mike had been taped. Whoever was monitoring incoming and outgoing calls at police headquarters must have been wondering. It didn't matter anymore. When they checked the number Gloria had called, they'd know it was Mike. Sooner or later the truth about Kimmy's adopted father was going to surface whether Lena wanted it to or not.

Gloria drove the short distance to her house gripping the steering wheel. She didn't know what to expect when she met with Mike. Lord, it had been five years. She had seen his picture once in the newspaper, and she'd been surprised and happy for him. Still, she didn't know whether he'd be glad to see her, angry or just plain distraught, as she and Lena were.

Hostage Negotiations, Gloria thought, that's the department the article had said he worked with. She remembered mentioning it to Lena, who hadn't had the time to read a paper in years, but her daughter had only put her hands stubbornly over her ears, cutting Gloria off. Now Gloria turned the corner onto her street and wondered how Mike held it together with his drinking. Maybe he'd cut down. Maybe he didn't even touch the stuff anymore. It didn't matter. So long as he could call in the troops, nothing mattered.

When she pulled up to the curb in front of her house she saw him in her headlights. He was standing next to his car, his hands jammed in the pockets of a leather jacket. Gloria got out, steeled herself against a surge of guilt and walked over to him. He looked the same. He was still a handsome man, tall and fair, that imperfect face set off with blue eyes that seemed to reach deep inside a person. Mike Quinn. Gloria realized instantly that she still liked him.

He nodded soberly. "Gloria," he said. "You're looking well."

She gave him a weary smile and they shook hands. Then, before she could say a thing, he asked her in a grave voice what on earth was going on.

"It's Kimberly, Mike. She's…missing."

He let out a quick breath. "What do you mean 'missing'?"

"I went to get her at school yesterday, like I always do, and she wasn't there."

Mike let it sink in and then he swore softly under his breath, still digesting the news. "And you and Lena have no idea, none whatsoever, where she is?"

Gloria shook her head slowly and leaned back against his car. She told him everything then, how they'd gone to the principal, phoned Kimmy's friends, checked everywhere they could imagine. And then they'd called the police.

"They spent all day today questioning people," she said. "Everyone. The teachers, the kids, even the mailman who delivers around the time I was to pick up Kimmy."

Mike listened quietly, but Gloria could see the stricken expression on his face. He asked some questions of his own, but nothing Gloria and Lena hadn't been asked a dozen times already.

"So you're saying that Kimmy disappeared from a relatively busy playground and no one saw a damn thing?" he finally asked.

"So far it looks that way."

"The cops are monitoring Lena's phone, I assume?"

Gloria nodded.

"And Lena?"

"She's in pretty bad shape, Mike. She's exhausted and frightened to death. I don't even know if she can think straight right now. I don't know that I can. I only know that you've got the connections to call in the troops. Surely your father and your uncle can call in markers, Mike, get us some real help. I never would have dumped this on you, but we're desperate."

Mike studied her face for a moment, then said, "Does Lena know you called me?"

Gloria shook her head. "You know how it is, Mike."

"Yeah, sure," he said, and she could hear bitterness creeping into his voice. "But she can't keep me out anymore. Kimmy's my legal daughter. Lena knows that. Dammit," he said. "She should have called me immediately. I'll head over there right now."

But Gloria grabbed his arm. "No, Mike, no! You'll make it worse. Lena's about to break. Just do what you can from the sidelines. *Please,* Mike, I'm begging you."

He studied her again, searching her face, and then finally, mercifully, he nodded. "All right," he said softly, "all right, Gloria, we'll do it your way for now. I'll go home and get on the phone right away." He turned to leave, then he hesitated. With his back to Gloria, he asked, "Does she really still hate me that much?"

Gloria bit her lower lip and then she sighed. "Yes," she said. "Yes, I'm afraid she does, Mike."

CHAPTER FOUR

THE FOLLOWING MORNING the Woodland Hills police decided to call in the FBI; they'd come to the conclusion that this was no simple case of a lost child.

Lena knew full well that the local police distrusted the feds and hated to call them in. She remembered so clearly how Mike and his partner Jeff would make fun of the ineffective, bungling "fibbies," and she certainly wasn't looking forward to their presence in her life.

Nevertheless, FBI Special Agent Alan Sabin came to interview her that morning. He was a small, wiry man with a sharp nose too big for his face, a square bony jaw and a horizontal slash for a mouth. He gave no hint of what he was thinking or feeling. He asked her and Gloria all the same questions, over and over, and recorded the whole interview on tape.

There had been no phone call, no ransom demand. If Special Agent Sabin thought that was odd, he gave no sign of it, nor could Lena glean any insight into whether he felt the lack of a demand was good or bad.

No wonder Mike hated the FBI, she thought. And as if having the FBI and the LAPD in her face wasn't enough, the news media were beginning to smell a good story. No longer were they just phoning the house, tying up the line, but they were beginning to camp out on the street—first one news van and then another and another, all poking mikes and cameras in everyone's face: the FBI agent's, the cops', Gloria's. It was becoming a circus. Lena wanted to scream at them all: Stop asking useless questions and *do* something!

The police were on the case. She knew that. They even had bloodhounds searching the area around the school. The handler had come for a piece of Kimmy's clothing so his dogs could get her scent. Lena had given him a T-shirt of her daughter's, and then she'd wept when she saw it in a strange man's hand.

After lunch, which Gloria fixed but Lena only picked at, she decided she had to pull herself together and get things organized for Al, even though it was Saturday and the shop was closed. Of course Al had forbidden her to come to work until she knew her daughter was safe, but she ignored his threats. She was going out of her mind sitting around the house. Gloria promised to stay there and call her instantly if she heard anything. But when she arrived outside the garage door and went into the cold, dim place, she burst into tears again.

She called home the second she got into the office.

"Nothing," Gloria said. "They're taking our guard dog away after today." The "guard dog" referred to the policemen who stayed at her house.

"What does that mean, Mom? That they're giving up?" Panic exploded inside her.

"No, no. It just means that they don't think there'll be a call or anyone coming to the house."

"If there's no call, then someone's taken her. God knows where. Or maybe they didn't take her far. They just…" She could never put into words the worst-case scenario. She couldn't say it, but she thought about it constantly.

"Shush," Gloria said. "Don't you even think that!"

"I can't help but think it, Mom," she said wearily.

She put a hand on her forehead. "Mom, what about all the reporters out front? The police aren't going to leave us alone to deal with them, are they?"

"No, no, honey," Gloria said. "There'll be a patrol car stationed here. It's just that they don't have the manpower to monitor the phone from inside. Everything will be okay."

"Sure," Lena said.

It took her all afternoon to get organized. She was so distracted she worked much more slowly than usual and had to check and recheck her figures.

Al came in about three. He walked into the office in his usual outfit—jeans and a T-shirt—chewing on his cigar stub. "I knew you were here," he said. "I spoke to your mother."

"I've got everything just about done," she said.

"I told you not to come in," he growled around the cigar.

"I don't care what you told me."

"You think this place won't run without you?"

"Frankly, no, I don't."

"Ah, hell, you're probably right."

"I'll leave in a little while," she said, rubbing her eyes with her thumb and forefingers. "It's hard. I can't think."

"I never had any kids," Al said, "but I can imagine."

"No, you can't," she said tiredly.

"No, I guess not. Listen, Lena, the guys all offer their support. If they can do anything, or if I can, just let us know, okay?"

"Thanks, Al. If there's anything, I'll tell you." She felt only a dull sort of gratitude, as if there was nothing left inside her but despair.

She showed Al a few of the more important details. "You can call me," she told him. "I'll be home."

Before he left he gave Lena a hug, a warm, fatherly hug, even taking the noxious butt out of his mouth when he did it. "We all care about you and Kimmy," he said. "We care a lot, Lena. You're like family, you and the guys. And don't worry about money. However long it takes, you'll get paid the same as if you were here."

She wished she could make a grand gesture and tell Al not to pay her while she was gone, but she couldn't. She needed her paycheck—her mortgage was due soon. So she just said, "Thanks, Al, thanks a lot," then her mind wandered elsewhere and she hardly heard him leave.

After turning on the computer, she started entering figures on the spreadsheets, trying to get everything up-to-date. All the while she tapped on the keys, her mind kept trying to escape the confines of the office, worrying, scared, wondering *why, why?* And *who?* Where *was* she?

Then she couldn't help remembering Gloria's advice: call Mike. Was she being too stubborn? Was this the time to back down on the promise she'd made herself five years ago? Could Mike really help? If he could, shouldn't she try every path, every possibility, however remote or uncomfortable or ridiculous?

She knew she was stubborn, but she'd always considered it a positive attribute. She reached her goals, she persevered, she didn't let anyone ride roughshod over her. Yet was her stubbornness jeopardizing her daughter now?

Call Mike. What if she did and he made things worse with his drinking and his fits of temper and black spells of depression? What if the whole awful, sick ordeal started all over again? And what if his parents and that self-righteous sister of his tried to get custody of Kimmy, as they'd threatened during the divorce?

A judge might say Lena was an unfit mother for allowing her child to get kidnapped from the school playground. A judge could say anything and take her child away. But, of course, none of that mattered right now, because Kimmy was already gone.

What should she do? The question gnawed at her, and she stared into space, thinking, weighing her options.

To see Mike again... She envisioned him, something she hadn't let herself do for a very long time. Tall and fair, deep-set blue eyes, a slightly off-center nose, a powerful chin. Endearingly homely. She'd loved him so much once, when she'd been young and naive. She'd always dreamed of a man like Mike Quinn who'd sweep her off her feet. And he had.

His drinking hadn't mattered at first, because they were young and everyone they knew partied and drank. She should have known after her own father had died of alcoholism, but she hadn't. Dumb, dumb.

Oh, how she'd loved Mike. And how he'd been destroyed by his partner's death and his descent into violence and depression. That one night had finally put an end to their marriage; she could never trust him again after that.

Could she trust him now?

She turned off the computer, wrote a few last notes for Al and stood, looking around the office. She had to go home now, home to that gaggle of reporters out front and her mother's unspoken fear and the waiting, the endless, terrible waiting. Her heart ached for her child, and she hoped, prayed, that Kimmy wasn't cold or hungry or lost or in pain. She prayed Kimmy wasn't suffering. The thought flew into her head unbidden that perhaps Kimmy wasn't suffering at all anymore, but she shut it off; it was unthinkable.

She turned off the lights in the office and walked through the dim, empty garage. It was quiet, too quiet, this Saturday afternoon—her footsteps echoed hollowly in her ears. She locked the outside door and went to her car. The sun was warm on her back; the sky was blue. Somewhere a dog barked, and a bird flew from a tree branch beyond the empty parking lot. She felt irrationally as if the beautiful weather was an insult, a slap in the face when her existence was pure hell. It should be cold and gray and raining.

She opened her car door and got in, rolling down the window. The car was hot inside after sitting all afternoon in the sun. She was about to insert the key in the ignition, when the passenger door opened, startling her. The door opened wider and a man slid in next to her. Shocked, she stared into Mike Quinn's eyes.

"Mike," she rasped, her hand at her throat.

"Sorry if I scared you," he said, watching her, studying her, feasting his eyes on her for the first time in five years. "But I thought this was the best way. You still don't lock your car, do you?"

For a very long moment she stared back at him in stunned silence, and then she whispered, "Mike?"

"Yeah, it's me."

Her face was pale and drawn, and she looked worn and tired, thinner than he remembered. But beautiful, still beautiful, maybe more so. Maturity had given her a grace and a confidence that were new, and his chest tightened to see her so afraid.

"How did you," she stammered, "how did you know where I was?"

He searched her face, trying to test the waters. Was her temper still as fiery as it had been? "I knew" was all he said.

"But..."

"Lena, I knew, that's all."

"Why are you here? Don't tell me you... Oh, God, my mother told you." She stared at him, her chin trembling. "You know, then."

"Yes, she told me. Don't be angry with her. She did what she thought was right."

"Oh, for God's sake, Mike, she's treating me like a child, and you're no better. Playing a ridiculous cloak-and-dagger game like this." She was angry, her dark eyes smoldering.

"Sorry," he repeated, "but I can help, Lena. There's no time for fighting between us—we need to find Kimmy."

"Oh, God."

She put her face in her hands, and her shoulders shook. He wanted so badly to touch her and comfort her, but he knew he couldn't; he'd forfeited any right to do that long ago. There could only be the business at hand between them.

"Lena, I can help," he repeated. "I checked out the case with the Woodland Hills department. I have some ideas...."

"What ideas?"

"Let's get you home, Lena. No sense sitting here in the car."

"Don't you patronize me, Mike!" she flared. "I've been taking care of myself and my daughter just fine without you...until...until..."

"I know," he said. "I only meant..." He paused. What had he expected—that she'd fall into his arms, that the past five years would be erased? "Lena," he said quietly, "let me help you on this. Forget the past. It's Kimmy who matters now."

He saw tears fill her eyes, and she bowed her head.

He followed her home in his own car. He'd never let her know that he'd occasionally driven by her house just to see where she lived, to see that she was okay. Of course he'd never parked in front of it or gone inside. He'd wanted to, so many times. He'd wanted to pick up the phone and call her; sometimes the temptation was so strong it hurt. But he hadn't, because he knew Lena's pride and stubbornness, and he respected her need to sever all ties with him. He figured it was better for her, and that was the important thing. How ironic that it had taken a tragedy to allow him back into Lena's life.

Gloria's face lit up when she saw him come into the house. "Thank God," she breathed.

"You should have told me, Mom," Lena said.

"You wouldn't have listened."

There was a policeman on duty outside the house, and he came in to investigate the visitor. "And you are?" he asked.

Mike took out his wallet and flipped it open, showing his badge. "Quinn, Metropolitan Area. I'm a…friend of Lena's. She's asked me to help."

"Hey, aren't you the one…didn't I see you on TV?"

"Maybe," Mike said.

"Glad to meet you." The cop shook hands with Mike. "My shift's over soon. It's good to know someone's here inside with the ladies, because the press out there are getting real antsy."

"Yeah, I know. I've been in touch with your captain."

"Are you taking over the case?"

"No, I'm just here to help," Mike said. He knew better than to step on toes. Nothing got cops more worked up than someone encroaching on their turf.

Gloria made coffee and the three of them sat around

the kitchen table. Mike couldn't help noticing the familiar items that Lena had kept from their marriage: some furniture, the teakettle, the cups Gloria poured coffee into. So familiar, yet so totally strange. Sometimes, for a split second, it was as if the intervening years had not existed, but then he'd become aware of the unfamiliar kitchen, the worry on Lena's face, and the time they'd been apart stretched into an unbridgeable gulf.

"Tell me," Lena said, "tell me what's going on, Mike. Is there something the police haven't mentioned? Are there any leads, any suspects, anything?"

He shook his head. "Nothing. They're not holding anything back, Lena."

"You know the FBI's on the case now?" she asked.

He nodded.

"Can they help?"

He shrugged. He didn't want to alarm her, but he had little faith that the FBI could find Kimmy—she wasn't anyone famous, after all. They'd only go through the motions.

"What could have happened to her?" Lena cried. "Why can't anyone find her?"

Gloria put a hand on Lena's arm. "It's only been two days, honey."

"Oh, God," Lena sobbed, putting her face in her hands, "it's been a lifetime."

Mike hated witnessing her suffering. He wanted, once again, to touch her, to hold her. His hands remembered the feel of her, and they itched to reach out and... He erased the thought.

She looked up at him. "How can you help? What can you do?"

"I've spoken to Pop and Uncle Ted. They'll take a

few days off and help out with the investigation. And Scott, you remember my cousin Scott?''

''Of course I remember him.''

''He'll help, too. They're trying to get off-duty guys to volunteer to canvas the neighborhood. *Someone* had to see something. The more men to saturate the area the better.''

''But the Woodland Hills police have already done that,'' Lena whispered, hopelessness filling her voice.

''It has to be done again,'' he said. ''And if there are no witnesses, we'll go back and do it once more. Show her picture, the works. Sometimes people don't remember what they saw—their memories have to be jogged.'' He hesitated. ''There's something else we can do. You can go on TV, Lena, and plead for Kimmy's return.''

''Oh, no... Oh, Mike, I...''

He put up a hand. ''I know how hard it'll be, but if the kidnapper is watching—and the local stations will play and replay the tape—you might be able to humanize the situation in his eyes, gain sympathy. And don't forget,'' he went on, ''someone else might recognize Kimmy from her picture. It's happened before. Look how well those national TV shows work, you know, like *America's Most Wanted*. It's worth a shot.''

Lena was listening, her eyes closed, her hands still white and shaky.

''Anyway,'' Mike said, ''I'll handle it. Don't even worry about it. In the meantime we'll start requestioning people, anyone who could possibly have seen anything.''

''And you think you'll find something new?'' Gloria asked.

''Listen, Kimmy didn't vanish without a trace. We know where she was last and when it was. That's good— that's real good. We start from there.''

"The playground at the school. Four o'clock Thursday afternoon," Gloria said.

"Yeah. One of the kids, I figure. One of her friends had to see something. She was there surrounded by kids when she was taken." He saw Lena flinch, and he felt the pain as if it were his own.

"Taken," Lena whispered. "You think, you *know* she was taken. How do you know? Tell me, Mike."

"It's the only logical conclusion. If she hadn't been taken, we would have found her by now. The bloodhounds couldn't pick up a scent. They milled around the school yard, went as far as the sidewalk, and that was it. So she didn't walk away or wander off or go on foot with anybody. It had to be a vehicle right there at the curb. Someone got her into a car."

"But she's been told a million times never to get into a car with a stranger," Lena protested.

"She's a little girl. Think about it. All a person would have to do is grab her arm and pull her, or even pick her up bodily. She had to be moved only a few feet. Five seconds maybe."

"Why? Why, Mike? What did they hope to gain?"

"I don't know," he said. Then, grimly, he added, "Not yet. But I will."

Lena had let her coffee go cold. She got up and poured it into the sink, then leaned on the counter. Mike met Gloria's gaze across the table, and he saw her pain, her helplessness.

He got up and went to Lena. He put a hand on her shoulder and felt her skin jump under his touch. "Listen," he said softly. "We'll find her. I swear to you."

She turned to face him, and he saw the flash of hope in her eyes, but then she backed away, her face clouding over, and he knew two things: he'd been too close to her, physically too near, and it frightened her. He also knew she didn't trust him. But then, she didn't know he'd quit drinking, did she?

She poured herself another cup of coffee, deliberately turning her back on him, then went to sit down at the table.

"I don't drink anymore," he said in the heavy silence. "In case you were wondering."

Lena looked up, a wry twist to her mouth. "That's nice," she said with pointed sarcasm.

She didn't believe him. Of course not. Why should she? He'd promised her before, and it had lasted—how long?—a day or two, maybe a week once. Nor was there anything he could say to convince her. Not Lena.

"I think that's wonderful," Gloria said. "I'm glad for you, Mike."

"Thank you," he said, noticing that Lena's mind was already elsewhere. He dropped the subject, sat down at the table and sipped some of his lukewarm coffee. Lena's head was bent over her cup, her hands gripping it, white-knuckled. She said something he didn't catch, then she looked up and repeated the question.

"What's the usual outcome in a case like this?" she asked. "Be honest, Mike. In your experience, what happens when there's no ransom demand?"

He was tempted to lie. But she'd know—Lena had always been able to tell when he was lying. He tried to frame his answer carefully. "Every case is different," he said. "There's no hard-and-fast answer."

"Come on, Mike, cut the bull," she said with a vestige of her former spunk.

"It usually means someone has kidnapped the child to…well, because they have a fetish. They're compulsive. They're sick."

"And what happens to these kids, Mike? Do you find them? Do you get them back?"

"There's every possibility that Kimmy will be found," he said in his professional voice.

But Lena pushed herself up from the table, leaned forward on her arms, her face white, her voice shaking. "Dead or alive, Mike? Dead or alive?"

"*Lena,*" her mother said.

"We'll find her, Lena," he said. "We'll find her, I swear."

She stayed there, still leaning forward, her eyes black holes of anguish in her white face. He could see the fine texture of her skin and the way a few dark tendrils of curling hair fell over her forehead. She took a deep breath, obviously trying to steel herself in front of him, wanting to hide her loss of control, but on the edge, held together only by a desperate effort of will. God, he had loved this woman.

She straightened up and caught his gaze and held it. "Find her, Mike," she whispered. "For the love of God, find my…find Kimmy."

"THIS WILL BE your room, Kimmy," Jane said as she pushed open the door to a bedroom at the back of the run-down adobe house. "It needs cleaning up, I guess, but we left in a hurry, see, to come and get you. It's not bad, is it? And you'll like Santa Fe."

The little girl—*my little girl,* Jane had to remind herself—was pretty dragged out from the trip and the pills. But she'd come around. Kids were real tough that way, or so Marie Carlin, who had the house next door, always said.

She switched on the overhead light and led Kimmy in and thought that it was good she'd talked to Marie because, really, Jane didn't know squat about kids, and Marie had five little round ones who all looked healthy. Yeah, Marie could come in handy.

"I want to go home." Kimberly's voice broke into her musings. "I want to go home to my mommy."

Jane felt her nerves rub against her skin. Kimmy was okay for a kid, except when she whined like this. At first she'd supposed the kid was going to be upset and cry and all that. But it had been days, all the way from California to New Mexico, and she was still griping. She and Danny had fed her, let her go to the bathroom, made her real comfortable in the back seat. They'd been friendly. You'd think the kid would quit whining.

It was then that Jane realized she was losing it. She needed a fix. "You wait right here, see?" she said to Kimmy. "I gotta do something and I'll be right back."

"Don't lock me in! Please!" Kimmy cried suddenly, but Jane had already closed the door and twisted the dead bolt Danny had put on it.

She went into the bathroom and lifted the lid of the toilet's water tank. Taped inside was a bag of crack cocaine and a syringe. Just seeing it had a calming effect on her, and within five minutes she was in the kitchen heating up a can of soup for Kimmy, the rush of well-being welcome and familiar.

When the soup was ready she went back to Kimmy, who was lying on the single bed on a pile of Danny's old jeans and T-shirts.

"Hey," Jane said, "it's okay, kid—Kimmy, I mean. Here. Here's something to eat. You'll feel better. Come on, now. Take a sip. I heated it for you myself."

Kimmy finally ate a little, and then Jane made her swallow half a sleeping pill. "Take the vitamin pill," she urged, handing her a plastic glass full of water. "Be good and take it.'' Then she waited in the room for Kimmy to settle down, and as she sat on an old stuffed chair in the corner, watching the flesh of her flesh, she thought again with surprise what a pretty child she'd had. Pretty, and smart, too. She wondered what Danny's plans were. He and his friends wouldn't really want to use this child for a movie the way they had that last girl, the one who had just disappeared one day. Surely Danny wouldn't do that to Jane's own blood.

I'll talk to him, she thought, emboldened by the drugs flowing in her veins. *I'll make him see that she's too young for that kind of stuff.* That other girl had been older.

But by the time Danny got home from visiting his buddies at the roadhouse, Jane's high was wearing off, replaced by the dulling effects of a couple of shots of tequila.

Danny, too, was drunk. ''Spaghetti again?'' he thundered. ''That all you know how to cook?'' Then he swore, sticking his face close to hers. ''You're no good for nothin','' he said. ''Can't even make your own sauce. Gotta buy that jar stuff.''

Jane cowered against the sink. ''Danny, please,'' she whimpered. ''We just got here a couple of hours ago. I didn't have time.''

He swore at her again, then finally backed off, eyeing her. ''That brat go to bed all right?''

''Yes, Danny.''

''You feed her something?''

''She ate. Sure she did.''

''I don't want her all scrawny like you.''

''No, Danny, she'll be fine.''

Danny scowled at her more fiercely. ''You are scrawny.''

"I..."

"Let's see how scrawny you are," he sneered, and he moved toward Jane again, his eyes darkening, moist.

She let him have his way, leading her into the bedroom, pulling off her sweatshirt and jeans, mounting her. Sometime during the act Kimmy awakened and Jane could hear her crying through the paper-thin walls. She closed her mind to it and tried to concentrate on Danny's movements. It was real hard, though, because something in the kid's plaintive sobbing reminded Jane of something from her own distant past. She'd been a kid, too. A real little kid. She'd been crying. And there'd been a man on top of her then, just like now.

CHAPTER FIVE

LENA FINALLY GOT some sleep on Saturday night, but only with the help of two glasses of wine. She slept fully clothed on Kimmy's bed, awoke, cried against her child's pillow and slept fitfully again. On Sunday morning it rained, a gray, misty rain that reached inside her and chilled her soul.

She showered, fought tears when she looked at Kimmy's shampoo on the shelf, then dressed in jeans and a clean white blouse with a dark green cardigan on top to keep warm.

By now it was only seven-thirty. She knew Mike wouldn't be there till nine or so, because that's what he'd told her last night before he'd left, something about having to make the end of a basketball game and he'd be out late. So when the knock came at Lena's front door shortly after eight, she was surprised and then relieved. Maybe it was Mike with some news.

It wasn't Mike at her door. Instead it was his older sister.

"Colleen?" Lena said, holding the door open, trying to fit her mind around the reality of the woman's presence. It had been years....

"Oh, my poor darling," Colleen said before Lena could collect her thoughts. "I had to come over right away. I just heard this morning. Not an hour ago. Oh, you poor, poor dear."

"Come in," Lena said, meeting Colleen's falsely sympathetic smile with one of her own. "This is quite a surprise."

"It's not too early...?"

"No, no, I've already had a half a pot of coffee. Would you like a cup?"

They'd never been friends. And as Lena led Mike's sister into the kitchen, she couldn't help remembering what Colleen had said on the morning of Lena and Mike's wedding: "We've never had a Mexican in the family. If you really cared about my brother, you'd live with him. There's no reason to get married. No reason at all. If you think this will better your station in life, think again."

Essentially Colleen had called her a gold-digging Mexican tart. Forget that Mike was hardly rich—quite the opposite, in fact. Never mind that Lena's family had been American citizens for longer than the Quinns. And forget that Mike had pursued *her.* Because, as Lena had pointed out to Colleen, it was none of her goddamned business.

After the wedding day she and Colleen had barely been polite. Lena might have considered a truce, although she felt then, as she did now, that Colleen owed her an apology. But Colleen wasn't here today for that. And as Lena grudgingly poured her a cup of coffee, she suspected that Colleen, single career woman extraordinaire, had come only to gloat.

Bitch, Lena thought as she handed her ex-sister-in-law the cup and saucer.

"You must be so upset," Colleen was saying. "I can't imagine."

"Mmm," Lena said. "Even if you did have a child, Colleen, it would still be hard to explain what a crisis like this does to you." It came out nastily, and instantly

Lena regretted her words. "That was low," she said. "I'm sorry. But I'm all grown up now, Colleen, and I try to deal in the truth. I don't think we were ever friends. And I can't believe you've come over here after all this time to offer your sympathy or your friendship."

Colleen stared at her for a moment and then finally nodded. "Well, you certainly have grown up," she said levelly.

"Yes, I have. I've had to."

"Then you won't mind if I tell you I've come here as an adult myself."

"Go on," Lena said cautiously.

"In a nutshell," Colleen said, "Mike is finally over you. He's met someone, a supernice lady with two small children. They're very much in love. They're talking about marriage, and I only came over here to warn you to—"

"Oh, please," Lena said, cutting her off, throwing a hand in the air, "give me a break. I'm not interested in Mike, and I'm sure he's not interested in me. What I care about…what *we* care about is the child we adopted six years ago. Did that ever occur to you, Colleen? Do you give a damn about Kimmy at all?"

"Well, of course I—" But she was interrupted by the sound of a key in the front door lock.

"It's my mother," Lena said. "I think this conversation is at an end anyway. I get your message, and you can rest easy. I'm not interested in your brother."

Colleen rose and put her cup and saucer in the sink, then turned to her just as Gloria appeared in the kitchen doorway with a bag of groceries. "I'm glad we had this talk," she said, and then she nodded at Gloria. "Mrs. Torres."

"Hello, Colleen," Gloria said. "It's been a long time."

"Yes. Nice to see you again." Then she turned to Lena. "I'll see myself out."

"Fine," Lena said coolly. "Do that."

When Colleen was gone, Gloria looked at her daughter, let out a long breath and said, "Phew. Want to tell me what *that* was about?"

But Lena only shook her head.

As promised, Mike arrived a couple of minutes after nine. And he had a surprise for her, something she hadn't at all been prepared for.

He'd come with a news team.

Lena stared incredulously at the lights and cameras being hauled into her living room, then she grabbed Mike's arm. "I...I can't do this! I can't go on TV and beg...."

He drew her into the kitchen. "I brought them this morning so you wouldn't have time to agonize over it. I knew if I told you, you'd go haywire. Let's just get it over with," he said.

She bit her lower lip. "I can't go on TV. I'll...I'll lose it, Mike."

"The idea *is* to lose it," he said in a calm voice. "I've arranged for the tape to air on all the local channels. You'll only have to do this once. I'll be right here with you. It'll take two, three minutes and it'll be all over."

"Oh, God," she whispered.

"I know," he said. "I know. Just think of Kimmy. Someone out there may have seen her. You need to do this."

She stood there shaking, her mind whirling. What was she going to say? And she knew she'd cry. She'd break down and spill her guts and her deepest, darkest fears to the whole world.

"Ready," said a voice from the living room.

Lena could see the bright lighting and a female reporter—she recognized the face—sitting right on her couch, waiting.

"The reporter will guide you through a couple of questions. It'll be easy," Mike was saying. "Then the camera will pan on your face and you'll ask whoever took Kimmy to return her. When they edit the tape, they'll keep flashing Kimmy's picture with a 1-800 number below. It's all taken care of."

"Mr. Quinn, we're ready," said the well-modulated voice again.

The reporter signaled the cameraman, a red light went on and the woman put a grim expression on her face. "Miss Portillo," she began, "can you tell us when and how your daughter, Kimberly, disappeared?"

Lena went on autopilot. She said something like, "We call her 'Kimmy,'" and after that she barely remembered what she said, other than, "If anyone has seen my daughter, please, let the police know. She had on blue jeans with pink hearts on the knees, a T-shirt and tennis shoes and a blue windbreaker. She has long brown hair and brown eyes."

All she could think of was to stay in control, to keep her dignity, to speak clearly, but the lights were shining in her eyes and the reporter was asking more questions, and she supposed she answered them. The only thing she could really remember afterward was that she looked directly at the camera and begged, yes, begged, the kidnapper to return her child. "Please, please, whoever has my little girl, please let her go." And then, in case Kimmy ever saw this, she said, "Kimmy, sweetheart, we're here waiting for you and trying to find you. We love you.''

And then it was over, and the crew cleared out of Lena's house and it seemed as if she gradually reoccupied her own body.

"You were wonderful," Gloria said, "absolutely wonderful."

All Lena could say to Mike was, "Thank God you didn't warn me."

Later, when she'd gotten her breath back, Mike brought them up to speed on the investigation. "I've already been by the Woodland Hills police station," he said. "Nothing new to report. I did get the full student list, though, and I'm going to work on it until something gives."

Lena took a calming breath and looked at him. "The police already interviewed all the kids in the playground that day," she said, hugging herself.

"So I do it again. And again if I have to. And right now Pop and Uncle Ted are out with several of the guys from L.A. Metropolitan talking to teachers and the janitor and the bus drivers. *Again.*"

"Something'll turn up," Gloria said, stacking the coffee cups and a few dishes in the dishwasher. "I know it will."

"I wonder," Mike said then, "I wonder if I could see Kimmy's room."

She nodded, understanding. After all, he'd been the caring man who'd taken the abandoned infant girl to the hospital in the first place, the man who'd stopped by every day to see how the little crack baby was doing. And it had been Mike who'd first suggested they talk to Social Services about adoption. They'd been planning a family soon anyway. But that had been before Jeff Davidoff's tragic death and Mike's descent into hell.

Lena shook herself mentally. "Sure," she said. "Down the hall to the right. I'll, ah, show you."

It hurt to see him standing in Kimmy's bedroom. Lena leaned a shoulder against the doorjamb and watched him as he eyed the room, the pink skirted dressing table, the dollhouse Gloria had given Kimmy for Christmas, the white toy chest with the painted lambs on it, the collection of stuffed animals on the windowsill. There was even the little brown fur rabbit Mike had given Kimmy as an infant.

He touched it. "I remember this," he said quietly.

Lena felt a flood of emotions then, each vying for ascendancy. There was resentment—Mike here, invading the special privacy of their lives again. Mike, the man who'd put a loaded gun to his head when his year-old daughter was sleeping only a few yards away. Yes, Lena resented Mike's presence. She resented needing his badge to pull the strings she couldn't. All these years she'd made it on her own, she and Kimmy, and now here he was in charge of their lives. She felt a surge of bitterness toward him and a peculiar kind of jealousy.

Mike stood in Kimmy's room, an invader, an alien, and Lena wanted suddenly to scream at him, *Look at what you did! If you hadn't been such a rotten drunk, my child,* our *child, would still be here in this room!* She said nothing. What good would it have done? And it really wasn't Mike's fault. It wasn't Gloria's fault or her own, either. She had to stop searching for someone to blame.

After a time the jealousy and resentment settled, and her heart actually began to soften toward the man who'd never gotten to know the child he'd chosen as his daughter, the man who'd sadly thrown everything away because of alcohol and a selfish sort of depression inherent in his work.

He looked awfully big and out of place in this little girl's domain, a giant among the dolls and fur animals. He'd opened a pop-up picture book and was smiling, then he caught Lena's eyes. "I missed a lot, didn't I?" he asked.

Out in the living room Mike picked up his leather jacket from the arm of the couch. "Half the kids I need to see will probably be at Sunday school or out to breakfast, but I'm going to give it a shot. If I hear anything, anything at all, I'll—"

"I'm going with you," Lena said.

Mike stopped short. "No way."

"I know these kids. I know most of their mothers. I can talk to them."

"And I can't?"

She sighed. "Right. You're working with Hostage Negotiations—I guess I knew that. But these are kids, Mike. They *know* me. You might intimidate—"

"Give me a little credit, Lena," he said.

"I can't sit here and do nothing," she blurted out. "Let me help. Let me at least tag along. Please."

"Haven't you been through enough already today? I don't think—"

"For my sake, Mike," she cut in. "I'm going stark raving nuts with this waiting."

Mike studied her for another moment, and Gloria said, "I'll man the telephone here, just in case."

And then he relented. "All right, okay. But you just sit and listen."

"Of course," Lena said, grabbing her purse. "I'll

drive, though—I mean, if it's okay? I know where a lot of these kids live and…''

"Sure," he said. "Whatever. You always did like to be behind the wheel."

Lena ignored his subtle jab. She was relieved just to be going along. Anything to keep busy. She'd steel herself against Mike's sudden control of her life; she'd do whatever she had to. *Just stay focused,* she told herself. *Forget Mike, forget who he is. Who he was.*

It wasn't a large school district, and Lena knew the streets fairly well. She drove her souped-up GTO smoothly as Mike read off the names on the list, beginning with *A.*

"Will Abbott," Mike said. "You know the kid?"

"Vaguely. I think his father's an insurance agent. Maybe he's a real-estate agent.

"They're on Keokuk Avenue."

"Okay," Lena said.

The Abbotts were all still in their pajamas and robes when Mike and Lena knocked on their door. Mike introduced himself, flipping his badge, and then introduced Lena. Will Abbott's father recognized Lena and asked them in immediately, mentioning that a policeman had already telephoned. "That was yesterday," he said.

The family was sick over Kimmy's disappearance. Will's mother hugged Lena and got teary eyed.

Mike chatted with the six-year-old in a friendly, quiet manner and then got down to business. "You know Kimmy, don't you?" he asked.

"She's in my class," Will replied, fiddling with the TV remote control before his father took it away.

''And you were in the playground area after school the day she disappeared.''

"Uh-huh."

"Were you playing with Kimmy?"

"Nah." He made a face.

"You don't play with the girls, do you?" Mike asked in a conspiratorial tone.

"Nah." Another face.

"I didn't either in first grade," Mike put in. "So tell me, were the girls playing with a soccer ball?"

"I...I think so."

"I only ask because my notes say that Ben Halloran thought the girls were tossing the ball around just before the school buses left. Does that sound right?"

"They always play with the soccer ball," Will said.

"Do you know which girls?"

Will screwed up his face, thinking. "I think it's Mary Lou and maybe Ally. And Marcia."

"And Kimmy?"

"Uh-huh."

"Will," Mike said in a very quiet, attention-getting voice, "did you see a stranger on the playground that day?"

Will shook his head.

"Maybe the stranger was outside the fence," Mike went on. "Maybe standing there or in a car."

"I don't know," Will said.

"There are so many parents who wait in cars," Will's father said. "You know, picking their kids up."

Mike turned to him briefly. "Something like eighteen or more that afternoon. Including Kimmy's grandmother."

"The girls get in trouble a lot," Will chimed in.

"How's that?" Mike asked.

Will shrugged. "They throw the ball into the street. Mrs. Martini says they can't play with it if they do it on purpose."

"Mrs. Martini? She was one of the playground monitors?"

"Uh-huh. She's my teacher."

Lena looked expectantly at Mike, but he shook his head. "She wasn't on the playground that day."

Then Will's mother spoke. "The kids are supposed to go straight to the buses or to private cars. They don't always, though. Tomorrow," she said, "a few of us are going to talk to Miss Trenholm about some after-school supervision on the playground. I think after Kimmy's... Well you understand."

"Of course," Mike said.

When they were back in Lena's car she checked the time. "My God," she said, "that took half an hour. If each interview takes that long, Mike, it'll be days more...."

"I know," he said gravely, "I know."

Before noon they'd talked to three more children. Getting anything out of a six- or seven-year-old was like pulling teeth. The only facts they had were that Kimmy, Ally, Mary Lou and a girl called Marcia had been tossing a soccer ball around. One of the children they interviewed corroborated Will's story about the girls frequently getting into trouble for throwing the ball over the fence into the street.

At a fast-food place where Lena and Mike stopped for a bite to eat, Lena pressed for interviews with Ally and Mary Lou. "I realize the police have already talked to them both a couple of times, but I think we should—"

Mike nodded. "We will. I just want to talk to a couple more kids first. If I can get one thing, one new viewpoint on what went on that afternoon in the playground—"

"We *know* what went on."

"No, Lena, we don't. All we know is that the kids

remember the usual routine. I'd like just one small break, something new to put in front of the girls before we talk to them. As it stands now, they've been asked the same questions and they've given the same answers. I want something, anything, to jar their memories."

Lena picked at her French fries and sighed. "I understand. But what if there isn't anything? What if both girls were gone by the time Kimmy disappeared?"

"Gloria was at the school on time. The buses hadn't even left yet. But Kimmy was gone. Believe me, something out of the ordinary happened, and someone had to see it. The trouble with kids is that their memories are short and they tend to recall only the mundane occurrences in their daily lives. That or something special," he added, "like a birthday party or a trip to Disneyland. You know."

"You're good with the kids," Lena admitted.

"Right," he said, skeptical.

She looked up. "No, you are. I'm surprised."

Mike made a grunting noise, dismissing her words. He went back to his food, and that was when Lena remembered his sister's visit, the news about Mike remarrying. The woman, according to Colleen, had children. A ready-made family for Mike. She wondered how he was really handling the booze. She'd heard what he'd said, but then she'd heard it all before. Her father had been a pro at denial. And so was Mike. Oh, she knew all about drunks who weren't drinking. It was only a matter of time before—

"Ready to go?" Mike said, breaking into her train of thought.

"Ah, sure," Lena said.

They went to two more houses that afternoon. One family wasn't home; the other family was, but the little girl was sick with a cold and not up to an interview. She'd been picked up at school early the day of Kimmy's disappearance, so the interview would have been a waste of time anyway.

Exhaustion caught up with Lena as they left the last house. She felt that now-familiar sinking sensation and pulled over to the curb, letting her forehead rest on the steering wheel. "Oh, God" was all she said.

Mike was very quiet for several minutes, and then he turned toward her, resting an arm on the back of her seat. It had begun to rain again, a monotonous drizzle oozing from a leaden sky. The wipers swished on the glass.

"Lena," he finally said, "you've held up like a trooper so far. Try not to let go now. Something *is* going to give. It always does."

"If Kimmy were... Oh, Mike, wouldn't I know it, *feel* it, if something awful had happened?"

"I think you would," he said. "Sure, you'd know."

"Liar."

He laughed softly. "Hey," he said, "where's that free spirit I pulled over for speeding? What was it—eight years ago now?"

Lena groaned, remembering. It had been a blazing hot summer day, the Santa Ana winds whipping down into the greater Los Angeles basin like breath from hell. She'd just had the rebuilt engine put into the car, and the top was down. She'd been speeding all right, doing ninety-three in a fifty-five zone, and Mike had rushed up behind her in his patrol car, lights flashing, siren wailing. When she'd pulled over and Mike had sauntered up to the car, ticket pad in hand, she'd slowly removed her sunglasses and taken the offensive.

"Officer," she'd said, "I realize I was going a little

over the speed limit, but I'm trying out a rebuilt engine, and you can't tell a thing at fifty-five.''

''Uh-huh,'' he'd replied, his eyes hidden behind mirrored sunglasses. But he was big and fair and intimidating as hell in his spit-and-polish uniform.

''See this invoice?'' She'd pulled the bill for the engine out of her purse. ''Eight hundred and ninety-six dollars. Would you pay it before checking out the car?''

''License and registration, please, ma'am,'' he'd intoned.

And that had set her off. ''You can't ticket me!''

''License and registration,'' he'd repeated, ''and your proof of insurance.''

''I'll...I'll lose my license!''

''So you've had previous tickets?'' he'd asked, deadpan.

''What do *you* think?'' she'd snapped back, and that had been the beginning of their relationship.

Mike had indeed ticketed her. But then he'd shown up in traffic court and allowed that Miss Torres might not have been going all that fast, his radar had been on the fritz that whole day, etc., etc. And after court he'd walked up to her and asked her out.

''You've got a lot of nerve,'' she'd said, ''but I suppose I owe you one.''

''How about going out with me, then?''

''This is extortion or something.''

''Uh-huh,'' he'd said. ''Either have dinner with me or I'll tail you everywhere you go.''

''You're not even that cute,'' she'd said.

''Dinner, Miss Torres?''

''All right, dinner. But it'll cost you a week's salary.'' In the end, Lena hadn't been able to do that to Mike. They'd gone to a cheap but good Italian place that was Lena's favorite. Six months later they'd been married.

"Remember?" Mike was saying now. "I clocked you at ninety-five on the freeway."

"It was ninety-three. Don't exaggerate."

He smiled. "Okay, I'll concede the point. I just want to see some of that old spark. You can get through this, Lena. If you hang tough, you'll make it."

"I'm trying," she said. "I really am."

The next family on the list was the Samsons. Ally Samson was Kimmy's best friend; she was also one of the last children who'd played with Kimmy in the school yard. Her mother had already told Lena that Kimmy had been there when she'd picked Ally up. She'd repeated this to the police, and Ally had been interviewed several times.

"Oh, Mike," Lena said, "what if she can't tell us anything else?"

"We'll see," was all Mike said.

The Samsons weren't home. According to a neighbor who was mowing his lawn, they had gone camping.

They had no more luck at the Meacham house. Then they drove to Mary Lou Shelton's and found the little girl just arriving home from spending the weekend with her father and his new family. Mrs. Shelton was very sympathetic, hugging Lena, sitting Mary Lou down and telling her to pay very close attention to the questions the nice man was going to ask.

Mary Lou sat on a footstool and looked at Lena. "Is Kimmy going to be at school tomorrow?"

Lena felt the hot burn of tears press behind her eyes. "If we find her, sure. She wouldn't want to miss school."

"Good," Mary Lou announced.

She was a precocious child who was better than most her age at recalling details. "I never left the playground," she told the group, "because Mrs. Martini gets real mad if we do. She said she'd take the ball away, too. So I never, ever throw it in the road.''

"That's good,'' Mike said, ''but didn't one of you throw the ball—by accident, of course—into the street that day?''

Mary Lou sighed and looked at her multicolored fingernails. "Marcia did, by accident.''

"I see,'' Mike said. "And did Marcia get the ball?''

"Kimmy did.''

"Oh,'' Lena said.

"That first time,'' Mary Lou added.

"So someone accidentally threw the ball into the street a second time?'' Mike asked.

"I think it was Marcia again.'' Mary Lou gave another sign. "But that time Kimmy told her not to be a brat and to get it herself.''

"So Marcia went into the street,'' Mike said. "And then what happened?''

"Nothing. She got the ball and that's when Mommy honked the horn for me.''

"Where was Kimmy then?''

"Waiting for Marcia at the fence. She was calling, 'Hurry up! My grandma's going to be here soon.'''

"And what did Marcia do then?''

"She had the ball. I remember she ran past me with the ball.''

"Why do you remember that?'' Mike asked.

"Because she bumped me and she looked like she was mad or something.''

"At you?''

Mary Lou shook her head. "I don't think so. But she looked mad.''

They left the Sheltons' shortly after that, and Lena wondered at Mike's silence. "What was all that stuff about? You know, about the ball? Are you thinking one of the girls might have seen something in the street?'' she asked, steering around a corner.

"I'm not thinking anything," Mike said.

But Lena knew that look of concentration. "Tell me. I'm not one of the kids, Mike."

"It's probably nothing," he said. "But I am wondering just what it was that made Marcia look so angry."

"Mike, little girls are like that. They have very complicated social relationships. Someone's always mad at someone else. It probably doesn't mean a thing."

"Complicated relationships," he repeated. "I'll try to remember that."

It was almost six that Sunday evening when they returned to Lena's house. Gloria came out to meet them and had very little news. "That FBI man was back this afternoon. Asking questions. He wants you to call him tomorrow. And several of the parents from school called to touch base, but other than that, zilch. I was hoping," Gloria said, "well, you know."

And then Lena walked Mike to his car. "A wasted day," she said, hugging her cardigan around her. "Another wasted day."

"Maybe not," Mike said, opening his door. "Remember the TV interview will be played over and over."

She tried a weak smile. "I want to thank you, Mike," she said.

"For what?"

"For all you're doing. You and the other guys. Really."

"Hey," he said, getting into his car and rolling down the window, "I'm Kimmy's father. No matter what you believe, I'll always be there for her." Then he added, "For both of you."

But Lena didn't have the courage to believe him.

CHAPTER SIX

A COLD SHOT of adrenaline awakened Mike at four-thirty on Monday morning. *Jennifer.* Holy cow, he realized he'd had a lunch date with Jennifer on Saturday!

Well, he couldn't telephone her at this ungodly hour. Still, he was wide-awake now, his mind working.

He got up and made coffee, showered and tried to listen to the twenty-four-hour news channel, but it was impossible to focus on anything but the desperate plight of his daughter.

Of course he'd have to go into headquarters this morning and talk to Joe Carbone. He'd need time off. How much? It was hard to say. They might get a break in Kimmy's case today. Or maybe tomorrow. Or maybe a month from now. The terrible truth was that too often missing children were never found. He himself was gut sick—but Lena. He couldn't begin to imagine what this was doing to her. The idea of never knowing Kimmy's fate was inconceivable.

At eight he phoned Lena, explaining there wasn't much they could do till after school was out. In the meantime he'd clear his desk at work.

"You're taking a leave?" she asked.

"Yeah," he said. "I'm due some vacation time. I'll also touch base with my father and Uncle Ted again, just in case. But as of last night, there was nothing new on their ends. They've been working the school-employee angle—bus drivers, teachers, janitor. Dad canvassed the immediate school neighborhood again yesterday. So far no dice.''

"Oh, Mike,'' she said, her voice trembling, "it's been four days. I'm starting to think…''

"Don't,'' he said tightly. "Don't start making up scenarios.''

"I can't help it.''

"Just wipe your mind clean. I'll be by at three-thirty to pick you up. Meanwhile I'll try to reach some of the parents we missed yesterday, set up appointments. This may take all evening.''

"That's fine,'' she said. "I'll get Mom to sit by the phone.''

"Lena,'' he said, "the chances of Kimmy's abductor calling after all this time are slim to none.''

"It's not just that. Kimmy knows our home number. She also knows 911. There's always a chance, well, that she could somehow get to a phone, you know.''

"She could,'' Mike agreed.

"She's very resourceful.''

"She gets that from you,'' he said.

Shortly after talking to Lena, Mike drove the few blocks to Jennifer's house. He would have telephoned her, but after forgetting their date, he figured his explanation had better be in person.

Jennifer had just gotten her kids off to school when he pulled up in front of her two-story, mission-style house. He parked his used beige Volvo behind her shiny new BMW. Their houses were only a mile apart. It might as well have been a million.

When she answered the doorbell, she was already in a leotard, tights and a light sweater, ready for work at her studio. A very attractive green-eyed woman with pale skin and long, curling auburn hair. She gave him a cool look and did not invite him in.

"Is my calendar wrong?" she asked.

Mike blew out a breath. "Something happened, Jennifer. If I could come in for a minute…?"

"I can't believe this," she said. "There's no reason on earth why I should let you into my house."

Jennifer was an independent nineties woman who didn't go in for games. She didn't have to. First off, her ex had left her and the kids pretty well-heeled, but second, she was one of those extremely good-looking women who took excellent care of herself. From the male attention Jennifer always drew, Mike imagined she could have all the dates she wanted. She and Mike had met through his sister, Colleen, and Jennifer had flirted with him. He figured she was one of those women who were drawn to the element of danger that was ever present in a cop's life.

He cocked his head and looked at her standing in her doorway, barring his way. Yeah, Jennifer would ditch him in a second if she wanted. "It's my daughter," he said. "You remember I told you about her? Kimberly. She's missing."

Jennifer's face fell. "Missing?"

"It happened on Thursday. Right from the playground at school."

"My God," she said, opening the door to him, "I had no idea. That must be what the message from Colleen was about. Oh, Mike."

He sat in her well-appointed off-white living room and told her all about it—everything that he knew, anyway, which was tantamount to nothing.

"Oh, Mike," she said, "you must be going out of your mind."

"I am. But it's worse on her mother. After all, I haven't seen Kimmy since she was a year old."

Jennifer nodded solemnly. "I know," she said, "and I've always thought the woman was, well, selfish not to let you help out, at least financially. Children need both parents."

Mike had explained to Jennifer about his partner's death and his drinking and about how Lena had severed all ties, even taken her mother's maiden name to hide from him. Jennifer never seemed to quite fathom it. Of course, he'd left out the part about putting the loaded gun to his head in a drunken fit of depression over Jeff's death.

"So it was this woman, Gloria, who was supposed to pick your daughter up at school?" Jennifer was asking.

"Gloria, yes," he said. "She's Kimmy's grandmother. Evidently she was on time, but Kimmy had already disappeared."

Jennifer closed her eyes for a moment, then sighed. "It's a shame, a real crime," she said, "that Lena wasn't at the school to pick up her own child."

Mike stared at her, frowning. That was the first real bitchy thing he'd heard her say since they'd started seeing each other. He was taken aback and he was disappointed. But then he thought about her statement and realized that her reaction was probably normal.

The only thing he said in defense of Lena was, "Kimmy's mother has to work long hours. She's lucky she's got Gloria to baby-sit."

Mike left the house by nine-fifteen, explaining that he didn't know when he'd be over again but that he'd keep her informed.

"How does it look for Kimmy?" Jennifer asked at the door.

He shook his head. "To be honest, not good. When something doesn't break in the first twenty-four hours, the odds get worse."

"Well, good luck," she said, and they kissed, a brush of their lips. Jennifer put a hand on his cheek. "Call me," she said.

At the LAPD Metropolitan Area headquarters, where Mike was stationed, everyone was surprised to see him walk in. Joe came striding out of his glass-enclosed office and confronted him.

"What in hell are you doing here, Quinn?" Joe asked, hands on hips.

"Don't start on me," Mike said, "I'm only here to dump my paperwork on one of the other guys."

"Already done." Joe folded his arms over his chest. "Now, I want you out of here for as long as it takes."

"Hey, Mike!" one of the other team members called from across the room. "I got your basketball kids all taken care of. Monday, Wednesday and Fridays. Right?"

Mike lifted a hand and gave him a nod of thanks. One less thing to worry about. He made a mental note to call Jay's mother. Jay was the kid he worked with in the Adopt-a-Buddy program. Maybe, though, by next weekend they'd have Kimmy home. *God willing,* he thought.

"I'd get out of here before the fibbies come back if I were you," Joe said then. "They've been a big pain in the butt around here all weekend. Especially that Special Agent Sabin. He's a real ass. And I sure don't like some of the questions they've been asking the guys."

"I can just imagine," Mike said, knowing the FBI would be looking into his background. His and Lena's. The parents were often the number one suspects in a case where a child disappeared and no ransom was being sought.

He frowned. "I suppose they want to question me."

Joe shrugged. "If they can't find you, they can't question you. Am I wrong?"

Mike nodded. "What about that class you wanted me to hold in Bakersfield? Do you think Raddo could handle…"

"Already done," Joe said. "Now, take off. And for God's sake, call me every day. And if anything breaks…"

"I'll let you know," Mike said.

"We're all praying for her," Joe said, "you know that."

"Thanks. I think we're going to need all the help we can get."

After leaving headquarters in downtown L.A., Mike drove to his dad's precinct in the Hollenbeck Area. Both his dad and uncle had been stationed there for their entire careers. Mike's father, Larry, was a homicide detective who could have retired ten years ago but figured he'd go bananas at home. Uncle Ted was also a detective, but with vice. His son, Scott—Mike's first cousin—was a patrolman. He was sort of a lazy kid who always took the least path of resistance. Riding around in a patrol car and responding to 911 calls suited him just fine.

Everyone at the Hollenbeck station knew Mike. They'd all heard about his daughter, too.

"Anything, anything at all we can do to help, just ask," he was told a dozen times as he wended his way through a clutter of desks to his dad's cubbyhole.

Larry Quinn looked up from a stack of paperwork. "Hey, kid," he said, rising, shaking his son's hand, "any news?"

"Not a damn thing," Mike said, and he sat down across from father.

Larry Quinn was a big man, too, taller than Mike by an inch, and he outweighed his son by twenty pounds. Not fat, but big boned. If his hair had been darker, he could have stood in for John Wayne.

"I've got a couple of printouts here from the national data bank on known child molesters in the area," Larry told him, and he handed Mike the sheets. "It's pretty recent. Ted's working the angle that our perp's a weirdo. He's out doing some checking on the streets right now."

Mike nodded. He didn't have to say how much he appreciated all the support—his family knew it without having to hear it.

"Now me," Larry said, "I've been thinking that maybe we could take a new tack here. What if someone, say a parent who'd recently lost a child, decided to remedy the situation? It's happened before. A grief-stricken mother just snaps one day. She sees a kid, a nice-looking kid around the age of her own, and she takes her. Just up and snatches her."

Mike let out a breath. "I don't know, Pop. Cases like that are few and far between."

"Could happen, though. This afternoon, soon as I clear some of this damn paperwork off my desk, I thought I'd get in touch with the county coroner's, try to get a list of kids, girls, around Kimmy's age who've died recently." Then Larry Quinn tapped his pen on a stack of files. "I still think we oughta try to find out where the birth mother is."

"I agree," Mike said. "The trouble is, she's not in any of the data banks. Doesn't have a driver's license, not registered to vote anywhere, zip. No one's heard or seen a thing since we found her and she signed the adoption papers six years ago. Chances are, the way she was using, she's dead by now."

"You've checked with Social Services and the adoption courts, you know, to see if anyone was trying to get info on Kimmy's whereabouts?"

"Woodland Hills cops did it first thing," Mike replied. "FBI checked some more. And keep in mind that Lena's been using her mother's maiden name. I just don't think that Jane Cramm, if she's even alive, could have traced Kimmy. Hell, I'm a cop. It took me a few weeks of pulling strings to find them."

"Yeah," Larry said, "I remember." Then he frowned. "I just hope there's nothing we're overlooking."

"So do I," Mike said. "So do I, Dad."

Mike arrived at Lena's a few minutes before three-thirty that afternoon and found her cleaning out the storage closet off of the kitchen.

"Staying busy," she said, giving him a weak smile. "I'll go change. Give me a minute?"

"Sure," he said, hands in his jean pockets.

"There's coffee made."

"I'll get a cup."

Mike poured himself some coffee, then wandered into the living room. He remembered most of the furniture, though Lena had had the couch recovered. He stood by the built-in bookshelves and stared at the many photos Lena had there. Pictures of her and Kimmy. Of course there were none of him. Idly he wondered if she'd thrown them away.

He noticed, though, that even if there were no mementos of his life with Lena, there were no photos of any other man, either. Did Lena have someone? Surely if there was a man in her life, he'd be present during this crisis. He could ask her. But then he realized he'd sooner burn in hell. Besides, he had a life of his own now. He had a woman, too, a good woman. They'd even spoken about marriage. Not planned anything. But both had mentioned not being entirely against remarriage.

Lena appeared in black jeans and a bright teal-colored cotton top, sleeves pushed up. She'd combed her long brown hair out of the ponytail she'd been wearing, and it fell softly against her shoulders. Mike stared at her for a moment too long before asking if she wanted to take his car or hers.

"Mine," she said, shrugging. "I know the streets."

She walked out to the road ahead of him, shoulder bag swinging against a full hip. God, how he remembered those hips. When they'd been married, he'd wanted to punch out more than a few guys for leering at that perfect fullness.

He got in the passenger side, slammed the door and told himself to forget it.

"Where to first?" she asked, sliding the gearshift into reverse, turning her head to back out.

"We'll go by the Samsons'. Ally Samson's. I talked to her mother this morning. She said she'd meet us at four."

"Oh, I hope Ally can help us. I know the police have talked to her before, but..."

He heard the desperation and hopelessness in her voice. And he felt it, too. There was no other way, however, to conduct an investigation. You simply had to go over and over what little you had and pray for a break.

Ally's mother was apologetic for going on the camping weekend. "If I'd known you needed to talk to us again, I would have stayed right here." Margy Samson showed them in, giving Lena a comforting hug. "Just tell me what we can do. Anything."

Mike started carefully, as always, with Ally, whom Kimmy had known and played with since preschool. He recalled Lena telling him he was good with kids. He didn't know about that. He was okay with adults, gentle and authoritative when it came to negotiating for a hostage's life. But kids? Truthfully, he was never sure how to handle them. Some were shy. Some forthright. Some were just downright obnoxious. He wondered what Kimmy was like. He wondered a lot about that. And he was beginning to wonder if he'd ever find out. It had been four full days without a single clue.

Ally was outgoing and very sweet. He imagined she'd be a sensitive young lady someday soon, the kind of friend who'd be close for a lifetime.

The interview went well, although they learned nothing new, except for the fact that it had been Mary Lou who'd first thrown the ball over the fence into the street. "Mary Lou calls Mrs. Martini a poop-face," Ally announced.

"Mmm," Mike said. "Is that because she disciplines you girls for playing in the street?"

"Uh-huh," Ally said. "Mary Lou and Marcia once had to go to Miss Trenholm's office."

Lena spoke up then. During all the interviews she'd sat in on, this was one of the few times she'd shown her frustration.

"For God's sake, Mike, we know all this," she said, leaving her chair, hugging herself as she walked to the front window and stared out.

He could see the quake in her shoulders, and he knew she was barely keeping in control. He met Margy's eyes for a moment.

To Lena, he said, "Just a couple more questions, all right?"

She didn't answer.

"Okay, Ally, so Marcia came back then, with the

ball," Mike said, "and Marcia bumped into Mary Lou. Like she was angry."

"She wasn't mad at Mary Lou," Ally stated positively.

"Oh?" Mike said.

Ally shook her head. "She was mad at those mean people."

Mike felt every nerve in his body tense. He noticed that Ally's mother had straightened in her seat and that Lena had spun around and was staring wide-eyed at Ally.

Mike took it very, very carefully. "You mean the people who were on the sidewalk?" he asked.

She shook her head, and that was when Lena took a step toward her. Mike put up a warning hand. He smiled at Ally. "So these mean people who made Marcia mad weren't on the sidewalk. Do you remember where they were?"

"In the car," she said without hesitation.

He couldn't believe it. He'd talked to how many kids? And until this moment not a single one had recalled anything like this.

"Okay," Mike said calmly, "Marcia was mad at the people in the car. Do you know why, Ally?"

Ally shook her head. "I think the mean man said something."

"And this was what—when Marcia got the ball?"

"Uh-huh."

"But you didn't hear what the man said?"

"No, my mommy was there for me."

"I see," Mike said, signaling both women in the room to keep their cool. "So tell me, Ally, was the man driving? Was he behind the steering wheel?"

"I don't know." She looked at her mother, who gave her an encouraging smile and a little nod.

"Ally," Mike said, getting her attention again, "was the other person a man, too?"

"I don't know."

"That's okay. I was only wondering because you said the mean people, so I thought maybe you saw another person."

Ally shook her head and then tears filled her eyes. "Did that man take Kimmy away?" she blurted out.

"We don't know," Mike said.

The interview went downhill from there. Mike ended the questioning when it was obvious they weren't going to learn another thing from Ally. Not today. But he knew that a police psychologist—one who dealt primarily with children—might have to be called in to do another interview.

At the door, Margy Samson said, "Do you want me to keep asking her?"

But Mike told her emphatically that he didn't want the Samsons to mention it. "The last thing we need Ally to do is make something up to please us. Okay?"

"Sure, I understand," she said.

In the car, Lena was clearly out of her mind with frustration. "Let me talk to her again," she begged. "Please, Mike, we both know Ally must have seen more. She knows me—she'll be relaxed. Mike, you've got to let me...."

He put a hand on her shoulder then, and surprisingly Lena burst into tears. He wanted so much to draw her close, to comfort her, but he knew she'd never allow it. Instead he kept his hand there, very gently, and let her cry herself dry.

Several minutes later she sniffed and raised her head. "Oh, God," she said, "what if it's the same story with

Marcia? What if she *does* remember these people and they have nothing whatsoever to do with Kimmy?"

Mike finally took his hand away. "Hey," he said, "why don't we just take this one step at a time? Let's go on over to the Meachams' and see what we can learn. Okay? You up to driving or do you want to—"

Lena gathered herself quickly. "I'm fine. I really am. I'm sorry I lost it."

"Don't be. If no one was watching," he said, "I'd do the same thing."

She shot him a look. "You're such a terrible liar, Mike Quinn," she said, and then she put on big round sunglasses and pulled out into traffic. He sat back, comfortable with her driving, and felt relief. The old spunky Lena was back. For now.

The Meachams lived in a more modest neighborhood of Woodland Hills in an old duplex, a wood-framed house that had seen better days. Lena didn't know them at all because Marcia was new to Jefferson Elementary School. Mike was slightly taken aback when a man in a wheelchair came to the door. Marcia's father.

"Nancy's still at work," he told Mike and Lena, "and me? I'm pretty much home, as you can see. Full government disability."

Mike nodded, then Gary Meacham called to his daughter, who appeared from the back of the house. "Marcia," he said, "these folks are here about your friend Kimmy. They want to ask you a few questions."

Marcia was a pretty little girl, though Mike could see the hint of deviltry behind her blue eyes. It wasn't hard at all to believe the playground monitor, Mrs. Martini, would have her hands full with this youngster.

As usual, Mike went slowly with the child, trying to gain her trust and put her at ease. Finally he began with the questions about the soccer ball and how it ended up in the street. "So you accidentally threw the ball over the fence," he said. But Marcia was quick to say that it had been Mary Lou who'd done it.

"Oh, I see," Mike said. "Sorry, I don't have my notes with me. Now, let's see. It was you, though, who offered to leave the playground and get the ball."

"Kimmy got it the first time," Marcia said, just to keep things straight.

"Right," Mike agreed. "But the second time's the one I'd like to talk about."

"Okay," she said.

"Was there anyone out on the street near the playground, Marcia?" he asked, hating to lead her on but needing to push. Time was growing short. "Someone in a car?"

She screwed up her face and thought. "Uh-huh."

Mike wanted to smile. This was corroboration. "Did you see the man in the car? Did he say anything to you?"

"He was mean."

Gary Meacham raised his brows. Obviously he'd been present when his child was first interviewed and nothing had been said about a man in a car.

Mike met his eyes reassuringly for a moment and then went on. "Okay, Marcia, let's see. Do you remember what this man said to you?"

"He said, 'Scram. Go away, kid.'"

"Why did he say that?"

She shrugged and looked at her feet. "The ball was kinda by his tire."

"Oh. But you got it anyway. Did he scare you, Marcia?"

"Sorta."

"And you got mad."

She nodded. "I didn't do anything bad."

"Of course you didn't," Mike said. "So tell me, did this man get out of his car or anything?"

She shook her head. "He leaned out."

"Of the window?"

She nodded.

"And what did the other person in the car do?"

"She just was sitting there."

"I see," Mike said. *She.* He met Lena's eyes calmly. Inside, however, his heart was beginning to pound. "Okay, so this woman didn't say anything to you. How about the other people in the car?"

"There wasn't anyone else."

"Oh. Okay. I was wondering, Marcia," he said smoothly, "did these people in the car look like anyone you know, or maybe like someone on TV?"

She seemed to think about that, then shook her head.

"Were they old?"

She didn't know. She did remember that they both had long hair about the color of daddy's.

"Light brown," Mike said.

"Uh-huh," she replied.

"Okay," Mike said, "about the car these people were in. Do you remember what it looked like, Marcia? Like its color, or if it was big or small?"

She screwed her face up and thought. "It had wood," she said.

"Wood?"

"Uh-huh. On its side."

"Wood paneling?" Lena suggested.

Marcia gazed back at her, not understanding.

"I mean," Lena said, "did the car have wood on its sides? One of those station wagons with wood sides?"

"It was like Jodi Pratt's car, only different," Marcia said.

"A Wagoneer. The Pratts have a wood-sided Wagoneer," Gary Meacham said.

"Only different," Marcia insisted. "It was old. The wood was coming off."

"An old wood-sided station wagon," Lena said. "Ford and Chrysler made them since the sixties. It was fake wood, either painted or a wood-grain kind of stick-on paper. I know 'cause we had one in the shop a few years back and Al had to repair the thing."

Mike smiled at Marcia. "Is that what it was, Marcia? A station wagon? You know what a station wagon is?"

"Like Janie Caudill's car," Gary Meacham prompted.

"Uh-huh," Marcia said, "only it was old and there was wood."

"You're a very smart young lady," Mike said, "and you've helped us a lot, Marcia." And then Mike couldn't help asking, albeit jokingly, "I don't suppose you got the license plate number, young lady?"

To everyone's utter shock, Marcia sat up very straight and said, "Daddy has the same one."

It was a long moment before anyone could speak. Finally, Mike said, "Come again?"

"My collection. Holy Toledo! She's talking about my license plate collection," Gary said, and he spun his wheelchair around and headed toward the back of the house. "Are you all just going to sit there?" he called.

He led them into a spare bedroom that was used as a den. TV, stereo, books and pictures and family memorabilia everywhere. On one wall there were dozens of old license plates.

Marcia studied the wall. After only a few moments she pointed up. "That one."

"Which one?" Lena cried.

"That one. The red one."

They looked up. Near the ceiling was a distinctive bright red-and-yellow plate: New Mexico.

Mike and Lena had an identical thought: how many old wood-paneled station wagons could there possibly be in a sparsely populated state such as New Mexico?

No one said a word, however, until Mike breathed, "Well, O-K-A-Y," and then everyone spoke at once.

FOR A SHORT AND WIRY man, Danny Hayden was very strong. He grabbed Jane by the hair and yanked her head back until she cried out.

"I'm goddamned sick and tired of your bitching," he grated out. "Now, stuff this pill down the kid's throat and get her ready."

"Please," Jane whimpered, but he only tugged harder on her hair.

"Get her the hell ready!" he said fiercely. "This job's worth two big ones, and I ain't lettin' her off the hook. Now, get in there."

It was useless to argue with Danny, and Jane did what she was told. When she unlocked the door to Kimmy's back room the child was huddled in a far corner, staring blankly at the old black-and-white TV they'd put in there to keep her quiet.

"Here," Jane said, holding a glass of milk in one hand, the tranquilizer in the other. "Come here and drink this."

Of course Kimmy didn't realize she was being drugged on a regular basis. Tranquilizers in the day, sleeping pills at night. Jane had told the kid she had to take her vitamins. What did a kid know, anyway?

Drugging her didn't bother Jane. But what Danny was

planning did. She'd argued against it ever since they'd first snatched the little girl, but he was unrelenting. They needed the money, and that was all there was to it.

He'd bought Kimmy a new T-shirt for what he called "tonight's party." It was a pretty, rainbow-colored shirt, and after Kimmy took the pill, Jane showed it to her.

"Do you like it?" she asked.

Kimmy just stared at her, in one of her brat moods.

"You sure are spoiled," Jane said.

"When can I go home?" Kimmy asked abruptly, looking up at Jane with big brown eyes.

"Soon," Jane said. "If you're good."

"When?" Kimmy persisted.

And Jane realized the kid didn't believe her. "I don't know when," she said, exasperated. "When Danny says, I guess."

"I don't like him," Kimmy said, pouting.

"You better do what he says," Jane warned, "or he'll get mad." Unconsciously she put a hand on her head where he'd yanked her hair.

Kimmy's own hair was tangled, and Jane tried to brush it out, but she kept hitting snarls, and Kimmy cried out every time she did.

"Mommy does it better," the kid whined.

"She's had more practice," Jane replied, losing patience.

"She puts conditioner on my hair so it doesn't tangle."

"Conditioner," Jane repeated. "Big deal."

"And sometimes she makes French braids."

"What the heck are French braids?"

"They're fancy and they're real hard, but Mommy does it for me, like when there's a party!"

Jane grabbed her shoulders. "Will you just shut up about your mommy? I'm your goddamned mommy."

Kimmy's lower lip began to tremble, and Jane realized she was going to cry. Danny would be furious.

"Shush," she said in a gentler tone. "Hey, don't you like you're new shirt?"

"It's okay," Kimmy said.

Jane sighed. "Now, you have to go with Danny tonight. You have to do whatever he says and be real, real good. Or else."

"I don't want to."

"You have to, Kimmy. Do you understand?"

"What for?"

"You just have to go, that's all." Jane tried to smile. Boy, this stuff with kids was hard. She'd thought you told them what to do and they did it. But it turned out that they had minds of their own, and they were smart and they talked back and argued. And they recognized a lie when they heard one. At least Kimmy did. How did mothers manage the little brats?

She took the child's hand and led her into the kitchen, where Danny was eating a bowl of cereal for dinner.

He looked at the kid and smiled, as if to disarm her. "Hi, there, Kimmy," he said with false joviality. "We're going to see some friends of mine."

Kimmy said nothing, but Jane could feel the child's little hand tighten in her own.

"So, you all ready?" he asked.

"Wait. Let me get her jacket," Jane said. It was cool in October in Santa Fe, eight thousand feet high in the mountains of New Mexico. It sure wasn't California.

Jane went back to Kimmy's room, got the jacket and helped her put it on. The child was obviously used to a grown-up doing this—she knew right when to put her arms up for the sleeves.

"Let's go." Danny was getting impatient.

"Be good," Jane warned once again, and then Danny took the child's hand and led her toward the front door.

Jane stood there and watched them go, watched Kimmy turn her head to look back at her beseechingly. Those big brown eyes. And Jane knew that when she'd been young, she'd felt that exact same way—scared, lonely, confused. *Poor kid,* she thought, and she wasn't sure whether she was thinking about Kimmy or herself.

She sighed when she heard the station wagon start up. She guessed Danny knew what he was doing. No one was going to hurt the kid. It was only a movie. Kimmy would be so drugged out she wouldn't remember a thing anyway. And they needed the money.

And today Danny had said they only wanted to *see* the kid. Well, when they saw how pretty she was they'd want her. Sure they would.

It would be okay, Jane told herself. And once this job was over, they'd be like a real family, the three of them. It'd be nice, she mused, to have something of her own for a change.

Her own kid, her very own.

CHAPTER SEVEN

IT WAS AFTER eight o'clock when Lena pulled into her driveway and turned her car off. She sat there for a minute, head bowed.

"You okay?" Mike finally asked.

"No," she said simply.

"But we've got a lead."

"Maybe." She shook her head. "Maybe it's nothing, some kid's father in the car who was in a bad mood."

"Listen to me, Lena," Mike said quietly. "I've got a hunch."

"Oh, great. A *hunch*."

"Okay, a hunch is a wild guess. What I have is intuition, and that comes from experience. A cop's intuition. This is a solid lead. That man and woman took Kimmy. They went to her school and waited and took her."

She turned her face to him in the darkness. "But why? Why Kimmy?"

"We don't know that yet. Either they took a random kid or they were really after Kimmy. It doesn't matter at this point. We'll find her." He hesitated. "Lena, do you believe me?"

"I don't know," she whispered. "I want to, but I'm so scared."

He put his big hand on hers where it rested in her lap. "Trust me," he said, and she felt the warmth of his hand,

and it frightened her how easily she remembered his touch.

"I can't, Mike," she said. "I can't risk it." She was afraid to move; his hand still imprisoned hers. "I can't risk Kimmy." Didn't he know how she felt? He'd let her down so many times. That's what drunks did best—they let people down. The closer the person, the more they got let down. She couldn't let it happen to her again.

"Come on," he finally said. "Let's go in, get something to eat. And I'm going to call Pop. He needs to know about the car."

Lena heard him on the phone. He sounded so hopeful telling his father the news. She wished she felt the same way, but the lead seemed so nebulous.

Gloria heard the phone conversation, too. "Oh, my God," she said, "you've found the people who took her?"

"Not quite yet, but it's a good lead," Mike said.

"Thank heavens! Oh, I know you'll get her back now."

"It's not that easy, Mom." Lena said. "They could be anywhere."

"Mike'll find them," Gloria replied. "Now, come on and eat. I made tamales."

Lena ate, so distracted she couldn't tell if the terrible, empty ache in the pit of her stomach was hunger or fear.

"What now?" Gloria asked over her prize tamales.

"We search the records for a wood-paneled station wagon with New Mexico plates. They should have them at the state motor vehicle department. Unless the plates or car are stolen or not registered. But neither of those cases is likely. No one'd steal such an old car, and there aren't many vehicles around that aren't registered at all." Mike paused. "Pop's coming over here soon. He's bringing Uncle Ted and Scott. We're going to make plans. Hope you don't mind. I thought it'd be easier.''

Lena looked up abruptly. "They are?"

"Don't worry, we won't bother you. Just go to bed, get some rest."

"I don't think so," she said. "I think I'd better sit in on your war council."

He shrugged.

"She's my *child*, Mike."

He studied her from under sandy brows. "She's mine, too," he said.

The Quinn men arrived as Gloria and Lena were doing the dishes. They crowded in the door, filling Lena's small living room, three big blond men, tall and broad. Four of them counting Mike. She hadn't seen them in five years, and she noticed that Scott had put on a lot of weight sitting in his patrol car.

They were very subdued as they greeted her and Gloria. "Long time no see. Sorry about the circumstances. We'll get her back for you, Lena. Looking good, Gloria. Yeah, I put on a few pounds."

They took up the couch and the armchair, and Mike brought two kitchen chairs in, one for Lena and the other for her mother.

"Okay," Mike's father said, "so we know a few things now." He reiterated the facts, then looked at Mike. "Right, Son?"

Mike nodded.

"The question is, who would come all the way from New Mexico to get one child? Did they have a reason or did they pick just any kid? If we knew the reason, we'd find 'em quick, but we don't, so we have to work backward, trace the vehicle. We're damn lucky it's not a common type of car, and we're damn lucky New Mexico has a relatively small population."

Uncle Ted spoke up. "We've got a two-pronged attack here. We trace the vehicle. We're also in the process of tracing this woman, Jane Cramm, Kimmy's biological mother."

"You don't really think…?" Lena put in.

"Hey." Ted turned to her. "We can't rule out the possibility. It seems to be a real trendy thing to do these days. Hell, fathers and mothers kidnap kids from each other. Biological parents get kids back from adoptive parents through the courts, even years later. Damn courts just hand them back. Maybe this woman, Cramm, maybe she's nuts enough to have done it."

"But she disappeared," Lena said. "It's been six years."

"Crazier things can happen," Ted said. "The FBI is trying to trace her, but they'll only have federal records. If she's never filed an income tax form, for example, they may not have her."

Lena sat there trying to listen, but in her head images whirled: two dreadful creatures in a run-down ancient station wagon, with Kimmy in the back, tied up, crying, scared to death, hungry, thirsty, not understanding why her mother didn't come and rescue her. She gave a short sob and became abruptly aware of Mike watching her, his brows drawn. Judging her. She felt hot all over, then cold, and she had to look away, pretend she didn't feel Mike's eyes on her, his gaze like a hundred tiny feet walking on her flesh. She despised her own weakness and hated even more for Mike to see it; she wanted no chinks in her armor where Mike Quinn was concerned.

She was so weary, so exhausted, and now all these men were crowding her house, familiar men out of a past she'd tried to forget, to erase. It was as if her life were turned back on itself and the past five years of hard work and independence had never existed.

"So, we have to trace this Jane Cramm. Do you have an address or a description, a Social Security number?" Scott was asking.

"I never saw her," Lena said. "I think they found her in a shelter, and she signed the papers, but we never met."

"No description, then," Larry said.

"She was in her twenties," Mike said. "I remember that. So maybe she'd be around thirty."

"Or she overdosed and died. Six years is a long time in an addict's life," Lena said.

"It's a possibility." Ted nodded.

"The thing is," Mike said then, "someone has to do the nitty-gritty work, the footwork. In New Mexico. Hell, before that. On the route there. Someone has to cover that ground and ask questions." He looked around at the circle of men. "I'm going to do it. I've taken a leave and I'll do it myself. Frankly I don't trust the feds to do it right. I don't trust *anyone* else to do it right."

Lena heard his words, but it was his tone that impressed her: serious resolve. She felt an unwanted stirring of admiration. This was not the man she remembered. Or was it all a big act? Would he go home tonight and hit the beer and whiskey chasers and forget his resolve by morning?

"Okay," Ted was saying, "you do New Mexico. I know a guy in Albuquerque, a detective there name of Hidalgo, John Hidalgo. Helluva good man. I'll call him and arrange things."

"I can only guess at the route they took back to New Mexico, if that's where they went. I looked at a map earlier. Interstate 40 is the easiest way to get there. Now, I realize they could be heading to the southern part of the state, but the population centers are on 40, so I have to go with it. And 40 goes straight to Albuquerque, where I need to end up anyway."

"Sounds good," Uncle Ted said.

"If these people in the station wagon left a trail, I'll find it," Mike said grimly.

Lena hadn't voiced an opinion until now, and frankly she was skeptical about Mike's hunch. These people could be totally innocent, parents or relatives who'd been at school to pick up a child. Or if they were the ones who'd taken Kimmy they might not have gone back to New Mexico. Maybe they lived in California and simply drove a car with out-of-state plates. Maybe they'd gone to Mexico or Canada. The thing was, Mike really *could* be onto a lead. And they had absolutely nothing else to go on. She'd be damned if she was going to sit here in this house frantic with worry when she could be doing something.

She took a breath and blurted out her thoughts. "I'm going with Mike."

The four big men turned leonine heads and stared at her.

"I'm going," she said.

Mike shook his head. "Lena, this is police work. Sorry."

"Not official police work," she said stubbornly.

"Lena," Larry said. "I know you're upset, but you can't do Kimmy any good by going with Mike."

"I need to get close to her," she said. "She needs her mother."

"I may be dead wrong about where she is," Mike protested. "I may…"

"You had a *hunch*," she reminded him. "And what else do we have?"

"Lena," Ted began.

"You can't…" Scott said simultaneously.

"I'm going," she repeated.

Gloria tried, too. "Lena, maybe…"

"No way, Lena," Mike said.

She shut up then, realizing not one of them would listen to her, but her mind worked incessantly, chewing away at the problem. She had to go with Mike.

"So I leave in the morning," Mike was saying. "I'll keep in close touch. You have the number of my cell phone. Any information you get, you call me. Anything."

The Quinn men nodded, rose and said they'd be going. They repeated their assurances to Lena, but she wasn't listening.

"Don't worry," Ted said, "Mike'll find her. Get some sleep."

Mike left last. He stood in the doorway for a moment, eyeing Lena. "Take it easy," he said. "I'll find her."

"Thanks, Mike," Lena said mildly. "You're leaving in the morning? For New Mexico, I mean?"

"Yeah, early. I've got to go home and get some shut-eye."

"You'll call me?" she forced herself to say.

"Absolutely."

"Okay," she said. "Good luck."

Then he was gone and she closed the door behind him and turned to see Gloria glaring at her, her hands on her hips.

"Okay, Lena," Gloria demanded, "now you just tell me what you have in mind."

LENA'S ALARM woke her at five-thirty. It was still dark out, and she felt heavy and almost as tired as when she'd dropped into bed last night. She hadn't slept well, tossing and dreaming of Kimmy, waking, dozing. God, she hadn't slept well in days, running on fear and adrenaline and desperation. She moved quietly so as not to awaken her mother, who would only try once again to talk her out of what she was going to do.

She threw a few things in an overnight bag, a jacket for cool weather, underwear, blouses, a pair of pajamas. Then, unable to help herself, she got the blanket from under Kimmy's pillow and her favorite teddy bear and threw them in, too.

The house was quiet, only the hum from the refrigerator audible. Outside, the sky was brightening, a faint mother-of-pearl glow behind the coastal range. She tiptoed out, leaving the door still locked behind her. No note. Gloria knew where she was going.

She started her car and backed it out of the driveway, headed down the street toward the Valley Freeway. She'd pried Mike's address out of Gloria, and she hadn't even bothered to tell her mother how sneaky and underhanded she thought Gloria had been to secretly keep in touch with Mike all these years.

The streets were empty at this hour; even the freeway was practically deserted. She made good time, racing through the dawning city, her lights cutting swaths ahead of her.

Mike couldn't have left already, could he? She couldn't have missed him. Turning south on the 405, she blasted through the just-awakening suburbs toward Santa Monica. It wasn't hard to find his address, just off the beach. His building was painted a ghastly color of salmon that glowed in the dimness of the early hour.

Lena breathed a sign of relief as she pulled up behind

Mike's Volvo, which was parked in front of the building. He hadn't left yet. She'd considered going right up to his apartment door and knocking, but she'd decided it would be better to ambush him at the last minute, when he wouldn't have as much time to argue with her.

She turned her car off and sat there, waiting. It was six-fifteen; she'd made excellent time. So far so good. But the hard part was yet to come. What would Mike do when he saw her? Would he be hungover and have one of his temper tantrums? She had no choice—she *had* to convince him to take her along. She'd follow him all the way to Albuquerque if she had to. If...*when* they found Kimmy, she had to be there.

She didn't have long to wait; at 6:35 Mike emerged from the shadows of the building. He was carrying a duffel bag and digging in his pocket for his car keys. It was such a familiar mannerism of his that she was instantly transported back in time; she could have been still married to him, waiting for him in the car, watching the way he moved, hunching up his shoulders that certain way. Despite her nervousness, she couldn't help noticing that he'd lost some weight since she'd last seen him. He looked lean and fit, and he'd even shaved, which surprised Lena. In the old days, he'd have been unshaved, puffy, irritable. Maybe he was taking this thing more seriously than she thought—maybe it had shaken him up so badly his mind was only on finding Kimmy. Well, Lena thought, good.

He tossed his duffel bag into the back seat, started to get behind the wheel, and that was when Lena got out and went up to the driver's side of his car.

"Mike," she said.

He stopped short in the process of putting his key in the ignition. He froze.

"Mike," she repeated.

"What in hell?" he said.

"I have to go with you."

"Lena, don't start. We've been over this. I thought you understood."

"All I understand is that I have to find my little girl. I have to be there when you find her. My God, Mike, she doesn't even know you. She'll be traumatized already, and then, for more strangers to take her... Don't you see, Mike? I have to be there."

He got out of his car. "Lena, I understand your concerns, and they're valid, but the minute she's found, I'll call you. You can talk to her."

Lena shook her head. "It's not the same."

"I don't even know if she's *in* New Mexico. It may be a wild-goose chase."

"I know, but it's better than sitting home losing my mind. Mom will be there if Kimmy is found in this area. I have to do this, Mike." She didn't want to beg, but she had to convince him somehow.

"You can't, Lena. You know that. I can't take you along on police business."

"But, Mike..." she began, and then she saw him focus on something behind her, and he frowned. Lena whirled around, but there wasn't anything except a blue BMW driving down his street; she turned back to him, ready to start arguing her case again, but he wasn't paying any attention to her.

"What...?" Lena muttered as Mike walked right past her.

The blue car had stopped at the curb, and Mike was approaching the driver's door. *It must be someone he knows,* she thought when a woman got out of the BMW and stood with the car door between her and Mike. Lena heard her say, "'Morning, darling, I thought I'd run by and see you off."

She was very attractive, whoever she was—the girlfriend Colleen had told her about, Lena supposed. She had an impression of auburn hair pulled back into a ponytail, clear, pale skin, a sweatshirt that read The Workout, but all she felt was impatience, the need to convince Mike and get on the road.

"Oh," the woman said, glancing at Lena. "I...is this...?"

Mike looked uncomfortable. "Jennifer, this is Lena. Lena, Jennifer."

Lena nodded brusquely; Jennifer smiled unconvincingly.

"I have to go now," Mike said.

"I know. I just wanted to say good luck," Jennifer said.

Lena stood there, the pale morning light beginning to illuminate the scene—Mike, Jennifer, Lena herself, an awkward threesome. And she wasn't sure what to do next; she only felt an irrational anger and a terrible impatience.

"Mike," Lena started.

"Lena, listen, you can't go with me." He seemed embarrassed, as if he didn't like airing dirty laundry in front of his lady friend.

"You can't stop me from following you," she said, not caring.

Jennifer looked from one to the other, surprised. "She can't mean... Lena, you aren't planning on going with him?"

"Excuse me, but I don't think this is any of your business," Lena said coldly.

"Lena," Mike said.

"I'm sorry—really I am. It's so awful about your daughter. I mean, Mike told me," Jennifer said, "but you can't go with him."

"Watch me," Lena said, tight-lipped.

"Lena, go home. Wait there. I'll call you. The second I know anything," Mike promised.

"No."

"Oh, please listen to Mike," Jennifer said. The fake pity, the possessiveness in her tone, grated on Lena's nerves. She turned to the woman and said fiercely, "It's not your child."

Jennifer drew back.

"Look, this is ridiculous," Mike said. "Lena, go home. If you try to follow me, I'll call in the LAPD. I'll put out an APB on you, and they'll stop you."

"I'll get there some other way, then," Lena said in a hard voice. "I'll show up in Albuquerque. You can't stop me. Kimmy's my child!"

"Oh, for God's sake," Mike said. "Jennifer, I'm sorry about this. I've really got to get on the road now...."

"Don't you apologize for me," Lena snapped.

"I'm leaving now."

He gave Jennifer a kiss, then closed her car door for her, leaning down and saying something to her through the window that Lena couldn't hear. Then, calmly, he watched her drive off, got into his own car and started it up.

Lena felt her heart drop into her stomach. He was leaving without her; he wouldn't listen. She stood there for a minute, defeated, and then, as Mike pulled out from the curb, she ran to her own car and got in, turned the key in the ignition, jammed it into first gear and took off down the quiet street after him.

She followed him for one block, then two. He kept

looking in his rearview mirror. He went another block, past apartment buildings and houses and a few shops. He was heading for the freeway; she knew exactly what route he'd take out of L.A.—Interstate 15 to 40. She'd follow him all the way if she had to, and to hell with what he or his girlfriend thought.

At the stoplight three blocks from Mike's apartment, he jammed on his brakes and came striding back to her car, angry.

"Dammit, Lena, go home!" he rasped.

"No," she said calmly.

The light changed. He got back into his car and drove away. She followed. Then she saw him jam on his brakes again and pull over. She stopped behind him. What now? A frisson of fear rippled through her. Was he angry enough to do something to her? Did he still have that awful temper?

He got out of his car again and came back to her. Leaning down, he said, "You mean this, don't you? Dammit, Lena…"

"Yes, I mean it."

He straightened and swore and then leaned down again. "Okay, okay. Goddammit, you can come."

"Thank you, Mike," she said, her heart pounding like a drum. *Be nice,* she told herself. *You won.*

"Let's go back to my place, leave your car there," he said, resigned.

"We'll leave *your* car there," she said. "Mine's faster, and Kimmy may see it and recognize it and…"

"I can't argue anymore. You win, Lena. Fine, we'll take your car. What the hell."

In five minutes she'd followed him back to his place, he'd parked and thrown his duffel bag into her car. Then he stood there, looking down at her in the driver's seat.

"Move over," he said.

"What?"

"Move over. I'm driving."

She was about to retort, but she clamped her mouth shut and slid over. Without a word he got in, adjusted the seat and put the car in gear. Neither of them said a word; the tension in the car could have been cut with a knife. He drove fast—skillfully, she had to admit—and she held her tongue so as not to antagonize him any further.

Silence except for the rushing wind and the hum of tires on the road. Then they were turning onto the freeway, and Lena took a breath, feeling as if she'd been holding it all morning. The commuter traffic heading into the city began to get heavy, and the sun backlit the buildings and the coastal range ahead of them.

Kimmy, Lena thought. *Sweetie, I'm coming to get you. Hang in there, baby.*

Mike drove, his muteness accusatory, but Lena didn't care anymore—she was on her way to finding her daughter.

"Admit it," she finally said, breaking the silence. "Admit it, Mike. I'm right to come. You wouldn't even recognize Kimmy."

"And whose fault is that?" he shot back.

And then Lena shut her mouth and turned her head away to watch the scenery flashing by, every second, every minute, possibly bringing her closer to her daughter.

She hoped. Oh, God, how she hoped.

CHAPTER EIGHT

THE TENSION in the car was unbearable, and finally Lena couldn't stand it anymore. She could afford to be the first one to give in now—she'd won the main battle, hadn't she? *Be mature,* she told herself. *Be reasonable.*

So she opened the glove compartment and found a road atlas. She studied it, rehearsing in her head the amiable tone of voice she'd use.

"I'm sure you're right," she began. "Someone from New Mexico would take Interstate 40. Ten is too far south. It makes sense."

Mike said nothing.

Later, as they followed the mountainous route on the edge of the Mojave Desert, she tried again, forcing herself to be pleasant. "I just wish we could be sure, you know, that we're on the right track."

"It's the only shot we've got right now," he said, pulling into the passing lane.

"I know, I know," she said. "I only wish, well...I've been doing a lot of hoping and praying. It doesn't seem as if Kimmy disappeared only five days ago. It seems like forever. I can't even remember what life was like before this happened."

"Mmm," he said.

Oh, she knew how ticked off he was. But really, what had he expected her to do? Sit at home frantic with worry while he was on the chase?

Two hundred miles along the route, outside of Needles on the Arizona border, Mike pulled into a truck stop to gas up. "This damn car of yours," he said under his breath. "What's it get—eight miles to the gallon?"

"Well, ten or better on the open highway," she said defensively.

"Great. It's a real economy model. I don't know why you've kept it all these years."

She opened her door. "You used to like it," she said.

While Mike filled the car, Lena went inside to use the rest room. When she was done, she showed Kimmy's picture to the cashier, explaining that the child was her daughter and that she'd been kidnapped.

The cashier was very friendly but of no help. "Jeez, lady, I didn't work on Thursday, and I never work nights," she said.

"Well, thanks anyway," Lena replied just as Mike was coming in to pay for the gas.

Outside again, he said, "No luck, huh?"

"I didn't think there would be."

"And just what is that supposed to mean?"

Hopelessness and fear overcame her, and her attempts to be mature and polite evaporated like steam in cold air. She stopped short and confronted him. "Do you know what the odds are that those people in the station wagon took Kimmy? Or how about the odds on them driving to New Mexico just because a car has New Mexico plates? But better than *that*," she said, "what are the odds that they gassed up here? There're hundreds of stops, and these places must have ten different cashiers to cover all the shifts."

They stood there under the hot desert sun, and he glared at her. "You got a better idea? If so, let's hear it."

Lena stared back defiantly.

"Police work is ninety-nine percent drudgery. You check dozens of possibilities to maybe get one small break. Hell, you're the one who begged to come along. Now is not the time to wallow in your doubts, lady. If you don't like it, I'll be glad to stick you on a bus home."

"Over my dead body," she said, and she turned on her heel.

"Just hold on a minute," she heard Mike say, and she stopped short, her back to him.

"Dammit, Lena, we can do this the hard way or we can do it the easy way, but we've sure as hell got to do it. It's your choice."

She stood there silently.

"I've been trying to give you a lot of room, but don't push me too far. I don't want to be stuck with you any more than you want to be stuck with me," he said harshly.

She whirled on him. "You don't have to remind me of that."

"Then act like you remember it," he said.

He walked to the car and got in, and there was nothing Lena could do but follow him.

Mike stopped often to flash Kimmy's picture that day. He pulled into two places in Kingman, Arizona, and every little dusty stop along the barren highway. Luckily, Lena thought, the turnoffs were few and far between in this isolated region of the desert Southwest.

They did very little talking. Even at their late lunch Lena had nothing to say to him. They were on a desperate quest, but that didn't mean they had to be friends; he was right about that. She'd tried to be civil, but obviously he wasn't going to cool off about her insistence on coming along.

She looked up from the grilled-cheese sandwich she was nibbling at and glared at him. Maybe he wasn't mad about her coming along. Maybe he was just hungover. She knew those sour moods of his. He could have left her house last night and gone to a bar, one of those cop hangouts he'd always loved so dearly. Sure he'd said he wasn't drinking anymore. But then, how many times in their marriage had he quit?

She studied him. His blue eyes were clear, but eye-drops could solve that. And maybe he'd showered off the alcoholic stench. It didn't mean a thing that he looked healthy. Her father had looked pretty darn chipper right up till the end.

It all came back in a sick rush—the nights Mike had come stumbling in drunk, sometimes passing out on the couch, waking with the hangover from hell. Never stopped him, though. She'd still loved him, idiot that she'd been. Loved him right up until he'd put that gun to his head. Then she'd turned her heart to stone.

She wondered how his lady friend, Jennifer, put up with it. They didn't live together, so maybe she hadn't gotten a full dose of his mood swings, the alcoholic bitterness and fits of depression. Colleen had said they were going to be married. Jennifer would get the full picture then. You bet she would, and no matter how much she loved Mike, she'd never be able to tolerate the binges.

Lena pictured the woman. Very pretty and very well groomed. She took care of herself: hair, skin, nails, clothes. This Jennifer was no slouch. How had they met? Lena wondered, but she shut off the question and erased from her mind the image of them kissing. It was none of her damn business.

They'd been taking shifts driving. It was Mike's turn again, and after they ate, he slid in behind the wheel.

Lena looked at him as he turned onto the on-ramp of the interstate. Five years, she mused. She hadn't seen this man in five long years, and yet he seemed to have barely changed. He still wore his dark-blond hair longish and there were no wrinkles on his face. He had a tan. When they'd been married, Mike had gotten little sun. She supposed he was outside a lot now with his new assignment.

She glanced at him. "What, exactly, is Hostage Negotiations?"

"Just what it sounds like."

"Come on, Mike, you can do better than that."

He draped a wrist over the top of the steering wheel and let out a low breath. "I'm a member of a team of six guys who're trained to talk people down from volatile situations."

"Mom said you were in the newspaper a couple of times."

"Mmm," he said.

"So you must be okay with the job."

"What are you getting at?"

She sighed and looked out the side window. "Nothing, really."

"Come on, Lena, I know you."

"Well, I, I guess it's hard for me to see you in control of your own emotions, much less someone else's."

"Oh," he said, "I get it."

"I'm not trying to tick you off, Mike. I'm just stating a fact."

"I don't think you know me anymore," he said coolly.

And then she couldn't help saying, "Tigers don't change their stripes."

He only shot her a hard look and then turned his attention back to the road.

Outside Flagstaff, as it was starting to grow dark over

the snow-capped mountains, Mike stopped at two gas stations and three motels, showing Kimmy's picture to anyone who'd been at work last Thursday night or Friday
morning. He got nowhere. Then, only a mile down the
road, he pulled off again at a string of motels, fast-food
joints and gas stations. Lena sat in the car biting her
lower lip, trying not to let panic swamp her.

It was after the sixth place he'd gone into that she
snapped. "This is the biggest waste of time I've ever
seen," she said hotly. "We should push straight on to
Albuquerque and have your uncle's friend start checking
on old panel wagons."

Mike turned to her slowly and deliberately. "I'm going
to say this just once," he stated flatly. "It's not going to
do us or Kimmy any good if we do find the owners of
that car and they're not even in the state. This way, *my
way,* we might just luck out and learn that they came this
direction. Then we'll know." He put a silencing finger
up. "And don't tell me again that the people in the station
wagon might not even have Kimmy at all. I know that
as well as anyone."

Lena glared back at him but kept her mouth shut until
Mike pulled off again two miles later. "I don't believe
this," she muttered, realizing that there must be a hun-
dred motels and restaurants and gas stations in Flagstaff.
She wanted to cry. "Can't we just go to Albuquerque?
We could be there in a few hours and..."

Mike leaned into the car and swore. "I promise, Lena,
one more word and I'll put you on a bus so fast your
head'll spin. I'm dead serious."

She glared at him. "I'll report that you stole my car."

"Good God, woman, don't you ever let up?"

"Not when it comes to Kimmy," she fired back. "*You*
I gave up on."

"You know, Lena, maybe if you had let me be a part of Kimmy's life, this wouldn't have happened," he retorted.

He might as well have stabbed her in the heart. Shocked, sick with anguish, she said, "You have the nerve to blame *me?* You were the one who put the gun against your head, Mike. And not ten feet from where my baby, *our* baby, was asleep. You're the drunk. Is that how you wanted her to be raised? Is it?"

He said nothing, and she knew she'd scored.

After another tense moment, he finally straightened. "I'm going into this motel to show Kimmy's picture. And then I'll go to the next place and the next. You can sit here and do nothing or you can take that other copy of her photo and start helping out. There's that gas station across the road and the minimart next door." He slammed the car door and strode into the motel.

She sat in the dark interior of the car for a few minutes, fighting tears and exhaustion. They'd never get a lead on Kimmy this way; they simply had to get to New Mexico and take it from there. But there was obviously no stopping Mike. He had to cross all the t's and dot all the i's before going on.

She opened the passenger door, got out and stretched, feeling so tired and dragged out her head was starting to spin. Still, she rummaged around in the back seat for the other copy of Kimmy's photo, then headed across the road toward the gas station. The cashier inside said he'd been on duty, a double shift, last Thursday, but he didn't recognize the picture, nor did he recall an old wood-paneled station wagon.

"I'm sorry, lady," he said. "Good luck, though."

Lena thanked him and left, crossing the asphalt drive to the twenty-four-hour minimart.

The place was busy, and she had to wait in line to show Kimmy's picture. She yawned, felt that weary, desperate sinking sensation in her belly. Maybe she'd get a tall coffee to go. This was going to be a long, long night.

Finally at the register she explained the situation and slid Kimmy's picture across the counter to the older lady behind the cash register.

"This is her most recent photo," Lena said dully.

The woman pursed her lips and cocked her head, studying the picture. "Hmm," she said.

Lena looked up.

"You know," the lady went on, "I think, well, I'm pretty sure she was here."

At first Lena thought she hadn't heard correctly. "What?" she asked, her heart beginning to pound.

"Well, I think I remember the child," the woman said. "It must have been last Thursday night or really early on Friday morning. This woman, see, was carrying the child, you know, into the rest room. I remember because the little girl was real dopey, sleepy. 'Course it was late. But then when they came out of the bathroom, the girl was walking and the woman was tugging her along. I thought at the time it was kinda mean, yanking the kid like that. I guess that's why I remember and all."

Lena had stopped breathing, and all the blood had left her head. *Oh, my God!* she thought. *Oh, my God!* "Are you sure it was her?" she managed to ask, and she realized her voice was trembling.

"I'm pretty sure," the woman said, staring hard at her.

Lena flew out of the store and dodged cars as she raced to get Mike. *He'd been right—he'd been right!* She found him walking toward the GTO, and the words came tumbling out all at once.

"Okay, okay," he said, putting both hands on her

shoulders, "take it easy. I'll go talk to the lady and see if she recalls anything else."

"Mike," Lena breathed, "they really did take her. Kimmy's in New Mexico!"

"It looks that way," he said, and he ushered her toward the car.

He was back in ten minutes, and he slid into the driver's seat. He was smiling. "Not only does the woman think it was Kimmy, but she said that maybe the car was a wood-sided station wagon. They'd evidently parked right in front of the door and left the headlights on. She said she noticed that, always does because it's annoying. But she doesn't remember the woman very well. Too bad."

"Oh, let's go, Mike, please," Lena pleaded. "I'm ready to burst. This is the first hope I've had in so long."

"I know," he said. "Believe me, I do know."

But then, only about five miles on the other side of Flagstaff, he pulled off the highway and into a motel parking lot.

"What on earth are you doing?" she demanded. "There's no reason to show Kimmy's—"

"We're stopping," he cut in.

"Why?"

"Because we're both exhausted. We need a few hours' sleep and then we'll take off. And you've got to be as hungry as I am."

"We'll…we'll get food to go," she protested. "I'm not tired at all now, and I can drive while you—"

"No," he said. "We're stopping. Quit arguing. We'll put a call in for 5 a.m. if you want. But neither of us is in any condition to be driving."

"Mike."

"No, Lena. And besides," he said, "we'd get into Albuquerque at one or two in the morning. There's nothing we can do at that hour anyway."

It was useless to argue. He parked and said he'd get a room and be right back.

There was a restaurant-bar nearby, all lit up, one of those false-front Western places. And then it hit her. Mike wasn't tired and he wasn't hungry. He needed a little pick-me-up. *Damn him!*

Shortly he came back with a key. Lena got out of the car and stared at him. "One room?"

"There's a pullout couch. I'll sleep there. If I sleep at all."

"I'm supposed to share a room with you?"

"Okay, fine, I'll get two rooms. They're not cheap, though. Does your budget run to that sort of thing?"

"No," she said sullenly.

Mike tightened his jaw. "I'm not going to molest you, Lena. For God's sake, grow up."

She looked up sharply and glared at him, refusing to get into an argument.

"Ready to get something to eat?" he asked.

"Sure," she said icily. "And how about something to drink, too?" Then she squared her shoulders and headed toward the restaurant, feeling the daggers in her back.

GLORIA TORRES HAD spent the day catching up on errands and bills and speaking to her boss at the restaurant. She knew that any other employee probably would have been fired by now, but her boss was a woman who had three grandchildren of her own. She could not have been more helpful or sympathetic. Just to be on the safe side, Gloria also had the telephone company forward all calls to a cell phone she'd rented a day after Kimmy's abduction. Still, whether she was at the post office or grocery store, she worried—what if Kimberly somehow made her way home in the few hours she was gone?

Of course she hadn't, and Gloria had returned to Lena's, dodging a persistent reporter, at five that afternoon. She'd had several calls on the cell phone that day. They'd all been for Lena. Concerned friends, teachers, Larry Quinn touching base. And there'd been a message from the FBI, asking Lena to return the call as soon as possible. Gloria had spoken to the man, Special Agent Sabin, but she'd said nothing about Lena's having gone to New Mexico. Thus far the FBI had only been a pain in the butt to everyone.

At seven she turned on the TV for company and cooked a light dinner. Nevertheless, she kept staring at the phone, hoping against all hope that Kimmy would somehow escape from her captors and call.

It was shortly before eight that there was a knock at the door. Her heart leaped. Kimmy? Could it possibly be Kimmy?

It was not her granddaughter. Instead, standing ramrod straight and wearing dark suits, were two men. They both held up ID cards. "FBI," the shorter man said. "We'd appreciate it if you could answer one or two questions, Mrs. Torres. It is Mrs. Torres?"

Gloria stared at the official-looking ID cards and said, "Ah, yes, I'm Gloria Torres. Lena's still not here, though, and I..."

"It's not Miss Portillo we want to talk to," the shorter man said.

"Oh."

"May we come in, please?"

The short, wiry agent who stood as if he had a steel pole up his back, introduced himself as Special Agent

Alan Sabin and the other man, taller, heavier and almost white blond, as Agent Miller.

Gloria made them coffee. She would have offered the devil himself coffee or tea because it was in her nature to be hospitable.

They sat in the living room and she asked if they had any news on Kimmy.

"Well, now," Alan Sabin said, "that, of course, is why we're here."

"Something's happened?" she said excitedly.

"No, not with locating the child, Mrs. Torres."

"It's 'Gloria,' please," she said.

"All right, Gloria," he said. "You see, we've run into a snag with our investigation, and you may be the only one who can clear things up for us."

"Oh," she said.

Miller took up the conversation. "The problem is—" he smiled at her "—that we've only just learned that Mike Quinn is Kimberly's legal father."

"That's true," she allowed.

"We were curious," he went on, "why your daughter lied to the police."

Gloria gave a tight laugh and shook her head. "I assure you," she said, "there's nothing sinister about it. My daughter simply didn't want to involve him. When she divorced him, well, there were bad feelings. She's had no contact since."

"And is that why she took on your maiden name, Portillo?"

"Yes."

Alan Sabin nodded. "I wonder," he said, "were those bad feelings over Quinn's drinking?"

"I don't think that matters," Gloria said quickly. "The

issue here is Kimmy's welfare. Whether or not Mike had a drinking problem has nothing to do with—''

Miller cut her off. ''You could be very wrong there, Gloria,'' he said, and he gave her another friendly smile.

''I don't see...'' she began.

''The thing is,'' Sabin said, ''we've been hearing some disturbing things in our investigation.''

Gloria looked from one man to the other, uncertain.

Sabin went on. ''You must understand,'' he said, ''that Kimmy's welfare is our primary concern here. We only hope it's not too late, Gloria. And we need to ask you some tough questions. Please don't be upset. We all have the same goal in mind and, as her grandmother, you'll want to help no matter how distressing it might be.''

''I'm afraid you've lost me.'' Again Gloria looked from one to the other.

''It's really quite simple,'' Miller said. ''We've gotten some off-the-record tips that there may have been child abuse.''

She sat stunned for a long moment, and then she leaped to her feet. ''That's...that's ridiculous!'' she gasped.

''Please,'' Sabin said, ''please sit down, Gloria. We understand how upsetting this is to you. But we need your help if you're ever going to see Kimmy again.''

She did not sit. Instead she folded her arms stiffly over her chest, presenting a steely front to the men despite her small, trim stature. She was a pretty woman; some called her handsome. But when she was angry, her Latin temper flashed in her dark eyes and most people knew better than to push her. ''And just what are these off-the-record tips you're talking about?'' she demanded.

Miller said, ''Please do sit down, Mrs....Gloria. If

there's been a mistake, then we want to clear it up. Your hostility won't help anyone, least of all your grandchild.''

Gloria eyed them warily, the blood pounding through her veins. She sat, looking down her nose imperiously at them.

''What we've learned,'' Alan Sabin said, ''is confidential, of course. Our sources asked that their names be withheld.''

''That figures,'' she snapped.

Sabin went right on. ''One of our sources is a neighbor of your daughter's,'' he said. ''Apparently this neighbor has heard some very unsettling things coming from this house.''

''Oh, bull,'' Gloria said, her temper barely in check. ''This is absurd. Lena would no more harm Kimmy than I would. What sort of jerk would make up such a story?''

''We realize,'' Miller said, ''that you'd have no way of knowing any of this. But you need to look at reality here. For Kimmy's sake. Your daughter, who most likely was abused herself by Mike Quinn, has been under an enormous amount of stress since her divorce. She's a single parent, working long hours, barely making ends meet. It's understandable that she may snap from time to time. My gosh,'' he went on, ''who wouldn't in that position?''

''Lena has never, ever laid a hand on her child,'' Gloria grated out. ''You've been lied to. That's the only possible explanation.'' Then, abruptly, her eyes widened. ''Oh, my God,'' she breathed, ''you think…you think Lena did something to Kimmy! You think my daughter harmed her and tried to cover it up. Is *that* where this is leading?''

It was Sabin who said in a quiet voice, ''I'm afraid so. It happens every day in this country. Too often. Either a single parent breaks under too much pressure or the other parent, the one denied custody, exacts some sort of revenge. No one, of course, means to harm the child, but things get out of hand.''

''Look,'' Gloria said, her heart hammering, ''neither my daughter nor Mike is capable of such a thing. No one lost control here. If some busybodies told you otherwise, then they're lying.'' *Or you are,* she thought.

But Sabin and Miller weren't listening. Sabin said, ''You could help us, Gloria. You could save Kimmy if it's not too late. You just need to take control of your emotions and look at the hard truth. If it's Lena or Mike, or both of them together, you need to help them, too. You can do it. The people we've spoken to tell us you're a very capable and moral person. We've come to you because—''

Suddenly Gloria stood up. ''I...I need to call work,'' she said, thinking fast. ''You don't mind if I take a minute to...?''

''Go ahead,'' Sabin said. ''We'll wait.''

Her fingers trembling, Gloria picked up the receiver while flipping through Lena's address book with her back turned to the FBI men. She found his home number and dialed Larry Quinn, Mike's dad. *Be there,* she prayed.

He was. ''Who is this?'' he asked.

''It's Gloria,'' she said. ''I can't come into work. There're these FBI men here and this will take a while.''

''What're you...?'' he began, but then he caught on. ''Oh, shit,'' he said. ''Just hold on, Gloria. I'll be there in ten minutes. Don't tell them a damn thing. Hold on,'' he repeated, and he hung up.

The ten minutes crawled by in agonizing slowness. She offered the FBI men coffee again. She knew she was chattering but she couldn't help it. She hoped they'd attribute it to nervousness.

"They're so nice at work," she babbled, "letting me off like this. And I can't even tell them how long it'll be."

"Mmm, that's helpful," Sabin said. "Now, Gloria, we'd really appreciate it if you could tell us if you ever saw bruises on your granddaughter, say, on an arm...or burn marks."

"Bruises?" Gloria repeated, delaying, pretending to think. "Well, she fell down last week, you know, the way kids do, and..." She smiled nervously. "Do you mind if I go to the bathroom?"

She took a ridiculously long time, sitting on the edge of the bathtub, her heart racing as she counted the minutes. *Hurry up, Larry,* she thought, flushing the toilet. She felt crazily like some kind of undercover agent. A spy.

Finally she returned to the living room, and Miller started right in on her. "Gloria, we appreciate how upset you are at this time, but if you could help us, we might be able to find your granddaughter sooner. Wouldn't you like that?"

The anger boiled up in her again. "There's nothing I can tell you that will help you find Kimmy. Why are you doing this? Isn't it bad enough that she's gone?"

"As I said before, Gloria, hostility is really not at all necessary," Sabin said.

And so it went, Gloria holding them off, alternating between angry replies and inanities. *Hurry, Larry,* she kept thinking, trying not to look at her watch. And then finally, mercifully, she heard his knock.

She leaped to her feet. "I'll get it," she said, smiling

shakily. When she opened the door, Larry took her hands and gave them a reassuring squeeze.

"It'll be okay now," he promised, and he strode in past her, tossed his hat on the couch and plumped down next to Agent Miller. "Hi, guys," he said, "Detective Larry Quinn here, LAPD. So, what did they try to pull?" he asked Gloria, looking at the two agents.

"They told me they had some tips that Kimmy was abused. They wanted me to help. I guess they wanted me to say that Lena was given to fits of anger from stress or whatever."

"Mmm," Larry said. "Well, boys, I think it's time you take a hike. You're barking up the wrong tree, but what the hey, you usually do." Then he turned to Gloria. "What they do is tell you a good lie, and it's supposed to make you break down and confess. It works, too. I've used it myself. The trouble is—" he looked at the FBI men "—the person being interrogated has to be guilty."

Gloria was awash in relief. She watched as the agents stood, tight-lipped, and strode past her to the door. Special Agent Alan Sabin paused with his hand on the door-knob and glared at her and Larry Quinn. "The issue's not dead," he said to Larry. "You've got to realize by now that without a ransom demand, the odds are damn high that either your ex-daughter-in-law or even your own son is at the bottom of the kid's disappearance. Think about it, Quinn." He started out the door.

To his back, Larry said, "No, you think about it, Sabin. I've got better things to do."

When they were gone, Larry rose and gave Gloria a long hug. "They're creeps," he said.

She sighed in his big arms. "You want some coffee?" she asked. "I've got a pot on."

"You bet," he said. "We've got five years to catch up on."

CHAPTER NINE

MIKE SAT AT THE TABLE, pretending to read the menu, but Lena could tell he was angry. She knew him so well there was no mistaking the tautness in his shoulders and the pitch of his head. She wished now she hadn't said anything; she'd been trying all day to stay on his good side. What if he packed her back home?

Finally he put down the menu. "I told you I'm not drinking anymore," he said with careful control.

"Sorry," she mumbled.

"You're pretty damn tough, aren't you," he said under his breath.

"Look, Mike, I..." But she thought better of saying the words aloud—that she trusted him about as far as she could throw him. *Let it lie,* she thought. *Don't push his buttons.* It was enough that he wasn't drinking in front of her, that Kimmy apparently mattered to him.

"Go on," he said tightly. "What were you going to say?"

"Nothing, really." She looked up and shrugged. "I can't even remember now."

"Uh-huh."

They ordered barbecued-beef sandwiches. Lena had a Coke, and Mike ordered iced tea. She tried not to ponder the iron control he was displaying. It was enough that he was trying.

Back in the motel room, Mike pulled out the sleeper sofa and then said he was going to take a shower.

"I'm going to call Mom," Lena said.

"Okay. I'll have to make some calls, too. Got to let everyone know about the new lead," he said.

Then he disappeared into the bathroom, and she heard the shower go on, and she saw in her mind's eye, without a bridging thought, Mike's naked body under the hot spray. It only lasted a moment before she shut it off like a bad program on TV, then she picked up the phone and dialed her home number.

"Hello?" Gloria said.

"Mom, it's me. I'm in Flagstaff. We've stopped for the night. Listen, Mom, we have—we *might* have a new lead."

"What?" Gloria asked. "Honey, Larry Quinn's here. He's going to want to know, but tell me, quick. I can't stand it."

Larry Quinn's there? "Okay, we stopped at a million places and showed Kimmy's picture, and at one place, a minimart here in Flagstaff, the cashier thought she remembered Kimmy."

"Oh, my God," Gloria breathed.

"Yes, isn't that wonderful? She saw her—she actually *saw* her. Mom, that means she's alive!"

"I know, honey. Oh, I always knew, but..."

"It isn't a hundred percent positive, of course, but it looks good." She paused. "Mom, why is Larry there?"

Gloria told her about the FBI men and their "good lie." "So I called Larry and he came over and chased them away. Thank heavens for him is all I can say."

"Those guys actually told you they had tips about me abusing Kimmy?" Lena asked, outraged. "From my neighbors? I can't believe it. I..."

"I know, I know," Gloria said. "It's an interrogation technique. Larry told me all about it. Don't pay any attention to it."

"Goddamn them!" Lena said between her teeth.

"Listen, Larry wants to talk to you. Here he is."

"Cool down, Lena," Larry said when he came on the line. "Like I told Gloria, it only works on guilty parties."

"I'll sue them," she grated out. "I'll—"

"You won't do anything. Now, tell me about this lead."

Lena told him, aware that the water was no longer running in the bathroom. She'd let Mike talk to his dad, then, because she'd probably leave out some important details of the story.

The bathroom door opened. "Here's Mike," Lena said into the receiver, then she turned and held it out to him. "Mike, it's your dad. He wants to…" She swallowed. Mike wore only a towel around his waist, and water droplets beaded his skin. His hair was wet and slicked back. "He wants to talk to you."

Mike strode over, his bare feet leaving damp footprints on the carpet, and he took the phone from her. Lena backed away swiftly, then went to her bag, turning away from the sight of him. *Oh, God,* she thought. *Oh, God.* He looked the same—his skin, the shape and curve and heft of him. The muscles sliding under the smooth, pale skin, the height and size, the unconscious proud carriage that had captured her heart all those years ago.

He was talking to his father, and she listened, afraid to turn around.

"Yeah, Pop, it looks good. I've got the woman's name and address. She'd make a convincing witness if we ever need her. Very clear, sure of herself."

Then he was quiet, listening. Finally she heard him swear.

"Those pumped-up jerks!" he said. "Those…" Then he listened some more. "Okay, okay, but I swear, if they ever try that again, if they… Okay, Pop, yeah, I know." He said to Lena's back, "You want to talk to Gloria again?"

"No," Lena replied, still facing away. "Just tell her I'm fine and I'll call her tomorrow."

He hung up and grabbed some clothes from his bag. "I'll get dressed," he said as if he could read her mind, then he went back into the bathroom.

Lena let out a breath she'd been holding too long. She was okay with him as long as things didn't get too…personal, too intimate. It was only Kimmy who mattered, she reminded herself, not Mike, not their past relationship. Only Kimmy. And Mike had been right about how to find her. He'd been right, and she had to admit it. His hunch had panned out. Was it pure luck or was Mike Quinn really such a good cop?

He came out of the bathroom then, dressed, and Lena took the opportunity to shower. She let the hot water cleanse her, and she felt, for the first time in days, an immense relief, a burden lifted from her shoulders. Kimmy was alive. A voice whispered inside her head that days had passed since that sighting of Kimmy, and something could have…happened to her after that, but she tuned it out. She'd go on believing Kimmy was okay— she had to.

She put on the cotton-knit pajamas she'd brought along. Unsexy, thick enough to hide any curves, very modest blue polka-dot pajamas. The last thing on earth she wanted to do was to give Mike Quinn any ideas. When she emerged from the steamy bathroom, he was on the phone again, and she couldn't help overhearing his end of the conversation.

"Flagstaff, that's right. No, it's pretty chilly here. It's up in the mountains." Pause. "Well, we may have found something. A cashier in a store saw a little girl who looked like her. Yeah, the timing is right."

Lena knew instantly from the tone of his voice whom he was talking to. *It figures,* she thought.

"Listen, Jenn," he said, lowering his voice, "I'm sorry about that scene this morning." Pause. "I know, but I had to."

Lena's temper suddenly flared. How dare that woman stick her nose into this again?

"Jenn, please," he was saying. "It'll only be a few days. We'll be in Albuquerque tomorrow. We just stopped to get some rest tonight. I—" He stopped talking, obviously cut off by something Jennifer was saying. "Yes, I got one room," he said, and then he apparently had to listen again.

Ha! Lena thought. *Take that, you silly twit.* And then she wondered at her reaction. Why the heck should she care what kind of trouble Mike was having with his girl-friend?

"Okay, Jenn, take it easy. Yeah, me, too. 'Bye."

Silence settled over the room when he hung up. He didn't move from the chair next to the telephone, and finally Lena sneaked a glance at him. He was sitting, rubbing his temples with one big hand.

"Giving you a hard time, huh?" Lena couldn't resist saying with mock sympathy.

He lifted his head and looked straight at her. "What in hell are you talking about?"

Lena snatched her eyes away from his, unable to hide a small grin.

"Goddamn women," she heard him mutter, and then she slid into the bed and pulled the covers up.

JENNIFER HILTY WAS fuming. She got her kids into bed, turned out the lights in their rooms and then stalked around her house, raging inside. Mike had actually admitted that he and his ex-wife were sharing a motel room! Either he was incredibly stupid, which Jennifer knew wasn't true, or he was incredibly naive, which she was beginning to suspect. Or maybe he was incredibly brazen.

It wouldn't have been so bad if Jennifer hadn't accidentally seen the woman that morning, if she could still believe that Mike's ex-wife was the faded drudge, the low-class tart Colleen Quinn had described.

Lena was her name. Funny, she couldn't even recall Mike's mentioning it. Lena. And she wasn't a faded drudge—she was exceedingly attractive. Dark, exotic looking, tall and curved in all the right places.

Damn him!

She paced the length of her white-on-white living room with its pale sandstone fireplace and copper lighting fixtures, and she couldn't help picturing Mike in a motel room with *Lena*. They were both undressing, and she could see Mike's nude body in her mind's eye: a great body, big, broad, honed to perfection, curling blond hairs on his arms and legs, a patch of soft blond hair on his chest. In Jennifer's line of work she'd come to appreciate a good body, and she couldn't keep her hands off Mike's.

Could it possibly be as innocent as he wanted her to believe?

Jennifer gave one last exasperated sigh, then she went to the phone and called Colleen.

"Mike just phoned me from Flagstaff," she told

Mike's sister without preamble, "and Lena, his ex-wife..."

"What about Lena?" Colleen asked.

"Well, she's with him, and they're both in Flagstaff sharing a motel room."

"Oh, for Pete's sake," Colleen said. "Is he crazy?"

"I don't know. Honest to God, Colleen, I just don't know. What's he doing? Does he still like her?"

"I don't know. Wow, this is nuts."

"I'm going out of my mind. He acted like it was nothing, him and this...this woman in the same room. I can't figure him out."

"Listen, Jennifer, just calm down. Look, how about I come over and we can talk."

"It's late. I hate to bother you like this. I'd meet you somewhere, but there're the kids, you know."

"No problem. I've got this great bottle of Chardonnay, and we can open it and sit around and gab like roommates."

"Would you, Colleen? That'd be so great. And you can tell me everything about Mike and this...his ex-wife, okay?"

Colleen was there in twenty minutes, tall and blond like her brother, her face rather severe, a feminine version of Mike's. She was a career woman, vice president of a large insurance firm, and she had a no-nonsense way about her that called for obedience at her job.

She was a good friend, though, and Jennifer appreciated that Colleen had come over at this hour, smiling, unperturbed, with a sweating bottle of wine in her hand.

"So," Colleen said, going straight to the kitchen and rummaging around for a corkscrew, "what did my sweet baby brother do now?"

"Lena showed up at his place this morning and wanted

to go along on this trip of his to New Mexico. I drove by, you know, just to say goodbye, and she was there. They were arguing. I *thought* he refused to take her. When I left, at least, that's the way it sounded, but she must have convinced him somehow, because when he called tonight he told me she was with him.''

"What an idiot,'' Colleen mused, pulling the cork from the bottle and pouring two glasses. "Here, this is good stuff.''

They sat on Jennifer's white sectional, Colleen's long legs stretched out in impeccable slacks, Jennifer sitting yoga-style in a sweatshirt and leggings.

Jennifer drank, the cool liquid sliding down her throat, then she held the glass in her lap, turning it in her hands. "Tell me about Lena, will you? I need to know her, to figure out what's going on here.''

Colleen held her wineglass up to the light and squinted through it. "Oh, she's a hellion, all right. A real hot temper, kind of a tomboy. She likes cars. *Cars!* She has this old convertible, all souped up. She's had it since before she met Mike. In fact, that's how she met him. He stopped her for speeding and gave her a ticket.''

"Cute,'' Jennifer said.

"I guess Mike thought so. They were married within a year. Lena was pretty young—too young, it seems.''

"How young?''

"Well, she must have been about twenty-three or so.''

"She's younger than I am,'' Jennifer noted.

"She had to grow up pretty quick. The baby, then Mike's drinking, then the divorce. She's done okay, though.'' Colleen took a drink and swirled the wine in the glass. "They were sure crazy about each other at first. I think Mike liked her energy. And she's smart, too. Manipulative.''

"She sure manipulated him this morning."

"Uh-huh, she could do that. To give her credit, she did try after Jeff was killed. She couldn't deal with Mike's drinking, though, and she came to Dad." Colleen shrugged. "Mike was pretty impossible then. He's told you this, hasn't he?"

"Yes, sure he has. It must have been terrible."

"It was. But if Lena could have stuck it out… Well, you see how he quit drinking and all. I never quite understood why she just ended it like that."

"Does she know Mike doesn't drink anymore?" Jennifer leaned forward, elbows on her knees.

Colleen shrugged. "Probably not."

"If she found out, would she want him back?"

"I don't know. Maybe. But it's been five years.…"

Jennifer unfolded her legs and stood up in one easy motion. "Damn it, Colleen, I'm here and he's there, with *her,* and he's probably telling her in that real sincere way he has how he's been sober for five years, and how he's changed. She's probably listening, out of her mind worried about her kid, and there he is, big, calm, understanding Mike Quinn, right there to comfort her. Oh, damn it!"

"Sounds like a possibility," Colleen said, nodding.

"What in hell am I going to do?"

"Go to Albuquerque. Tomorrow. Leave the kids with your ex and just go."

Jennifer stared at her for a long moment. "You mean just show up? But I don't know where he is."

"Easy. Call the Albuquerque police and ask for John Hidalgo. He's Uncle Ted's friend, Mike's contact. He'll know where Mike is."

"Just show up out of the blue?" Jennifer repeated.

"It might not be a bad idea," Colleen said thoughtfully.

"Won't Mike be ticked off? I could make matters
worse."

"You don't know Lena the way I do," Colleen said.
"You might just want to make that trip, Jennifer."

MIKE WAS HAVING a helluva time getting to sleep. The
pullout bed was lumpy, but that wasn't it. Nor was it the
television, which Lena had left on low before she fell
asleep. He was hesitant to turn it off, because it might
wake her up, and he knew how exhausted she was. She'd
been a trooper, though, doing a lot of the driving. Finding
the woman in the minimart—that'd been incredibly
lucky.

He tried to sleep, closing his eyes, wrestling with the
blanket and pillow, endeavoring to be quiet so he
wouldn't awaken Lena.

Everything about her was achingly familiar, and if he'd
let himself realize that this enforced proximity was going
to be so damn difficult, he'd have gotten two rooms—no
matter how much they cost.

The way she moved, every gesture, was a stake driven
into his heart. He thought of how she'd emerged from
the bathroom with a towel wrapped around her wet hair.
How many times had he seen her like that when they'd
been married? And how many times had he gone to her,
pulled the towel off, enfolded her damp body in his arms
and they'd fallen onto their bed together, Lena all soft
and warm from her shower?

The TV set droned on, flickering blue light on everything, on Lena where she lay on the bed, curled up on
her side, the same way she'd always slept. She'd fit into
the curve of his body as if they'd been molded together.

He recalled without wanting to the many nights they'd slept together like that and he'd smelled the scent of her hair as he fell asleep.

He opened his eyes and sat up. He couldn't sleep. He searched for her shadowed form, and while he watched she moved restlessly, the blanket falling away from her foot and her calf. A slim beautiful foot and a smoothly curved calf. He could feel her skin under his hand, feel the satiny warmth of her, still, after all this time, and he burned with shame and desire.

He'd hated her for a long time for leaving him when he was falling apart, but then he'd come to realize that he hadn't allowed her, or anyone, to help him. It wasn't until later that he'd been ready to accept help, and then it had been far too late for reconciling with Lena. Joe Carbone had been there for him, thank God, and Joe had made him understand that Lena had done what she had to do in order to survive.

It had been his fault, he'd come to realize, but that was all water under the bridge now.

They'd been okay together all day, once the clash that morning had been over, but that remark she'd made about his getting a drink had cut right to the core. She didn't believe he was sober now, but then, she had reason to suspect his truthfulness. Alcoholics lied routinely, or evaded the truth or conveniently forgot what they'd promised; he knew that now, and he tried to see the situation from Lena's point of view.

Was she dreaming? Or was she having nightmares? He heard her make small noises in her sleep, soft, distressed sighs, and she seemed restless. She was single-minded in searching for Kimmy, that powerful maternal instinct, and she was probably too preoccupied with that to give him much thought. It was just as well, he mused. He had his life and Lena had hers. Maybe there was some guy, as well, for all that she professed not to date. An attractive woman like her.

It seemed she was doing okay, too, with her job and her house and her friends. Better than okay.

He watched her sleep, and regret washed over him. It was warm in the room, and he threw off the cover and lay with an arm behind his head, staring up at the ceiling, trying not to hear the rustling and murmuring that came from Lena's bed.

Next time he'd definitely get two rooms.

THE FOLLOWING MORNING they left early, getting back on Interstate 40, heading toward Gallup, New Mexico, then the final leg into Albuquerque. It would take most of the day, what with stopping to show Kimmy's picture along the route.

Mike was tired, a result of his restless night, and he let Lena drive while he dozed, head back on the seat. They stopped wherever there was a gas station or café or Navajo curio shop, and both of them fanned out to display Kimmy's photograph.

It was a desolate stretch of highway, past the giant meteor crater outside of Flagstaff, past ocher-and-dun-colored hills covered with dry brush and stunted trees. They descended, leaving behind the mountains around Flagstaff, only to rise again as they approached Gallup, just south of the huge Navajo reservation. They ate lunch at a burger place right off the highway, where they'd stopped to show Kimmy's picture. No one had seen her, though. No one had seen her all day.

"Maybe they didn't stop here," Lena said, sighing. "Or maybe no one we talked to was working last Thursday or Friday, or maybe…"

"Don't torture yourself," Mike said. "We had one lucky break. Can't expect another so easily."

He took over the wheel when they left Gallup, with its honky-tonk bars and Indian trading posts, and to keep himself awake he asked Lena what Kimmy was like.

"What's she like?" Lena repeated, staring out the side window. "That's a tall order."

"I missed her growing up," Mike said. "I only remember a little baby. Big brown eyes, fat wrists. She'd just learned to say *dada*."

"She's a very serious little girl. Oh, she plays like crazy," Lena said, "and she giggles with her friends. She listens, though, and she seems to have a real mature sense—oh, gosh, it's hard to explain, but she seems to understand how people feel. She's sensitive. And she loves her grandma and Al and the guys at work. I think she's a pretty well-adjusted kid."

"Sounds like you did a good job with her."

"All I did was love her, Mike. She felt that from the day we brought her home."

"I loved her, too."

She didn't answer, and he felt regret eat away at him.

"If...when we find her, I don't know what to tell her about who you are," Lena finally said in a small voice.

"What *have* you told her about me?" he asked, his heart sinking.

"I just said you had to go away because you were sick. I said you always loved her."

"Mmm." It could have been worse, he thought. Lena could have said terrible things about him.

"I guess I've been overprotective in some ways," Lena said defensively, "but I couldn't let anyone, anything, hurt that child, not after what she'd been through."

Was this Lena's attempt at rationalizing her behavior? Or could it be a stab at an apology?

"She had a loose tooth," Lena said. "I was going to pull it out for her, and then we were going to put it under her pillow for the Tooth Fairy. I wonder..." Her voice broke, and she put her face in her hands.

"God, Lena, don't," Mike said, and he reached out a hand and touched her arm.

"I can't help it," she said, her voice muffled.

"We'll find her," he promised. "And you can introduce her to me. You can tell her I'm her father and that I'm not sick anymore."

Lena took her hands away from her face and said fiercely, "If you ever hurt her, Mike, if you ever lie to her or let her down...I'll murder you with my bare hands!"

"For God's sake, Lena, give me some credit," he said heatedly.

"Why?" she asked, and then she settled back against the seat and turned her head away from him, watching the rough, arid landscape slide by. Mile after monotonous mile.

CHAPTER TEN

JANE STOOD in the cramped bathroom and touched the swollen corner of her eye. It was turning purple already. She choked back tears. She'd been struck before, and not just by Danny. The bruises always went away.

It had started over the empty cereal box in the cupboard. He'd gotten up late and in a bad mood, hungover and hungry. He'd rummaged around in the fridge, looking for eggs. There were none. Then, swearing, he'd gone for the cereal, and there had only been a few spoonfuls left.

"Do you ever go to the goddamned store?" he'd yelled, breaking a coffee mug in the sink. Then he'd turned on her and, without any warning, he'd punched her.

Kimmy had seen it, too, and she'd cowered in the corner, crying. He'd almost gone for her then, but instead he'd grabbed Jane's purse, taken her money and said the guys were picking him up in a few minutes and he'd just stop and eat somewhere. "When I get back, there'd better be food in the house, you hear me?"

Jane had whimpered that he'd taken the last of her money. He'd thrown some bills onto the kitchen table and stormed out, and the last she'd seen of him, he was sitting on the curb, waiting for his buddies, smoking a cigarette.

She looked at the bruise again. *I hate him,* she thought.

And she knew what he was up to today with that bunch of creeps he called friends. They were making last-minute arrangements to use a no-questions-asked rental house up in Espanola—the house where they were going to do the film with Kimmy.

Jane washed her face and shut the thought out of her head. They were flat broke, and there was no other way. She didn't even know if she had enough money to buy enough groceries.

While Kimmy lay on the bed in the back room, locked in again with the TV turned on, Jane cleaned the broken glass out of the sink, then fixed a cup of instant coffee, which she proceeded to lace with whiskey because yesterday she'd run out of the drugs she kept stashed in the bathroom. Just thinking about having to do without them made her sweat. She drank the coffee quickly, then fixed another cup, pouring in more whiskey, not giving a damn that Danny would notice the bottle was now two-thirds empty.

By noon she was drunk. She unlocked Kimmy's door and stood over the bed, watching as the child lay dozing, last night's sleeping pill still in her system.

"Hey, wake up, kid," she said, slurring. "I gotta go to the store. Wake up."

Kimmy stirred and rubbed her eyes. "Is he…gone?" she asked.

"Yeah, he's gone. For now. Hey," Jane said, "you gotta be a good little girl while I run to the store. No tricks. Okay?"

Kimmy sat up. "You're leaving?"

"Store's only a few blocks away. I'll be right back. Your door'll be locked so…"

"I don't want to stay here," Kimmy cried suddenly,

and she wrapped her arms around Jane's waist. "Please don't leave me alone!"

Jane sat on the bed completely at a loss, the kid clinging to her. She felt a rush of warmth in her stomach. Her kid, her *own* kid, was hugging her.

Maybe it was the alcohol flowing in her blood, or maybe it was maternal instinct, but abruptly she made up her mind. "Okay," she said, "I'll take you along. But you've gotta be a real good little girl. No talking to anyone. Okay?"

Kimberly looked up. "Okay," she said.

"You gotta promise."

"I promise."

Danny had ridden with his buddies, so Jane took the station wagon. She was really too drunk to be driving, but she was past caring.

"Okay," she said when she parked the big wagon near the front of the store. "Here we are. You keep your mouth shut. I mean it. And no telling Danny about this, either."

"All right," Kimmy said, opening the passenger door.

It felt strange and special to walk into the familiar grocery store with a kid holding her hand. How many times had Jane seen mothers leading their kids along, letting them push the big carts? This was her kid, too, her flesh and blood.

Kimmy was awfully well behaved going down the aisles, but she did keep asking for stuff Jane couldn't afford. Once Jane had to take her by the shoulders and scold her. "Put that back. Who said you could have that?"

Then Kimmy shied away and said, "Your breath smells."

"Just be quiet," Jane snapped, and she moved along.

It happened in the cereal aisle. One minute Kimmy was right behind her, the next she was gone.

Jane's heart lurched when she realized it. Quickly she hurried up the aisle and down the next, then backward, pushing the cart, frantic. Where in hell *was* she? *Oh, God,* Jane thought, maybe the kid had conned her!

She left the cart and rushed outside, stumbling once, righting herself, desperately searching the parking lot. Damn it. Danny was going to murder her!

She dashed down one row of parked cars, past the station wagon, then up another, her breath rasping with the exertion. Where in hell was that brat?

Then she spotted her, and the rush of relief almost made her pass out. She raced toward the street, where Kimmy was standing, waiting for the light to change, ready to cross and run away.

"Kimmy!" Jane yelled. "You get the hell back here! Kimmy!"

She caught her and spun her around, then started to drag her back toward the car. The damn kid was sobbing and crying that she wanted her mother.

"Shut up!" Jane kept yelling, pulling at her. "Shut the hell up!"

Jane had almost reached her car, when a lady shopper walked over. "Is everything all right?" the woman asked, eyeing Jane and Kimmy.

Oh, hell, Jane thought, and she pushed Kimmy toward the car.

"I want Mommy," Kimmy was crying.

Considering her state of inebriation, Jane reacted quickly. "Get in the car," she ordered, then she turned to the woman. "That kid," she began, "she's been a pain all week. She's my niece, see, and I'm baby-sitting." Then she turned away.

The woman stared at her for another moment and then walked toward the store, looking back over her shoulder a couple of times. Jane got into the car, gulping in a breath of relief. Then she grabbed Kimmy's arm and dug her nails in. "You sneaky little brat!" she said, shaking her. "You tell Danny about this and I swear you'll get the spanking of your life. You hear me?"

She didn't remember the groceries till she was halfway home, nor did Jane realize that the woman who'd confronted her had gone into the store and immediately asked where she could find the manager.

IT WAS NINETY MILES to Albuquerque, and Lena was driving again. They hadn't spoken much since Lena's last outburst, and she was desperately casting about for something to say, something that wouldn't get Mike's back up. She felt like a crazy yo-yo, alternating between polite conversation and five years' worth of harbored resentment. Things just burst out of her, and she couldn't help it. But she kept trying. They had to stay together, after all, until they found Kimmy.

The subject she chose was not a good idea, and she knew it the second the words were out of her mouth. But it was too late by then. "So," she said, modulating her voice to careful neutrality, "what's with you and Jennifer. Are you going to get married?"

"Huh," he said, and the reply held a wealth of irony and doubt but no surprise.

"What does 'huh' mean?"

"It doesn't mean anything."

A devil inside Lena wouldn't quit. "Well, are you? Are you madly in love?"

He gave her a sidelong glance. "Awful curious, aren't you?"

"Just trying to make conversation."

"You want to pick another subject?"

She was glad she was driving; she could keep her eyes on the road, her face straight ahead. She shrugged. "Sure, whatever." But inside, the devil plied his pitchfork. Yes, she had to admit to herself, she was curious, damn curious. And, even worse, she was just a tiny bit jealous. God, she hated that lack of control on her part.

"You might want to slow down," he suggested.

"No," she said. "I figure if I get pulled over, you can flash your ID and get me out of a ticket."

"This is New Mexico," he growled.

"You'll get me off," she said complacently. His grousing about her speed had never gotten him anywhere, and it wouldn't now.

The interstate rose again as they neared the Continental Divide. The distant peaks to the north were already snow-capped, but here the land was still dry, and the few stunted trees had to fight for a patch of dirt in which to grow.

Shortly after four they began to descend as they approached Albuquerque. They drove through the Acoma Indian Reservation and then the Laguna Reservation. Ahead was the Rio Grande, a green line bisecting the high, arid plain, and from its banks Albuquerque sprawled eastward to the dry Sandia Mountains.

Lena and Mike turned off the interstate at a downtown exit, and they were instantly lost among the hodgepodge of old colonial streets: San Pedro Drive, Lomas Boulevard, Indian School Road. Mike had to use the cell phone to call police headquarters and get directions. It was located near the central plaza and the convention center in the heart of the city. It was also a stone's throw from gang-infested neighborhoods.

Lena looked for signs to the Galleria Convention Center. "Do you think this detective friend of your uncle's...what's his name?" she asked.

"Hidalgo," Mike said, "John Hidalgo."

"Do you think he'll be there?"

"I really don't know."

"If he isn't... Well, do you think the police will help? We're out-of-state, after all, and..."

"Stop worrying," Mike said. "It's a reciprocal thing. Cops help one another. Doesn't matter where they're from."

Lena let out a low whistle. "I just hope the FBI doesn't try to butt in."

Mike laughed humorlessly. "So do I, so do I."

Detective John Hidalgo was at headquarters when they parked in the visitors' lot, strode into the tall building and checked in with the desk sergeant. He came down to meet them, and Lena had the instant impression of an attractive, smart, self-assured man about her own age.

On the drive Mike had told her what he knew of John Hidalgo. He'd met Ted Quinn at a police convention in Colorado in the winter, and a group of cops had tried skiing, including John and Uncle Ted. They'd struck up a friendship. He was of Spanish descent, from one of the original seventeenth-century land-grant families. Despite herself, Lena had been impressed. Her family had been from Spain, but they sure hadn't owned any land grants.

Lena studied him, the pale complexion and perfect razor-cut dark hair, the long, narrow Don Quixote face. His dark eyes had depth and intelligence. He was wearing a sport coat and light wool trousers, while the other guys were mostly in jeans.

"I've been waiting for you," John said, shaking both their hands, escorting them through the security doors, up in the elevator and into the enclave of police headquarters. As they walked, he explained that he'd done some preliminary work on the case. "I had motor vehicles run a printout on every old wood-sided station-wagon model registered in the state," he told them as they arrived at his desk in a large, open room where the vice detectives were stationed. "There're eighteen or so. The question is, did these characters in the car even return to New Mexico?"

Mike sat next to Lena across from Hidalgo and explained about the clerk in the minimart.

"All right," John said, "good legwork there, Quinn. At least we can assume they're back in the state. That's a real break."

"And Kimmy's...alive," Lena put in, closing her eyes for a moment. Even the notion of the alternative was too difficult to contemplate. She felt Mike's brief, gentle touch on her shoulder, as if to say it was okay, they were all having the same thought.

John pulled the motor vehicle printout from under a file and held it up. "This is it," he said. "I know eighteen doesn't sound like a lot, but it'll take a while to check them all out. New Mexico's a big state. Lotta territory to cover. We'll get them, though. If they're here, we'll get them."

"Can we start now?" Lena asked expectantly, but Hidalgo said this couldn't have been a worse time at headquarters.

"It's what we call a roundup day. Happens every twelve months or so. Trouble is, I've got to help with the arrests. It'll take the whole damn evening to process them. But tomorrow morning, bright and early, we'll meet here and divide up the list on those station wagons, start making calls. I hope that's okay."

Lena felt disappointment settle in her stomach. There was nothing she could do, though. Kimmy had been unharmed when the lady at the minimart had seen her. Surely she was still okay. How could anyone hurt such a sweet, loving child?

"Tomorrow morning," Lena said, "I want to help make those calls."

"Lena—" Mike began.

But John smiled and cut in. "I don't see why not," he said. "I can find you an empty desk and a phone and you can take some of the names on the list."

"I'll need to know what questions to ask," she said. "I assume we won't be calling to ask if anyone kidnapped a little girl out in California."

"No, we won't. I'll make up some cock-and-bull story and give you a prompt sheet," John said.

"Okay," she said, and she was able to smile. She'd be doing something, actually helping to get her child back. "Thank you," she breathed.

"My pleasure," John said, and then abruptly he snapped his fingers. "Damn, I almost forgot." He pushed aside papers and files and then snatched up a note. "Here it is. Came in for you this morning, Mike. It's from a Jennifer Hilty. I guess she's here in town, checked into the Desert Inn. She wanted you to call when you got in. Number's right at the bottom." He handed Mike the note.

Mike stared at it. "Oh, boy," he said, then he looked up. "Mind if I use the phone?"

"Sure," John said. "Just dial nine for an outside line."

Lena sat in shocked silence, staring at Mike as he dialed. She couldn't begin to imagine what he was thinking. Was he happy? Angry? Surely he must find this pretty darn unusual—possessive, she thought.

She tried not to listen, but it was hard.

"Jenn?" he said, and he turned away, the phone against his ear. For a moment he listened, then he said, "This is crazy. I mean, I'm going to be maxed out here." Again, he listened. "Well…yes, I suppose we could do that. But I really don't have much time." There was another period of listening, then he said, "All right. But you'll have to wait in your room. I'll call when I can." A pause. "No, haven't had time to get a room…two rooms, that is," he added.

John met Lena's eyes and shrugged, a quirk of a smile on his lips. Lena kept her countenance expressionless, but inside she was both amused and irritated. This woman had no right to take up Mike's time during a crisis like this. No right at all. Still, it was kind of funny how jealous his lady friend must be. If only she knew.

John had to get busy helping with the roundup, so after Mike's call he walked them out to the parking lot, promising to meet them back at headquarters at 8 a.m.

Then he saw Lena's car. "Is this yours?" He walked around it. "Wow, this sucker is great. What's the horsepower?"

Lena told John all about her prize vehicle, where she'd bought it, how she'd fixed it up.

"I'll bet you get your share of tickets in this," he said, hands in his pockets.

"Oh, not too many," Lena said.

"Right," Mike put in.

Hidalgo laughed. "I'd better get going," he said. "If you're looking for a good deal on motels, try the Red Rocks out on Route 66. It's clean, too. They've got a few two-bedroom suites, if that's what you're looking for," he added diplomatically.

Mike groaned.

"See you *mañana*," John said, and he left.

Lena got behind the wheel of her GTO and started it up. "Look," she said, "I can drop you at this Desert Inn place and then I'll go get us a couple of rooms. Or maybe you want to, you know, just stay with your friend and I'll pick you up at a quarter to eight tomorrow."

But Mike was shaking his head. "No," he said, looking straight ahead. "Let's go check out this Red Rocks Motel. I'd feel better if I knew you were safely in a room. If they have a suite, that'll work."

She cocked a dark brow. "Then you won't be staying with Jennifer?" she asked in a neutral voice.

Mike shook his head. "No, I won't. As soon as you're settled in, I'll borrow the car, though, if you don't mind."

"No problem," she said, and she backed out of the parking space. He wasn't going to spend the night with Jennifer, then. *Interesting,* Lena thought, and she squelched a momentary stab of satisfaction before driving off, her mind settling back on Kimmy.

CHAPTER ELEVEN

MIKE STARTED LENA'S GTO, his thoughts on what he was going to say to Jennifer. He had directions to the Desert Inn but had to concentrate so hard on finding his way through the unfamiliar streets of Albuquerque that by the time he pulled up at the posh glass-and-stone facade of the motel, he still had no idea what he was going to say or why Jenn was there.

He asked at the desk, found her room and knocked. She didn't answer immediately, and he stood there waiting, resenting his need to do this, and at the same time feeling guilty for his resentment. Damn. How in hell was he supposed to handle this?

She finally opened the door, and her perfume wafted out around him.

"Mike, oh, Mike, I missed you so much, darling," she said in that lovely, throaty voice that could send ripples of desire through his gut, and she pulled him inside and clung to him.

"Hey, Jenn, what's this all about? I haven't even been gone for two days," he said.

She leaned back in his arms and looked up at him. "It was your being so far away. I almost went crazy missing you."

He wasn't sure whether to be flattered or irritated. "Where are your kids?" was all he could think of to ask.

"Bob took them. He was a sweetheart about it. I just hopped on a plane and here I am. Aren't I bad?"

"Well, Jenn, like I said, I really won't have any time to see you. Tonight's the only free time, because Hidalgo's tied up, but starting tomorrow morning, hell, I'll be lucky to get a bite to eat."

She pouted a little. "Mike, I came because I want to be here for you. Don't you understand? This is a terrible thing for you to be going through, and you need someone here for support."

"That's great of you, Jenn. It's just that I'm going to be so busy."

"Then I'll wait for you. I'll be here whenever you have the time. That's what a relationship is—or at least that's what I always *thought* it was."

Mike held her, one hand on each of her arms, and he studied her face, trying to read her, trying not to hurt her feelings. "Look, this isn't about relationships. It's about Kimmy and about police work."

An expression he couldn't name flickered across her face, then disappeared. "So why is Lena here with you? She isn't a policeman."

"She's Kimmy's mother. She was half out of her mind. I couldn't leave her behind."

"That's not what it sounded like yesterday morning."

"No, I…ah…it's complicated, Jenn. You'll just have to trust me on that."

"Did you really share a motel room with her last night?" Jennifer asked, coyly fiddling with the end of the zipper on his leather jacket. "Are you sharing one with her tonight? Is that why you don't have time for me?"

"Jennifer," he said, "for God's sake, you're getting all upset over nothing. I don't have time for this. We have separate rooms, okay?"

She looked up at him, searching his face. "You're mad. I blew it, didn't I?"

"Nobody blew anything. I'm just trying to explain to you..."

She threw her arms around him then and laid her head on his chest. "I love you," she breathed. "I can't help it."

He stroked her hair. "Take it easy, Jenn. I'm not angry. I'm just, you know, preoccupied." He put a finger under her chin and tilted her face up, and he saw with dismay that there were tears shining in her eyes. "Come on, let's get something to eat. We'll talk."

They ate in the Desert Inn steak house, off the lobby of the motel. The food was excellent, the decor very Southwest, and romantic notes from the piano bar accompanied the mouthwatering smells of grilled meat.

Jennifer ordered chicken—she never ate red meat—and Mike ordered the filet, medium rare.

"What a change from burgers and pizza," he said, cutting the butter-soft steak.

Jennifer was still busy with the plate she'd heaped high from the salad bar. She ate silently for a time, then put down her fork and asked him directly, "Do you still love Lena?"

He almost choked on his mouthful of filet. "Damn it, what kind of question is that?" he retorted.

"Kindly answer my question," she said coolly.

"No, I do not love Lena." He glared at her. "This is how you give me *support,* Jenn?"

"I think I have to know, don't you?"

"Well, now you know."

"Why'd you break up?" She leaned over the table, her face lit by the candle in the glass cylinder. "Why did you leave her?"

"I told you all that. My drinking. Look, can we eat in peace? I *was* enjoying this meal."

"What kind of marriage did you have? I mean, was it wildly romantic, practical, purely physical?"

"You're not going to let up, are you?"

"No. I need to know, Mike. I mean, you just took a leave, left L.A. with your ex-wife, and I don't understand it."

"I wish I could tell you in twenty words or less what kind of marriage we had. Hell, it only lasted a few years. We were in love, we thought it could work, it didn't." He shrugged and turned back to his food.

"Was your drinking the only problem? Or was it money or your job or something else?" She toyed with the salad, then picked a crouton off the top and ate it slowly.

"It was my drinking, as far as I know. You've heard all this, Jenn. Why the third degree?"

"Because she's back in your life."

"Only out of necessity. Believe me, she doesn't like it any better than I do."

"You're sure of that?"

"Yeah, I'm sure. She hates my guts."

"Hmm," Jenn said, and then she dropped the subject, and the meal went much, much better.

He was really glad she hadn't pushed any more, because he didn't much like recollecting the sordid details of that final scene of his marriage. Only he and Lena and Joe Carbone knew, and he'd like to keep it that way.

She started again, though, over coffee. "Was it the baby that put pressure on your marriage?" she asked. "I mean, with her being adopted and sick and everything?"

"No," he said. "Believe me, Kimmy had nothing to

do with it. We both loved her. We wanted more kids, too, but... Well, that never came about.''

''I think you were very brave to take that baby.''

''We never thought of it that way,'' he said. ''But the media made a big deal of it. We were really surprised, but I guess it was a human-interest kind of story. It was sort of embarrassing.''

''You're too modest.''

''You wouldn't believe the fuss. Phone calls from papers and TV shows all over the state. We had to change our phone number, for God's sake. Lena was going nuts trying to get in and out of the house without being followed.'' He laughed and shook his head, remembering.

''Didn't it make you feel good?''

''Hell, it was a pain in the butt.'' He thought back. ''The only time I remember enjoying the publicity was the day we went to the hospital to bring Kimmy home. We'd tried to keep it secret, but someone at the hospital must have leaked the information, because there were some photographers and video guys around when we left. And we did let them take some pictures. I still have the newspaper article. It has a nice picture.''

''I didn't know you were famous,'' Jenn said playfully, reaching over the table to put her hand on his.

''It was just for a little while. But it *was* a nice picture. Lena and me, and she was holding the baby, and Gloria was there, grinning like crazy....''

''Gloria?''

''Lena's mother. We looked so damn happy in that picture. It was on TV, too.''

''Mmm, that's nice.''

''Yeah, it was.'' He could close his eyes and recall the scene as if it were yesterday—Lena holding Kimmy proudly, him standing behind her, Gloria beside her, and the caption: Policeman and Wife Save Baby. And their names and...

Gloria's name! Gloria Torres, right there in the article, and it even said she was from Woodland Hills, where she still lived! Someone could easily have found Kimmy through Gloria, who picked her up at school every day. Someone who followed Gloria to the playground and saw her pick her granddaughter up and then went early one day and grabbed Kimmy and...

Mike was vaguely aware of Jennifer saying something and the muted tinkle of china and silverware and conversation, but his whole being was focused on this new hunch, this *cop's* hunch. After six years, someone had found Gloria and then Kimmy through that newspaper article. And who would still have that? Who and why? The who was pretty easy—Kimmy's birth mother, Jane Cramm. She might have abandoned her baby, but she might not have been entirely without feelings. She would have seen the newspaper and kept the article, and since Lena was virtually untraceable, she'd searched out Gloria.

"Mike?" Jenn was saying. "Mike, what's wrong?"

"Nothing," he muttered.

"You didn't hear a word I said. I asked if you—"

He cut her off. "Listen, Jenn, I've got to make a call. I'll be back in a second."

"Mike, what...?"

But he'd pushed back his chair and was striding out to the lobby. He went straight to the public phone and dialed his folks' number. His mother answered, and he had to talk to her for a minute before she put his dad on, and he tried not to sound impatient. Finally Larry was on the line.

"Pop," Mike said, "it came to me. Who it is, who it

probably is. It was that newspaper picture of us getting Kimmy at the hospital.'' He explained the whole thing. ''So it could be her, Jane Cramm.''

''By God, you're onto something there,'' Larry said. ''It's worth a try. There's got to be a record of her somewhere. I'll push the FBI. She has to have left a trail.''

''Do that. They may find something. We're going to work the vehicle angle at this end. Hidalgo's got the list of wood-sided wagons for us. We'll go to work on it tomorrow. And hey, Hidalgo says to say hello to Uncle Ted.''

''I'll tell him. How's...uh, Lena?''

''Okay,'' he said offhandedly. ''Why—how's she supposed to be?''

''Well, since Jennifer's there, I wondered...''

''How in hell do you know Jenn's here?'' Mike asked angrily.

''Colleen told me. Why—is there a problem?''

''Damn it! I *knew* there was something... Colleen set the whole thing up—I know it.'' He took a deep breath to stave off his anger. ''Tell that sister of mine to mind her own business,'' he said.

''Maybe you'd better tell her,'' Larry said. ''I'm sorry I ever mentioned it.''

''Okay, okay,'' Mike said, trying to stay calm, ''forget the whole subject. I'll call you tomorrow about the case. And now I've gotta go and try to convince Jennifer to go home. Nice job, huh?''

''You'd rather walk on hot coals?'' Larry suggested.

''Something like that, Pop.''

Mike wasn't sure whether to be more aggravated by Colleen or Jennifer, but he sure wasn't in a very good mood when he sat down across from Jenn.

''Business,'' he muttered. ''Sorry.''

"Something about the case?" she asked carefully.

"Yeah." He'd decided not to say a word about Colleen. It would only cause an unpleasant conversation, and he didn't feel like dealing with it.

Jennifer insisted on paying for dinner; they argued about it and finally decided to split the bill. It was just another irritation in an evening that was degenerating moment by moment.

He walked Jenn back to her room, and she turned to him, her eyes luminous, and said, "Do you want to come in for a while?"

It was a laughable come-on, seeing as he and Jenn weren't exactly strangers to each other, but frankly he wasn't in the mood.

"Look, Jenn, I'd love to, but it's late, and I've got to get up early tomorrow. Helluva day ahead of me. I'm beat."

She looked at him, her mouth a tight line.

"How about I drive you to the airport in the morning?" he suggested, hoping to soften the blow.

"So I'm getting dumped?" she asked, stepping back from him.

"No," he replied wearily, "you're just going home." Then he kissed her on the cheek. "I'll see you in the morning."

She turned her back and unlocked her door.

"Good night," he said softly.

The door closed in his face. He stood for a moment, looking at it, then shrugged and walked off down the hall, and before he'd even reached Lena's car, his mind was whirling with ideas, plans, possibilities. Jane Cramm, eighteen vehicles to trace, records—the phone company, driver's license? Credit card? Probably not, if she was a druggie. Social security? Drug arrests?

Maybe the station wagon was a dead end, or maybe it was connected. He didn't know yet; he only knew the pieces of the puzzle were starting to fit together—only the outside rim of it for now, but he'd find more, and eventually the whole picture would emerge. And there, at the center, he'd find Kimmy.

Back at his motel, he let himself into the suite quietly, yawning, figuring Lena was in her own room, fast asleep.

She was asleep, all right, but she was on the couch in the living room, the TV still on. He crossed the floor and stood looking down at her. She'd fallen asleep on her side, her head resting on one hand. She had her pajamas on, the polka-dot ones, and she looked so young, so peaceful, lying there. Her dark hair spread over the cushions, and the light touched her features, as if a finger brushed them with gilt here and shadow there. He gazed at her too long, a feeling of regret for the past, for what he'd lost, tightening in his chest.

Then he leaned over and shook her very gently. "Lena," he said, and her eyes flew open and she gave a startled gasp.

"Lena," he said again, "you fell asleep here."

She rubbed her face. "Oh, God, sorry, I…"

"Go to bed."

"Uh-huh." She sat up. "I was dreaming that we found Kimmy and we were back home, and I was so happy. Oh, Mike, I was so relieved and happy."

"Mmm," he said.

"Will we find her?" she asked imploringly.

"Yes, Lena, I already told you that."

"It's the only thing keeping me sane," she breathed.

"Go to bed," he said gently.

She got up and gave him a shaky smile. "Good night."

"Mmm," he said again, and he watched as she padded

across the floor, barefoot, and disappeared into her bedroom, closing the door behind her.

Two doors shut in his face tonight, he thought. *Good work, pal.*

THE NEXT MORNING over breakfast he told Lena about how Jane Cramm might have traced Kimmy. She held a mug of coffee, her elbows resting on the table, and watched him with her dark, slightly slanted eyes.

"The newspaper article had Gloria's full name in it. They couldn't find you or me, so they located Gloria, followed her, maybe staked out her house for days," he said.

"Why?" she asked.

He shrugged. "Some kind of belated maternal instinct? A ploy to get welfare maybe, aid to dependent children, something like that?"

"Kidnapping is a federal crime, a capital crime. Wouldn't she know that?"

"Ah, who knows what's going through her mind—if it's her." He went on. "It'd be too much to expect the wagon to be registered to her. Probably the guy's."

"You mean the guy with her, the 'mean man' Marcia saw."

"Yeah, whoever he is."

"I hope these leads aren't dead ends," Lena said, frowning. "We've wasted so much time on them."

"It's all we have to go on. Lena, don't worry. I've got a hunch the connection is this Cramm woman."

She gave him a quick smile that disappeared so swiftly he wasn't sure he'd seen it.

"I like your hunches," she said softly.

He dropped Lena at police headquarters just before eight. "Tell Hidalgo I'll be back soon."

"Okay. Maybe we'll have already found the car," she said, trying to be cheerful. "At least I can *do* something."

He watched her walk into the building, her shoulders set, her jeans tight over her rear end, a perfect fit. Then he pulled out into traffic and drive to the Desert Inn to pick Jennifer up and take her to the airport.

When she didn't answer his knock at her door, he looked in the coffee shop to see if she was eating breakfast. She wasn't there.

The clerk at the front desk answered his inquiry by punching keys on his computer. "Mrs. Hilty, Jennifer Hilty?" The clerk looked up from the keyboard. "She checked out an hour ago, sir. Asked me to call her a cab."

DANNY HAYDEN WAS on the phone, trying to clinch the movie deal, and Jane was doing a pile of dishes left over from the night before. She was making too much noise, fumbling, dropping things right and left, and Danny knew she'd been sneaking booze again. It made him mad as hell.

The little girl was sitting at the table, eating cereal out of a bowl, real quiet and scared, her big brown eyes just showing above the bowl. She was starting to look pale with shadows under her eyes. They'd better make that damn movie fast.

"Okay," he said into the phone, "so you got all the equipment lined up?"

"Don't worry about our end of things," the man said. "You just deliver the kid, all clean and nice and smiling."

"No problem," Danny said. "And the money?"

"Like I said, half when we start, half when it's done."

"Cash?"

"Cash."

When he hung up, he whirled around and yelled, "For God's sake, keep that racket down, will you?"

Jane dropped the lid of a pot, and it clanged in the sink. "Sorry," she whispered.

He shook his head in disgust, deciding not to bother swatting her because it made the kid cry, and he couldn't stand the goddamn screeching all the time.

Yeah, Jane was drunk again. And he knew why. Well, besides the fact that there was no money for drugs—it was the damn little brat. Jane wanted to keep the kid.

Once he'd realized that she really meant it, he played along just to shut her up. A kid. Sure, she was a cute kid, and for a minute here and there he'd thought it might be fun to have a kid, like a puppy or a kitten, but he knew it was far too much trouble to take care of her, not to mention too expensive. And what would happen when she grew up and starting asking questions and talking back?

No, fatherhood was not in the stars for Danny Hayden. Jane, of course, was a different story. The kid was Jane's real child.

He'd been pretty damn clever once Jane had told him she'd had a baby that she'd given up for adoption. He'd worked on that maternal instinct, and it had been easy as pie. The grandmother was right where the newspaper article had said she was—unbelievable luck—and all he'd had to do was call Information to find that out. Almost too easy.

Jane was staggering around the kitchen with that stupid grin on her face, the one she got when she drank. And her one eye wandered, walleyed, so you couldn't tell exactly where she was looking.

"Go take a nap or something," he said. "You're driving me nuts."

"In a minute," she said.

"Now."

She shot him a frightened look. "But I told Kimmy we could go out for a walk."

"In your condition?" He laughed.

"I'm okay, Danny."

"The hell you are. Go on, like I said. I'll take care of the kid." He was aware of the girl looking at him, scared, dropping her spoon.

"Danny…"

He walked up to Jane, stood chest to chest with her; he wasn't much taller than she was. "I said," he breathed, low and deliberate, "go take a nap."

She switched her eyes to Kimmy, once, hesitated, then her shoulders slumped and she turned and shuffled off.

"Okay, kid," he said. "You finished?"

"Yes," the little girl whispered.

"Let's go."

She walked down the hall in front of him, went into her room. Then she looked up. "Can I go for a walk with Jane later?"

"Maybe," he lied. Like hell he'd let the neighbors see this kid—or any cops who might be driving down the street. For all he knew there was a nationwide APB out on her, with her picture and everything.

"When can I see my mommy?" she asked in that little, piping voice of hers.

"If you're good for the next couple of days, maybe you can see her then."

"Promise? Cross your heart and—"

"Yeah, yeah, sure, kid," he said impatiently. "Cross my heart and hope to die."

CHAPTER TWELVE

IT WAS ALREADY A ZOO at police headquarters when John Hidalgo met Lena at the security desk downstairs.

"Lawyers," he said, shrugging. "After yesterday's busts, there must be fifty lawyers in here arranging bail."

"I'll be in the way," she said, apologetic.

"Nonsense," he replied. He took her arm and led her to the elevator and the maze of offices while she explained, as best she could, where Mike was.

"You were once married?" John asked en route to his desk.

Lena nodded.

"And Kimmy's adopted, by both of you?"

"Yes," she said. "It was Mike and his partner who took Kimmy to the hospital when she was only a day old. The guys were really concerned. Mike and Jeff tried to visit her every day. She was a crack baby, and the doctors weren't sure if she'd make it."

"So you and Mike adopted her. That was a…very special thing you did."

Lena shrugged. "We were lucky to get her." She told John about Mike's hunch, how Kimmy's birth mother might have kept track of her through Gloria, who still lived in Woodland Hills and was a big part of the child's life. "That's what Mike thinks, anyway," Lena said.

"But you don't?"

"Well, I don't have that cop's nose, you know. But

he has his dad out in L.A. stepping up the search for the woman. Jane Cramm's her name. At least it was then...."

"Is the FBI...?"

"Oh, yes," Lena said. "They're supposedly conducting their own investigation. But what they're really conducting is a farce. A sick farce." She told him about Special Agent Sabin's visit to Gloria. "That moron," she said under her breath.

Hidalgo laughed.

He shuffled files at his desk, then found what he was hunting for—the prompt sheet he'd made up for Lena. "Ah," he said, "here it is. Why don't you sit here a few minutes and look this over while I try to find you an empty desk and a phone."

She sat in the wooden chair across from his desk and began reading the prompt sheet, familiarizing herself with the questions he'd concocted for the phone interviews with the station wagon owners. While she read, she was aware of a lot of male eyes on her. They were no doubt wondering who she was. John's girlfriend? Someone he was interviewing? A poorly dressed lawyer?

Lena couldn't help smiling. Lots of times, long before Mike had joined Hostage Negotiations, she'd visited him or met him at his station. She'd known most of the guys then, and they'd all been teases. "Soon as you dump that creep Quinn, I'm next in line. Okay?" they'd said.

Back then she'd liked cops. Just as she enjoyed the company of her fellow workers at Al's. Sometimes they seemed to her to be no more than little boys playing games: cops and robbers or race car drivers. She found, too, that the boldest and most flirtatious of them turned to mush if she called them out on their teasing. She'd bet this lot of Albuquerque cops was no different.

"What do you think?" John asked.

She started, realizing she'd been daydreaming of by-gone days, missing the life, and she was surprised. "Oh," she said, "the phone questions. They're good, John, really."

He found her a desk and phone near the window over-looking the plaza below. "This is Swartz's spot," he said. "He's on vacation." John then produced the list of eighteen names and addresses. Some had phone numbers; others didn't. "Why don't you take, say, five of these and start from there. Try Information if you haven't got a number. Okay?"

Lena took the list he handed her and nodded. "I hope I do this right."

John put a hand on her shoulder and said, "You'll do fine. Just keep good notes and we'll see where it all leads."

She smiled and took a breath. "Okay," she said. "Just leave me alone or I'll get even more nervous than I am."

"Done," he said, and he left her there with her list of names.

The first person on Lena's list, a man from Alamo-gordo, wasn't home. She didn't even bother to leave a voice message. What would be the point? Next to his name she put a star and a notation: try after work. It was going to be a long day.

She picked up the phone again, ready to try the next number, but found herself glancing toward John's desk. Mike wasn't here yet. And she wondered if he was still at the airport with Jennifer. Was he waiting for her flight? Having coffee with her, leaning close over a little table? She thought about last night. He'd been home relatively early. Still, he'd had plenty of time with Jennifer to…to go to bed, she thought, trying to tamp down the image. *Had* he made love to her?

Get a life, she told herself, and she shook off the images and dialed the next number.

She reached Hannah Grueter in Farmington on the second ring.

"Hello?" said an elderly woman.

Lena's heart quickened. *Do this right. Concentrate,* she told herself firmly.

"Good morning, Mrs. Grueter," Lena began. "My name is Anne Berringer, and I'm from Roper's National Survey. I wonder if I could have a minute of your time."

"Is this one of those sales calls?" the woman snapped.

"No, it isn't," Lena went on. "We aren't selling a thing. In fact, Roper's is being paid by the automobile manufacturers to conduct a very important survey that will be a benefit to car owners such as yourself."

"Go on," the woman said, albeit suspiciously.

Lena took a breath. "I understand that you still drive a 1961 Ford station wagon, ma'am."

"Yes, I do."

"Good, good. And could you tell me how many miles are on your odometer?"

"Oh, for heaven's sake, I have no idea," Hannah Grueter said.

"Over one hundred thousand? Two hundred?"

"Over a hundred. Maybe it's around a hundred fifty."

"That's fine," Lena said, ad-libbing, beginning to feel more confident. "And are you the sole driver, Mrs. Grueter?"

"It's *Miss.* And, yes, I'm the only one who drives my car."

"I see. Then there's no nephew or niece who would borrow your automobile occasionally?"

"No. My nephew's a bum. I wouldn't let him touch it with a ten-foot pole."

Lena allowed herself a friendly laugh. "How about your mechanic?"

"Slacks? Well, sure, to test it or something."

"Slacks?"

"Slacks Kerry."

"Mmm. Okay. Do you often have to leave your car for a few days with him?"

"Sometimes. Transmission went out a few years back. You know."

"Okay," Lena said, underlining the name Slacks Kerry on her notepad. "Has there been a recent break-down, Miss Grueter?"

"Had my winter tires put on, is all."

"And that was…?"

"My show's coming on," Hannah Grueter said, annoyed.

"Only two more questions," she said pleasantly.

"Oh, all right."

"Have you taken your car on a trip recently?"

"Yes."

"To…?"

"Colorado Springs."

"Uh-huh. And it ran well?"

"Just fine, young lady, and now I'm going to watch my show."

"Thank you for your time," Lena said, and she hung up. *Phew!* she thought. She'd had to wing it a lot. But then, she spent half her days on the phone at Al's. She knew how to talk cars.

She called the next number on her list, having to get it from Information. It belonged to a Daniel Hayden of Santa Fe. There was no answer and no recorder. She put a star next to the name: call later, no answer.

It was then that Lena noticed Mike at John's desk,

talking to him. He was standing, leaning over with his hands on the desk, one knee flexed, and she couldn't help noting that Mike was as tall as anyone in the room, and certainly as handsome in his jeans and pink shirt with the cuffs rolled up. She'd always liked looking at Mike, the way his dark-blond hair fell softly over the top of his ears and curled a little at the back, the way he carried himself, the pitch of his head when he was concentrating, as he was now. She couldn't help wondering if Jennifer saw those same things in him or if his nearness made her stomach tighten the way Lena's used to.

Mike turned his head, as if sensing her eyes on him, and their gazes met for a moment before Lena collected herself and looked back at her notes. And then she was aware of him approaching her, but she kept her head down, studying the list in front of her.

"How's it going?" he asked.

"Oh," she said, as if surprised. "Well, I got one person so far."

"Good," he said. "Good."

"She doesn't look like a suspect."

"Mmm."

"So—" she clasped her hands on the desk and looked up "— did you get Jennifer off all right?"

"Oh, yeah, sure," he mumbled.

"Good," she said, idiotically repeating Mike's words. "Well—" she smiled brightly "—I'd better get back to work here."

"I guess so."

She switched her gaze to her notes, aware of Mike moving away. Still, she couldn't help searching her feelings, and it was rather like probing a sore tooth with her tongue. Was she glad he'd shipped his lady friend off? *Yes,* she thought, trying to convince herself it was only because Mike needed to concentrate on the job at hand. Yet she couldn't help remembering that he'd come home early last night. *Had* he slept with the woman?

Damn it, she thought, letting out a breath. How could she possibly have room in her mind for such triteness? Kimmy was what mattered. She was *all* that mattered. And yet, somehow, there was room in Lena to wonder about Mike and his life. And she hated that.

With determination, she forced her thinking back to Slacks Kerry, the mechanic. If he had access to Hannah Grueter's car, he *could* have driven it to L.A. and back in two days. He might warrant checking out.

She dialed another number, someone named Ralph Martin right here in Albuquerque. He answered, and she went through her routine.

"If you're trying to sell me a new car, forget it, lady. I like what I have. I'm out of work, too, so trying to get money out of me won't fly."

"This really is a survey, sir," she said. *Nasty man. Angry,* she scribbled on her notepad. "We merely want to determine how many of these wagons are still on the road. It helps the auto manufacturers with engine design, torque, suspension, all those things."

"Yeah, so?" he said.

"Could you tell me how many miles are on your engine?"

"Two-forty-five."

"That's a lot of miles. Is the engine the original or a rebuilt one?"

She went along those lines until she was sure he wasn't suspicious of the call. Then she switched gears. "Are you the only driver, Mr. Martin?"

"Yeah, sure. Well, sometimes my wife uses it."

And then Lena ventured, "Is that your wife, let's see, Jane?"

"Where in hell do you people get your information? Her name's Polly."

"I'm sorry. I'll make that correction, sir. Now, do you feel comfortable driving your '68 wagon on a trip?"

"Would you?" he said curtly. "Hell no. We take my wife's car. It's a Buick, by the way."

"I see. So in, say, the last six months your car hasn't been out of New Mexico?"

"Hasn't even been out of this damn city," he grumbled.

"Thank you, sir. That will do it," Lena said.

"Yeah," he said, and he hung up.

Just before lunch Lena tried the first number she'd called and still got the recorder. She tried Daniel Hayden again, too. No answer. Then she tried the last number on her list, but the car owner had passed away last June and the car was at the junkyard. Lena put a line through the name.

She finally stood and stretched, aware, after the fact, of every eye in the room turned to her. She was wearing jeans and a white round-necked T-shirt with long sleeves, and she realized it wasn't much of a cover-up, not around this group.

Mike was looking at her, too. He was at a desk near John's, on the phone with his own list, talking. Nonetheless she felt his gaze, and a hot ripple of tension ran along her limbs. She felt suddenly as if she were betraying herself.

She walked to John's desk, her list and notes in hand. He wasn't on the phone, so she sat and asked how his calls were going.

Hidalgo frowned. "Not so good. Yours?"

"Well," Lena said, aware of Mike hanging up the phone and coming toward them, "two I can't reach yet. One's deceased, the car's junked. There was a man—" she glanced at her notes "—a Ralph Martin, whom I'd say is not a possibility. But there was this woman, a Hannah Grueter, who's got a mechanic who could possibly be our man. I know it's not likely, but I've got his name. He's in Farmington."

"If we have to, we'll check him out," John said. Then he looked up at Mike. "How's your list going?"

"About like yours," Mike said. "The trouble with me is I'm afraid I don't come off very well as a telephone surveyor. I had two people cuss me out and hang up."

Lena looked down at her hands and cleared her throat. "I...well, I seem to be doing okay on that end. I mean, I do spend half the day on the phone at my job. Maybe I should, you know, take a few more names from you guys." She studied her nails.

"Well, now," John said, "what do you think, Mike?"

She heard Mike give a short laugh. "What the hell," he said. "When it comes to cars, Lena really can hold her own."

"Okay, then," John said. "Let's get a bite to eat and then, Lena, well, you can have at it."

"Really?" she said, perhaps too eagerly.

"Really," John said.

They ate at a popular local diner, a real blue-plate-special joint. The restaurant wasn't old, but it was decorated in the style of the 1950s. The menu, too, was reminiscent of the fifties: burgers, hot dogs, grilled cheeses, BLTs, fries, malts and shakes and cherry or vanilla Cokes. The prices were 1998.

Lena had a grilled cheese; the guys chomped down on chili burgers. They all had iced tea.

John was easy to be with. He had a quick smile and sharp, humor-filled black eyes. His jokes were bad, though, a little too raunchy for Lena, who had already heard most of them at Al's. She told the only joke she remembered, a feminist joke. Lena laughed, but John said, "I don't get it." Then all three laughed.

"I didn't know you'd become a feminist," Mike said, staring at her, his head cocked.

Lena took a drink of iced tea and raised her eyes. "There's a lot you don't know about me, Mike Quinn," she said levelly.

After lunch they walked back to headquarters under a perfect October sky. Lena commented on how blue it was.

"It's from the dryness," John said. "A lot of desert out there."

And then the reason she was here, walking with these two policemen, came crashing back into her head, and she couldn't believe she'd actually forgotten it for a few minutes. *Kimmy.* Perplexed at herself, she started across the street against the light.

Mike grabbed her arm and pulled her back onto the curb. "God, you trying to get killed?"

She let out a breath and had to shake off her thoughts. "Sorry," she said. "I was thinking about Kimmy."

She could feel the warmth of Mike's hand on her arm, the strength, and she wanted to lean on him, to put her hand on his chest and beg him to tell her it was all going to be okay. She felt the warmth of his fingers still gripping her arm, a searing heat that turned her flesh to liquid. *No, no, no,* her brain kept repeating, a mantra that her heart ignored. And when he finally released her and they crossed the street, she was certain her knees were going to buckle. After all these years, all these days and months and years, how could this be happening?

Back at the station she was immensely grateful to have the lists to occupy herself, to drag her mind back to reality. Between her, Mike and John, they'd spoken to eleven of the eighteen station wagon owners, and according to everyone's notes, there were only two questionable car owners, and neither of them seemed too promising.

Before going on to a few of the names from the other two lists, Lena redialed the car owners she hadn't been able to reach earlier. Again she got the recorder on one of them. But the other picked up.

It was Daniel Hayden's number in Santa Fe.

A woman spoke. "Hello?"

Lena went into her routine patiently, being very careful not to arouse suspicion. The woman was a bit of a pain, too, a little paranoid, one of those people who were sure everyone was out to sell them something. She wouldn't even give her name, only said she was a friend of Daniel Hayden's.

"You're familiar with his station wagon?" Lena asked.

"Uh-huh."

"I wonder if you could tell me approximately how many miles are on it."

She didn't know.

And so the Q-and-A session went. The woman was timid, her voice uncertain, and Lena jotted down in her notes: confused.

"Just a couple more questions," Lena finally said. "Does Mr. Hayden trust his car on long trips?"

"I don't know."

"Does he take trips, say, out-of-state?"

"Well, maybe, sometimes."

"Hey," Lena said, "it must be a great old car."

"Uh-huh."

"Do you sometimes go along with Mr. Hayden?" Lena ventured.

"Sometimes."

And then she pushed; even though John had warned her about not arousing suspicion, she pushed a little harder.

"Would Mr. Hayden trust his car on a trip as far as Chicago or perhaps California?" Lena asked matter-of-factly.

There was a pause, then the woman said, "I gotta go," and she hung up.

Lena sat back in her seat and whispered, "Wow." It certainly crossed her mind that this woman—the very woman she'd just spoken to—could be Jane Cramm.

She took a moment to collect herself, then she rose and went over to John's desk, where he and Mike were compiling notes.

"I may have something," she said neutrally.

Both men stopped and looked up.

"It was this woman, up in Santa Fe." She went on to tell them about the conversation, referring to her notes. "I mean, she could have been tired or hungover or even stoned. I don't know."

"Interesting," Mike said. "Very interesting." He glanced at John. "How far a drive is it up to—" he was saying, when abruptly he stopped, his attention drawn to something over John's shoulder. He swore.

Lena followed the path of his gaze and her heart froze. Coming straight toward them were two men in dark suits, both men wearing sunglasses. "Oh, no," she breathed. "It's them."

John swiveled in his chair. "Swell," he said.

Before any of them could say another word, FBI Special Agent Alan Sabin and his sidekick, the big blond Miller, were at Hidalgo's desk. Lena felt her limbs go stiff and her pulse grow heavy.

Taking off his sunglasses with measured practice, Sabin introduced himself and Miller to John. Lena just glared at him, and Mike rose to his feet, towering over Alan Sabin.

"I can't say this is a pleasure," Mike said coolly.

Sabin smiled. "Thought we'd drop by and compare notes. It's still our case, Quinn, and for your information, interfering with an FBI investigation is a federal crime."

"Who's interfering?" Mike said. Then he added, "That was a nasty little trick you pulled on Gloria Torres. Big man, aren't you?"

Lena had had about enough male posturing. "Do you have any new information on my daughter's kidnapping?" she asked Sabin. "Or would you rather trade insults with these guys?"

Sabin eyed her up and down and took his time answering. "It so happens we do have a lead," he finally said insolently.

Lena's breath stopped. "Tell me," she said, "what is it?"

"Well, now," Sabin began, "you haven't exactly been cooperative, Miss Portillo, or is it Mrs. Quinn? Never really got that straight, did I?"

"What is it?" she demanded, her cheeks hot, fury battling with exhaustion, desperation clawing at her.

He grinned, taunting her.

"Tell me," she said harshly, and all her control fled in that moment. She started toward him, not knowing what she was going to do, not caring, only determined to force him to tell her what he knew.

There was a hand on her arm, and Mike spoke into her ear, "Take it easy, Lena."

She pulled in a deep, rasping breath, her hands in fists, trembling with emotion, then she whirled abruptly and walked swiftly into the ladies' room, banging the door. She stood for a time, eyes closed, calming herself, then she bent over a sink and splashed cold water on her face.

Mike opened the door, stuck his head in and looked around.

"Lena?" he asked uncertainly.

"I'm okay," she answered.

He came in and stood next to her, his expression concerned.

"You're not supposed to be in here," she said dully.

"The hell with that. Listen, the FBI found out that Jane Cramm had a waitress job four years ago. She paid taxes. Place called Malaga." He put his hand on her arm and brought her around to face him. "Malaga, New Mexico."

It was a moment before his words sank in. "Then..." She licked dry lips. "Then this Jane Cramm really is here? Here in New Mexico?"

Mike was smiling softly. "Looks like it. Looks like she gave up the baby six years ago and then, for whatever reason, she stole her back. And," he added, "I can't think of one single reason she'd want to harm her."

The tears came then. A flood of relief and worry and desperation. She fell against Mike's chest, her fingers convulsively gripping his shirt, and she let herself cry. She wasn't aware of Mike's fingers in her hair or the look of pain and regret etching his face.

When Lena and Mike emerged from the bathroom everyone avoided eye contact with them. One of the women officers edged past them and went into the ladies' room. "Ah, excuse me," she said, and Lena wished a hole would open up and swallow her.

Mike was forging a path back to Hidalgo's desk, to the FBI agents. *The goons,* Lena thought. She forced her feet to move and told herself firmly to get it together. Now was not the time to fall apart. And they had a lead on Jane Cramm. The woman had been in New Mexico. Years ago, true. But she'd been here, and Lena prayed she still was. With Kimmy. Yet, amazingly, when they reached John's desk, Sabin and Miller were back on the same refrain.

Lena overheard Miller saying, "That vehicle list you're checking out is a wild-goose chase."

And John. "How's that?"

"Statistics," Miller went on, and he gave Lena and Mike the once-over.

Sabin took up the conversation. "Jane Cramm or no Jane Cramm, statistics say it's usually the parents behind a kidnapping."

Lena stared incredulously at him while feeling the sudden energy flowing from Mike. He seemed to swell, to grow larger than life. It was almost as if she could see him gathering himself for a confrontation, but John Hidalgo forestalled him.

John said, "There's no evidence whatsoever that this is the case. If you'll recall, Kimberly was even spotted by a clerk at a minimart in Flagstaff. I don't see how you can—"

"Oh, right," Sabin chimed in. "And who did the clerk *allegedly* tell this to? Quinn? Miss Portillo here? I don't suppose you checked it out yourself."

"Now, look—" John countered.

Sabin cut him off. "These two have put up a good

show, I'll give them that. But my money's on that poor kid still being in L.A. They probably dumped her—''

Lena gasped at the very moment Mike lost it. One second he was standing next to her, hands in his jeans pockets, the next he had the FBI man sprawled across the top of John's desk, papers and files flying, his fist raised to strike.

"Take it easy, Quinn!" one of the cops yelled, and three more joined him to pull Mike off. They had to hold him and talk him down while Sabin righted himself and puffed out his chest, straightening his shirt and tie.

He glared at Mike. "I'm pressing assault charges, Quinn, right here and now," he rasped.

"Be my goddamned guest, you bastard," Mike shot back, and he struggled against the cops who still held him.

Sabin turned to his partner. "You witnessed that, Miller. You can corroborate this officer's assault on me."

"Yes, I certainly can," Miller intoned.

Sabin swung around to John. "You saw the whole thing. Write up an arrest report."

John shrugged. "I didn't see a thing."

Sabin glared at him, then pivoted, facing another one of the crowd. "You saw what he did!"

"Not me, buddy."

"Then *you* saw it!" Sabin snapped at another onlooker, a woman.

"Saw what?" she said.

Lena watched the whole thing, frightened by the violence, by the atmosphere of pure male testosterone, but glad that Mike had stood up to Sabin. She was sickened by the necessity but perversely thrilled by the vanquishing of the FBI man.

When the FBI men were gone, John looked at Mike,

who was tucking his shirt into his jeans. "That was cute, Quinn."

Mike, his face still flushed with anger, shrugged. "He's lucky I didn't kill him."

Drawing in a deep breath, her hands shaking, Lena picked up the papers and files scattered on the floor, placed them on John's desk, then headed back to her own private spot. There was still work to be done. Later, when Mike was calm, she'd tell him that if he hadn't tried to punch Sabin, she would have done it herself.

The afternoon waned. Lena reached three more people on the list, but no one fit the bill. By five she'd only reached one more. That car, too, had been junked this past year.

At five-fifteen, Mike came over and interrupted her. "'Scuse me," he said, standing in front of the desk. "I got hold of the owner of the restaurant in Malaga where Jane Cramm worked. No luck. He said they get a lot of transients, go through waitresses by the dozens. He can't remember Cramm at all."

"You know," Lena said, "we don't have one single station wagon registered there, either. Of course, we know it's not registered in her name, anyway."

"That's true," Mike said. Then he gave her a half smile. "You'd make an all-right cop, Lena."

"Really," she said, shaking her head. "I think I'll stick to cars, though. A lot less stress."

"You're doing okay," he stated. "I always knew you would."

Lena looked up. "You checked, though, Mike. You kept tabs on me."

"Only to see if you were okay. You and Kimmy. I make no excuses."

"Mmm," she said.

Mike changed the subject. "John's going to have Hayden and that Slacks guy run through the computer first thing in the morning, see what turns up."

"Something's got to give," she said, sighing.

"It will. Always does."

At seven they called it a day. They'd reached sixteen of the eighteen car owners. That was good. What wasn't so good was that other than the two John was going to do a computer check on, they had zip. Lena held on to the fact that the woman at the minimart had identified Kimmy, and the fact that Jane Cramm had once worked in New Mexico. She had to still be here. She simply had to be the one who'd taken Kimmy. And Mike said, over and over, that they'd find her.

"Let's get a drink," John suggested when they were through for the day.

Lena's heart skipped a beat. *Oh, no,* she thought. He'd take them to some cop hangout. She knew it. And what would Mike do? He'd been awfully good this past week, but in a cop bar?

Still, she herself could use a drink. Two, maybe. Her nerves were raw, and every muscle in her body thrummed with weariness.

"Well?" John asked. "How about that drink?"

"Okay," Lena said, and she picked up her sweater, threw it over her shoulders and glanced at Mike.

"Fine," he said.

John took them to a nearby bar, one of those narrow, shotgun places with pool tables lining one side, the long bar on the other and tables in the back, near the kitchen. It was dim and smoky and jammed with cops. Loud. All three pool tables were busy, and two electronic dartboards were in use. A big matchup was in progress.

"I'll find us some barstools," John said over the din.

But Mike put a hand on his arm. "Let's just get a table. That okay?"

"Sure," John said. "They've got great food in this joint."

"I smell garlic," Lena said, following John toward the rear.

"Spaghetti, garlic bread," he said over his shoulder. "And the lasagna's the best in the city."

It had occurred to Lena that if Mike and John began on beers and shooters—Mike's favorite—the car was only four blocks away, at police headquarters. She could always leave, drive to the motel and order food in. No big deal. She just hoped Mike wasn't hungover in the morning. That would be the icing on the cake.

A barmaid came over when they were seated. "The usual?" she asked John.

"Yeah, in the bottle. And back it up with a shot of tequila. Don't forget the lime, eh?"

"I look like a moron?" she said. She turned to Lena and raised her brows. "And for the lady?"

"Ah, how about a vodka and OJ."

"One screwdriver comin' up." She turned to Mike.

"What do you have for nonalcoholic beer?" he asked.

She rattled off three brands.

Mike chose one.

Lena cocked her head.

"Don't drink?" John asked.

"Let's see," Mike said, looking at John. "It's been sixty-one months and... Hell, I don't know how many days anymore."

Lena sat there mute, stunned. Sixty-one months? That would have made it... *Oh, my Lord,* she thought. Mike was saying he hadn't had a drink since that night? She stared at him. Sixty-one months.

CHAPTER THIRTEEN

IT TOOK A WHILE before Lena's mind stopped whirling with the new realization, and she wondered if Mike and John noticed how quiet she was. She sat there and sipped her drink and was glad for the dim light that hid her expression. She kept staring at Mike across the table, studying him, and she wondered with a sense of shame how on earth she could have missed the signs of his sobriety.

She hadn't believed him. But how could she have? The one thing in a relationship that alcoholics eroded most was trust. Only once did he glance in her direction, and their gazes met and held for a mere breath of time before he looked back to John and replied to something the detective had asked him.

They ordered dinner from frayed old menus—John didn't even need to look—and still Lena watched Mike, thinking back over the past week. How could she have failed to notice how healthy he looked? The alcohol bloating gone, the clear eyes. And he'd never smelled of liquor. Had she just not wanted to see it?

My God. Five years and Mike hadn't had a drink and she hadn't known.

He was talking to John, something about the FBI, and she saw his brows draw together. John replied, obviously something humorous, because Mike's expression cleared and he flashed a smile that lit up his face like a boy's.

The waitress came with their dinners and asked if they wanted refills on the drinks. Lena nodded. She needed to relax, to erase from her mind the awful ups and downs of the day, to try to wind down.

"You want to work the phone again tomorrow?" John was asking her.

"Oh, yes, of course."

"Okay. You did a good job," he replied, smiling, his long Spanish face creasing pleasantly.

"Do you think that Daniel Hayden could really be a good lead?" she asked anxiously.

"Maybe. It's worth the computer check, and we'll run that Slacks character along with Jane Cramm. It's too bad we couldn't trace her through that restaurant, but we'll keep trying. At least we know she was in New Mexico."

"Years ago. She could be anywhere," Lena said, playing devil's advocate.

"We'll find her," Mike stated.

She gave him a rare smile and thought there were so many things she should say to him now, needed to say. An apology to start with. And maybe, just maybe, she and Mike could be friends, and if, *when,* they got Kimmy back, he could indeed be a father to her.

They ate, Lena quiet, the men trading police talk. She was impatient, she realized, for dinner to be over, for her and Mike to return to their motel alone so that she could say the things that were building up inside her.

She didn't eat much, but she finished her second drink, and eventually she relaxed, her limbs liquid, a slight buzz in her head. Maybe she'd be able to get a good night's sleep.

It was eleven before John walked them back to the parking lot to Lena's car.

"You drive," Lena said, handing Mike the keys.

He didn't say anything, only waved good-night to John and started the car. Lena rested her head on the seat back, her eyes closed, and listened to the reassuring rumble of the engine.

"You're the only person I ever let drive this car," she finally said.

"That so?"

"Uh-huh."

"You mean, in all these years you never let anyone else touch it?"

"That's right."

"What about the men you dated?"

"Fishing, Mike?"

"No, dammit, just plain curious."

"You can count on the fingers of one hand the men I've dated, and they all had their own cars."

The car slowed and turned, and Lena rested, her eyes still closed. She was thinking about what to say, how to ask, but the words came out before she framed the right question. "Why didn't you tell me years ago, Mike?"

"Tell you what?" he asked maddeningly.

"That you really stopped drinking."

"Would it have done any good?"

She had to think for a minute, and, ruefully, she had to reply no.

"Question answered."

"Maybe you should have tried, told Gloria, had your mom or dad tell me... Well, try to tell me."

"I thought about it, but you disappeared, and frankly, I didn't have the energy or the nerve. I was fighting my own battle. And then it was too late."

"I ran," she mused. "I ran for my life."

"I know," he said. "I understood after a while, and I figured it was better not to dig up old bones."

"Maybe you were right," she said. "Or maybe..." Her voice died.

He pulled into the motel parking lot and stopped the car. "We're here," he said quietly.

She stayed there, unable to summon the energy to move. "I'm so tired, Mike," she said.

"Come on, let's get inside and get you to bed. You sure are a cheap drunk, Lena."

"I'm not drunk."

"No, only comatose."

He came around to the passenger side and opened her door, and she roused herself to open her eyes and stand and breathe in the fresh night air.

"You're not going to be sick, are you?" Mike asked.

She shook her head.

Inside, she sank onto the couch.

"Lena, it's late. Go to bed."

She looked up at him. "Should I have stayed with you?"

He sighed in exasperation. "Is this really the time to discuss it?"

"Should I have?"

"I don't know. I honestly don't know."

"Maybe I should have, but I was so scared. I couldn't deal with it. After my father... And I loved Jeff, too, you know."

A shadow crossed Mike's face. "I know you did. It was a real bad time, Lena, for all of us."

He paused, and she could see the effort he made to smile.

"But we survived, we managed, didn't we? And we're both doing okay."

"I owe you an apology," she said, her gaze on his. "I'm sorry."

"Not necessary."

"Oh, but it is. For years I thought every bad thing there was to think about you. I hated...I thought I hated you."

"Forget it," he said gruffly. "It was my fault. I was the one who drank. I almost killed myself. I chased you away, almost lost my job. I deserved everything that happened."

She looked down at her hands. "I'm ashamed of myself. I didn't believe you. I'm so damn stubborn. I couldn't give you credit for changing, and I..."

"Stop it, Lena."

"It isn't *me*," she went on. "It's Kimmy. I deprived her of her father. I'm so sorry, Mike."

"Lena..."

"No," she said, waving a hand, "let me say it. I made you miss all the years she's been growing up. It was a terrible thing I did."

"You did what you thought was right."

"Why are you being so damn nice to me?"

"Why shouldn't I be?"

"Oh, Mike. Maybe you'll never get a chance to know Kimmy now. Maybe she'll never get to know her father. Maybe it's too late, and it's all my fault," she said wretchedly.

"Lena, don't torture yourself. It's the booze talking. We'll get Kimmy back."

"You could be wrong. What if it's too late and she's..."

"Stop it, Lena," Mike said sharply.

She tried, but every horrible possibility she'd ever imagined flashed before her eyes. Her baby, her little girl, tortured, dying, screaming, her little body lying... No, she couldn't allow herself to think those things. She closed her eyes for a minute, taking deep breaths, feeling the hideous shuddering terror retreat into a corner of her mind.

"Lena, you okay?" Mike asked.

"Yes, sure, I just... I'm going to take a shower," she said, forcing her voice to remain calm.

She thought the shower would be soothing, but it wasn't. It was as if all the tears inside her were raining down on her skin, and slowly she slid down the tiled wall to sit crouched, face in her hands, moaning in anguish, the water pounding on her back.

A knock on the bathroom door barely roused her. She heard Mike calling her name, asking if she was all right, but it didn't seem to matter; she couldn't stop crying.

The door opened, and he came in. She was aware of it, but it had no reality; only her pain was real.

"Lena?" he asked in an anxious voice, then, "Damn, I knew those drinks were too much... Lena?"

She couldn't move. The water was hot, but she was shivering; that didn't matter, either. Then the glass door slid back, and Mike reached in and turned the water off.

"Come on, Lena," he said softly. But she couldn't respond; it was too much effort.

A towel was thrown around her, and she was pulled upright. His strong arm supported her, and she surrendered to her need and clung to him, not caring that she was wet and naked and water was streaming into her face from her hair.

"Mike," she sobbed, "I can't go on if anything's h-happened to her. Oh, Mike."

He held her and stroked her hair. "Shh," he said. "It'll be all right. I promise you. You're just tired. It'll be better in the morning."

She trembled convulsively from cold and fear, and she

shook her head, droplets of water flinging off her hair. "No, no, it won't be better till I have her back."

"You will. You'll have her back."

"Oh, Mike," she cried, tilting her face up to his, "if only I'd known you'd changed! If I'd let you be a part of her life, maybe this wouldn't have happened."

"Don't be silly, Lena. It could have happened if I'd been there. It isn't your fault. It isn't anything you did wrong."

She buried her face in his chest, wetting his shirt, but he only pushed her hair back and tried to dry it with a corner of the towel. Gradually she stopped shaking, and as she felt his heart beating against her cheek, she calmed down, her tears stopped. She took a deep, quavering breath.

"Better?" he asked.

She nodded wordlessly.

He held her still, and his arms, his chest, felt so good she never wanted to leave their shelter.

"When you hold me," she whispered, "I can almost believe everything will be all right."

"It will."

She knew she had to let go of him—this had only been an interlude—but she couldn't bear the desolation it would bring.

"Lena," he began.

"I'll go to bed now," she said, but she didn't move.

She felt him shift his position; he was going to disengage himself from her, he was… But his head bent and his cheek brushed hers and somehow, miraculously, his lips were on hers.

A voice in her head cried danger, but she didn't care. His smell, his warmth, the strength of his hand on her back, the wetness of his shirt from her tears and her hair—they were too important, too vital to her existence. He murmured something, and she felt his hardness against her nudity, and he pulled her closer.

She opened her mouth to receive him, and it was as if it had been a century since she'd been with this man—or a minute. Time ran together in jerky moments, endless and fleeting.

She opened her eyes to find him looking at her, everything he was in his eyes, in the gaze he fastened hungrily on her.

"Lena," he said again, and his fingers tightened on her back. "Lena."

Something inside her burst free, and she knew suddenly and irrevocably that she still loved this man. Nothing mattered, not his history with his lady friend, protection, nothing. Only the fact that she loved him.

He swept her up effortlessly and carried her into the bedroom. His strength held her in thrall—she was not a small woman. The towel fell away, and she was on the bed, naked, reaching up for him, and he leaned over her, his weight on both arms, his clear blue gaze on her face.

"Are you sure of this?" he asked.

Her answer was to unbutton the first button on his shirt, then the next. Her fingers shook, and impatiently he sat on the bed and pulled his shirt off.

He lay next to her, on one elbow. "I never thought I'd do this again," he said.

"Neither did I."

His arm moved in a swift arc, pulling her close, and now she could feel his bare skin. How long it had been, how endlessly long.

They lay together on their sides, mouths and fingers halting wherever they wanted, in a sanctuary of their own making, touching, stroking, murmuring sounds that were not words.

He undressed, dropping his pants on the floor, and returned to her. His mouth was on her skin, trailing exquisite sensations, on her nipple. His hand brushed her wetness, and she gasped, her hips rising, her body twisting.

Time was suspended, reality was suspended, and Lena lost herself in a maelstrom of pure sensation. There was an absence of everything that had marked her life for so long—no haste, no fear, no worry, no ambition, a banishment of all that she'd thought important for so long, of all that mattered in the daylight.

When he entered her, she stopped breathing for a second, then two. It felt so different, so perfect, and she wanted to hold him there, to keep him, to stop time.

But he moved over her, and she felt his hardness growing inside her, and her body wouldn't stop; it was on its own relentless search for fulfillment.

She rose, pressing against him, trying to touch as much of his skin with hers as she could, desperate to pull him into her, more of him. They moved together easily, without hesitation, as if their bodies remembered, despite their stubborn minds. No words were needed, the changes in rhythm understood between them.

She felt her body on the brink of explosion, moving faster, her breath quick, almost desperate, and he thrust into her hard—once, twice—and their mouths found each other, hot and searching, and she shuddered, a cry rising from her to meet his.

They lay silent afterward. Lena was stunned, her mind unable to comprehend what she'd done, but her body seemed to have learned something her brain didn't know. She was afraid to speak, for there was nothing either of them could say, and she didn't want to spoil what had happened between them.

She felt herself drifting into sleep, roused briefly when Mike pulled the covers up over them. Then she drifted again, and she wasn't sure whether she dreamed it or imagined it, but she thought that Mike leaned over to kiss her on the cheek, and said, "I've always loved you, Lena."

KACEY CRAWLEY ALWAYS got to police headquarters before anyone else except the desk sergeant, who was on all night anyway.

"'Morning, Kacey," he said, pressing a buzzer to allow her entry into the enclave. "It's two minutes till seven—you're early."

Kacey tossed her blond ponytail. "Oops. I'd better go out and come in again. You know how they feel about overtime."

"Boy, do I ever," he replied, and then he watched her walk to the elevators. No one looked better in a uniform than Kacey, recently divorced, Crawley, with those blue eyes and those endless long legs.

Kacey took the elevator down to her department, Juvenile Division, and switched on lights as she walked the long corridors. This was her favorite time of day, early morning, when she felt most alive and most efficient.

Switching on more lights, she made her way to her cubbyhole of an office, turned on her computer and stuffed her purse and sweater into the empty drawer of her file cabinet. She sat down, punched her private password into the computer and waited for the screen to read "Good morning, Kacey, code accepted. Have a nice day."

She was anxious to start on a particular search.

It had begun at five that morning. She'd awakened before her alarm rang, something gnawing at her. She'd made coffee, showered and been blow-drying her hair, when the first clue slipped into her brain. It had to do with that cop from L.A., Quinn, who'd punched the FBI agent yesterday afternoon. The story had spread through headquarters like wildfire, everyone snickering, laughing and embellishing the episode until, by the time it had reached the basement, the agent was in the hospital with a broken nose and ribs.

Kacey had asked a fellow juvenile officer what the cop from L.A. was doing in Albuquerque.

"Don't really know," he'd replied. "Something about his kid being missing and doing a search here for a car involved in the abduction."

Then somebody two desks away had called over, "The L.A. cop's looking for one of those old wood-paneled station wagons."

"Interesting," Kacey had said, and she might have recalled the report from Santa Fe she'd read on the computer, except the chatter went back to the big, good-looking city cop who'd decked the fibbie.

"I hear he's a real hunk," one of the women in the office had said.

"Forget it, Flo," another one said. "Guy brought his wife along."

"Ex-wife," someone else had called out.

But at 5 a.m., Kacey had awakened, and the station wagon had nagged at her. A missing kid, an old station wagon.

As a juvenile officer, Kacey read reports of child abusers, kidnappings—mostly by angry ex-spouses—teenage crimes, everything having to do with kids under the age of eighteen on a statewide level.

Each day she cataloged hundreds of reports that poured in from other police departments around the state. It took most of her day. Some reports stuck in her mind; others did not. Why the mention of the station wagon jarred her was a mystery.

"But what day?" she said aloud. "Monday? Tuesday?" It had been recent. She was sure of that.

She began searching the original reports that had come in on Monday. By eight-thirty, when the building was buzzing, she sat back and rubbed her eyes, realizing she didn't really have time for this. Another hour or so, she thought, and she'd give up. The chances of this station wagon thing in her head being connected to the L.A. cop's missing kid were remote at best.

She began searching Tuesday's reports, scrolling through page after page after page.

Waste of time, Kacey thought.

MIKE SAT ACROSS FROM John Hidalgo and frowned. He'd just gotten off the phone with the Malaga cops, having asked them to run Jane Cramm through their local computer records, but they'd never had contact with her—no misdemeanors, no traffic violations, nothing.

He glanced over at Lena, who was working the phone on the last of the station wagon owners. How many times had he promised her they'd get Kimmy back? He'd never tell her, not in a million years, of the doubts that were beginning to assail him.

Lena was speaking to someone on the phone, writing in her notepad at the same time, her long, shining brown hair forming a curtain over one side of her face. He recalled without a bridging thought the way her hair had fallen against his cheek last night and brushed his chest as she'd taken the top position in their lovemaking. He could almost feel the warm, silken flesh of her hips in his hands when he'd guided her, the way she'd unfolded to him like a flower, her back arching. She had the most beautiful hips and breasts, full and womanly, and goose bumps raised on his arms just thinking about the firm roundness of her bosom, the taste of her.

He kept staring, lost in the memory of last night. If anything, it had been even better than during their marriage, when Lena had been younger, more shy. Him, too. But now they fit together like a pair of gloves long separated. He'd never had a night like that. Not with anyone. Not with Jennifer...

Mike tore his gaze away and let out a low breath. Jennifer. Holy cow. He hadn't once thought about her till this very second. Guilt surged through him, then rested hot and burning in his gut. How could he have made love to Lena and not once given Jenn a single thought? And Jenn had suspected that was exactly what was going to happen. How could he have been so naive?

"Ahem." John cleared his throat. "You with me here, Quinn?"

"Ah, yes, sure," Mike said, distracted. "What were you saying?"

"I wasn't. Just wanted to show you these printouts from Records." As he handed Mike the computer sheets, he glanced over at Lena, then back at Mike.

Oh, God, Mike thought. Was it that obvious?

There were three sheets. One was on Jane Cramm, one on Slacks Kerry and another on Daniel Hayden.

He read Cramm's. It was a single line. She'd gotten a driver's license from the Department of Motor Vehicles four years ago. The records didn't even say where, exactly, she'd taken the test. It had an address—in Malaga—which Mike knew was useless. The license had expired last year. There'd been no renewal.

"Dammit," he muttered.

He put aside Cramm's sheet and looked at Slacks Kerry's. Now this dude had an interesting past. In '89 he'd been arrested for possession of a controlled substance, given probation. In '91 he'd been jailed for thirty days in Farmington for auto-parts theft. Then, in '96, he'd spent ninety days in the slammer for failure to stop his vehicle when a state trooper had tried to pull him over for a traffic violation. *A loser,* Mike thought. Maybe a friend of Cramm's? Both real losers. Maybe this Slacks character had been the man in the car at the school. Maybe Jane Cramm had been the woman. There were sure a lot of maybes.

He looked at Daniel Hayden's sheet, and it was even longer. Hayden had been arrested seven times in the past ten years. Of those ten years, he'd spent nearly six in prison. The conviction that had sent Hayden to the state penitentiary was a doozy. The idiot had stolen a car in Santa Fe to make a court appearance on drug charges right here in Albuquerque. Unbelievable. And rather than heisting a nondescript car, the rocket scientist had taken a bright pink VW bug convertible.

"Look at this," Mike said, handing John the printout. "What an idiot."

John read the report and chuckled.

"I wonder," Mike said, "if we could get the mug shots of these two guys faxed to my pop in L.A. He could show them to the little girl who saw the driver of the station wagon. She's a sharp little kid. Who knows? Maybe she can finger one of them."

"If one of them's our perp."

"There is *that,*" Mike said gravely.

"Well," Lena said over Mike's shoulder, "I'm through with the list."

"Anything new?" John asked.

Lena shook her head, but Mike was barely aware of what either of them said after that. All he could see was her: the jut of her chin, the sensuous curve of her mouth, the tilt of those sable-colored eyes. She was standing, and her breasts beneath the oversize dark blue sweater she wore were on a level with his eyes. He could see the firm round curves, and despite all his efforts, he couldn't think about anything but touching her, cupping those breasts, drawing the hard nipples into his mouth.

Mike broke into a sweat sitting there in the middle of the crowded vice squad office. If they'd been alone, he would have swept Hidalgo's desk clean and taken Lena right there and then. He couldn't believe what was happening to him. It was like a mad charade being acted out in his brain despite everything he tried to do to stop it.

He looked up and met Lena's eyes, and he knew that she knew. He felt heat crawl up his neck. Quickly he rose and mumbled something about having to use the bathroom.

"Be, ah, right back," he said, and he got the hell away from her.

When Mike left the men's room, Lena and Hidalgo weren't alone. A woman police officer was with them, uniformed, with pretty, long blond hair in a ponytail, and every eye in the room was fixed on her legs.

"Mike," Hidalgo called, waving him over, "listen to this."

She introduced herself, shaking his hand. "Kacey Crawley, Juvenile Division."

Mike was aware of the smile on John's face and of

Lena—she was biting her lower lip and wringing her hands.

Kacey went on. "If you hadn't hit that fibbie," she said, "I never would have made the connection. Anyway—" she handed Mike a computer sheet "—here's what I've got. A couple of days ago, up in Santa Fe, a lady shopping at a grocery store reported a child-abuse incident to the store manager. Evidently some drunken woman was giving a child—little girl around six or seven years old—a hard time. The woman said she was her aunt, but the lady shopper felt something wasn't ringing true. Anyway, she reported it and the manager called the police. It got put on the statewide network."

Mike drew his sandy brows together. "The shopper didn't happen to notice the car…?"

Kacey grinned. "That's what made me think of you," she said. "The inebriated woman was driving an old wood-paneled station wagon."

It took a moment for that to sink in and then Mike looked at Lena. "Hayden. Daniel Hayden lives in Santa Fe," he said in a harsh whisper.

Lena had tears in her eyes now. "And I'll bet any amount of money that the woman was Jane Cramm."

"Wow," Mike breathed, and he put his hands on Lena's shoulders, a rush of hope and relief flowing between Lena and him.

CHAPTER FOURTEEN

JANE HEARD DANNY'S CAR stop outside the house, and she threw the rest of the drink down as fast as she could, ran water into the glass and rinsed her mouth out with the mouthwash she kept under the kitchen sink.

Danny came in, leading Kimmy by the hand, and Jane was heartened by his expression, which was neutral for a change. She put a smile on her lips and asked, "How'd it go?"

"Okay," Danny said, nodding. "She did good."

"Lucky it didn't rain," Jane observed.

"Yeah, it was okay. All she had to do was run around and pretend to chase butterflies and stuff like that."

"She behaved?"

"Damn right she did. It was hard to make her laugh, though. See, they wanted her to look happy and all."

Jane turned to Kimmy. "I told you to do what the men said, and you promised."

Kimmy looked at her feet and sulked.

"She'll do better this afternoon," Jane assured him.

"Damn right," he growled.

"You'll do what the men say this afternoon," Jane said to the child, "won't you, Kimmy? It's like a game. It's playacting, is all."

Kimmy said nothing.

"I'm hungry," Danny said. "The cheapskates didn't have no food, nothing."

"I'll make you some sandwiches, okay?" Jane hastened to say.

"What kind?"

"Bologna. And cheese."

"Okay, but put plenty of mustard on. I like mustard," he said.

"Okay, Danny."

She even cut the sandwiches diagonally, to make them pretty, and she cut Kimmy's twice, to make little wedges for the girl. Then she opened a beer for Danny and poured a glass of milk for Kimmy.

"Here it is," she said brightly. "Lunch for everybody."

Danny sat and started to eat quickly, his head down, his shoulders hunched. Jane smiled benignly on her daughter and took small, ladylike bites of her own sandwich. Kimmy sat there perfectly quiet, not eating a thing.

"What's the matter?" Jane finally asked.

"I'm 'lergic to bologna," she whispered.

"'Lergic?"

"It makes me, you know, sick," Kimmy said.

"Eat it, kid," Danny said.

"I'm 'lergic."

"Eat the goddamned food."

Kimmy began to whimper.

"Take the bologna out, then," Jane said, reaching over to Kimmy's sandwich.

Danny slapped her hand away. "She can eat it the way it is."

Kimmy was crying for real now.

"Goddammit!" Danny yelled.

Jane got scared then. She always got scared when Danny was mad. And now, with Kimmy, it was worse, because Jane had learned how to placate him, but Kimmy hadn't yet, and it seemed every little thing the kid did aggravated him.

"Be quiet," she murmured to Kimmy.

"I want my mommy!" the child wailed.

"Be quiet now. Shh," Jane said.

"Danny promised. He said if I was g-g-good!" Kimmy cried.

"You did, Danny?" Jane asked. "You promised she could see her mother?"

He shook his head, disgusted. "Yeah, sure, so what?"

"Oh," Jane said, understanding. He'd lied to Kimmy. She wasn't sure whether she was relieved or not.

"Shut up, kid," Danny said.

"I want my mommy!" The little girl's eyes were streaming and her nose was running.

"I said shut up!" Danny stood over her, his hand raised, and Kimmy cowered.

"No," Jane said urgently, "no, Danny, you'll…"

He backed off, obviously realizing he couldn't hit her because she had to look good for the filming that afternoon, and Jane heaved a sigh of relief.

Danny swore and strode out of the kitchen. At the door he turned around and snarled, "Have her ready when I get back." Then he left, slamming the door behind him.

Jane sat there for a minute, feeling the sandwich she'd eaten rebel in her stomach. Then, slowly, shakily, she got up and went to the cupboard, got out the bottle and poured herself a healthy shot, drank it down, then poured another.

She felt better after the second, so she put the bottle back, turned around and said pleasantly to Kimmy, "You need to eat lunch, you know. I'll fix it up for you." Jane went to the table, pulled the bologna out of the sandwich and replaced the bread. "There, now it's a cheese sandwich, see?"

Kimmy sniffed, rubbed her nose with the back of her hand. "I'm not hungry."

"Sure you are." Jane smiled. "Come on, Kimmy, please. Eat just a little bit. A nice cheese sandwich."

Eventually the girl started nibbling at a corner of one of the wedges. She drank some milk.

Jane felt good, as if she'd really accomplished something. She was getting better at this mother thing.

Gosh, she wished this darn movie were over, then she'd find out if Danny meant what he'd said about keeping Kimmy. But it worried her, the way he went and got so darn mad at everything Kimmy did. Maybe he really wouldn't let her keep her daughter. The last kid had just up and run off, after all. But then, that kid hadn't been Jane's flesh and blood, had she?

Jane sat there and watched Kimmy eat, and she nodded and smiled to encourage her. Then she got another of the pills from the bottle and gave it to Kimmy. "Here, take your vitamin pill," she said. "Drink it right down with your milk."

"It sticks in my throat."

"Come on, take it. It'll make you strong and healthy. Danny specially wants you to take it," she wheedled.

"But…"

"Take it, Kimmy. We don't want to make Danny mad, do we?"

LENA, MIKE AND JOHN left for the Santa Fe police station shortly before noon. Hidalgo had called ahead and told the Santa Fe cops the whole story, specifically asking them to do nothing whatsoever until they arrived, especially not to post an unmarked car near Hayden's house.

"The guy's streetwise, got a rap sheet the length of my arm," John had said, "so please sit tight till we get there."

"How far is it?" Lena had asked anxiously.

"Hour. Not far," John had replied.

Lena drove Mike in her car, following John's police cruiser. She was a wreck. She was sure they'd found the man who'd stolen her daughter; at the same time she was terrified she was mistaken or that if it was the man, he would be gone and Kimmy gone with him.

It was about seventy miles north to Santa Fe, and Lena chafed at how slow John was driving, at how long it was taking, at how close she might be.

"Relax," Mike kept telling her.

"I can't. What if this Hayden is leaving Santa Fe this very second, taking Kimmy somewhere else? What if he's hurting her?"

"He has no reason to hurt her."

Lena shot him a look.

"Watch the road," he said, "or let me drive."

The previous night had fled from Lena's mind almost as if it hadn't happened; she was entirely focused on one thing, with no room for considering what she'd done, what *they'd* done, what it meant, what would happen next. She'd think about that later.

"Lena," Mike said, "she's going to be okay." He put a hand on her thigh as she drove, a familiar touch. "Lena…?"

She bit her lip, blinked back panicky tears and shook her head, driving on, keeping Hidalgo's car exactly the correct distance ahead.

The Santa Fe police were ready for them; they'd started organizing a command center, rounded up off-duty policemen, called in their SWAT team. Mrs. Goodfriend, the woman who'd reported the child-abuse incident outside the Santa Fe grocery, was supposedly awaiting their arrival at police headquarters.

"I wish we had a picture of Jane Cramm," Lena said to Mike. "Maybe the woman could identify her."

"Well, we don't," Mike said. "I guess we'll find out soon enough."

"God willing," she whispered.

They met with Captain Bill Hunt at the police station, and John introduced Mike and Lena. He told Hunt that Mike was on the L.A. Hostage Negotiations team, not defining his present status; no sense admitting he was on his own time.

"Mrs. Goodfriend is waiting," Hunt said. "How about I go in with you?" Then he turned to Mike and Lena. "You can watch through the one-way mirror. I think too many people will confuse her."

So John entered the room with Hunt, and Lena stood outside at the window with Mike. Her heart was beating so hard she was afraid everyone in the squad room could hear it.

Selma Goodfriend was a pretty woman, dressed in a fussy, old-fashioned way, with wire-rimmed glasses, her hair permed. She was holding tightly to the strap of a patent-leather purse that rested on her knees.

Bill Hunt introduced himself and Hidalgo and had Mrs. Goodfriend tell in her own words what she'd seen the previous Wednesday afternoon in the parking lot.

"I used to be a teacher," the woman told them, "so I'm very aware of children's behavior. I'm retired now, but I still notice children, and I knew this little girl was not a happy child."

Lena recoiled from the words. What did the woman

mean? Had Kimmy been bruised or hurt or crying? Oh, God.

"And the woman with her, the *aunt*," Mrs. Good-friend said, "well, she smelled like alcohol something fierce. I thought at the time, when I saw them getting into that old car, that she shouldn't be driving that little girl anywhere. And there probably weren't even seat belts, either."

John Hidalgo pulled out Kimmy's photograph and showed it to Mrs. Goodfriend. "Is this the little girl you saw on that occasion, ma'am?"

The woman peered at the picture for a second, then two. Lena held her breath. Next to her, Mike moved rest-lessly. He put a hand on her arm, as if to reassure her, and she was grateful for his touch.

Finally the woman nodded. "Yes, that's definitely the little girl I saw."

Lena drew her breath in sharply and felt her knees turn to water. It was Kimmy! This woman had seen her right here in Santa Fe.

Captain Hunt went on to try to get a description of the woman who'd been with Kimmy in the parking lot, but Selma Goodfriend wasn't much help. "She could have been thirty or fifty. She looked...worn, shopworn, if you will. You know, bad hair and skin, ghastly teeth. Trashy looking."

"Uh-huh," Bill said. "If I had a police artist work with you, could you remember enough details to help with a sketch?"

"I could try."

"All right," Hunt said. "We may not need the artist, but just in case, where can you be reached during the day?"

On he went, and all Lena could think was that they

weren't going to need a police artist or anyone else. They could get Kimmy right now. They had Hayden's address; they had all they needed.

"Thank you very much, Mrs. Goodfriend," John was saying on the other side of the glass. "You've been a great help."

"Let's go," Lena said, whirling on Mike. "Let's go now! She's there, Mike. Oh, God, let's get her quick!"

"Not so fast," Mike said. "We can't just rush up to this man's door and tell him to hand her over. Think about it, Lena. He's dangerous. You saw his rap sheet. If we go in without a plan, we could endanger Kimmy's life."

"Mike, she's right here, a few minutes away, and you're telling me I can't go to her?" Lena cried.

John came up to them. "He's right, Lena. We have to make a plan to ensure your daughter's safety. And it's the local police who have to do it. We're only spectators here."

"Oh, my God," Lena breathed. "I'll go. I'll just go by myself and get her. Please..."

"Lena, try to understand," Mike said. "This is for Kimmy's safety."

"I can't just wait here," she said. "I'll go out of my mind!"

"We can't do anything more, Lena. It's out of our hands now," Mike said. "We located her. We confirmed her identity. Our job is done."

"No, I can't..." Lena put her face in her hands.

"Come on, let's get some lunch," John said. "This place'll be a madhouse for at least a couple of hours."

It was the hardest thing Lena had ever been faced with, to know Kimmy was so close, yet be unable to do anything. She had to swallow her wild impatience and go to lunch. She must have eaten something, but she never remembered. She must have made conversation, but she couldn't recall that, either.

Finally they went back to police headquarters, walking the few blocks through scenic Santa Fe, with its square adobe buildings, some ancient, some brand-new, but all conforming to the historical style of the 1600s when Spaniards had built the frontier outpost from native materials. Lena barely noticed, even though John pointed out historical gems on every block.

"This city was here before the Pilgrims landed," he told her proudly.

"Mmm," she said, not hearing him, "that's nice."

The station was in an uproar when they returned. There was a map drawn on a blackboard, the street Daniel—Danny to the local police—Hayden lived on. There were Xs and arrows marked on it. The phones rang constantly. Hunt spoke to a group of detectives in one corner; the SWAT commander was there, dressed in black fatigues, thick boots and a cap, a gun slung over his shoulder. He studied the crude map with his men. Police were on the phones, calling in the troops.

Talk filled the air: parameters, rounds per second, caliber of weapons, unmarked cars, surveillance.

Lena sat on a chair in a corner and hugged herself, trying to keep calm. But the men talked and talked, groups shifted and reformed, and there was more talk. And meanwhile Kimmy was in the hands of that awful, dangerous *criminal*.

Mike and John joined a group, listening, giving an occasional suggestion. Especially Mike, because his experience could be invaluable if this case turned into a hostage situation.

That, of course, was the last thing anyone wanted.

It was two o'clock, then two-thirty, and still Hunt was talking and organizing and phoning. At two forty-five, FBI Special Agents Sabin and Miller walked in.

Lena's heart lurched. Not them! Dear Lord, would they interfere and slow everything down? Would everyone have to start over?

"Well, well, if it isn't the feds," John Hidalgo said.

Mike's face froze, but he didn't open his mouth.

Sabin went right to Hunt. "Agent Miller and I would like to be apprised of the current situation," he said. "We have jurisdiction here."

"For the love of God, Sabin," Mike said through clenched teeth. "No one has time to apprise you of a goddamned thing."

"Excuse me, gentlemen," Hunt said, coming between them, "I really think we can find some common ground here."

It was insane. Jurisdiction! Lena only wanted her little girl back, and she had to sit on her hands and wait while grown men argued and rattled sabers and played games. And what really made her grate her teeth was that the FBI owed her and Mike an apology. They owed Gloria one, too. But they just stood there dickering.

Someone do something! she wanted to scream.

She got up and went outside, unable to sit for another moment. She stalked back and forth in front of the building, not even noticing the clear, bright air or the autumn-hued mountains. Taking deep breaths, she told herself that John and Mike and the other men knew best; they'd handled these situations before and knew how to get the captive person back unharmed. Then she'd remember the many news reports she'd seen about this sort of situation, where there were gunfights and deaths and terrible injuries. Where the cops had blown it and the hostage was killed.

Her nerves were jumping under her skin, and there was a strangling tightness in her chest. *Please,* she prayed, *hurry up and get my baby out of there.*

She saw Mike exit the building and look around, worried.

"Oh, there you are," he said. "I was afraid you'd lost it."

"I have lost it," Lena said.

"Everything's under control. Right now they're checking with a doctor to see how tear gas will affect a child."

"Tear gas?"

"In case it's needed."

"Oh, Mike, this waiting…"

"I know, I know."

"Can't they just *go?*"

"Not until everyone knows exactly what to do."

"Will you be there, Mike? Will they let me come along?"

"Yes, I'll be there. Yes, you will be, too."

"When?"

"Soon."

Mike returned to the interminable plan making, and Lena pulled the cell phone out of her purse, then dialed her home number in California. Gloria answered on the second ring, her voice, as always, anxious.

"Has something happened?"

"Yes and no," Lena said, and she explained about Selma Goodfriend's ID of Kimmy in Santa Fe.

"So you're in Santa Fe now?"

"Uh-huh," Lena said, "but the wheels of justice are grinding awfully slowly. Mom, Kimmy's so close… Every minute we delay… That could be the minute…"

"You just hold on, sweetheart. Don't think about that. I'm sure the police know best. You'll have Kimmy back so soon you'll forget all this. Oh, Lord," Gloria breathed, "I'm so anxious for all of you. I wish I were there."

"I know, Mom."

"You'll call the instant you have Kimmy?"

"Of course."

"Promise?"

"Of course, Mom."

"How's Mike holding up?"

"He's calm, used to this sort of thing. Can you imagine?"

"God, no," Gloria said. "And you two are getting along?"

Lena paused a heartbeat too long. "Sure," she said.

"Mmm," Gloria said. "Am I reading something into this?"

"We'll discuss it later."

"*Lena.*"

"Forget it, Mom. I've got to go back inside now. I'll call you soon."

"My prayers are with you," Gloria said.

When Lena reentered the building the scene seemed unchanged. Groups of men with serious faces, phones ringing, talk, talk, talk.

Then she heard the unmistakable sound of Alan Sabin's voice raised in anger—and Mike answering him.

"I strongly suggest you wait till my team gets here from L.A.," Sabin was saying. "I can't be responsible otherwise."

"You aren't responsible anyway," Mike retorted. "You're out of the goddamned loop on this one!"

"This is a federal case. I have jurisdiction, Officer Quinn!"

"You know what you can do with your jurisdiction, Agent Sabin?" Mike yelled.

It was the last straw, the two of them shouting at each other. Something snapped inside Lena, and she was either going to get hysterical or she had to *act*. What she'd told her mother was true. Every minute they delayed, every second they strutted and postured, might be Kimmy's last.

Unnoticed, she took a good look at the blackboard with its map of Danny Hayden's neighborhood. There was his house, marked with an *X*, the name of his street, the house numbers.

Three-forty-eight Rio Blanco Street. She closed her eyes and committed the address to memory.

Several other cops had joined the argument between Mike and Sabin, and not a soul observed Lena slipping out. It was so very easy, she thought, that she should have done it hours earlier. She simply got into her car and drove out of the parking lot. For the first time in days she felt calm and in control—she was *doing* something.

Stopping at a gas station, she asked directions to 348 Rio Blanco Street and fixed them in her mind. It wasn't very far away, but then, Santa Fe wasn't a huge city like Los Angeles. She drove carefully, watching street signs.

Yes, there was Rio Blanco, running up into a ravine, lined with small, run-down adobe houses. She finally caught a house number and drove on, slowly now, watching like a hawk. Her mouth was dry, her heart beating slowly, heavily in her chest. She wasn't scared, wasn't out of her mind anymore, just ready. Yes, ready.

There it was: 348. Cracked, patched adobe, crooked window frames, a tilted porch. Daniel Hayden's home sweet home. And perhaps Jane Cramm's, too. Could the woman who'd borne Kimmy really harm her own flesh and blood? *No,* Lena's mind said, *no.* Yet Cramm had taken crack during her pregnancy, and Kimmy had suffered.

Lena stared at the house. What kind of people were those two? If the condition of the house was any indication, they were slobs, pigs, mindless human beings.

And Kimmy was with them.

She saw the car then, the wood-sided station wagon, parked around the corner from the house. They were home, then. They were home, and Kimmy was probably in there. A momentary panic squeezed her heart, but it was gone instantly, and deadly anger took its place. They'd stolen her child!

Lena parked across the street. She hadn't made any plans, hadn't thought ahead. She'd been running on autopilot ever since she'd gotten into her car.

She sat there for a time, watching the house, hoping, praying Kimmy really was inside, waiting for a door to open, someone to emerge, a clue to tell her what to do.

But the house squatted there, surrounded by its squalor, utterly silent.

A minute went by, then another, and Lena was no closer to knowing how to approach the house. She'd figured it would be easier than this, and now she wondered if she'd been insane to come here. She told herself sternly not to be a wimp. *Count to ten,* she thought, *then get up and knock on that door.*

She'd gotten to six, when the front door opened. Surprise took her breath away. A man moved into the sunlight, a skinny, homely-looking guy, scruffy, with a short-man's swagger. Danny? Was this the infamous Danny Hayden?

He turned and yelled something to someone inside— Lena couldn't hear the words—then a woman appeared in the doorway. Jane Cramm? She was thin and haggard, much older looking than her real age. Used up. And then, squeezing out from behind the woman, a child, her head ducked, a little girl with long brown hair and...the T-shirt, the blue jeans!

Kimmy! My God, it was her!

That was the last coherent thought Lena had. She didn't remember flying out of her car or racing across the street. She only knew her baby was there, her daughter who'd been stolen from her, and she had to get her back. She ran across the dead brown grass of the yard to where the man was leading Kimmy to the car.

She'd almost reached them, ready to cry out her child's name, when the man sensed something and turned on his heel to face Lena.

"What the hell?" he rasped.

Lena dodged, reaching for her daughter, but Danny yanked Kimmy away.

"Mommy!" Kimmy cried, joyfully, tearfully, glad and scared all at the same time.

The cry wrenched at Lena's heart.

The man stood there in dirty jeans, holding a struggling Kimmy behind him, his skinny legs wide apart.

"You let her go, you son of a bitch," Lena whispered harshly, her hands clenched into fists. *"Let her go."*

IT WAS ALMOST FOUR in the afternoon when Mike realized he hadn't seen Lena in quite some time. A little voice in his head chattered warningly, but he refused to take it seriously.

Excusing himself from the group he'd been talking with, he checked the coffee room, even the ladies' room, embarrassing himself when it wasn't empty.

Hidalgo noticed him and called out, "Getting in the habit of using the girls' room, Quinn?"

"Very funny. I'm looking for Lena. Seen her lately?"

Hidalgo thought. "Not for a while."

"How long?"

"Hmm. Quite a while."

"Shit," Mike said under his breath.

"You think…"

But Mike was striding outside to where he'd found Lena earlier. She'd be there, sure she would, muttering and threatening, as jumpy as a cat.

He walked all the way around the building and didn't find her, then it occurred to him to check the parking lot.

The empty parking space stared back at him like a blind eye. He was filled with a bright explosion of panic.

The GTO was gone.

CHAPTER FIFTEEN

WHEN LENA AWAKENED from the blow Danny had dealt her, she was aware of being in a car, her head lying on a warm lap.

Her eyes flew open despite dizzying pain, and she looked up and realized it was dark out and that it was Kimmy's lap—her own child's little lap—on which she rested.

A rush of emotions surged through her: immense relief and joy, followed by mounting alarm. Whose car...? Where were they?

"Mommy?" said a small voice. "Are you awake, Mommy?"

"Oh, yes, baby," Lena breathed, and she licked dry lips. "Oh, yes, sweetie, Mommy's awake." Tears sprang from her eyes, and her arms went around Kimberly's waist, a waist that had grown smaller. She clung to her child desperately, her brain reeling from both the pain and the release of so many fears. And despite their predicament, which was becoming clearer by the moment, she basked in the relief that her daughter was alive.

Kimmy was clinging to Lena in the dimness just as tightly as she was to her. "Mommy, Mommy," her child kept saying, "I want to go home."

And then the voice from the front seat came, jarring Lena into full reality.

"Shut the hell up, kid."

Daniel Hayden, of course. She and Kimmy were in the car with Hayden, driving somewhere. But where?

Mike, she thought suddenly, where was Mike? But she'd slipped away from the police station, gone to Hayden's by herself. How many hours ago? Did Mike realize what had happened? Oh, God, what had she done?

Lena came to a sitting position, the blood rushing to her head, making pain crash against her skull. She closed her eyes, willing herself not to pass out, and that was when she became aware of the car coming to a stop, the headlights piercing nothing but a vast, empty plain.

Hayden turned to her, resting a gun against the back of his seat, its barrel aimed straight at her.

"'Bout time you woke up," he said.

Lena was instantly disgusted by the figure this man, this *animal* presented. Even in the dimness she could make out his scraggly hair and the unevenness of his front teeth. He had a ferretlike face and his eyes were lifeless holes. He smelled unwashed.

He reached toward Kimmy with his other hand, as if to grab her hair, but Lena drew her more tightly against her side. "Don't you touch her."

Hayden made a grunting sound and swung the gun barrel from Lena's face to Kimmy's and back. "You shut your mouth," he said, "or I'll come back there and shut it real good for you." He turned around in his seat and opened the driver's door. "Get up here now—you're driving," he said, pushing the door all the way open with a booted foot.

Lena tried to think. "I...I can't drive. I'm too dizzy."

"Get up here!"

"I'll...pass out. Really I will."

"You get the hell up here and behind this wheel or I'll beat the tar out of your sniveling brat."

"Mommy," Kimmy sobbed, "I don't want you to leave me!"

In the end, Lena was forced to do as he said. As Hayden warned them, he didn't need two hostages. One would do just fine.

With Kimmy trying to cling to her, Lena had to force herself to open the back door and disengage her child's embrace. She felt as if part of her own body was being torn away. "It'll be okay, sweetie. I'm just going to drive. I'll be right here."

"Shut up!" Danny kept yelling. "Shut the hell up! Haven't you done enough to ruin everything as it is!"

Lena got out and swayed against the side of the car, her head whirling. There was no use arguing, though, because he was right: Hayden did not need to keep them both as hostages.

She got into the driver's seat, while Danny slid in on the passenger side, then slammed the door. "You better know how to drive," he muttered, and he waved the gun in the air.

She tried to ignore him and the sudden nausea that rose in her throat. Her head was pounding and her fingers shook as she found the gearshift and put it in drive. "Where are we?" she breathed.

"Never you mind where we are. Just drive," he grated out.

Wherever they were, Lena realized as she steered onto the two-laned road, there wasn't another car in sight. Not one single car. They might as well have been driving on another planet. *Oh, Mike,* she kept thinking, *why didn't I let you handle it?* She looked in the rearview mirror a hundred times, praying to see lights coming up from behind: Mike, coming to rescue them. How could she have defied him? Stupid, stupid, stupid. And yet she was with Kimmy, her baby. Hadn't she prayed for this moment?

Kimmy huddled in a corner of the back seat, barely visible in the rearview mirror. The headlights stabbed at the blackness ahead, and even when she finally passed a road sign—Route 44—it meant nothing to her. Only the NM below the route number told her they were still in New Mexico.

Danny Hayden eventually leaned his head against the window and muttered something about his not going to sleep. "I was in the army, see," he said, "and I don't need no sleep. Even if I did, I'd hear a dime drop and wake up. So don't try nothin' cute."

Army, Lena thought, *sure.* She'd read his rap sheet. The only time this lowlife had ever done was in prison.

She closed her eyes for a second against a sudden pounding in her temples, then opened them. She had to stay alert. Still, her vision was hazy and she was pretty sure she had a concussion. She glanced again in the mirror at Kimmy, who was so quiet she might have been sleeping, and then she looked over at Hayden, leaning against the window, the gun in his lap aimed at her.

She took a breath. "Where's Jane?" she dared to ask.

He muttered something, and Lena heard the word "bitch." It seemed to be his only adjective to describe a woman.

"Why didn't Jane come along?" Lena asked again.

"None of your goddamn business," he said.

But that was all Lena needed to hear. Jane. Jane Cramm. It really had been her all along.

She passed another road sign. It read Blanco Trading Post—6 miles. Where was that? She looked at the stars, a million bright points of light, but she didn't recognize any of the constellations. Then again, she barely knew them anyway, much less where they were located in the night sky.

Mike. By now he had to know she'd been kidnapped along with Kimmy. Surely he'd found the GTO across from Hayden's house. And maybe, just maybe, he'd found Jane and had learned where Danny was taking them. Maybe Mike was following right now, hot on their trail. He'd spot the station wagon, and somehow she could stop the car and keep Hayden from using the gun. Even if Mike wasn't on the road searching for them, there'd surely be a statewide APB out on this car by now. When it finally got light out, they'd be spotted.

She thought about Jane Cramm, wondering if the woman really did know where Danny was taking them.

Lena cleared her throat. "Why isn't Jane here?" she asked for the third time.

"Shut up," he muttered, stirring against the seat.

"Does she know where we're going? Is she going to meet us or—?"

"One more word," Hayden growled, "and I'll make you sorry. Just drive."

It was no good. He wasn't going to tell her a thing.

She drove through the eye blink of a town called Blanco Trading Post, and that was when she saw the sign, Farmington—28 miles.

Farmington, she thought, the northwestern part of the state. But what lay ahead? Colorado? Arizona? It didn't matter anyway, not if he hadn't told anyone where they were heading. For all she knew, he was taking them deep into the high desert, far, far from civilization. And once he felt safe, once he was certain no one was going to find them, he might turn that gun on them and that would be it. He could dump them here, right out in the open, and no one would find their bodies for years. If ever.

MIKE FIGURED THAT THIS was what it felt like to go stark raving mad. Despite all his training, despite his being used to commotion and confusion during a hostage crisis, he was losing it.

He tried to take a calming breath as he stared at Hayden's house, which was garishly lit up by three spotlights. Around him were no less than fifteen cop cars, blocking the narrow street, parked helter-skelter. Cops and FBI agents stood in groups, some arguing, some just quietly watching the house, others trying to keep the neighbors inside their homes, but to little avail. The one thing Mike knew from experience was that there were a lot of itchy trigger fingers out here.

Then there was the negotiator who'd flown up from Albuquerque in a helicopter. This was his turf, not Mike's, and he'd taken over the bullhorn. They'd tried dozens of times now to phone into the house—they could even hear Hayden's telephone ringing. But no one had answered, which was highly unusual.

"Think they're in there?" John asked at Mike's side.

Mike shook his head. "Frankly, I don't know. Hayden's car is gone. For all we know they could be hundreds of miles from here." He stared at the run-down house with its dirty windows and dusty patch of lawn, and he couldn't help the frustration that surged through his gut. *Was* anyone in there?

The negotiator, Ted Laraby, picked up the bullhorn and tried again. "Danny," he began, his voice friendly, well modulated. "This isn't getting any of us anywhere. You know you can't escape. If you give up peacefully, things will go better for you. You don't want to harm anyone, Danny. I'm going to call on your phone again. Please pick it up this time. We need to talk, and not over this bullhorn, okay?"

Mike knew that Laraby was doing the best he could, trying to keep things calm, peaceful. It was his job. The last thing a hostage negotiator wanted was for things to get out of hand, for violence to erupt. Hell, Mike taught negotiation tactics; he knew the routine as well as anyone. On the other hand, the rest of the cops dealt in violence—they were keyed up, on the edge, getting real tired of the waiting.

To make things worse, the media had begun to arrive en masse. Reporters and their camera crews, satellite vans, pushing in around the cordoned-off perimeter, vying for camera position, making everyone crazy.

John nodded toward a cameraman who'd sneaked in too close and was being escorted out of the area. "What a mess," John said in disgust.

Mike frowned. "I don't know how long things will stay peaceful. Hayden should have responded to the phone calls by now. It's just putting everyone more on edge." He didn't want to step on toes, but Mike finally went over to Laraby and introduced himself, giving the man a rundown of his involvement with the hostages.

"This must be rough on you, Quinn," Ted Laraby said.

Mike nodded. "If Hayden would only respond to the phone calls, we'd get a better read on the situation inside. As it is…"

"I'd sure like this to stay peaceful," Laraby said, "and I know you would, too."

"Damn right," Mike said, and then he looked over at Captain Hunt, who was calling the shots. "I'd like to go in under a white flag," Mike said, "approach the house unarmed. The trouble is, Hunt would never let me."

"No, he wouldn't," Laraby said. "You're the last person he'd let near that house."

Mike locked his jaw. "Well, something's got to give here, and soon. If it doesn't—" he nodded toward the SWAT team "—Hunt will give them the go-ahead to assault the house."

All Laraby could do was agree.

Mike watched eight-thirty come and go. The tension outside the house was palpable. He kept his eye on the eight SWAT team guys in basic black: trousers, shirts, bulletproof vests, knit caps and face paint. Each one held an assault rifle trained on the house. If shooting started, Mike knew they'd tear the walls apart with those high-powered guns and no one inside would be left alive.

Nine o'clock arrived. "There should have been some movement from the house by now," John said.

Mike nodded gravely.

"What do you think?"

"You've asked that sixteen times," Mike snapped, then caught himself. "Hey, sorry. It's really getting to me."

"Understandable," John was saying, when they both noticed Agents Sabin and Miller approaching.

"Quinn," Alan Sabin said. "Pretty unusual situation here."

"Oh? And how's that?" Mike asked.

"Hayden should have responded to the telephone by now. We're starting to believe the house is empty."

"And?" Mike said, knowing what was coming.

"We'll give it a while longer, but then I've got to advise Captain Hunt to go in. Maybe his team can get close enough to—"

Mike swore. "You've got no way of knowing if my wife and child are in there!"

"Ex-wife," Sabin said.

Mike ignored the pointed remark. "Just because the

car isn't here doesn't mean Hayden's not in there. He might be inside and armed to the teeth. If he feels the slightest bit threatened…''

"No one said anything about threatening him."

"Right," Mike said sarcastically.

"Look—" Sabin began.

Mike cut him off sharply. "We wait. We wait for days if we have to. Whatever it takes."

Alan Sabin frowned. "Hayden may lose it anyway. There're two schools of thought here, Quinn, and you know it. By waiting we might drive him over the edge, and—"

"Then send in someone under a white flag," Mike said, starting to lose it. "Send just one unarmed man.…''

"I can't risk that," Sabin said, "and you know it. Now, I think SWAT can handle—"

"No," Mike said hotly, "you send even one single armed man anywhere near that house and you could start a Waco-style nightmare. If that happens…" But John put a hand on his arm and Mike tried to collect himself. He shut up, turning away from the FBI men, but he knew what he had to do. At 9:31 he made his move. He took two deep breaths and stepped out and away from the patrol car that had been protecting him.

At first no one noticed him because of all the commotion. But when he approached no-man's-land in the middle of the street, voices began to reach him.

"Hey!" "Hold up there!" "What in hell do you think you're doing?" "Quinn, I'm ordering you to stop!"

Mike ignored the protests, and step by slow step he kept going, empty hands held up to show that he was unarmed, entering the bright circles of the light from the spotlights trained on the house. When it was plain he wasn't going to retreat, a hush fell over the crowd, as if all air had suddenly been vacuumed from the scene. He felt as if he couldn't breathe.

Another step. Another.

Mike kept his eyes on the windows. Ever since they'd arrived the curtains had been drawn, and he watched for the slightest movement, feeling the gun he wore concealed under his armpit, cold steel against his flesh.

He stepped onto the curb. Along the sidewalk to the sandy patch of lawn in front of the house.

Had that curtain just moved?

He felt his pulse burst, and goose bumps rippled up his limbs.

Keep going. Slow, slow. He reached the walkway to the tilting front porch. The door was ten, fifteen feet in front of him.

Sweat broke from every pore in his body, and the spotlights felt like spears of heat on his back. He kept moving slowly and breathing. *Keep your cool, Quinn.*

Mike neared the front door. He had no idea what to expect. He knew that door could fly open at any instant and bullets could slam into his body.

He raised his hand to knock, sweat pouring off his brow, blinding him, and he rapped once on the door, twice. Another scenario tore through his brain. They might all be inside and, hours ago, before the cops had even arrived, Danny had panicked and put a bullet in each of them, then stuck the gun in his mouth.

Mike knocked a third time.

ON THE FAR SIDE OF Farmington Danny spotted a dirt road and ordered Lena to pull onto it.

"Is this where we're going?" she asked. Oh, God, she thought, it was exactly what she'd feared most—a dirt road in the middle of nowhere. "Why are we turning?" she asked again, her voice quivering.

"Just keep going," he said, "a mile, two. I'll tell you when to stop."

OhGodohGodohGod. Desperately, Lena stole a side-long glance at the gun. Could she get to it, fight him for it? He was a small guy, but wiry. And even if she did manage to struggle with him, the damn thing might go off, and Kimmy was right there....

What to do? She wasn't going to let him kill them so easily; that much she knew. First she'd refuse to get out, then, if he tried to drag her out, she'd fight tooth and nail. She'd never go meekly. And maybe she could buy Kimmy a little time to run and hide. It was dark, no moon. Surely Kimmy could evade him somehow. She had to.

"Here," Danny said. "Pull off here behind that boulder." Lena's heart lurched.

"Hey, do what I tell you!" he yelled, and he smashed the butt of the gun against her shoulder.

Hot searing pain shot down her arm. "It won't work, you bastard," she said.

"What the hell're you talking about?"

"The cops know you've got us. They'll give you the chair, Danny, the electric chair. You'll fry. Your best bet is to let us go. Just leave us right here and drive off. Maybe you can make it to Mexico or Canada or—"

"Shut the hell up!" he yelled. "I need some rest. I got gout in my foot and I gotta put it up."

Lena stopped the car. "What?"

"You're gettin' in the back with the kid. I'm gonna lock the doors, and believe me, I'll hear the locks pop if you try to open them. I gotta get this foot up. You make any move toward me and I'll blow your head off. The kid's too.''

"You're not...?" But she decided not to finish. Why give him any ideas?

Eventually Lena did lie down on the back seat, Kimmy alongside her. She knew Danny had given her child something to knock her out, but she decided not to say anything, not now. But if he tried to give her child anything else, he'd have one helluva battle on his hands, gun or no gun.

She remembered the cell phone then—it was in her purse. She'd put it there after talking to Gloria this afternoon....

It wasn't going to work, though. Even if the battery was still strong enough, how could she make a call without Hayden hearing her? Damn it. But she'd think of something. Eventually there'd be an opening and she'd somehow slip through.

Oh, Mike, she thought, *where are you?*

Against her side Kimmy stirred, her warmth seeping into Lena, the most beautiful warmth.... For a long time she pressed her nose to Kimmy's hair, drinking in her scent, and tears filled her eyes. *We're alive,* she kept thinking, and that was all that mattered right now. Alive and together again.

CHAPTER SIXTEEN

MIKE STARED WEARILY at the woman and realized he almost felt sorry for her. *Almost.* But Jane Cramm had made her own choices. And they'd all been bad.

He glanced at the wall clock in the interrogation room—it read 3:22 a.m.—and he looked over at John Hidalgo, then at Captain Hunt. The captain shrugged.

Mike had found Jane alone in the house in an alcoholic stupor, and since then they'd pumped five cups of coffee into her. Still, after almost six hours, she was scarcely cognizant of her surroundings and her situation. There'd been no activity at Hayden's house despite the host of cops that remained stationed there—just in case Danny Hayden returned. Which wasn't going to happen, Mike was sure.

"Jane," Mike said for the umpteenth time, "we really need your help here. Kimmy needs your help."

She sat slumped in the hard metal chair across the table from the men, arms folded tightly over her thin chest, straight, dirty hair hanging limply in her dull brown eyes.

"Jane?"

"I hear you," she said in a barely audible whisper. "I don't know anything."

Mike sighed. He looked down at her hands; they were white and trembling. She had the shakes.

"She ought to be in the hospital," Hunt said under his breath. "She ought to be in detox."

"Give me a few more minutes," Mike said, not wanting to beg. But, damn it, he would if that's what it took.

They'd been after Jane for hours now, trying to find out where Danny had gone. But thus far the poor woman either didn't know or she was too scared of Danny Hayden to tell.

"Now, Jane," Mike said to her, "everyone realizes Kimmy is your natural daughter. You're not the first mother who wanted her child back. Courts take these things into account."

Jane glanced up, then looked back down at her lap.

"The thing is," Mike said, pressing on, "if Kimmy or Lena is harmed in any way, well, I'm afraid it will be a lot rougher on you. We know that Danny's with them. All we need is a clue, one word as to where he's gone. Jane? Are you listening?"

"Yes." A whimper.

"Danny doesn't have to know. We can always let him believe it was the cops who spotted him. No one will tell."

Jane bit her lower lip.

"Look," Mike said, leaning across the table, "you've got my word. No one will tell Danny. Now, please, Jane, help us. Help your child."

Mike glanced at the clock again. Damn. In a matter of minutes some court-appointed attorney was going to show up—even on Saturday and at this early hour—and advise Jane to keep her mouth shut. It was her right. Mike knew the law and he appreciated it. But in this case...

"Jane? You have my word. Come on, where did Danny go?"

"Don't know."

"Yes, you do. Think of Kimmy all alone and afraid. She's probably missing you right now."

She raised her eyes. "She's got that woman. Lena."

"But she's used to *you* now, isn't she? You've been feeding her and combing her hair and putting her to bed. Jane, she's *your* flesh and blood. I know you couldn't live with yourself if anything happened to your child."

Tears began to ooze from the corners of her eyes.

Gotcha, Mike thought. *Come on, woman, come on.*

"Look," Hunt said, rubbing his face, "I really think—"

But Mike held up a hand. "Come on, Jane, for God's sake help your daughter."

Jane said something. They all sat up and leaned toward her.

"What was that?" Mike asked, his tone calm despite the urgent thumping of his heart. "Jane?"

"Ver...Vernal," she whispered.

Mike pivoted to John and Bill.

John reached out and touched Jane gently on the shoulder. "Was that Vernal?"

She nodded, barely.

"Vernal, Utah?" John asked.

Again, a nod.

"Does Danny know someone there?"

Another nod.

"A friend? A relative?"

"His...brother."

"Is his brother also named Hayden?"

"Uh-huh," Jane said. Then she looked up and met Mike's eyes. "I feel real sick," she said.

"I know," Mike said. "I know you do. And you can go to the hospital now."

Tears rolled down her cheeks and spotted her stained T-shirt. "Thank you," she whispered.

IT WAS BARELY DAWN when Lena pulled into the only open gas station in the Navajo reservation town of Shiprock. She'd seen Danny slip the gun into the back waistband of his jeans, and he'd made it very plain that if she said one single word to the cashier, he'd kill them all on the spot.

They visited the rest room, and Lena used her own money to buy stale sandwiches and a bottle of juice. There was never an opportunity to signal the young Navajo cashier or make solid eye contact. She wondered if the Indian boy would even remember them if asked.

"It's going to be a nice day, huh?" Lena said. "What do you think?"

"Yeah, sure," the youth replied, not looking up.

Lena gathered the juice and sandwiches, aware of Danny standing close now, Kimmy right next to him.

She thought frantically. "Could I have a sack for this stuff, please?"

"Let's go," Danny said behind her.

"I don't want to get the car all messed up," she said, praying the Navajo boy would notice the vintage wreck they were driving. He handed her a plastic bag, never directly looking at her.

Damn, damn, damn, Lena thought as she went back to the car.

Danny was a mess in the morning, in a foul mood, nasty and uncommunicative. Kimmy ate her sandwich in the back seat and remained quiet for the most part, obviously intimidated by Danny's very presence. *I could kill him,* Lena thought, *I really could.*

They left Shiprock, passing the giant slab of rock for which the small town was named, and it did jut up from the high-desert floor like a schooner under sail across the vast, empty spaces of the Four Corners region.

As dawn inched across the land, Lena saw other immense rock formations in the distance, thrusting pinnacles that interrupted the land's arid flatness. They passed canyons whose walls were maroon and ivory in the early light, bands of earth colors against the clearest sky she'd ever seen.

They were in Arizona now, still driving through the huge Navajo reservation. Occasionally she passed a single car or truck, and every once in a while there was a hogan, a round squat Navajo house, off the road, smoke curling up in a question mark from the chimney.

Lifeless, Lena thought. It was like driving on the surface of an uninhabited alien planet. The sun finally rose behind them over a distant chain of mesas, and shadows retreated, crawling across the desert. Lena glanced at the gas gauge. Over half a tank left.

She tried something anyway. "Will we be stopping soon?"

"Shut up," Danny mumbled, his bony knees propped on the dashboard, the gun in his lap.

"I only asked because we'll need gas again unless we're almost where we're going."

"We don't need no gas."

"Then we will be stopping soon? In Arizona?"

"Jeezus," he said. "You never shut up."

"Will we be?"

He uttered a string of oaths that made Kimmy cower, then said, "Utah. We're going to Utah. Now, just drive."

"What's in Utah?"

He sat straight up, leaned over and pushed his face at hers. "One more word and I'm going to climb in the back and give that kid of yours a real licking. You hear?"

Lena subsided, but she thought, *I could kill him with my bare hands.*

For the next hour they drove in silence, Danny lethargically staring out at the empty land, Kimmy resting with her eyes closed in the back, whatever Danny had given her obviously still in her system. Lena drove, biting her lip, thinking about Mike, wishing to God there were a way she could know if he was in pursuit.

Of course he is, her mind would tell her, and then her thoughts would flip-flop. The only way he could know was if Jane Cramm had told him, and only then if *she* knew.

Utah, Jane thought over and over. What lay ahead for them in Utah?

The spurts of anger began at midmorning. It was as if Danny had finally come alive and was shifting into his usual gear.

"Stupid bitch women," he muttered, "ruined everything. Everything!"

Lena gave him a quick, sidelong look. "What's everything?"

"Shut up!"

"Are those the only two words you know?" she taunted boldly.

He waved the gun and grinned wickedly, his yellow, stained teeth showing. "I'll shoot you—you better believe it."

"While I'm doing sixty-five miles per hour?" she fired back, fed up, sickened by the very sight of him.

"Think you're real smart, don't you," he rasped. "Well, you're so smart you let your brat here get snatched."

"What do you mean?"

"Your mother, *stupid.*"

"Gloria?"

"Yeah, that Gloria Torres. Said right in the paper years

ago, right under the picture of you and that cop at the hospital, said her name and where she lived."

"So you staked out my mother?"

He laughed. "Only took a day. No big deal."

"Well," Lena said, "that was nice of you, Danny, to try to get Jane's child back for her."

He took the bait. "You are one dumb bitch," he said.

"Look," Lena broke in, "call me anything you want, but I'm getting real sick of that word."

"Bitch, bitch, bitch," he said gleefully.

Oh, he was easy, she was learning. Dumb as a post. "So you didn't steal Kimmy for Jane's sake?" she said. "I thought…"

"That's the trouble with women," he sneered. "They oughta give up thinking. No, stupid, the kid was making a movie. A movie, you know? But you had to come along and ruin it. Two big ones. I'm out two big ones."

A…movie? And then she knew. "You dirty rotten…"

He laughed, and that was when Lena slammed on the brakes and the car skidded halfway across the road and came to rest on a sandy shoulder.

Danny was gripping the dashboard. "What the…?" he cried.

Lena held on to the steering wheel, ignoring Kimmy's, "Mommy?" coming from the back seat. "How far did it go, you bastard?" she demanded, glaring at him. "How far?"

Danny righted himself, looked confused, and then he grinned. "Well, ain't you a real hothead."

"Tell me!"

"Not far enough" was the answer she got, and he refused to say more.

THERE WAS NO WAY Mike could be positive he was on the right road. He was going solely on the advice of John

Hidalgo, who had a cousin who lived in Salt Lake City.

"Trust me," John had told him back at police head-quarters in Santa Fe, "this is the shortest route. Right through the reservation, buddy. Any other route will take our boy Hayden hundreds of miles out of his way." He'd folded up the map he'd taken from his police cruiser and handed it to Mike.

"Make sure they get that APB out in all four states," Mike had said, opening the door to the GTO. "New Mexico, Arizona, Colorado and Utah."

"I know the drill," John had said patiently.

"And call Vernal. Alert the police. Maybe ask them to put a stakeout on Hayden's brother's house. Okay?"

John had smiled. "I really do know the drill, Mike."

"Right," Mike had said. "Sorry." And then he and John had clasped hands.

"You drive carefully," John had said when Mike was in the car, starting the big engine.

"Like hell I will," Mike had replied, and they'd said goodbye, John promising to look him up when he was in Disneyland that winter with his kids.

"I'll see Lena, too," John had assured him, "and Kimberly."

"God, I hope so," Mike had said, and he left rubber in the street.

Now the immense territory of Four Corners stretched ahead of him, endless country, an ancient geologic bat-tlefield littered with the results of unimaginable violence, eroded by wind-driven sand and severe temperature fluc-tuations.

Indian country. And somewhere in this immensity were Lena and Kimmy. Were they afraid, intimidated by

Hayden as Jane was? Or was Lena holding on, that temper of hers keeping her going, keeping her sharp?

He drove through the unearthly land of the Apache and Zuni, the Paiute and Hopi, the Ute and Navajo, and he sped by the monuments to their past. He registered only that Lena and Kimmy should be with him, protected and safe, enjoying the scenery, but they weren't. Danny Hayden had them.

He looked at the speedometer. Pushing ninety miles per hour. He knew he was on the Navajo reservation now. If he was stopped by the tribal police, would they listen to him, respect his badge, or would they lock him up and throw away the key? This wasn't like crossing a state line, after all; the Navajo Reservation was a nation unto itself. White-man's law meant little here.

It was outside the Indian town of Shiprock that Mike pulled over to fill up. He pumped the gas—damn car of Lena's took the highest octane—then hurried inside the trading post to grab a sandwich and soda to go. It struck him at the counter that maybe, since gas stops were almost nonexistent, Hayden had stopped here, too.

He looked at the young Navajo clerk, a handsome teen whose face looked as if it were carved out of the rock of the nearby mesa.

"I wonder," Mike began. "You wouldn't have been on duty last night or real early this morning?"

The kid nodded.

"You were?"

"Yep."

"Would you remember a man, a scruffy-looking man in his thirties, who might have been here with a woman and a child... Hey," Mike said, "I've got a picture of the child. It's in the car...."

"Guy in an old station wagon," the boy said.

Mike's heart clutched. "That's right. Wood paneled."

"Sure," the teen said.

"You're positive?"

"My grandpop drives one. A real dog."

"What?" Mike said.

"Car's a real dog."

"Oh," Mike said. "Thanks. Thanks a million."

The boy only shrugged.

Relief surged through Mike as he rushed out to the car—he was so close, so damn close to overtaking them... And then it struck him out of the blue. *Gloria.* No one had told her about Lena. It had been hours and hours, and no one had even bothered to call her.

He stopped in his tracks, pivoted and eyed the pay phone on the wall outside the trading post. Every ounce of his being told him to get back on the road, but hell, this had to be done.

He went to the pay phone, found a quarter in his pocket and shoved it impatiently into the slot, then used his credit card to dial Lena's number. *Come on, come on, come on.*

"Hello?" said Gloria, her voice a nervous croak.

It occurred to Mike that he could lie to her, but then he decided to tell the whole truth. It took him too much time, though, and Gloria had too many questions.

Finally, he said, "Gloria, I know you're a wreck. But I've got to go. Every second I spend on the phone..."

"Go," she said, "go. But for the love of God, Mike, you get my babies back for me."

"I will," he said, "I promise. Safe and sound."

Mike hurried back to the car, frantic to be on the road, knowing every second counted. He started the engine, shoved the gearshift into first, and then it hit him. *Jennifer.* Why hadn't he taken another minute to call Jenn?

He glanced at the pay phone. It would only take a short time to do the right thing and call her. She'd be home. And she'd be up by now, even on a Saturday. *Do it. Call her,* his brain said, but something stopped him cold. No matter the danger Lena and Kimmy were in, Jennifer would still ask him at least one pointed question: had he slept with Lena? He knew in his gut she'd ask. He couldn't lie to her, either.

He looked over at the phone again, and guilt stabbed him. He frowned, exhaled, then, a moment later, he let out the clutch and sped out onto the reservation road, putting the whole situation with Jennifer right out of his mind.

The morning sun painted the land in pastels as Mike crossed the border into Arizona. He was due south of the Four Corners area, where Utah, Colorado, Arizona and New Mexico met in a perfect square, and there was only this single road that ran west into Arizona for a hundred miles before it turned north into Utah. Hayden had to be on it. But how far ahead? He'd snatched Lena sometime after 3 p.m. yesterday. But when had he left Santa Fe? And had he pulled over during the night to sleep? Maybe. Maybe. That old beat-up station wagon wouldn't be doing ninety, either. Maybe they were just ahead, somewhere around the sweep of that mesa.

It occurred to Mike that Jane might have been lying about Vernal. She *might* have been. But he doubted it. She'd been too scared, too out of it to fake her answers. Or had she?

Mike rubbed his face and realized he was running on adrenaline alone. He hadn't slept in what? Over twenty-four hours? He'd gone on little sleep before, especially during a hostage-negotiation crisis. But this was different. This was Lena and Kimmy. He wondered then if he was up to the inevitable confrontation. Was his judgment as sound as it could be? Should he have asked John to come along?

"Ah, hell," Mike said, and he pressed the accelerator to the floor. The GTO sprang forward, and the needle read one hundred mph as he sped off, moving deeper and deeper into the vastness of the reservation.

CHAPTER SEVENTEEN

"TURN HERE," Danny said, pointing at a road sign, but when they got to 191, which cut up into Utah, there was a sign that read Bridge Out.

Lena felt like laughing hysterically. Bridge Out. No detour sign, nothing. And it wasn't as if there were alternate routes out here. They were lucky if they passed a dirt road every fifty miles.

"What now?" she said, slowing.

Danny swore a blue streak, calling the Navajos every name in the book.

"Where to?" Lena said, disgusted with his filthy mouth.

"Just keep going, I guess. There's a road up in Kayenta. Maybe fifty miles."

"Okay," Lena said. "I just hope for your sake there's a gas station there."

"Shut up, will you?" Danny said, and he rubbed at his swollen foot.

As the morning proceeded, exhaustion took its toll on everyone. Kimmy was whiny, antsy, grating on Danny's nerves, and Lena wasn't sure how long she could keep driving these endless miles of eroded red washes and prairies dotted with sagebrush and pinyon trees. To make it worse, there were no fences on the reservation, and what few cattle and sheep there were had the freedom of the roads. The road signs read Open Range. Twice already this morning she'd had to hit the brakes hard to avoid a steer in the road. Her nerves had about had it. Cattle, sheep, coyotes and deer. An occasional car or semi barreling past. That was it.

By midmorning it was getting hot out, too, a dry desert heat that shimmered across the barren land and up the sides of the distant mesas. Danny rolled his window down, and Kimmy whined some more from the back seat.

"It's blowing me," she whimpered. "Mommy, the air's blowing me."

"Shut up!" Danny yelled, then he lifted his gun, stuck it partway out the window and took a few potshots at a road sign indicating a deer crossing.

"That's really adult," Lena said under her breath.

Danny pivoted toward her and pointed the gun. "Bam, bam," he snickered. "You're dead."

God, how she hated this man. She gave him a withering glance. "Why Utah? What's there?"

"A big surprise," he said, still playing with his gun.

"What surprise?"

Danny shrugged. "You'll find out."

"Tell me now. I'm curious."

"Ha!" he said. "But if you must know, my brother's there. He's got real good connections, see."

"Connections?"

"In South America."

"Just what does South America have to do with any of this?"

"He knows some folks who like white women." Then his face lit up. "Of course, you're probably too old. But the kid..."

"Oh, that's a *great* idea," she said sarcastically. "And just how do you plan on getting us out of the country?"

He laughed. "You think it doesn't happen every day? Huh? There're ways."

"Mommy," Kimmy said from the back, "I have to go to the bathroom."

"Just hold it, brat," Danny said, and silence fell over them for a while.

The town sprawled on the flat, reddish desert with red rocks showing through everywhere in big round domes. A hot wind blew dust across the road, and there was a tall water tower with the name Kayenta on it.

Danny told Lena to stop for gas, and no sooner had she pulled up to the pumps at a trading post than a cop car pulled in, too. It was a big white Blazer, and on its side it said Navajo Tribal Police.

Her heart flew into her throat. This was the break she'd been waiting for.

But Danny thought quickly.

Before Lena was even out of the car, he said, "Kid stays here with me. I'm gonna keep the gun trained right on her, see, and if I even *think* you're trying to pull something, I'll kill her. I got nothing to lose. Now, get the gas and pay with that card of yours and don't even look at that cop. Hurry it up."

Lena got out and lifted the gas nozzle off its cradle, her hands shaking so badly she could barely press the correct buttons on the pump to start it up. *Oh, God,* she thought, starting again, trying desperately to concentrate: cash or credit, pay inside or outside. Why couldn't they make these machines easier? And all the while the tribal cop on the other side of the pump was eyeing her, which made her mouth dry and her heart leap sickeningly.

Finally the policeman stepped over the concrete island. "Need some help?" the big man asked. "These things can be pretty confusing."

"Ah...sure," Lena said, her lower lip trembling. "I, ah, want to pay with a credit card, outside."

The policeman helped her, even going so far as to start the gas. He seemed friendly enough, and she thought desperately of some way to signal him, but he did glance twice into the car, making eye contact with Danny.

Oh, God, oh, God, Lena thought.

Then Kimmy, her window in the back now open, piped up with, "I have to go to the bathroom."

"Okay, let's go," Danny said, obviously thinking fast. "I'll walk you over while Mommy finishes pumping the gas. Come on now." Then he was out, opening the back door, taking Kimmy's hand and leading her away. Lena didn't see the gun, but she knew he'd keep it real close. Danny watched her, too. Even while Kimmy was inside the ladies' room, he never once took his eyes off Lena. The policeman finished pumping his own gas, tipped his black Stetson at Lena and disappeared inside to pay. He was still inside when Danny and Kimmy got back. They drove off, Lena at the wheel, without seeing him again.

"Take Route 163," Danny said, nervous himself, "right there." He pointed.

Lena bit her lower lip and wanted to cry. That might have been her last chance.

"I'm thirsty," Kimmy said from the back, and the litany between Danny and her child began anew.

North of Kayenta the distant obelisks and flat-topped mesas and chimneys and lines of cliffs and spires of Monument Valley stood against the horizon like a prehistoric cityscape. Closer, right by the road, the huge sail-shaped rock called El Capitan jutted up. Across from it stood Owl Rock, a perfect stone replica of folded wings and eyes and beak. Lena steered the curves of the two-lane road and realized she'd seen this scenery before—

seen it dozens of times in Westerns. She drove and stared and even in her awful fear and weariness, she saw the beauty of it.

For miles the city of stone went on, and even Danny started looking out his window. They crossed the state line into Utah, the monuments becoming fewer in number, and Lena grew desperate to keep her daughter's mind off her predicament.

"Look, Kimmy," she said, "isn't that a pretty mountain?"

Danny muttered something.

"I'm still thirsty," Kimmy complained, ignoring the spectacular sight. "Mommy..."

Lena turned a little, ready to reassure Kimmy that they'd get something to drink soon, and her eyes went off the road for a split second. The deer bounded out of nowhere, the movement catching Lena's eye, and she hit the brakes in a reflex action. The car swerved, lurched, skidded sideways. It tossed them around as it bounced across the gravel, Lena fighting the wheel, and then stopped abruptly, nose down in a gully, throwing everyone forward, dust rising around the car in the sudden silence.

It had all happened in a heartbeat, and yet to Lena the accident had run before her eyes in slow motion. She lifted her head from the top of the steering wheel and drew in a long, quavering breath, mentally searching her body for injuries.

"Mommy?" Kimmy said.

Lena pivoted.

"Mommy, what happened?"

"Are you all right?" Lena asked in an urgent, rasping voice. "My God, Kimmy, are you okay?"

"Uh-huh," she whimpered, shaken and afraid.

Trying to clear the cobwebs from her own brain, Lena looked over at Danny. He wasn't moving, and there was blood showing on the dashboard where his head rested.

The gun, she thought abruptly. *Where's the gun?* And then she saw it near his feet. Carefully, carefully, she reached down and took hold of it, her eyes never leaving Hayden.

The gun in her hands, Lena became slowly cognizant of two things: there was steam coming up from the radiator and they were nose down in a deep wash. *Have to get out of here,* she thought.

"Kimmy, Mommy's going to climb out and then help you. Okay?"

"Uh-huh," Kimmy said.

Lena glanced again at Danny. She knew she should probably disable him right now—if he was even alive—shoot him in the kneecap, somewhere, anywhere. But she couldn't. She simply couldn't.

Climbing out of the car was a task, and her feet kept slipping on the loose sand and gravel on the steep sides of the gully, but eventually she and Kimmy were scrambling up the bank, gripping rocks and roots, bloodying their hands until they were standing on the flat desert floor.

Kimmy got her breath and clutched Lena's hand. "Is Danny dead?" she asked innocently.

"I don't think so," Lena breathed. "I think he's just unconscious."

"We can get away now," Kimmy said.

Lena suddenly remembered the cell phone. She reached into her purse, felt the gun and then found the phone. *Oh, please work,* she prayed. But it didn't. It was dead as a doornail.

"Can we go, Mommy?"

"Ah, yes, sweetie, we can," she said, and she thought about Danny down there in the wrecked car. They could go; they could actually escape *if* he didn't wake up, she was thinking, and that's when she saw the doe lying on the shoulder of the road at the end of the black skid marks.

Oh, no. "Kimmy, honey," she said, "I want you to stay here for a minute. You sit on this rock and Mommy will be right back. I'm only going over here a couple of feet. Okay?"

Kimmy nodded.

The poor doe was dead, and Lena was thankful at least for that, because the animal never would have survived the injuries and might have limped off to die in some sort of terrible pain.

It was time to go, though. She and Kimmy didn't dare stay around in case Danny woke up. She took her gaze off the deer and searched the road. No one. Not a single car in sight.

She walked back to Kimmy and took her hand. "Sweetie," she said, "we have to leave." Then she stood on the rock where Kimmy had been sitting and searched the land until she spotted something off to the east—a hogan, a Navajo hogan, sitting almost at the foot of a red rock spire. How far could it be? Not even a mile. If they walked on the road, Danny might wake up and be able to spot them. But crossing the desert floor...

"Are you up to a little hike?" Lena asked her child, and Kimmy nodded.

"Okay, let's go, then."

They started off across the dry, uneven land, the squat round top of the hogan just barely visible. But someone would be there, Lena thought, and she could get help. The sun was baking now, rising on hot waves off the sand and rock. A mile or so, Lena thought, that was all they had to go. And they'd be safe. She clutched Kimmy's hand, gave her baby a reassuring smile and put one foot in front of the other. Still every fifty yards or so she couldn't help looking over her shoulder, her heart beating a little too fast.

MIKE HAD his second break when he finally took the time to stop at the Navajo Tribal Police headquarters in Kayenta. He realized he should have stopped back in Shiprock, but he simply hadn't known what kind of reception he'd get. Now, however, he needed help; ever since passing the closed road with the Bridge Out sign, he wasn't at all certain which route to take.

Mike went inside the worn-out trailer that was the Kayenta headquarters and introduced himself, showing his badge and giving the dispatcher at the front desk a thumbnail version of the pursuit he was on.

"I've been following them all night," he began, and that's when a tribal policeman stepped out from the back room.

Mike looked up.

"You say a man in an old station wagon with a woman and child?" he asked, thumbs in his jeans pockets.

"That's right," Mike said, eyeing the big Indian cop. *Wouldn't want to meet him in a dark alley....*

"Well, mister, I think maybe I just helped the lady pump some gas right here in Kayenta."

Mike cocked his head, hardly believing his ears.

"That's right," the cop went on. "Couldn't have been much more than an hour ago."

Mike let out a breath he seemed to have been holding for days. "They were all right?"

"Appeared to be, though the lady was nervous. I didn't

give it much thought." Then the Indian grinned. "Too bad you didn't stop when you first drove onto the res. We'd have had your man in custody by now."

The cop introduced himself as Sergeant Bob Yazzie, and he led Mike into the back room, where he picked up a two-way radio handset. "It's Saturday," he said to Mike. "Not many of us on duty. But I'm sure you've noticed by now there aren't many roads, either." Then he put the information out over the radio. When he was done, he said he'd take off down Route 160 through the Black Mesa region of the reservation. "You head up 163 toward Utah," he said. Then he narrowed his eyes. "That your car out front?"

"Ah, no," Mike said, "it's my ex-wife's."

"Uh-huh. Well, you just keep it under a hundred and don't push your luck. We like to cooperate with outside police, but this isn't L.A. Okay?"

"Sure," Mike said.

"And when you get to the Utah border, you find a phone and let us know. Hear?"

"That's a promise," Mike said, and he shook the man's hand.

Outside the station, as Mike was getting back into the GTO, Yazzie put a hand on the hood and said, "By the way, you carrying?"

Mike stopped short, feeling the weight of the gun under his armpit. "Yes," he said.

"Mmm," Bob Yazzie said, then he moved away. "Happy hunting."

Ten minutes later Mike was heading up 163 toward Utah. He was thinking that Lena and Kimmy were probably exhausted and scared to death. He felt a moment's flash of anger at Lena—what had she been thinking when she went alone to Hayden's?—but then he realized he'd have done the same damn thing. She had courage; he'd sure give her that.

He drove, wondering if he could possibly overtake them in that old station wagon, *if* they were even on this road, when he remembered the other night—Lena sobbing in the shower, the scent and taste and feel of her. He'd wanted her so badly, wanted to hold and protect her and make endless love to her. Had it been just an interlude, the two of them in need of human companionship? He knew he still wanted her; always had. But how did *she* feel?

No time for this, Quinn, he was thinking, driving around a long, sweeping curve in the road, when he saw the skid marks.

Mike downshifted and slowed, and he saw the deer lying by the side of the road. It had been hit recently, too, because the buzzards were just circling overhead.

He downshifted again, into second gear, his eyes following the skid marks that disappeared into the sandy—

"Oh, my God," Mike whispered harshly. There it was, the station wagon, the tail end of it sticking out of a ravine.

He slammed on the brakes and skidded to a stop on the shoulder, then jumped out, his hand under his jacket, reaching for his gun. *No, no, no!* his brain shouted. *Don't let them be dead!*

He scrambled and slid down the side of the wash, his heart pounding against his ribs. The car was empty, completely empty. And then he noticed the blood on the dashboard of the passenger side. Lena's? Kimmy's?

Where in hell were they?

Mike looked up and down the wash but saw nothing. Then he made his way back up to the top of the gully and began to scan the area. He climbed a nearby boulder, shoes sliding on the smooth rock, and stood on top, searching first the road and then the desert, and that was when he thought he could make out a movement near a hogan about a mile away.

Were those people out there?

Binoculars, he thought, but he didn't have any with him. He felt a tightening in his chest—anger, fear, frustration—but he pressed it down and strained his eyes. It had to be people out there. Had to be. But who? All three of them? Or merely some Navajos who lived here?

He made his decision in a flash, jumped off the rock and hurried back to the car, starting it up. He put it into gear and let out the clutch. The GTO lurched forward onto the barren desert, its tires skidding, the chassis bottoming out, and he left a cloud of dust behind him, hanging in the hot dry air, marking his passage.

THE PLACE WAS EMPTY.

Lena looked around and felt her heart sink to her feet. *Empty.*

"Mommy, I'm so thirsty," Kimmy said at her side.

Lena had to force her weary, sun-fried brain to think.

"Okay," she said, standing in the center of the abandoned hogan, "guess we'd better find some water." She smiled down at Kimmy reassuringly.

"There's no water, Mommy," the child said.

Lena felt like laughing—she never could put anything over on Kimmy.

"Maybe out back," she said, "a well or something. Let's look."

There was one, an old wellhead pump sticking up out of the bone-dry ground. Lena licked her parched lips and touched the handle. *Just a cup,* she thought, *just one lousy cup....*

She began to pump. "Go inside and see if you can find a cup, honey, anything to hold water."

"It'll be dirty."

"We'll rinse it out. Now, go on."

She kept pumping, listening for a gurgle, her eyes fixed on the antiquated spigot. *Oh, please,* she thought.

It took ten minutes, but finally, mercifully, a few drops began to trickle onto the sand and then a small stream of dirty water. Kimmy rinsed out the broken plastic cup she'd found, and they filled it and drank greedily. Somewhere in the back of Lena's mind she knew you weren't supposed to gulp water when you were dehydrated, but she simply didn't care. It was probably an old wives' tale, anyway.

"Better?" she asked Kimmy.

Kimmy nodded eagerly, and Lena thought that now all they had to worry about was if the water was okay.

They went back inside, out of the bright sunlight, and Lena put her hands on her hips and frowned. How was she going to get the two of them safely out of here? Then she saw him through the front door: *Hayden.* Terror kicked her senses wide open.

"Oh, my God," she breathed, and she cast around desperately, as if a hole would open up magically and they could somehow hide.

She looked out the door again, gut-wrenching panic seizing her. He was still coming, maybe only a hundred yards away. She could see him limping, and make out the bloodstains on his filthy shirt. But it wasn't stopping him.

Horror swept her, and she had to close her eyes to calm herself. *Think, think.*

She opened her eyes. "Kimmy," she said in as even a voice as she could summon, "Mommy wants you to go out back and find a place to hide. Maybe in that shed.''

"But, Mommy…" And then Kimmy saw him, too. The little girl froze in fear.

Lena crouched down and took her shoulders firmly, staring her in the eyes. "Go outside and hide," she said sternly. "I'll be fine. *We'll* be fine. I have the gun, Kimmy."

"But Mommy…" Kimmy's lips were trembling.

"Danny is not going to harm us. I won't let him. Now be strong for me and do as I tell you." Lena stood up. "Go," she said in the voice she used when she meant business, and finally Kimmy disappeared out the back door.

Lena took a breath and turned toward the entrance. He was there. *Right there.* Shaking, she reached into the waistband of her jeans and pulled the gun out and raised it, holding it in both hands.

Danny stepped inside, shielding his eyes. She saw the wound on his forehead and all the drying blood—so much blood—but he'd made it here, hadn't he?

"You bitch," he said, standing there, swaying. "You left me for dead." He took a staggering step toward her.

"Stop right there," Lena said, and his eyes seemed to adjust to the dimness. He stared at the gun, which was leveled right on him.

"You ain't gonna shoot me," he said, and he licked his cracked lips. "You'd have done it back at the car."

"Don't count on it," Lena said, and something, something just over Danny's shoulder, caught her eye. It was a cloud of dust, like a rooster tail. She heard it then, the grinding sound of an engine.

A car? *My God,* she thought. *Hurry! Whoever you are, hurry!*

But there was no time. Danny was moving toward her. She could see the car now—hers? she thought in amazement—and she backed up, backed all the way up until the far wall stopped her.

"I'll shoot," she said. "I'll do it."

Danny grinned ferociously. He kept coming, oblivious to the approaching vehicle. "Give me that," he said.

"No."

He kept coming. He was only three feet from her.

Lena lowered the barrel of the gun toward his knees. Surely, surely he'd know she'd do it. "Stop," she commanded, her pulse racing. "Don't make me do this."

"Pull the trigger, bitch," he said, and he reached toward her.

Lena aimed, closed her eyes tightly and pulled the trigger.

The gun went click and her heart stopped. Completely stopped beating.

Her eyes flew open.

"Empty," he sneered, so close his breath was in her face. "Emptied it at the road sign, you stupid..."

And then his hand was at her throat, and she stood there, terror ripping through her.

He shoved her head against the wall and something inside her, some primitive instinct, took over. She started to struggle, fighting his hands, kicking and thrashing, forgetting everything but survival. She never heard the car pull up outside. She never saw the shadow of a man fill the door. She was only aware that if she didn't stop Danny, she and Kimmy were as good as dead.

She sank her teeth into his arm. Danny yelled and swore, and she saw his hand going back, back, forming a fist. *No, no, no!* tore through her brain when, from out of nowhere, something, *someone,* grabbed his fist and

Danny was being spun around like a top. Before she could blink he was sprawled on the earthen floor, a look of utter shock in his pale eyes.

Lena dragged her gaze up from Danny, and it was a long moment before she could fit her mind around what she was seeing. She tried to say something. Tried again. But the sound only echoed silently inside her brain. *Mike?*

SERGEANT BOB YAZZIE turned Hayden's gun over in his hands. "Empty," he mused. "So then it was empty when I saw you at the gas station?"

Lena nodded and shifted Kimmy's weight in her lap, trying not to dislodge the blanket and the teddy bear that Kimmy was clutching. Thank heavens they had still been in Lena's bag in the GTO. "If only I'd known. I kept trying to think of a way to signal you," she told him, and that was when Mike appeared in the doorway of the police trailer.

"You want the good news or the bad news?" he asked Lena.

"How about the good news," she said, although she knew what was coming, really—her car was broken down. Badly. Heck, they'd barely limped back into Kayenta.

"The good news is that the axle can be replaced," he said.

"And the bad news?" she said.

But Bob Yazzie answered. "Let me guess. It's going to take days to replace it."

"Uh-huh," Mike said, and he gave Lena an apologetic shrug.

She looked down at Kimmy and stroked her head, which was resting against her breast. "I don't want to leave the car,'' she stated emphatically. Then she glanced back up at Mike.

''We'll see.''

By midafternoon Tribal Police Headquarters in Kayenta was becoming a hotbed of activity. Lena and Mike heard through another Navajo policeman that Danny Hayden was still being patched up at the local clinic. ''Put twenty stitches in his head,'' one of the cops said in Bob's office. ''You should have heard him whine. Just like a baby.''

And then, before they could even transport Danny to the jail and lock him up, Special Agent Sabin and his entourage arrived by helicopter to cart him off. It was quite an event in the tiny Indian town, and all the residents stood outside their shops and homes to get a look at the helicopter, which had landed in a cloud of dust in a field behind the police station.

Lena was still sitting in Yazzie's office, Kimmy asleep in her lap, when Special Agent Alan Sabin poked his head in.

''We're all very glad to see you and Kimberly safe and sound,'' he said as if he were her new best friend.

She looked at him, too weary to be anything but indifferent. All she could say was, ''Thanks.''

Mike, however, had a lot more to get off his chest, and she could hear his voice outside the office as he spoke to Sabin. ''No thanks to you they're safe. If you hadn't spent so much time treating us like suspects, this might have been over a helluva lot sooner.''

''Just doing my job,'' Sabin replied.

There was some talk then about the rights of the Navajo nation versus FBI jurisdiction. Lena heard Bob Yazzie say, ''We could keep this Hayden character here if we wanted, but frankly, I'd hate to waste even one jail meal on him.''

The men went on talking, but Lena shut their conversation out—she was through with Hayden and hoped she never heard his name again. She turned away from the open door, carefully shifting Kimmy's weight, and pulled the desk phone over, then dialed her home phone with her credit card number.

She reached Gloria on the first ring. "Oh, my Lord! Oh, my God! Lena, baby! It's really you!"

Lena told her everything, and she even woke Kimmy up to say hello to Grandma. Then, when Kimmy was off the phone, Lena said to her mother, "The axle's shot on the GTO. They say it'll be days before it's fixed."

"I'll send you plane tickets," Gloria said anxiously.

But Lena wasn't too sure. "Let me think about it, Mom. Maybe Kimmy needs some time away from it all."

"Mmm," Gloria said. "And will Mike stay, too?"

"No one said I'm staying, Mom. I haven't decided. All this only happened a couple of hours ago. The one thing I do know is that if we return to L.A., the press is going to drive us crazy. I don't think Kimmy can handle it yet. I'll just have to work this all through."

"Well," Gloria said, "if you stay, then Mike should, too."

"Oh, really?"

"For Kimmy's sake, honey—that's all I meant."

"We'll see," Lena said, and she promised to call in the morning after they'd all gotten a real night's sleep.

While Bob Yazzie finished up the paperwork on Danny, Mike rejoined Lena. "You get hold of Gloria all right?" he asked, looking down at Kimmy.

"Oh, yes," she said, "and I had to tell her everything.

Kimmy talked to her, too. Mike, she said she'd send plane tickets...."

But he only shook his head. "Later. We'll figure it out later."

The helicopter lifted off as Mike was on the telephone to his father in L.A. They talked some about everyone who'd want a piece of Daniel Hayden: the LAPD, the state of New Mexico, the FBI. It seemed it was going to take a while to sort it all out. Lena half listened, but the only thing that mattered was for Hayden to be behind bars. And, she hoped, for a very, very long time.

Mike also phoned John Hidalgo, and at one point he signaled Lena to pick up the line. The first thing John said to her was, "That was an A-number-one stupid thing you did, Lena. But congratulations anyway. Now, get some rest."

"I will," she said, "and thanks for everything, really."

"Oh, payback will come. I'm vacationing with the family in L.A. this winter. You could cook us a real meal."

"Done," Lena said. Then she asked, "How's Jane Cramm. Mike told me...?"

"She's under psychological evaluation, not to mention drying out."

"What will happen to her?"

"Depends. A judge will have to decide if she's competent to face charges. It's going to take months."

"I almost feel sorry for her," Lena said. "I think she only wanted Kimmy. It was Danny with the bigger plans."

"You may be right," John said. "Kimberly wasn't his first, either. We're about to tie him into another kidnapping. The child got away. She was older than Kimmy, and she disappeared. We may have a line on her now.''

Lena squeezed her eyes shut. ''Oh, God, I hope you find her. You'll let us know?''

''Of course,'' John said, and Mike took over the conversation from the other phone.

It was a long, long afternoon before Bob gave them a ride to the Holiday Inn—owned and operated by the Navajos—a few blocks down the road.

Lena was exhausted. Still, Kimmy needed dinner and, she guessed, so did she. She and Mike got two adjoining rooms, then met in the dining room.

As they were being seated, Mike mouthed over Kimmy's head, ''Do we tell her who I am?''

''Tomorrow,'' Lena said. ''We'll tell her in the morning.'' She gave him a weak smile.

By nine they were all in their beds. Kimmy had fallen asleep instantly, but Lena lay there, her body thrumming with weariness, overtired. She kept one hand on her sleeping daughter, not quite believing she had her back. She watched the TV for a half hour or so, trying to settle her thoughts, but it was no good. It wasn't Danny or her ordeal that was keeping her up. It was Mike. Just on the other side of that door. The last time she'd put her head on a pillow he'd been there with her. An eternity ago. Or was it only moments? she wondered, and she could almost feel his phantom touch on her skin and the way he'd held her all night; long, long after their desire was quenched, Mike had held her.

CHAPTER EIGHTEEN

IN THE END Mike insisted on staying with them in Kayenta while the car was being repaired.

"But don't you have to get back to work?" Lena asked over breakfast at the Holiday Inn coffee shop.

"Don't worry about it. I've got some time coming."

"What about the basketball team? Surely they're counting on you…"

"Called last night, and I've got it covered."

"But…"

"Lena, I'm staying. You'll need help on the drive home anyway."

She looked at him for a moment and then nodded.

Mike cleared his throat. "There's a more important matter right now." He glanced at Kimmy, who was putting far too much syrup on a waffle, and Lena knew exactly what he was getting at. It was going to be difficult, more than difficult telling her the whole truth. She wondered if Kimmy could handle it all. Were kids that resilient?

She looked at Mike again. "Are you sure?"

"Yes," he said firmly.

Lena had been mentally preparing for this moment for years, ever since they'd adopted Kimmy. She'd read all the books on how to tell adopted children where they came from, and they all agreed on one thing: regardless of the age, never lie to a child.

She let out a breath. "I'll do it. Let me do it, okay? After we eat. Maybe you could… Well, I'll need you there."

"Okay," he said, and he turned his gaze on Kimmy. "Hey, now, aren't you drowning that poor waffle?"

She looked up at him with big brown eyes. "You can't drown a waffle," she said.

"If you're going to pour all that syrup on it, you'd better eat it, sweetie," Lena said.

After breakfast they went outside and sat in chairs in the autumn sun by the side of the empty swimming pool. The day promised to be warm again, but the morning air was cool in the high desert this time of year.

"Come here, Kimberly," Lena said. "I want to talk to you."

Kimmy came, standing between Lena's knees, regarding her mother with great, dark, serious eyes.

"It's about Mike," Lena began, feeling her face grow hot with discomfort.

"Uh-huh," Kimmy said.

Lena looked at Mike, as if for help, then she tried again. "Well, see, sweetie, Mike and I… Mike is…" She faltered, and gave Mike a look that said she needed him.

"Come here, Kimmy," Mike said.

Mike took the girl's hand and tugged her over to stand in front of him. He put his big hands on Kimmy's arms and looked her straight in the eye. "What your mother's trying to say is that I'm your father, Kimmy."

Silence held them all for a moment, then Kimmy asked, "Is he really my daddy, Mommy?"

"Yes," Lena whispered.

Kimmy cocked her head and studied Mike. "You're my daddy?"

"Yes," he said.

Kimmy frowned. "But my daddy is far away. He's sick."

"I'm better now, sweetheart. All better."

Wordlessly Kimmy retreated to the shelter of her mother's embrace. She didn't say anything, but she watched Mike while Lena held her, watched him with a disconcerting child's stare.

Lena kissed the top of Kimmy's head. She hoped this wouldn't backfire—the poor child, so much heaped on her shoulders. "It's okay, Kimmy. I know this is confusing, all this stuff happening."

"I want to go home," Kimmy mumbled against Lena's chest while the two adults locked gazes above her head.

"We will, sweetie. We'll go home as soon as the car's fixed. Grandma's there taking care of everything."

Kimmy peeked at Mike. "Are you my real, real daddy?" she asked.

"Yes," Mike replied, "and I love you very much. Even when I was…sick, I always loved you."

She turned her face into Lena's chest again, and Lena felt her warm little body and worried that Kimmy couldn't take this, that it would damage her. What kind of scar would this leave on the innocent child's psyche so soon after the kidnapping?

Kimmy looked at Mike again. Shyly, still holding on to Lena's shirt with both hands, she asked, "Am I supposed to call you 'Daddy'?"

Mike smiled at her. "You can call me anything you want."

"How come you're my daddy?" she asked.

"Well," Mike said, "see, your mom and I were married."

"You were?"

"We used to be married, and then I got... Well, I was sick, and we got divorced, and that's why you don't remember me. You were a tiny baby when I...went away."

Kimmy thought about that for a time, then she asked Lena, "Why did that lady say she was my real mommy?"

Lena told herself to stay cool. She'd known the time would come. "Oh, Kimmy, it's kind of complicated, but you're a big enough girl to understand." She set her child on her lap and held her very close. "See, it's like this, Kimmy. You know babies grow inside mommies, right? Like when Ally's mother had her baby brother, remember?"

Kimmy nodded.

"So, this lady, Jane, was your birth mother. That means she gave birth to you, sweetie, you understand? But she couldn't keep you—she had lots of problems—so your daddy and I adopted you. You were our own little girl then."

"You 'dopted me," Kimmy repeated.

"Yes, we did. See, that makes you very, very special, because we picked you, we chose you, out of all the babies in the whole wide world."

"Did that lady want me back?"

"I think so," Lena said softly. "She loved you, too. She just... Well, she can't take care of you."

Kimmy didn't seem upset; she appeared to accept the explanation the way children did when they were confronted with clear truths. *Never lie to a child,* Lena told herself again.

Kimmy nodded solemnly. "That lady wasn't pretty like you, Mommy," was all she said.

They took a walk, the three of them, across the street to the shopping center, down the street, then back. Wher-

ever you went in Kayenta you could see the line of striated bluffs on one side and the big red fist of smooth
rock that stuck up above town on the other. Eddies of
red dust blew across the street, running before the wind.

Kayenta was tiny, and there wasn't much to do, but
Lena was still so worn-out by her ordeal that the peace
seemed blissful. Just to walk under the vast blue sky
without fear was a blessing. She hadn't realized how constant fear had depleted her energy.

Kimmy walked between them, holding her mother's
hand. The only sign of her experience was a tendency to
stay close to Lena, to hold on to her and to keep her
teddy bear and blanket close, although she'd thought herself too old for them at home. She'd cried in her sleep
the night before, and she seemed more subdued than
usual. But it could have been much, much worse, Lena
knew.

"I hope the press doesn't get word of what's going
on," Mike said. "I asked everyone to keep quiet about
it, but you know the media. They'll figure it out pretty
soon. Someone will leak something."

Lena sighed. "I can't face anything like that right now.
I really can't."

"You won't have to," Mike assured her.

They strolled farther, stopping to look in a store window at the display of silver-and-turquoise jewelry.

"Let's go in," Mike said.

It was very beautifully crafted stuff, authentic Navajo
designs. The owner was named Madeline Begay, and she
was glad for someone to chat with.

"Well, the summer crowds are gone now, but there
are still a few tourists, so I stay open," she told them.
"My family makes the jewelry, and there are a lot of

them—my mother's whole clan—so I'm always supplied with plenty of pieces.''

"Mommy, look," Kimmy said, her face glued to a glass display case.

Lena went over to her daughter to see what she was interested in.

"Look, Mommy, see?"

It was a necklace, a fine silver chain holding a tiny silver-and-turquoise bird.

"Oh, it's a bluebird, Kimmy," Lena said. "How beautiful."

Madeline Begay opened the case, took the necklace out and hung it around Kimmy's neck. "There, isn't he a nice bird?"

"Now, Kimmy," Lena started, but Mike interrupted her.

"We'll take it," he said, pulling out his wallet.

"Mike, you don't have to…" Lena began.

"I know I don't, but I want to."

"I can keep it?" Kimmy asked, wide-eyed, her hand on the tiny silver bird.

"Yes," Mike said. "It's yours."

"What do you say?" Lena asked.

"Thank you, thank you very much," Kimmy said shyly, "Daddy."

They walked back to the motel. Kimmy kept her hand on the necklace, and there was a smile on her face. When Lena next glanced down, she saw that her daughter had silently taken Mike's hand, walking between them, occasionally skipping or hopping, holding on to them both, and it seemed as natural as breathing for her.

Tears burned behind Lena's eyelids, but she blinked them back. She stole a sidelong glance at Mike; he was studiously staring straight ahead, but she could see a muscle working in his jaw. Her heart felt full, and she tried to banish any thoughts of the future. This was good enough for now—it was better than good; it was wonderful.

They had lunch, and Lena relaxed into the slow, easy pace. Mike went to his room to make some calls while Lena and Kimmy walked a block to the gas station where they'd towed her car.

"The part's on its way," the mechanic said. "Had to order it from Phoenix. Don't see too many of these around nowadays. Those old 409s were fast. Still runs good, does it?"

"Oh, it runs great," Lena said. And they swapped car stories until Kimmy grew restless.

"So you think it'll be done in a couple of days?" Lena asked while Kimmy tugged at her hand.

"Two or three, depending on how busy I get."

"Well, you know where to reach me," Lena said.

Time stretched out before them, uncluttered. There was absolutely nothing to do. It occurred to Lena that Kimmy would need to be examined by a doctor and a psychologist, but not now, not yet. For now, she just wanted to luxuriate in the peace and quiet of this special little town in the middle of nowhere.

She bought a couple of children's books in the grocery store and a paperback for herself, although she felt as if she'd fall asleep if she tried to read. Her mind and her body had slowed down, recovering from trauma.

Kimmy hadn't slowed down, though. Her natural childish exuberance and energy were reappearing as if by magic. She swung on Lena's hand, dancing, hopping. She sang one of the songs she'd learned at school, then she stopped to hold up her bluebird and admire it.

"He's a nice man," she announced on their way back to their room.

"Do you mean Mike?" Lena asked.

"My daddy," Kimmy said. "I mean my daddy." She looked up at Lena. "Not like that mean man, that Danny."

"Did Danny hurt you?" Lena asked carefully.

"No," Kimmy said, skipping, "but he yelled at me. He yelled bad stuff. At Jane, too."

"He was a very bad man," Lena said.

"I know." Kimmy nodded wisely.

Lena took a breath. Of course she and Mike had discussed when to talk to Kimberly about the movie. It was a difficult subject to bring up, and they'd decided to wait for an opening. She had one now. She only wished Mike were there, too.

She took another breath. "Kimmy, Danny wanted you to be in a movie. Did you understand about that?" *Oh, God,* she thought. How much *had* Kimmy understood?

"Uh-huh," Kimmy said, not the least bit shy or afraid. "I played hide-and-seek outside one day."

"And someone took pictures of that?"

"Uh-huh."

"And that was…all?"

"Uh-huh. I was sleepy, so Danny took me home. He wasn't even mean that day. He got me a candy bar."

"Oh," Lena said, her emotions flying between relief and anger, and she wondered if the FBI could get Danny Hayden to name the other men involved. She prayed that they could.

"Well, listen, Kimmy, if you ever want to talk about Danny and Jane, or if you remember something they did that you didn't like, you tell me, okay?"

"Okay, Mommy."

"You may have to talk to some people when we get home about it. The police, for instance. They may want to know all the things Danny did."

"Okay."

She squeezed her daughter's hand. "That's a good, brave girl, sweetie."

While Kimmy took a bubble bath that afternoon, Lena and Mike sat in her room and talked, Lena telling him that she believed the movie had never gone further than the preliminary stages. "God, I hate that Danny Hayden," she said. "I hope they lock him up and throw away the key. But, Mike, what if he tries to make a deal? You know, by ratting on the other men involved?"

"Oh, he'll probably rat, all right," Mike said. "But it won't get him anywhere on a kidnapping charge."

"You're sure?"

"Absolutely positive."

"Good," she said staunchly.

They made small talk over the sounds of Kimmy's splashing coming from the bath.

"You got all your calls made?" Lena asked.

"Yes."

"To your father and everyone?"

"Yes, Lena."

"Mmm," she said, picking up a brochure from the table and leafing through it idly. "Did you get hold of your friend, Jennifer?"

He was silent for a moment, then said, "Yes, I did."

"Mmm," Lena said again. "I imagine she must be upset. Well, you know, about your being here in Kayenta and all." *Babbling,* Lena thought, *you're babbling.*

Mike didn't reply.

"Of course it's not my business," she went on recklessly, "but I just hope it works out now, you know, what with your marriage plans and all."

Mike looked up sharply. "I never said that."

"Colleen told me."

He swore loudly, then stopped abruptly, remembering Kimmy. "It's not like we set a date or anything, for God's sake. Colleen doesn't know a damn thing about it."

"Mmm," Lena said, and she couldn't help wondering if Mike had told Jennifer everything. If the roles were reversed, would she herself have the guts to confess to a fiancé that she'd slept with her ex?

Lena sneaked a glance at him. Mike would tell all, she suddenly knew. He'd tell the truth no matter what the consequences. So what *had* Jennifer thought?

At an early supper that evening Lena was still wondering, studying him, watching how he interacted with Kimmy. He'd changed; he really had. He'd certainly changed more than *she* had. All those qualities she'd fallen in love with were still there, but the overlay of bad ones were gone. How he must have suffered, she thought. His partner dead, his drinking out of control, his wife gone with his baby daughter. He'd been totally alone, trying to deal with his pain. Oh, sure, he had his family, but the Quinn men lacked the kind of sympathetic touch Mike would have needed. They were all macho, admitting to no weaknesses, and they wouldn't have been much help at all.

It kept coming back to Lena, the feeling of guilt—she should have been there; she should have stayed with him. He'd needed her, she realized now, far too late, but she'd been unable to handle his drinking.

He didn't blame her, it seemed. His anger and his anguish appeared to be washed away, and she was so very glad for him. And she wondered whether she could forgive Mike as completely as he forgave her.

THE NEXT DAY went by as slowly and uneventfully as the first. It rained that day, though, black thunderclouds amassing to the west over the striated mesas and the stark rising remnants of ancient volcanoes. Lena read to Kimmy, sitting in bed, cuddled together. The books she'd found were Navajo stories about clever foxes and mischievous coyotes and ravens and stars in the sky.

Mike knocked on the door at lunchtime and brought them a bag of fast food, so they all ate together.

"Bob Yazzie's gotten several calls from TV stations and papers," he said.

"I knew it," Lena said dejectedly.

"He's instructed all his men to keep quiet. No comment, that sort of thing."

"Maybe the car will be fixed before they inundate the place," she said hopefully.

"How's it coming?"

"The part's here. He'll install it tomorrow. We can probably leave the next day."

"We're going home?" Kimmy asked, jumping on the bed in her stocking feet.

"In a couple of days. Stop that, Kimberly."

"I'm bo-o-ored," Kimmy said, jumping, bouncing.

"Let me take her for a while," Mike suggested.

"It's raining."

"I've got a plastic poncho with me. You get some rest."

"Why—do I look like I need it?" Lena asked.

"No, you look fine. I just thought Kimmy and I could get to know each other."

"You're going to spoil her."

"Yeah, probably." Mike grinned. "It's my pleasure."

"Come on, come on, let's go," Kimmy chanted, running to put on her shoes. "I can tie my laces," she announced proudly. "I learned to a long time ago. Grandma taught me." She sat on the floor, concentrating on the shoelaces, her mouth half-open.

"God, she's cute," Mike said.

"She seems okay, doesn't she?" Lena asked quietly. "No trauma?"

"She seems fine. Remarkably."

"I worry, you know, what something like that can do to a child."

"Sure you do. So do I."

"I'm trying not to be overprotective," she said, "but it's hard."

"Nothing like that will ever happen to her again."

"My brain knows it, but in my gut I'm still terrified. I don't want to let her out of my sight."

"You're going to have to for a little while here," he said. "For starters, anyway."

"I will. I have to. She's got to go back to school, too."

"She'll be fine."

Lena only bit her lower lip, and Mike took her hand and stroked the back of it, holding on to her fingers. "She'll be okay, Lena, and she'll probably get over the whole thing before you do."

"Kids." She gave him an uncertain smile.

"Yeah, kids."

He took Kimmy with him out into the rain, and Lena sat propped up on the bed and read the book she'd bought. The print began to swim before her eyes, and her head nodded, and the next thing she knew, there was knocking at her door and Kimmy was calling, "Mommy, Mommy, let us in!"

Her daughter danced into the room, decked out in a colorful Navajo dress with a silver concho belt and leather moccasins. Someone had even braided her long brown hair.

"My goodness!" Lena exclaimed. "We've got a real live Indian girl here."

"Isn't it pretty, Mommy? And the lady braided my hair, too."

Lena met Mike's gaze. "You're spoiling her rotten."

"I know," he said proudly.

That evening they were invited to Bob Yazzie's house for dinner. He lived within walking distance in a neat bungalow with his wife, Betty.

Lena put on one of the few as-yet-unworn articles of clothes she'd brought, a red V-neck blouse. At least it was colorful. And *clean.*

Mike knocked on the door at six, so they could walk to the Yazzies' house.

"You look fantastic," he said to Lena.

"It's not too loud?" Lena asked.

"It's perfect. You know, you had on a red blouse when I first saw you."

"When you stopped me?" she asked, surprised.

"Uh-huh."

"You remember what I had on all those years ago?"

He shrugged.

She smiled, feeling her cheeks flush. "You're embarrassing me."

He met her gaze and held it. "I got you something."

"Oh, Mike…"

He dug in a pocket and took out a small white jewelry box. "Here," he said.

The box held a pair of earrings, silver-and-onyx, an intricate geometric design. Lena drew in her breath.

"I thought they looked like you," he said matter-of-factly.

"Mike," she whispered, and she felt an odd melting sensation, as if her insides were liquefying and flowing, warm and soft and joyful. "You're spoiling both of us."

"I'm enjoying the hell out of it," he said. "Making up for lost time."

A pang of guilt stabbed at Lena again, but she put it aside. This interlude could only be lived in the present, no anxiety about the future, no recriminations from the past. Only *now*. Her daughter, safe and sound, and Mike, her bastion against the outside world. "Thank you," she said, her eyes brimming.

"Put them on," he said, his blue eyes fastened on her, very serious, very intent.

She put the earrings on, looking in the mirror, then turned around. "What do you think?"

"You look pretty, Mommy," Kimmy said.

"Thanks, sweetie."

But Mike was silent, his gaze devouring her, until she had to turn away and make a big fuss putting Kimmy's jacket on over her Navajo dress.

Dinner at the Yazzies' was very pleasant. No exotic Indian food, but meat loaf and mashed potatoes and gravy, with ice cream for dessert.

"This is such a treat," Lena said. "Home cooking after days and days of restaurant food. Thank you so much."

"You sure are looking better than that first time I saw you at the gas station," Bob said bluntly.

"I must have been a sorry sight."

"You sure were."

"Bob, you're insulting our guest," Betty said.

"Oh, no, he's right, and I guess it was a good thing, because he noticed me. He remembered," Lena said.

Kimmy fell asleep on the Yazzies' couch, and Mike carried her all the way back to the motel.

"She's heavy," he said.

"I haven't carried her in years," Lena said. "She got too heavy for me when she was three, I think."

He shifted the sleeping child in his arms. "I kind of enjoy carrying her."

"She likes you, Mike," Lena ventured.

"Yeah, she seems to," he allowed. "She's a great kid. You did a good job with her."

Lena ducked her head. "It would have been better to have had her father around," she murmured.

"Well, she has him around now."

When they reached the motel, Mike came in with Lena and laid Kimmy on her bed.

"Thanks," Lena said.

He seemed reluctant to leave, standing there, so big in the small motel room. "This has been nice," he said finally, "this time together."

She nodded wordlessly.

"It's going to be over soon," he went on, "but I hope you'll let me see Kimmy when we get home."

"Of course I will, Mike."

"That's good. And you, too, Lena. I'll see you, and I don't want... I'd like it to be friendly between us."

Friendly. "I don't see why not."

"Good. Well, see you tomorrow."

BY THE FOLLOWING afternoon, Lena's car was repaired. It was too late to start that day, so they made plans to leave early the next morning. Lena called her mother to tell her, and Mike called his family and Joe Carbone at work. They ate their last dinner in Kayenta in the Holiday Inn dining room, which had become very familiar to them by now. The waitress knew their names and suggested menu items for Kimmy.

Lena was both anxious to get on the road, to get home, to take up the reins of her job again, and at the same time a little afraid of the new route her life was going to take. Not only would she have to deal with any problems her daughter might have, but she'd also have to deal with Mike in her life again.

After dinner they took a walk, said goodbye to Bob Yazzie and his wife, then watched TV in the motel lobby while Kimmy colored in a book on the floor. Peaceful, quiet, relaxing hours and minutes. But these were the last easy hours—tomorrow it would all end.

Lena said good-night to Mike at the door to her room, tucked Kimmy into bed and turned the TV set on low while she changed into her pajamas and brushed her teeth. The whole time her mind was working, though. The one thing that was still a wedge in her newfound friendship with Mike was the apology she truly did owe him. She'd basked in this interlude, this protective cocoon here in Kayenta, and she'd avoided talking to him, coming clean.

She rinsed her mouth and stared at herself in the mirror, painfully aware of Mike next door, painfully aware of the need to bare her soul.

She left the bathroom, and in the dimness of the bedroom she threw on her jeans and a shirt, then pulled open her side of the double doors to Mike's room and stuck the room key in her pocket. She glanced at Kimmy, who was fast asleep, and then let herself out and stood before Mike's door. She lifted her hand and knocked softly. *Crazy,* she thought. *This might be a crazy idea.*

Maybe she should do this another time. *I hope he's asleep,* she was thinking, but he opened the door before she completed the thought.

"Something wrong?" he asked. He was in his boxer shorts, no shirt, his blond hair mussed.

"Oh, I'm sorry. You were asleep," Lena said, backing away. "I'll…"

"Are you okay?"

"Yes, sure, no problem. I just wanted to… I'll, uh, go to bed now."

"Come in," he said, reaching out to draw her into the room.

She was terribly ill at ease, knowing she never should have done this. Good Lord, what had she been thinking?

But Mike was sitting on the edge of his bed and running a hand through his hair. He looked up and said, "What is it, Lena?"

She stood there, in a room that smelled distinctly, uniquely, of this man, feeling lost and frightened and very foolish. "I'm sorry. I shouldn't have—"

He cut her off. "What's on your mind?"

"I…well…" *Oh, God.*

He stared at her, his eyes in shadow, backlit only by a lamp on his night table. "Come on, Lena, I know you. Something's bugging you. Come here." He held a hand out.

She went to him, not knowing what else to do. She sat next to him on the bed, stiff, her hands clasped on her lap, her shoulders tense. "I wanted to apologize, Mike. I was wrong. And it's hard for me to admit that, but I was wrong all these years. I should have let you be part of Kimmy's life. I was selfish and…"

"That's what was bugging you?" he asked.

"Yes." She looked down at her hands, her shoulders hunched.

"Ah, Lena," he said, his voice a low caress.

"It was because of my father, I guess. His drinking…and then he was so sick…and I couldn't face it all over again. I was so scared, Mike."

"I know," he said. He took her hand, stroking the smooth underside of her wrist. "And I owe you an apology, too. For what I did to you, to our marriage."

"But then you changed, Mike, and I didn't. I just went on being…"

"That's all over now," he said. "It's all over, Lena."

"Is it, Mike?"

"Yeah, it is."

He drew her close, and she laid her head on his bare shoulder, drawing in his scent, feeling his warmth and the smooth hardness of him. His heart beat beneath her ear, slow and steady, and she put her hand on his chest to feel it. He kissed her then, a long, slow mingling of their mouths. He pulled back and looked at her. "You know how long I've been wanting this? Every night. I almost knocked on your door every night."

"Maybe you should have."

"I had no right."

She pulled his head down and pressed her lips to his, sipping the sweet nectar of his mouth, and his arms encircled her, crushing her softly. Her heart raced, and a slow heat began to burn inside her. She moaned with her need, and he laid her on the bed, stroking her face, her neck, bending to kiss her, trailing fire with his mouth, unbuttoning her shirt.

Her hands couldn't get enough of touching him, her mouth of tasting him. She felt whole in his closeness. Her jeans kicked off, her shirt trailing off one arm, she ran her hands up his back to the hair at the base of his neck, then down to his buttocks, pushing at the waist of his shorts, feeling his hardness pressing into her belly.

"Now," she whispered. "Please, now." There was no shame, no holding back, nothing but nearness and slick hot skin under her hands as he rose above her and into her, and her breath stopped in her throat for a moment, then caught and she was breathing again.

"Is it good?" he asked, his voice a rasp.

"Yes, yes, yes," she replied, and he rolled, pulling her with him, so that she was on top, raising and lowering herself. She felt ready to explode, but he moved once again, and she was beneath him, and he plunged into her, wild with his own need, again and again.

Something inside her burst, and she felt her body bucking under him, and her voice cried out.

He thrust into her once more, then groaned and convulsed over her, spilling his essence, and then he collapsed onto her, breathing fast, heavy, warm and damp and hard muscled.

Lena lay there, her chest rising and falling under Mike's weight, and nothing mattered just then—not tomorrow and not yesterday. It was, she guessed, just one more moment of her strange interlude. And then she closed her eyes, wallowing in the sensation of his body on hers, and let herself feel her own remorse and relief and love.

CHAPTER NINETEEN

WITHIN HOURS OF returning home, Lena was assailed by the media, with satellite vans in front of her house, reporters with video cameras and microphones at all hours of the day and night, incessant phone calls. The Woodland Hills police finally blocked off the street and tried to keep the vans away. She changed her phone number, never went out without sunglasses and a hat and tried desperately to keep Kimmy insulated from the firestorm of publicity.

Still, she was treated to the sight of herself on the local news, slinking around, or Mike or Gloria or Kimmy caught with a telescopic lens, strangely wavering, disembodied by dancing electronic spots.

"Never talk to strangers" became a mantra that her daughter heard every day.

The furor died a natural death after several weeks and, except for one offer of a TV movie, Lena's world eventually settled down.

Kimmy was back in school, and her teacher had met with Lena. So far Kimmy seemed fine, but they were all keeping a very close eye on her.

Miss Trenholm had asked for parent volunteers to patrol the school playground after school, and the program was so successful that other elementary schools in the district were adopting it. Nevertheless, Gloria picked Kimmy up the minute classes were over. She got there so early that her granddaughter began to complain that she didn't get to play with her friends.

Lena had taken Kimmy to her pediatrician, who'd declared her perfectly healthy, which made Lena heave a giant sigh of relief. The doctor had nonetheless recommended a child psychologist, and Kimmy went once a week, just in case.

"She's an amazingly resilient little girl," the psychologist told Lena. "I don't think there'll be any lasting effects. Just make sure she has the opportunity to talk about her experience without feeling uncomfortable."

They saw Mike quite a bit. He visited; he ate dinner with them a couple of times a week; and sometimes, on weekends, Lena drove to Santa Monica to the salmon-colored apartment building where Mike lived. Kimmy loved it, as it was only a block from the beach.

"She's fine," Mike said one Sunday afternoon, "isn't she?"

They were sitting in the sun by the beach promenade, watching all the in-line skaters, the bicyclers, the teenagers with purple hair and nose rings. Kimmy was watching a juggler, fascinated.

"She seems to be fine," Lena replied.

"I swear she's grown since we got back."

"She needs new shoes already," Lena said, "and I just got her some before school started."

"You want me to take her shopping for them?"

"No, really, I wasn't hinting around, Mike," Lena said, laughing.

"I put money in an account every month for Kimmy, you know," he said. "You wouldn't take anything from me, so I just put it away. It's there, Lena, whenever she needs it."

"Oh, Mike," she breathed. "We're doing okay. You don't have to..."

"She's my daughter, and I should be supporting her."

They'd had this argument many times over the past month. She was distinctly uncomfortable with the notion of Mike supporting Kimmy, and he was getting more and more frustrated at being shut out.

"I told you, save it for her college education," Lena said.

"I'll get her those shoes," Mike growled. "Maybe even two or three pairs."

"Oh, for goodness' sake." Lena sighed.

"Okay, okay, we'll discuss it later."

Lena turned her face up into the warm November sun and thought about the tentative relationship they had. When they'd first gotten home after Kimmy's ordeal it had somehow been easier between them. But then, she knew, that had been before Mike's breakup with Jennifer. He never told her the details, but he had sat at dinner in her house one evening and said, "I saw Jenn last night. We had an honest talk and decided it wasn't going to work."

Lena had looked up. "God, is it my fault? I mean..."

"Absolutely not," he'd said. "It's my fault if anyone's. In retrospect, it would never have worked out anyway. We were oil and water."

He'd left it at that, and a part of Lena had rejoiced, while another part had withdrawn in fear. And since then she simply didn't know how to feel. She was on an emotional tightrope.

Unspoken, but always in the forefront of their thoughts, was their daughter's welfare. Neither, it was understood, would do anything to jeopardize that.

"How's work?" Lena asked, switching to a safer subject.

"It's okay. I'm supposed to go up to San Francisco next month to do a seminar."

"That's good, Mike."

"I'd like you to meet Joe one of these days," he said. "He's been hearing a lot about you lately."

"Anytime." *Oh, Lord,* she thought, it was as if he were asking her to meet his family. *Dangerous.*

"Maybe we can all get together next week. There's a restaurant near here, sort of halfway between your place and his."

"Fine. I'd like to."

"My treat," Mike said.

That night after dinner Lena spoke to her mother.

"Yes, everything's fine," Lena said. "We're getting along fine. Kimmy adores him."

"So what's going to happen next?" Gloria asked.

"Next? The same thing. It's working very nicely. We meet, Kimmy enjoys herself, we go home to separate places, everything's great."

"You two can't go on like this."

"Why not?"

"Because it's not natural, honey."

"Oh, Mom."

"Okay, don't listen to me, but something's got to give sooner or later."

"Don't hold your breath, Mom."

But Lena had to admit that it was becoming harder and harder to keep Mike at arm's length, to stay neutral. It was so natural to want to touch him, to accept his chaste good-night kiss and wish for more, to confide in him. Watching Kimmy climb all over him, pull on his arms, kiss him with big smacks on his cheek, was wonderful, but his face, his whole demeanor, changed when he spoke to Lena. Then he was guarded, and the easy affection was transformed into stiff courtesy. Oh, how Lena would have loved to see him turn his open, boyish grin onto her.

Their last passionate meeting was a taboo subject. Yet it had happened, and just as the psychologist told Lena that Kimmy needed to deal with what happened, Lena knew the time of reckoning would come. The time when they'd both have to deal with the results of their actions.

The only certain things in Lena's life were her daughter and the clear knowledge that her love for Mike was like a delicate spring bud, dormant for so long and yet ripening with each passing day. She was terrified that it might blossom, yet thrilled at the same time. She wondered constantly, too, how he felt. Did he dream of her?

The dinner with Joe Carbone turned out to be a big affair. All the Quinns were there, and Mike had reserved a private room in the restaurant for the crowd. They all ate barbecued spareribs, a messy but cheerful meal, with paper bibs and sticky fingers.

"You're good for Mike," Joe told her after the meal was under way. "He's a happy guy these days."

She liked Joe—he was as bald as a billiard ball, with terrific character lines on his face. "Oh, I don't think it's me. It's Kimmy," she told him.

"Don't be too sure about that, little lady."

She smiled politely but didn't dare believe a word Joe said. It was good to see all the Quinns together, although they drank a lot of beer. But for once she didn't have to worry about Mike—he had plain old soda with a lemon wedge in it.

The only rough spot in the evening came when Colleen arrived just after dessert. Lena's heart clenched—Mike's nosy sister had to realize what had gone on between them. She was, after all, Jennifer's friend. But she said hello to Lena politely, and Lena wondered if Mike had lectured her. It didn't matter, really, because Lena and Mike had every right to be friends. Or so Lena told herself—friends.

Later, as Lena got into her car, Mike was there, leaning down to the open window. "Thanks for coming," he said. "Everyone enjoyed seeing you."

"It was a great evening, Mike. Thanks. And I like Joe a lot."

"Yeah, he's a good guy." He paused, then said, "You drive carefully, hear?"

"Yes, Officer," she replied pertly.

He smiled and raised a brow. "Tell Kimmy," he said, "that we'll do something on Sunday, okay? Saturday's out—got that basketball game with the guys."

"Okay," she said.

He reached in the window then and drew the back of his hand across her cheek. "See you Sunday."

"Uh-huh," she got out, her throat closing.

On Sunday he arrived with a new Barbie doll for Kimmy.

"You've got to stop this," Lena scolded.

"Do I tell you what to do? Let me be, Lena," he said, and the whole afternoon, while he was out with Kimmy at a movie, Lena kept wondering why she was pushing him away. Was she hiding from the truth, in denial?

The following Saturday she had to work. Normally Gloria would have watched Kimmy, but this time Mike was free and offered to take her for the whole day. He had big plans—they were going to Disneyland.

"Is it okay with you," he asked Lena, "if I take my

Adopt-a-Buddy along, too? Jay's a good kid, and he could use some fun.''

"Sure. It'll be good for Kimmy to share you with someone for a change.''

"I'll pick her up early, okay? Around eight.''

"You sure you can handle two kids all day at Disneyland?''

"If I can run a hostage negotiation, I'll bet I can manage two kids.''

Lena only grinned.

That day she got her work done, then did her grocery shopping on the way home. She even cleaned her house, not used to so much time on her hands. She cooked dinner, not sure whether Kimmy would eat out or not— Swedish meatballs and new red potatoes.

She heard Mike's car stop outside at a little past six, then Kimmy burst into the house, full of stories.

"Mommy, we rode all the rides, and we did the Small Small World one twice, and I saw Mickey Mouse, and the spaceship rocked like we were taking off, Mommy.''

"Wow. Sounds like you had a good time.''

Mike came in then, his shoulders sagging. She gave him a glance, then said, "You look beat.''

"I am. They ran me ragged.''

"I warned you.''

"And, Mommy,'' Kimmy went on, "Jay wasn't bad at all. He held my hand when I got scared in the spaceship.''

"That's wonderful,'' Lena said. "Did you guys eat?''

"She ate enough to feed an army,'' Mike said.

"Junk, I suppose.''

"Sure, lots of junk.'' He shrugged tiredly.

"What about you?''

"The cotton candy did me in, but some real food might revive me."

Kimmy nibbled at a meatball, still talking about her adventures. "The jungle ride was so cool, Mommy, and all the animals jumped out at me. Jay thought it was funny." But she was winding down, her eyes getting that glazed look of utter exhaustion.

"She's on overload," Lena said to Mike.

"What's that, Mommy?"

"You're tired," Lena replied. "I can tell."

"I'm not, I'm not."

They put Kimmy to bed early. Mike read her a story while Lena did the dishes, an inadvertent smile on her face as she listened to Mike's voice coming from down the hall.

He emerged from Kimmy's room, shutting the door quietly. "She's out," he said.

"Thanks for taking her. I never got around to it. I kept thinking I was going to, but, you know...."

"Sure, I know. You're busy."

They sat at the kitchen table across from each other. The house was silent. Mike sipped at a cup of coffee, and Lena rubbed at some crumbs she'd missed on the tabletop.

He broke the silence with a surprising suggestion. "I was wondering," he said hesitantly, "if we should consider moving in together. For Kimmy. All this commuting back and forth, well, it must be confusing for her."

Lena's heart gave a lurch, then settled down to beat slowly, turgidly. She couldn't meet his eyes. "I don't know, Mike, I..."

"I thought we could ask Kimmy about it first."

"She's only a little kid. I'm not sure it'd be good to put so much on her head," she fumbled.

"It was a thought."

Silence fell between them again, and Lena still felt her heart beating too heavily. He'd caught her off guard, completely off guard. And yet... Wasn't this the most honest he'd been since Kimmy's abduction?

She could barely face it, barely even begin to examine her feelings. *Don't deny* ran through her brain. *Talk to him. Be truthful.* But what was the truth?

"Well, what do you think?"

Be honest. Don't be a coward.

"I...I'm not sure. Do you think it could work?" She dared to meet his gaze.

"We could make it work," he said softly.

"God, Mike, it scares me to think about it. You know..."

"Sure I know."

"I've made a good life for myself. I've worked so hard. Mike, I can't go through it again and start over. I don't have it in me anymore."

"Believe me, I understand. But sometimes you have to take a risk, Lena, to get something better. Joe taught me that."

She clasped her hands together tightly. "I don't know."

He leaned toward her. "I'd never hurt you or Kimmy. That's a promise."

She looked at him hard, and she knew suddenly that more than anything in the world, she wanted this man. She'd always wanted him. Wanted her family together. Her heart felt as if it had shattered, too fragile to stand up to so much pressure all at once. She bit her lip and could say nothing.

Mike finally leaned back in his chair. "Well, think

about it. There's plenty of time.'' He pushed the chair back and stood up, stretching. ''I'd better go, I guess.''

She wanted so much to say, *Stay, hold me, love me, be with me,* but she was held immobile. *Coward,* she thought. *Sniveling coward.*

He came around the table and took her hand. ''You'll think about it?''

''Yes, I will,'' she breathed, and she offered no resistance when he carefully brought her to her feet and held her against him.

''Promise?'' he asked, his breath tickling her ear.

''Yes,'' she whispered.

He tilted her face up and brushed her lips with his. She couldn't fight it. She sighed and opened to him as he kissed her deeply, his tongue searching out the sweetness of her mouth.

He pulled back then, leaving her afloat without a life preserver, alone, chilled. She shivered.

''I'd better not start something I can't finish,'' he said with a wry smile.

She tried to smile back. ''Drive carefully,'' she said, a sad substitute for the feelings that were locked in her heart.

''Uh-huh.''

''Good night.''

''Bolt the door after me.''

''I will.''

''Good night, Lena.''

Later, as she drifted into sleep, a realization came to her out of the blue, something she hadn't considered or thought about or paid any attention to in the last month. She was late; she hadn't gotten her period last month.

MIKE QUINN REMEMBERED the day with utter clarity. It was a cool, drizzly November evening; he'd had a tough day, talking down a desperate man who'd lost his job and was holding his family hostage, threatening to kill them and himself. Mike had succeeded, but it had been a long, hard battle, and he'd had to call on every ounce of empathy and training he had in him.

All he wanted was to flop down in front of the TV set, put some food in his mouth to stave off his stomach's growling, then go to bed.

He saw the blinking red eye of his answering machine, and he was tempted to ignore it till morning, but there was always the possibility it was Kimmy—and she couldn't wait.

He pressed the replay button and stood, one shoulder against the wall, his arms folded, while he waited for the message to play.

It was Lena. "Please call me, Mike. It's important." That was all. Not even her name, but of course he knew her voice. And she'd sounded strange, upset maybe—or just tense. Had she made a decision about their living together? If so, her tone of voice did not bode well for him. Or, God forbid, had something happened to Kimmy?

He dialed her number quickly, worried. She answered as if she'd been waiting for the call. "Hello?"

"Lena, it's me. What…?"

"Oh, Mike, I'm so glad you called."

"What is it? Is Kimmy okay?"

"Yes, she's fine. It's not Kimmy. Oh, Mike…"

"For God's sake, what is it?"

There was a moment of absolute silence on the line, and Mike just had time to feel his hand on the receiver growing slick with sweat, when she spoke. Two simple words in a flat tone: "I'm pregnant."

He must have heard her wrong. "What?" he said.

"Mike, I'm pregnant."

This time the meaning sank in. Lena was pregnant. With his child. Lena was…

"Mike, are you there?"

"I…I'm not sure." He took a deep breath, feelings batting around inside his head like a cageful of agitated birds. "Wow."

"What are we going to do? What do you…?"

"I'm coming over," he said in a rush. "I'm not discussing this over the goddamn phone, Lena."

"You're angry. Oh, Mike, I knew you'd be angry. I'm sorry, I…I…"

"I'm not angry, Lena. I'm in shock."

"I didn't know what to do."

"You did the right thing, and I'll be there in half an hour. Don't move."

"Okay."

"Listen, I'll be more coherent by the time I get there—I swear I will."

"You're not upset?"

"Are you kidding?" he asked, then he hung up, his weariness forgotten. He grabbed the sport coat that he'd just thrown on a chair and strode out to his car.

All the way across Los Angeles, his mind churned with the news. It must have been that last night in Kayenta, he figured. He'd never thought, never considered. God, they'd acted like irresponsible teenagers! He should have… But he was fiercely glad it had happened, more than glad. Elated. He realized there was a dumb grin on his face, and it wouldn't go away.

Lena pregnant. A baby. His baby, his and Lena's. A little sister or brother for Kimmy.

It all seemed so simple to him. He loved Lena and she

was having his child—hell, she already had one of his children—and there really wasn't much else he could do about it but marry her. Sure. Marry her *again*. Only this time, it'd stick.

Of course Lena might have other ideas. She was one stubborn, independent lady now, no pushover. His joy faded for a moment. What if she didn't love him and didn't want to marry him?

Well, he'd damn well convince her. Those kids of his needed a father.

Convince Lena? he thought. *Good luck.*

He was a nervous wreck by the time he pulled up in front of her house. She opened the door just as he got to it and stood there looking at him. Her eyes were red. She'd been crying.

He took her arm and steered her inside, closing the door behind him. He'd decided to come on strong right from the first, to brook no dissent. He was the child's *father,* for God's sake.

"We're getting married," he said firmly. "Lena, I've thought about it, and it's the only thing to do, and damn it, I don't want any argument about it."

"Married," she said faintly.

"Yes, married. You know, with a ring, in the church, all the folks there. So your kids have their father."

She looked at him for a breath of time, then whispered, "Okay."

"What?"

"I said okay."

"So, it's a deal?" he said, his gaze on her disbelievingly.

"It's a deal," she breathed.

He held his arms out, and she came to him, nestling there as if they'd never been apart. He kissed away her tears. "I never thought I'd be so lucky a second time," he said softly.

"We have to tell Kimmy. I haven't said a word to her. I was worried you'd... Well, that it wouldn't work out."

"Where is she?"

"In her room coloring. I didn't even tell her I'd called you or that you were coming over."

"We'd better face her, don't you think?"

Lena nodded.

They went to Kimmy's room together, holding hands.

"Hi, Daddy," Kimmy said, looking up from the floor where she knelt amid her crayons.

"Hi, sweetheart. Mommy and I have something to tell you."

Kimmy waited, her big brown eyes on him.

"Well, see, your mother is going to have a baby, and so we thought we'd get married."

Kimmy thought a moment, then she said guilelessly, "I'd like a little sister to play with."

Mike and Lena looked at each other. "Is that all you have to say?" Lena asked.

Kimmy considered the question, her brows coming together. "Well, I guess a brother would be okay."

Mike looked at Lena; she stood there, her hand over her mouth, baffled. Then she gave a little hiccup of laughter and put a hand on his arm, trying to say something, but she was laughing too hard. And then he was laughing, too, and Kimmy was watching them, puzzled, but they couldn't stop, and everything good and worthwhile in the world was right there in that room.

His family.

You Were On My Mind
MARGOT EARLY

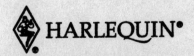

HARLEQUIN®

TORONTO • NEW YORK • LONDON
AMSTERDAM • PARIS • SYDNEY • HAMBURG
STOCKHOLM • ATHENS • TOKYO • MILAN • MADRID
PRAGUE • WARSAW • BUDAPEST • AUCKLAND

PROLOGUE

Jenny Hix, Tennessee
November

"PEOPLE MUST BE GETTING their Christmas packages in the mail early."

"Before Thanksgiving?" Tara laughed. "I doubt it, Mom." The line was creeping, but Tara recognized several faces from the midwifery conference she and her mother and her sister, Ivy, had just attended. The conference, hosted by a local midwifery school, must have doubled the size of the small town of Jenny Hix. And sure, they'd be in this line for twenty minutes, but "You know, I'm so high from the conference that not even this line can get me down."

Her mother sighed.

"You don't have to wait, Mom. Why don't you go find Ivy, and I'll meet you guys at the deli?"

"No." Francesca sighed again. "Let's stick to our plan. If I try to find Ivy, she'll probably come back here, and I'll miss her. You know how it is."

If she sighs one more time, I'm going to lose it. The sighs asked more plainly than words why Tara needed to mail a check to the phone company right now, today. Tara saw no reason to share that particular war story with her mother, though she'd told Ivy; there was nothing you couldn't tell Ivy. She'd realized that soon after meeting Ivy seven years ago. Ivy was special, which was most of why Tara had suggested to her mother that they adopt her, make Ivy part of their family. It wasn't a legal adoption, but they'd had a ceremony, and Ivy had taken Francesca's last name as her own.

Anyhow, if she tried to explain to Francesca about the last time her phone was cut off, her mother would suggest she quit working at Maternity House—the birth clinic on the border paid very little—go to nursing school, get certified as a nurse-midwife....

That conversation just wasn't going to happen. No way was she going to bow to the political pressure to become a certified nurse-midwife. She'd attended over two thousand births in three countries, with just one stillbirth and one Down's baby—unavoidable outcomes in each case. If anything, the midwifery conference had strengthened her conviction to remain a direct-entry midwife, whatever the legal and financial ramifications, whatever the personal cost.

The post office line moved again. Francesca was rubbing her temples. Irritated, Tara faced the posters on the corkboard above the desk. Wanted posters, missing persons. It looked like no one ever changed the posters; one of them was for a man who'd disappeared in 1984.

Tara studied the faces of two missing girls. She wished she knew them, had seen them alive and well. She wished she could reassure their families. But the faces were unfamiliar, and she moved on to another poster, showing a woman who had disappeared from Guyandotte, West Virginia, a decade ago.

Gasping, she grabbed Francesca and spun her around. "Look. *Look.*"

"Oh, God. Now what?"

"Keep my place." Tara climbed over the cable and crowded up against a trash can to scrutinize the poster. The woman was blond and blue-eyed, born 9-13-66. Her suntan brought out a light smattering of freckles. Tara studied the small, straight nose, the wide smile and even white teeth. Only the hair was different—shoulder length and turned up at the ends in the picture, long and straight now.

She took a deep breath and read the instructions, what sheriff's office to contact. She should write down the number. Oh, hell…

"Tara!" her mother hissed as Tara tore down the poster. "I think that's illegal."

Tara had been in jail so many times she'd lost count. Student demonstrations, practicing medicine without a license, standing up against oppression in Chile—and plain old bad luck in Mexico. Ignoring her mother's protest, she climbed back over the cable and handed her the flyer. When she spoke, her voice cracked. "It's *Ivy.*"

CHAPTER ONE

Guyandotte, West Virginia

SOMETHING HAD HAPPENED. Cullen knew it.

To Gabriela?

Or to Daddy...?

The sheriff of Guyandotte County, West Virginia, had not come into Mountain Photography for a new campaign photo. He was wearing his got-news-for-you face.

"Hi, Orrin." Cullen waited for bad news the way he had ten years ago, for news that Gina's body had been found.

"Cully." Orrin Pratt had known him since he was five years old and licking an ice-cream cone in his daddy's chambers at the courthouse. The sheriff arranged his bulk in one of the customer chairs in front of the reception desk. "How's business?"

"Good." He'd just finished up school photos and he had four weddings booked before Christmas. *Say it, Orrin. Whatever it is, you're making me nervous.*

The sheriff flipped open the album on the desk, skimmed the graduation photos and baby pictures. Then he shut the book with a bang.

He wouldn't be acting this way if someone was hurt.

Or dead.

"Found your wife, Cully. And she's alive."

THE STUDIO HAD NEVER seemed so quiet. The name, phone number and address the sheriff had left stared up at Cullen from the counter. *She figured you might have remarried. She wanted you to have the chance to contact her when you felt ready. But count on it, if you don't, she'll contact you. We had to tell her the basics, Cully.*

The basics were a husband.

And a daughter. Gabriela.

Cullen massaged the bridge of his nose and reread the slip of paper.

Ivy Walcott, P. O. Box 39, Precipice, Colorado.

She'd changed her name.

She's had a head injury, Cully. Has no recollection of her life as Gina Till. Or Gina Naggy, before she'd married him.

How would he tell Gabriela? Not just Gabriela, either. He shut his eyes and pictured the faces in his life. His daughter, his parents, his sister and her husband, his sister-in-law...

Matthew.

And one more face, the face he really didn't want to see, especially after he shared this news.

Tracy would recover fast and say how wonderful for Gabriela. She would back off from him and respect the bonds of his marriage to a woman the sheriff had assured him would be a perfect stranger—and would consider him a stranger, too.

As he reached for the phone, an idea occurred to him, casting a new slant on his ambivalence, on all his confused feelings.

If Gina didn't remember him, had *she* found someone else?

Precipice, Colorado

"IT'S FOR YOU." Blue eyes somber, Francesca handed the phone to her daughter, the daughter she'd adopted as an adult when Ivy had admitted to Tara and Francesca that she had no family of her own—and no past she could remember. Now, seven years later, Ivy's unremembered past was on the phone. Covering the receiver, Francesca said, "It's him."

"Thanks, Mom." Ivy tried to make her smile reassuring.

Tara, who had decided to stay in Precipice until Ivy's husband contacted her, left the living room of the Victorian house Ivy and Francesca rented. Her mother followed. Ivy knew they'd done this to give her privacy.

But it felt like desertion.

She forced herself to speak. "Hello?"

"Hi. This is Cullen Till." The unfamiliar voice was deeper than she'd imagined, his slight drawl interesting, almost musical.

What did you say to the husband you hadn't seen for ten years and couldn't remember? The husband you would never remember. "Hi," she replied. "Thanks for calling."

"Yeah. You, too." He laughed, but not with humor. "I understand you've had brain damage."

"A temporal lobe lesion. Fortunately, I escaped a lot of the problems that usually go with a head injury. In fact, I'm a midwife—"

His sharp intake of breath stopped her. "Go on."

"But I lost my entire personality. My earliest memory is from ten years ago, in a hospital in Boulder. Someone found me down by the creek and brought me in." It was then that she'd walked into her own life in the second act, with no idea what had happened before.

And this man... She told him, "I'm so sorry. It must have been bad for you." The Colorado police had tried to learn her identity a decade ago, with no success. She'd known that someone, somewhere, must be worrying. "My sister... Sorry, that'll confuse you. My friends saw the flyer in a post office in Tennessee. We'd been at a midwifery conference. We called the sheriff right away."

"He told me." In his studio, Cullen held his head in his hand. She was a midwife. *You didn't lose as much of your personality as you think, Gina.*

Ivy settled on the nineteenth-century couch that Tara hated and Francesca treasured. It was a couch that made you sit on the edge of your seat, and there was no way she could do anything else. There was no other way she could ask the questions she must.

"I understand we have a daughter."

"Yes. Gabriela. She's twelve."

The sheriff had said her parents and grandparents were dead, that Cullen and Gabriela were her only known family. "And...have you remarried?"

She had time to untangle the phone cord halfway before he said, "No."

"I hope you didn't suffer much. Worrying."

After a pause he asked, "What about you? Involved with anyone else?"

"No."

He cleared his throat, away from the phone. "Then I'd like to see you."

To see me?

"I want you to come home."

Eight, nine, ten years ago, she would have donated an organ to hear someone say those words. Then, while she was in nursing school, she'd met Tara and Francesca at a midwifery conference. For the first time in her new existence, she'd found friends; it had been Tara's idea to invite her into their family. Now, Tara was her sister and Francesca her mother—the only family she had.

No. She had a family she couldn't recall in Guyandotte, West Virginia. A family who wanted Gina Till to come home.

But Gina Till was as dead as her husband must have feared.

"I want to see Gabriela. I definitely want to know my daughter. But I'm not the woman you remember. I won't know your face. I'll never share your memories."

"Unless I share them with you."

It sounded intimate, a man who'd loved the woman she used to be, carefully filling her in on her missing past.

A man and his daughter were waiting for her to come home. They'd waited ten years. She shivered. The man was a stranger to her; so was their daughter. A daughter she'd given birth to, and held and nursed and loved.

She said, "Do you mean…come there to stay?"

A long breath from the other end of the phone.

"I'm telling you, Cullen, I'm not the same."

"Nobody is after ten years. But I married you for the long haul. You have a home here with us if you want it."

He was brave or honorable or crazy—she didn't know which. She whispered, "The man who sets his sights firmly on the outcome will avoid the entanglements that befall people in relationships."

"What's that?"

"The *I Ching,* I think." She'd made him promises, too, in her former life. For richer for poorer, for better for worse, in sickness and in health.

This was the worse part.

Was it right to try to keep those vows? She wished the issue was black and white; instead it was foggy, obscured by mist and mountains. How many times during those first hours in Tennessee had she gazed northeast? They could have driven on to West Virginia, but she and Francesca had had pregnant clients waiting at home in Colorado.

Maybe Cullen still loved Gina Till. Maybe he was simply honoring his promise. In any case, he wanted her "home."

Who was this man? What did he look like? What did he believe? What did he eat for dinner? Was there any chance at all that they could be compatible? Given her usual disagreements with the men she dated, she didn't think so.

But they had a daughter.

She stalled. She asked him about himself and Gabriela.

They lived on her—Gina's—family property in a hundred-year-old cabin. She heard the satisfaction in his voice as he described the additions he'd made, how he'd tried to modernize without compromising the integrity of the building. He told her about his work, portrait and freelance photography. He drank little and didn't smoke. His parents and siblings lived fifteen minutes away from him and Gabriela. Gabriela took ballet. Gradually, he filled in some of the blanks in her life, as well as the years they'd spent apart.

Ivy remembered how she'd arrived at the Boulder hospital. The unanswered questions were all relevant.

"What kind of marriage did we have?"

Just a brief hesitation. "Loving. We were friends first. Like…the pillars of the temple."

"What do you mean?"

"The pillars of the temple must stand apart. Kahlil Gibran on marriage."

"That's beautiful."

In his studio, Cullen clutched an arm around himself. Gina had picked that reading for their wedding.

Ivy Walcott had never heard it.

Ivy said, "You never answered my question. If you're hoping I'll come to stay."

It seemed to her that his next pause wasn't hesitation. It was something else. "Yes."

"Because of Gabriela."

"Partly."

He has reason to want me back. For him, there were more than promises. There were memories. *But I have none of him.* She had only this conversation and the way the sheriff had spoken of him—with respect and familiarity. But Cullen Till held the keys to her past.

And they had a child.

"All right. I'll come…home." *This* was her home. With Francesca, in Colorado's San Juan Mountains. "I just want to request one thing."

"What's that?"

"That you please call me Ivy. It'll help you remember—that I'm not Gina anymore."

Silence on the line. "Sure. Ivy. Anything else?"

She couldn't think. "No. No."

A thousand miles away, Cullen wondered how much brain damage she really had. Because if he were a woman going to a strange town to move in with a perfect stranger, there was one more request he would have made.

GABRIELA HAD BALLET after school, and as Cullen walked to Tracy Kennedy's dance studio to meet his daughter, he wondered what to say. To both of them.

This is insane. Only two or three years had passed since he'd stopped hoping Gina would return, since he'd made a deliberate decision to let go. He and Tracy had been seeing each other for the past year. Now he didn't know what to feel.

Class was over, and students were leaving as he hurried through the glass door and the small foyer and past the dressing-room doors to the arch that led onto the polished oak dance floor. There was Gabriela, her hair in a loose ponytail as Gina used to wear hers. She swung her backpack onto her shoulders over layers of dancing clothes and joined her teacher, who was saying goodbye to a parent.

Tracy had gathered her frothy brown curls in a chignon at the base of her neck. She'd danced with the New York City Ballet before coming home to Guyandotte to open a studio. Cullen had known her younger sister in high school. Within a week of Tracy's return, Cullen had noticed her—but Gabriela had been her student for three years before he'd decided to ask her out. At first, it had seemed awkward, because she was four years older than him. That had faded on their first date.

She spotted him and waved, her smile accentuating her high cheekbones.

He returned the wave and waited for her and Gabriela to come to the door. No hiking boots allowed on the floor.

"Daddy, can we go to Tracy's for dinner?"

"Not tonight. School night."

Gabriela snapped her fingers in an "Oh, darn" gesture and made a face at Tracy.

Tracy's arm was already around his waist. "How was your day?"

An unanswerable question. His mind saw Gina's soft hair, her Joni Mitchell smile. "Interesting."

She released him, still keeping her hand on his back. The touch he'd once enjoyed suddenly irritated him, and he had to resist stepping away.

"Anything wrong?"

He opened his mouth. Hesitated. "I'll come by while Gabriela's doing her homework."

His daughter's mouth fell open. "That's not fair!"

"Of course it is. I don't have school tomorrow. Been there, done that."

"Oh, shut up." She elbowed him good-naturedly.

What is this going to do to her?

"If I hurry with my homework, can I come with you?"

"I don't know yet." He wasn't sure how he'd feel leaving Gabriela alone after delivering this news, but he didn't want her present when he told Tracy. If he owed Tracy anything, it was sensitivity. Especially now.

And already her dark eyes were searching his face, trying to read his feelings, guess what he had to say.

He wanted to tell her that he'd cared about her, that he'd always respected her. He would leave those things unspoken. There was little he could say beyond *I'm sorry.*

"DO YOU THINK YOU MIGHT marry Tracy?"

Cullen nearly drove the Camaro into the oak tree with three trunks at the end of Missing Girl Hollow, at the start of their road. Naggy's road. It had been Gina's grandmother's place, and Gina had put his name on the deed when she married him. *I'm grateful, Cullen. I want to give you something.*

Gabriela's question was the perfect lead-in.

"No." As he steered over the rutted dirt road and the cabin finally came into view through the dense trees, he formulated his words.

"Oh, I didn't want to be pushy, Dad. You know I'm happy with just the two of us. It's just…"

He parked the Camaro, the same car he'd driven in high school. Gina had ridden in this car. She wouldn't remember.

Ivy wouldn't remember.

"…if you were going to marry someone, I think it would be pretty cool if it was Tracy."

He switched off the ignition, unfastened his seat belt and turned in his seat. "Gabby, I don't know how to tell you this. I had a big shock today, and it's going to be a big shock for you, too."

Her face dropped. "Did Grandpa die?"

"No. No." He shook his head. "He'll probably live for years." Another problem pricked him. *One thing at a time.* "What happened is…I learned that your mother's alive. I talked to her on the phone, and…she's coming home. At least for a while."

Gabriela looked like she might throw up.

Quickly, trying to make everything clear, he filled

her in, sharing everything he knew. Especially the incomprehensible horror of Gina's lost memory. "She wants me to call her Ivy. And she doesn't seem like the kind of lady to insist that you call her Mom." He paused. "It's going to be hard for all of us."

"*Hard?* Some perfect stranger is coming to live with us? And what? You're just going to dump Tracy? Tracy's cool, and this other person sounds weird."

It was the last reaction he would have expected from Gabriela. In grade school, she'd tortured him with questions about Gina and made up amazing fantasies about her mother that she'd described to him. He'd always nodded solemnly as she went through those scenarios and said, "Could be." Could be she'd been kidnapped by a circus and taken behind the Iron Curtain. Could be she'd hit her head and gotten *amnesia*....

Oh, Gabby.

Hero worship for Tracy Kennedy was behind her rejection of Gina—Ivy.

"This other person," he said, "is your mother. And my wife. That's why she's coming home. However bad things have been for you and me, you can bet they've been just as hard for Ivy Walcott. Harder, even. Imagine waking up one day with no idea who you are and no one to take care of you. Imagine suspecting that people are worried about you, but you don't know who or how to reassure them."

Her blue eyes, eyes like Gina's, stared hard and angry at the dash. "I'm really sorry for her."

He'd had about two years to get sick of that smart-ass tone of voice, what he thought of as her Alanis Morissette act. This time, he let it go. "Gabby, I loved your mom. I still love her, in my heart." He touched his heart.

"Could have sworn you loved Tracy yesterday."

"Enough, Gabriela. Ivy is your mother. I'm not going to let anyone hurt you. But you need to respect her."

"How can you call her my mother? She's not even the same person you married!"

"She carried you inside her for nine months."

"I'm honored. I bet we'll make a really happy family." She overenunciated each syllable in "family."

"Gabriela. Start being honored. Start now."

"ON YOUR WAY TO MAKE Tracy's night?"

He zipped his parka. "Gabby. Would you please clean the bathroom before I get home?"

"Oh, that's *such* punishment." She lay on the couch that had been Ivy's grandmother's, reading Gelsey Kirkland's *Dancing on My Grave*. With her hair twisted up in a knot, she was a dead ringer for Gina at seventeen or eighteen. Already, boys were calling. Boys whose voices had changed. Cullen wanted to put her under lock and key.

Instead, each day she slipped further away from him.

He touched the knotty maple door frame, noted a place where the chinking was coming away from the logs. When he and Gina were married, he'd built on the loft upstairs and the sunroom addition in the back. Since then, he'd added onto the sides of the cabin, with a room for Gabriela and a place for her to practice ballet.

What would Ivy Walcott think of this place, the place where she'd grown up as Gina Naggy? Where she'd lost her mother when she was two—the same age at which Gabriela had lost hers.

Gabriela was reading again—or deliberately ignoring him.

"Why do you talk to me that way?"

"What way?"

"Put down that book and look at me."

She did. Almost.

"I asked you a question. Does it pain you that I pay for your ballet lessons and give you a clothing allowance? That I spent last December driving you to Charleston four times a week so you could be Clara in *The Nutcracker?*"

She blushed.

Her eyes sneaked a look at him. "I'm sorry, Daddy."

Only an ogre wouldn't forgive that expression, that voice.

"Thank you," he said. "Enjoy your night. And please clean the bathroom."

NOEL NATHAN WAS fourteen years old to Gabriela's twelve and a half. She lived next door to Grandpa and Grandma's house, Coalgood, and she was Gabriela's best friend, the only person with whom she could possibly share this abysmal news.

"So, it's like this *stranger* is coming to live with us. A brain-damaged stranger. Bet she's lively." Holding the phone against her ear with her shoulder, Gabriela painted her toenails black. She would put white moons and stars on them next. Her cheek pushed the button on the phone, interrupting Noel's reply with a loud beep. "Sorry, sorry. I'm painting my toenails."

"I said, she's your mother. Aren't you excited to meet her?"

"If you hadn't seen your mother since you were two and in the meantime she hit her head and forgot you existed, would *you* be excited?"

"You've got a point." Noel wasn't stupid. "But is your dad excited? I've seen her picture. She's totally beautiful, and you look just like her."

"Thanks. I guess he's excited. He gave me all this 'Honor thy father and mother' crap today. At least, that's what it felt like."

"What's Tracy going to do?" Noel was in Gabriela's ballet class, and everyone knew the ballet mistress was going out with Gabriela's dad.

"Get over it, I guess."

"Your dad's a hunk. Gosh, Gabs, you could drive your mother away like the twins did to the icky fiancée in *The Parent Trap*."

Gabriela snorted. "Excuse me? We are talking about my mother."

"Sorry," answered her friend. "Sorry, sorry. Well, I hope she's cool."

"Yeah. Me, too." Drive her away... *Real funny, Noel.* But at least her friend hadn't brought up all the speculation. It was crazy to grow up never knowing what had happened to your mother. Some people thought she'd walked out on her husband and daughter. Others thought she'd been murdered.

Dad had always said, "You know, Gabby, anything could have happened. There's no way of knowing, but I'll tell you one thing. Your mother loved you." And that had pretty much kept Gabriela from losing her mind thinking about her mother walking out on her family.

She *had* thought about her being murdered, though.

When Noel had to get off the phone, the cabin was suddenly horribly quiet, and Gabriela wished she hadn't been a jerk to her dad. She loved him more than anybody in the world.

And what frightened her most, in a list of about a hundred things, was that Ivy Walcott—her *mother*—would steal him away from her.

CULLEN'S PARENTS' neighborhood was isolated, a circular street separated from the town of Guyandotte by a highway and a steel trestle bridge over the river. Beyond the bridge, the cloudy moon shone on tall roofs with many gables, brick palaces, stucco-and-beam mansions built by coal barons when coal was still king. Cullen's father, the district judge—retired—was the grandson of such a baron. His home was called Coalgood.

The half-timbered and masonry Tudor perched on its own hill of velvety blue grass, crowning two acres, the largest plot on Ore Circle. Leafless maples sprawled on either side of the recessed entry, high above road level. From the attic windows, Cullen and his sister, Zeya, used to peer down at the houses on the island that was the center of the circle. They still, occasionally, sledded down Coalgood's hill with Gabriela and with Zeya and Tom's five-year-old daughter, Scout. Tonight looked perfect for sledding; all was smooth and white with snow, the roof eaves glowing softly with tastefully placed holiday lights.

Cullen drove past the house, noticing cars. Shelby's VW bug was in the driveway with Zeya and Tom's ancient Volvo. Matthew's XKE, Mother's Oldsmobile and Daddy's Lincoln would be in the garage. The judge didn't drive anymore—unless he forgot and no one stopped him.

The lights were burning downstairs, behind the steel casements and the leaded glass. Maybe he'd stop by after he talked to Tracy, tell everyone about Gina—Ivy.

Maybe he wouldn't.

Tracy lived on the other side of the island in a brick house with cast-iron lacework everywhere. She'd grown up in that house and bought it from her parents when they moved to Logan. Cullen had spent the night there twice, while Gabriela was at slumber parties. Tracy had never slept in his bed.

Now he wished he'd never so much as kissed her.

Her porch light was on, and she opened the door as he climbed the steps. She shut it behind him when he entered the foyer, and he saw she'd changed into jeans and a sweater.

Her living room was ivory, with a black baby grand piano in the corner. Sitting on the kind of furniture that always made him want to check his clothes for mud, he told her his wife was alive and returning to Guyandotte.

He told her everything, as he'd told Gabriela.

"What are you going to do?"

He went still, then told himself it was a reasonable question. "She's my wife. And Gabriela's mother."

Her mouth trembled some, then steadied. "That's the right thing to do, Cullen. I'll miss what you and I have shared. But I know Gabriela will be happy."

There was nothing left to say. He wouldn't tell her his reasons for making the choice he had. He would never say to Tracy, the other woman, *She was hurt. I have to be there for her if she needs me.*

No point in saying that the promises he'd made thirteen years ago still mattered to him. He could never explain why they mattered so much.

"I'm sorry, Tracy. I really thought she was dead."

Tracy sat tall and straight, her hands folded in her lap. "It would be easier if you weren't sorry, Cullen. But I know you are. And I want you to believe that I wish you the best. All three of you. Of course, I'll still see Gabriela in class."

"Yes." Contemplating his hands, Cullen thought,

Wedding ring. It was in the top drawer of his dresser with a picture of Gina, the picture they'd put on the missing-person poster. What had happened to her rings?

In a restless movement, Tracy rose. "What can I get you to drink?"

He got up, too. "Actually, Gabriela's home alone. And I wanted to stop and see my dad."

Excuses for parting. *I'm sorry, Tracy. I'm sorry.*

He was sorry for hurting her.

But after the last few minutes, he was sorry most of all that they'd ever become involved.

OUTSIDE COALGOOD, Cullen leaned on the steering wheel. He didn't think he could tell the story again.

And he wasn't ready to tell it to at least one person inside that house.

Numb and half-crazy, he lingered, undecided, till the front door, way up the hill, opened wide. He unfastened his seat belt then, and when he stepped from the Camaro, his father's voice called down, "Cully, that you?"

Someone else warbled a call from inside. The tone was fear. "Sam? Sam?"

Sam Till came down the flagstone steps cut into the hillside of glittering white. *Watch out for the ice, Daddy.* The judge skidded but didn't fall, and Cullen started up the walk to meet him.

"Sam?"

The porch light snapped on. A head of smooth blond hair, recently colored, peered out. The woman vanished then returned, her red sweater and green plaid pants bright as the holidays. She carried his father's wraps.

Cullen waved to his mother.

"Sam, you need your coat." Mouth tight, she picked her way down the walk after her husband. She clapped his wool driving cap over his head, wound his muffler round his neck. Helping her husband into his coat, she cast Cullen a look that said, *You won't let him go anywhere, will you?*

Later, if she was alone with Cullen or with Cullen and Zeya, she would say, "He's almost the same as always, don't you think?"

The judge did seem sharp tonight. Blue-gray slacks creased. Fresh red polo shirt under a cashmere sweater. His small round glasses winked back the starlight, and below the sides of his cap, his bald head gave off a satin sheen. He walked tall. Tall and handsome, smart and good.

Fitting on his gloves, the judge made it down to the sidewalk. "You've been a stranger."

"Busy."

The lights in a neighboring white Colonial flashed on. Big front room with a grand piano. A young girl sat down to play, her ponytail waving over her straight spine.

"Let's take a walk," said the judge.

They walked together in the empty street, on the fresh snow, avoiding the narrow sidewalks. "You all right, Cully?"

"Yes." Sure. Fine. No. Lousy. "Gina's been found. She has total amnesia."

His father's look was blank, either over Gina or amnesia. It was a funny word to forget, but there it was. That was how they'd begun to notice he was sick. That—and forgetting other things.

Cullen straightened his insides. Daddy was sick. He couldn't expect any advice, any intelligent comment. As far as he could tell, his father hadn't even recognized Gina's name.

The judge said, "I'm sorry about this. About the way I am."

It wasn't the first time he'd mentioned his illness to Cullen. Cullen hoped the conversation wouldn't take its usual course.

"I guess it happens," he said, "when we get old." It could happen to him. The odds were good.

His father's arm settled across Cullen's shoulders. A shaky surprise. "This is just between you and me. I've always loved you best."

His father's gift had a history. *Your Honor, why couldn't you have loved one of your other children best? Matthew, for instance. I don't deserve the favor, thank you.*

"And that's why I'm asking you this," the judge said.

Cullen braced himself. The judge had asked him for this thing twice before; he probably didn't remember.

Cullen wished he could forget, too.

"Should have done it...earlier. But I thought about

it right from the start. No impaired judgment. No guilt, Cully.'' A breath. ''I want you to help me die.''

Shit.

''You're the only one with the integrity. Matthew's got the guts, but he wouldn't trouble to keep the secret from your mother.''

Matthew was better at keeping secrets than the judge knew. And Cullen already had more secrets than he wanted.

''Someday I'll wander off. You could help me into the river—down a mine shaft. Promise me, Cully. It's for your mother.''

Not hardly. His mother would hate the idea.

But his father wanted it, and she might go along with it for him. She'd surprised Cullen most of his life.

''Daddy, you need to talk about it with Mother.''

''Your mother will never agree, and it's my life.''

And if she did agree and if the judge died in an ''accident,'' there would be life insurance fraud, which was a crime in spirit and in law. Whereas assisted suicide… There was enough here for a university ethics class. Cullen changed the subject. ''Daddy, do you remember Gina?''

The judge walked with him, their bodies linked by that arm across the son's shoulders.

His profile showed nothing. Blank.

Suddenly, he seemed to come back to himself. He glanced at the house. ''We'd better get in for dinner.''

Cullen didn't bother to tell him that it was almost ten and that the judge had already eaten.

CHAPTER TWO

"WE REALLY HAVE TO GO to Coalgood for dinner tonight?"

"It's Grandma's birthday."

"I'm totally traumatized by the concept of meeting my mother for the first time. I don't want to go."

Twenty-four hours had passed since he'd told Gabriela about Ivy. That morning, Ivy had called him at the studio to say she was on her way and should arrive the following afternoon, Wednesday, the day before Thanksgiving.

Gabriela had blanched at the news.

"We're going."

"Have you told them?"

About Gina. "No. I will tonight."

Dragging her feet toward her room, she muttered, "I bet *they'll* be thrilled."

His antenna went up. "Why do you say that?"

She acted like she hadn't heard.

"Gabby. Why did you say that?"

In slow motion, she turned and leaned against the doorjamb. After four years of ballet, she could still slouch. "You think I'm stupid? Grandma and Grandpa don't like my mother in a big way. You got married too young. I've only heard *that* about fifty times. If only you'd gone to college like Matthew and Zeya.'' She shook her head sadly in a dead-on imitation of his mother.

He bit his tongue but couldn't hide his smile. "Go get dressed, brat."

She made a face at him. "*You're* the brat."

She was so pretty, so much like Gina—or like Gina might've been if her childhood had been different. If she'd known at least one of her parents.

He realized too late that she'd been studying his expression. She played the moment for all its worth. "Can I have a raise in my allowance?"

DINNER THAT NIGHT was served in the dining room, one of Coalgood's great halls, with mullioned and transomed stone windows and crown moldings and rich cherry furniture. Cullen sat between Gabriela and Scout, who was trying to interest him in some Playmobil bandits under the table. While his niece whispered, "Uncle Cullen! Bang bang!" he tried to figure out how to break the news about Gina. Maybe at the door, right before he and Gabriela left?

"Scout." Zeya, one year older than Cullen, frowned at her daughter. "Please put away the cowboys."

"If Uncle Cullen promises to play Playmobil with me after dinner."

"Yes."

Tom Tormey, Zeya's black-haired, blue-eyed husband, winced at the promptness of Cullen's answer. "We're trying not to make a tyrant of our daughter."

Cullen winked at Scout. "Am I the one who opened the biggest toy store in the Appalachians and bought every Playmobil set imaginable?" He and Scout shook their heads at each other, and her black corkscrew curls bobbed. "No, I'm not."

"No, you're not, Uncle Cullen. My parents have the biggest toy store in the whole world."

As Zeya held out a hand for the bandits, her mother said, "Zeya, please don't reach across the table. It sets a bad example. Scout, honey, don't you want some lamb chops?"

That's the problem, Cullen wanted to tell Zeya, *with living at home. Mother wants to raise your daughter.* It was a bigger problem because Zeya, Tom and Scout were all vegetarians, an anomaly at Coalgood and in Guyandotte.

His family lined both sides of the table, Mother at one end and Daddy at the other. Matthew's wife, Shelby, sat on the judge's right beside Scout. Her husband sat across from her, next to Zeya. Matthew was Cullen's half brother, the son of the judge's first marriage. He'd been fourteen when Cullen was born. When Cullen was three, Matthew had transported him halfway to the second floor of Coalgood in the dumbwaiter and left him there. On another occasion, he'd held him by his heels from an attic window.

It was family tradition to fly in Matthew's plane to each newly completed building that he'd designed. Though Matthew was touted as the South's most brilliant architect, Cullen never entered one of his buildings without noticing that a child could be launched

down the grand staircase in a red wagon, without seeing all toilets as objects to climb on when trapped in
a bathroom with a six-foot black snake.

Scout, deprived of her toys, pulled on one of
Shelby's dark red curls, corkscrews like her own.
"Shelby, can I go to your office tomorrow?"

Shelby turned serious eyes and gold-rimmed
glasses on her niece. "Sweetie, I have to go to court
to defend a really creepy guy."

"Oh, Shelby!" Scout frowned. "I bet you'd rather
be with me."

The judge muttered, "Shelby likes the low-life
sons of bitches, and she doesn't believe in the death
penalty, either."

Shelby patted her father-in-law's hand. "But you
and I can still eat dinner together, even live in the
same house."

"Your husband's a sponge."

Matthew's dense eyebrows lifted. "Her husband,
your son, pays most of the upkeep on this turn-of-
the-century monstrosity."

The judge's next utterance was profane.

"Daddy!" exclaimed his wife. "There are children
present."

Tom scooped up some millet pilaf from his plate.
"That's all right, Mitzi. Teaches 'em how to talk.
Scout, Gabby, you catch all that?"

Every summer, while Gabriela was at dance camp,
Cullen and Tom completed thirty-mile-a-day treks on
the country's longest trails. The Appalachian Trail,
the John Muir Trail... They grew beards, ceased all

bathing and brushed their teeth but not their hair. They yipped with coyotes, cawed at black-winged scavengers and devised elaborate schemes for outwitting fat marmots and bears. They maintained silence in the presence of eagles and hawks. Cullen usually enjoyed his brother-in-law's wit. Tonight, it grated.

Restless, Cullen retrieved his camera and began photographing family members in black and white. Shelby talking earnestly to Scout. Zeya's family eating different food from everyone else at the table. His parents' servant, Lily, bringing the coffeepot. Gabriela scowling at the camera. Daddy blowing out the candles—on Mother's cake.

"It's time for presents," announced Zeya, jumping to her feet. "Mother, this one's from Daddy."

The judge started. "It most certainly is not."

Cullen put his head in his hands and silenced his suddenly giggling daughter with a glance, which she aped to Matthew a second later and her uncle aped right back.

"I forgot her birthday," the judge said. "Like always." He winked down the table at his wife.

Everyone laughed then, at the joke, which was a sign of the judge's sharpness, a sign the disease was moving slowly.

During the opening of the gifts, Gabriela caught Cullen's eye. With an agonized look, she mouthed, "Can I go to Noel's?"

"After the presents."

It would give him a chance to talk to his family

without Gabriela's seeing their reactions. What she'd said earlier still bugged him. She didn't miss much.

The minute Mother had opened her last gift—a framed photo of Cullen and Gabriela—Gabriela said, "May I be excused?"

"Of course, darling."

Her grandmother lifted her face, welcoming a kiss, and Gabriela obliged. "I love you, Grandma."

The judge said, "Thanks for the presents, everyone."

As Gabriela hugged him, too, then left, Matthew opened the sideboard. "Drinks anyone? Chablis, Mitzi?"

His stepmother responded with a dazzling smile that suggested the ritual was annual rather than nightly. "Why thank you, Matthew."

"Health fanatics, I recommend the Merlot. I'm told it's loaded with antioxidants."

"Too yin," Zeya said.

Shelby smiled at her husband. "Nothing for me, Matthew."

Cullen heard the front door close behind Gabriela. "Gina's coming back."

Glass hit glass. Matthew getting clumsy with the wine.

Daddy snapped his head up. "Who?"

"Gina?" exclaimed Mitzi and Zeya.

Tom said, "Your *wife?*"

"She goes by Ivy now. Ivy Walcott." His throat was full, confessing this, that she had changed her name. Especially her last name.

From the sideboard, Matthew coughed. "Guess we all need some excitement, Cully. I'm glad you brought it up tonight at this family gathering."

Out of compassion for Shelby, Cullen let it pass. *Surely* you're *not excited, Matthew?*

"But your wife's dead!" Scout blurted. "People don't come back from the dead."

"She was never dead. But she can't remember her life with me. She has a head injury. Permanent brain damage."

"Oh, God, how awful." Zeya shuddered.

"Oh, Cullen." His mother shook her head. "Surely *you're* not going to take care of her? What about Tracy?"

"An interesting question." Matthew spilled Mother's Chablis in her lap. "Oh, jeez. I'm sorry, Mitzi."

"What's the matter, Joe? Got butterfingers?" Daddy said in that slow voice that wasn't really his anymore.

Joe was Daddy's brother. Joe had died in Korea before Cullen was born.

Lily peered in from the kitchen and hurried for a damp towel to mop at Mother's dress. "It's just the white, Mrs. Till. It'll come right out."

Returning to the sideboard, Matthew collected his own glass of Merlot. "Where's she staying?"

Cullen met his eyes. "With her husband."

Shelby stood up from the table too fast, and he wanted to shoot himself. "Hey, Scout," she said. "Did you mention a Playmobil party?"

THE NEXT DAY, Ivy wondered if West Virginia was a place of gray skies. She hadn't seen blue since she'd crossed the state line, though she'd seen plenty of snow since reaching Guyandotte. And this hollow…

Missing Girl Hollow. Cullen had said "holler" the way people in Tennessee had. She'd grown up here.

There was the oak with three trunks that Cullen had described to her. The road looked rutted, the passage between the trees narrow, but the Saab would make it easily.

Branches wound together above the car, creating a long corridor of tree limbs. They were gray and brown now, streaked white with the snow collecting on them. But in summer, this would be a forest of green.

As her windshield wipers stroked back and forth, she took a sip from her travel mug of nettle tea. She carried tea balls and herbs with her, and she'd made tea with gas-station hot water all across the country. It was almost two days since she'd slept.

That's the cabin. Light-headed, she parked beside a black vintage Camaro with pinstripes and an intake scoop.

The cabin door opened, and through her snow-flecked windows, she saw the tall figure behind the screen. Then the screen pushed out. His hair was light brown, overlong and wavy. His wool shirt hung on broad shoulders, his faded jeans on narrow hips and long, muscular legs.

What am I going to say to this man? What will he expect?

Closing her eyes, she held on to one thought. She'd contacted the midwifery association in West Virginia and been assured that a midwife in the Guyandotte area could provide much-needed services. There wouldn't be much money in it. *You'll be eating rice and beans, but the women in those hollers really need help.*

Naturally, she wouldn't start a local practice until she knew she'd be staying. But Cullen had already said he hoped she'd stay. And her heart and soul pointed in that direction, too—toward honoring their commitment, toward joining Cullen in raising Gabriela.

Any comfort, any sense of continuity, came from one source. She was a midwife. Her key ring, an over-size diaper pin bearing the logo of Mountain Midwifery and holding a cluster of functional diaper pins, reminded her of this and her connection to Tara and Francesca. The same was true of the birthing-woman pendants Francesca had bought for them all at the midwifery conference in Tennessee. And the friendship bracelets Tara had made with kids at the birth clinic in Texas. Ivy was a midwife, the daughter of Francesca Walcott, the sister of Tara Marcus.

And the wife of Cullen Till.

He had left the porch, and when she opened her door, he stood six feet away, beneath the naked trees. His green eyes were the missing leaves, the missing shoots of spring. Ivy's chest tightened oddly, her pulse racing, her stomach hot. Heat ran down her legs, and she couldn't move.

His smile cut grooves on each side of his mouth. Beautiful teeth and a yin-yang post in his left ear.

Precipice, Colorado, was a town of celebrity second homes, a land of handsome adventure-seekers, rugged mountaineers and suntanned skiers. But this was the finest-looking man she'd ever seen, and she'd bet he could climb mountains or hike for miles without rest.

Her lips parted. *Husband.*

He'd come closer, close enough that she noticed a button in the middle of his shirt was white, while the others were black.

Like the hair on his chest.

And his eyelashes and eyebrows.

Cullen searched her eyes, hunting signs of recognition. No, he could tell she didn't recognize him, though he knew her. He knew her smooth golden skin, her fine nose. Her wide mouth. *It's you.*

But it wasn't.

Ivy Walcott wore a cream-colored turtleneck, a sheepskin coat and jeans that made her legs a mile long. Cowboy boots, too. She was ski-resort Western chic, like an ad for Aspen.

Or Precipice.

Gone was Gina in her gingham and secondhand clothes. Gone were Gina's eyes that always looked sideways when she spoke to you.

Ivy Walcott looked right at him, her mouth soft and vulnerable.

He wasn't sorry he'd asked her back.

She held out her hand.

Ignoring it, he stepped close and put his arms around her.

Cullen's body trembled at the contact. *Gina.* He meant the hug to be simple, a welcome.

It was intense and complicated, with her head making one nervous turn against his chest, with her arms reaching to hold him in a way that reminded him that, for her, this was a first meeting. His jaw rested on her hair, and he shut his eyes. Different shampoo.

There was nothing to say, nothing to make it sane.

When he released her, slowly, she said, "That was nice."

Nice was inadequate. Nothing could express what he felt.

He didn't respond.

The black Saab was filled with boxes and a couple of suitcases. There was a loaded luggage rack on the roof, and cross-country and alpine skis strapped to the back. Through the rear window, Cullen saw ice skates and snowshoes, too.

"I didn't know how much snow you have."

"Quite a bit, here. There's actually a ski area a half hour away." He laughed. "Not that I'm sure *you'd* call it a ski area."

Ivy looked toward the cabin. "Where's Gabriela?"

"School. You can come with me to pick her up."

Her watch read two o'clock. Which meant an hour or so alone with Cullen in this deserted place.

But she liked the cabin. It was log and stone, rustic in a way the log houses of Precipice would never be. The roof peaked steeply into the trees above tall windows and a circular stained-glass panel showing a falcon and a red wolf. The upper story looked new, while Ivy could easily believe that the central cabin was a hundred years old. Neatly stacked firewood filled half the porch.

"See anything familiar?"

Was he hoping? She searched his eyes, trembling inside just from the visual contact. "Nothing. I knew I wouldn't. My memory won't ever return. The loss is permanent."

He didn't look away. "Then we have some catching up to do. But I have to tell you, I'm not as sure as you are that your past is all gone."

Oh, Cullen, don't. Don't believe that. Don't hope for it.

"See..." His voice sounded uneven. "Your grandmother was a midwife. And so was your mother. And so were you."

Midwives... She'd been a midwife when she was Gina Till? Was that why catching babies, identifying the sagittal suture, assessing a baby's lie, had always felt so natural to her, like something she'd done before?

I was a midwife, and...

And she didn't remember, nor had she ever seen this man, the husband who'd made love to her, who'd made a child with her. Her mouth filled with saliva, and she felt dizzy, her legs unsteady.

Her head swam, and his face became too vivid, the edges too sharp, and then everything went away.

ON THE COUCH, horizontal, she came around.

Kneeling beside her, Cullen watched her eyelashes flutter, watched the shades of violet appear. Panic when she saw him. She closed her eyes, then re-opened them, calmer. "I'm sorry. Did I faint?"

"You fainted. Any idea why?"

She held her hand against her eyes, half-shielding her face. "I, uh, haven't slept real well the last two nights."

Neither had he. "Did you stop last night? On the road?"

"No." It was embarrassing. "I was wide-awake."

"Could you sleep now?"

Ivy tried to sit up, and he let her, slowly.

Sleep... Could she sleep now? No, Ivy decided. Not a chance. Not until she met Gabriela. She shook her head. "I'll be fine till tonight." She put her feet on the floor. The cabin was hot. Roasting in her coat, she pulled it off, and Cullen took it from her to hang up.

When he returned, he moved a pillow on the couch to sit next to her.

As she blinked, catching the details of the room, he said, "I apologize for shocking you. Do you re-member what I said?"

"Yes. I'm afraid it's just a coincidence. Please don't—don't hope that my memory will return. It cat-egorically, absolutely, will not. Neurologist certified, short of an act of God. And I'm not talking about one doctor. I've seen a dozen, psychiatrists and brain doc-tors."

Cullen believed her. "It's okay. Let's talk about something else." If she hadn't slept for two days, she was more nervous than she let on. At the moment, he didn't trust her judgment. "I'll give you a tour in a minute. Gabriela's room is in there." He nodded toward the door. "There's a loft upstairs with a turn-of-the-century tester bed. Narrow. And there's a day-bed up there, too. Also, there's this couch. So…there are options."

Ivy met his eyes. She knew things about him already. That he was a gentle man. That his house was clean and that there was a pair of toe shoes, for ballet, at the end of the couch and a copy of *Seventeen* on the coffee table. That he took his commitment to her seriously. At least, seriously enough to ask her to "come home."

"Ivy, I need to be straight with you. I don't expect a commitment tonight or this week even. But I've never brought lovers to this house. I didn't want to do that to Gabriela. She doesn't need a walk-on in her life."

Ivy had pondered this question ever since he'd asked her back. What would be best for Gabriela? What was reasonable to expect of Cullen and herself?

Now she was here, and she found him attractive and kind.

"I should warn you. Gabriela had a mixed reaction to the news that you were coming back. She's twelve. You know?"

Ivy understood.

"I told her I hoped you'd stay. That's still how I

feel. I know things are different, but I see your face, and you're still my wife.''

The same urges that had prompted her to return to a situation she couldn't foresee urged her answer now. "I will stay."

"You shouldn't make that decision yet."

"It's obvious to me. And better for Gabriela if we decide immediately."

Cullen tried trusting her and could not and knew he should not. He and Gabriela would be at her mercy, at the mercy of a stranger.

As she was at theirs.

"Then—" his mouth was dry "—I think you should sleep upstairs. In the daybed, if you like. You can trust me to leave you alone."

His teasing smile was gentle and friendly, not threatening.

"For a while anyway."

Ivy's heart gave several hard thuds. What would it be like when he *didn't* leave her alone? *I need to say something. To warn him.* Tara and Francesca and ten years of unavoidable awkwardness had taught her that honesty was the best policy. "I haven't had a lover."

Every time she met his eyes and spoke, she ceased to be Gina for him.

Cullen deliberately closed his mouth. No lovers.

He considered the implications. *Think about her.* "Do you remember what sex is like? Do you imagine it?"

Her pelvic floor tingled with increased blood flow. He'd asked like a man who had the right to know.

The space behind her eyes was hot. *He loves me. Or he loved me once.*

As far as she knew, no other man ever had.

Eyes on his lips, she made the words come out. "I…imagine it. I might remember the sensation. I'm not sure. It's probably like being pregnant or having a baby. I *think* I know what it feels like. But I've completely forgotten the experience itself."

Cullen took a long breath. *There's a lot you've forgotten. More than you'll ever guess.*

Her cheeks were bright beneath her tan, and she tensed initially as he relaxed against the back of the couch. A sadness nudged him, and Cullen shoved it away just as something familiar hit him. Her scent. He knew that scent. *You smell the same.*

Did she know his scent? Could she remember that much?

He focused on what she'd said. About sex. It should have been a dream come true—the chance to be Gina's first. But she wasn't Gina. "How do you feel about the prospect of making love with me? It must seem like an arranged marriage."

"No." She drew her lower lip between her teeth, a nervous gesture of Gina's and one that had never failed to excite him. Even now. "It feels safe. I must have liked you."

He had no answer for that. Except to continue putting the pieces on the table. "So. I slept with Gabriela's ballet teacher a couple of times. I've been seeing her…for about a year." He found her steady, clear-eyed gaze. "I thought you were dead. I'm not promiscuous."

"That's an attractive quality."

He laughed. The dark sadness, the highs and lows of familiarity tugged at him again.

"Does she know?" asked Ivy. "The ballet teacher? That I—"

"I told her."

"And?"

"She's a nice person."

Ivy wasn't surprised. "Are you in love with her?"

"No." He'd thought he might be, until he knew it was over. Time to get off this couch, carry in Ivy's things. "Let me bring your stuff from the car, and I'll show you around. A lot of the things in this house were your family's. Your grandmother, your mother, you and Gabby were all born here, in this cabin."

Quilts. It was then that she noticed the quilt on the couch, another quilted piece on the wall. *I know how to quilt.* Gently she touched the soft fabric. There was a beauty and timelessness to this heritage.

He was giving it back to her, and she wanted to embrace him again, to thank him. Before he went out, she said, "Cullen? What about my father?"

"Died in the mines when you were a baby. There are photos of both your parents—and your grandparents on your mom's side—at my studio. They're yours, of course. I'll take you down there before we pick up Gabriela."

"Please." *You have my past. You are giving me my past.*

Had he told her the whole truth about the ballet teacher? Had he made love only twice with a woman he'd dated for a year? And what did he mean by making love?

A new distance had sprung up between them at the mention of his lover. A year was a long time to be involved with someone. Did that explain his sudden quiet, the way he went outside without looking at her again?

Turning to peer out the window, she watched his athletic strides over the snow, watched him stop and put his hand to his face. His shoulders trembled slightly.

I wish I could see your face.

His body told her enough.

Something hurt. And until she knew for certain what it was, she'd sleep in that daybed.

DON'T THINK ABOUT IT. Don't think about it.

Cullen had stifled the thoughts as long as he could. Outside, under the trees, they descended on him like mosquitoes in July.

Memories of a woman with Ivy's looks, an Appalachian lilt in her voice, a down-to-earth practicality and weaknesses he'd loved and loathed. He'd wanted to *talk* to her. All morning, he'd imagined hugging her, talking to her, watching her tomboy ways, watching her assess the change between the two-year-old she'd left and the twelve-year-old she'd come home to, then sit down for a heart-to-heart with Gabriela and turn a mouthy adolescent into an angel.

She'd been at her best as a mom.

But she was gone, and tears came against his will. Postponed grief. Gina was as dead as if her body had died, too.

He was married to a woman he didn't know but whose scent was like Gina's. Who looked like Gina. Who had felt like Gina when he embraced her.

A woman he couldn't help wanting.

A woman he did not love.

CHAPTER THREE

HER CONVERSATION with Francesca was brief—but long enough for her mother to ask, "Ivy, is that wise? Staying there? With him?"

Cullen had put on his coat and was gathering film canisters and manila envelopes—undoubtedly containing photographs or proofs, things for work.

Regretting what she'd told Francesca, Ivy said simply, "I hope so. In any case, it's what I'm going to do."

Francesca's sigh traveled across miles. "I wish I could come out there, at least meet this man."

If only Cullen wasn't listening. "It's not about him." She didn't want to see his face, his reaction to that. "We have a child."

This time, the other woman's long breath contained all the emotion of what motherhood meant. "Yes," she murmured. "I see. And you feel you're safe?"

"Very."

"Well… Then please give your family a hug from me and Tara. I think I can get away after Lori Sheffield's birth, in December."

"I'll love seeing you, Mom."

She couldn't help noticing that Cullen watched her quizzically. When she'd given Francesca Cullen's address and phone number and hung up, she said, "So you're wondering why I suddenly have a mother."

She liked his smile.

"Sure."

"I'll tell you in the car."

THEY TOOK THE SAAB, and she let him drive. On the way downtown to his studio, she told him how Francesca and Tara had befriended her and informally adopted her as an adult. "Charlie, that's Tara's dad, wanted in on it, too, but he and Francesca have been divorced twenty years, and she said one mutual child is enough. Still, I call him Dad. But he lives in Alaska. I've only met him about five times."

What was Cullen thinking? It wasn't till they reached a traffic light, at the turnoff from the highway and onto Main Street, that he met her eyes. "I'm glad someone took care of you. I'll be happy to meet them."

She didn't know how much of what he said was simply good manners, but she trusted it was sincere.

And in her weariness, her sense of unreality in an unfamiliar world, she trusted *him*. Although she wasn't sure she could tell Francesca why.

CULLEN LEFT IVY ALONE with the photos while he went to develop the roll he'd shot at Coalgood the other night. Rather than opening the albums he'd brought out for her, Ivy rose and walked through the studio. The walls were a gallery of photos. Not portraits—more like photojournalism, in black and white and in color. Appalachian places and faces worthy of the best magazines. Cave interiors, hill-country farms. And when she opened one of the books on the counter, she discovered he had sold to magazines. All his magazine work was in plastic sleeves in the album.

You're good, Cullen.

Choosing a dark blue overstuffed chair, she finally settled down with a brown album of faded photographs. *My grandparents.* Each line on their faces spoke to something inside her. Through these portraits and snapshots she could know the family, the places, that would otherwise be completely lost to her.

Mountain faces. Her father's skin blackened with grime from the mines. In other shots, the grime never seemed completely gone. Her mother and grandmother, carrying midwifery bags. Her mother was blond, too, dressed simply in sixties style—so similar to the clothing worn by her grandmother in the earlier photographs. It was as though time had stopped in these mountains.

This is my place. This is my country.

She knew she would never return to Colorado to live.

She had truly come home.

The second album opened another world, captured through Cullen's lens.

She'd nursed Gabriela. A newborn. Ivy had seen the tester bed that day. She'd seen the quilts, on the tester bed, on Gabriela's iron bed downstairs, on the daybed in the loft where she would sleep that night, a dozen feet from him.

Gabriela was born at home. But who had been there? Cullen had said Gina's mother died when she was just five, that her grandmother died when Gina was eighteen, two years before Gabriela was born.

She would have to ask Cullen. She turned pages and finally found a single picture of him holding the newborn Gabriela. With a shock of memory, she recalled a detail of her stay in the Boulder hospital. It was something she'd tried to put out of her mind for the last decade—with limited success. The baby photos brought it back. She must tell Cullen, but she couldn't tell him suddenly. He'd be upset.

"Hi."

He'd emerged from the darkroom.

She gestured to the photos on the studio walls. "You're wonderful."

"Thanks."

She turned another leaf in the album. "We look so young."

He peered at the album, at upside-down photos. "We *were* young. Twenty. Our wedding photos are at home. I think they're in Gabriela's room."

"Who attended her birth?"

"Me. You told me what to do."

And these were the memories lost to her? The birth of her child? Nursing her infant daughter?

"What happened? What was the birth like?"

"I was taking photos for the paper. I came home, and you said you were in labor, and suddenly your water broke—all over my shoes.'' He grinned, then averted his eyes.

She understood. Grief. That was why he'd been upset outside the cabin. She whispered the why. ''I'm not her.''

Cullen crouched beside her to look over her shoulder at the photos. As if she hadn't spoken, he said, ''You'd always planned to do your own birth, so you'd lined me up with midwifery books to read. *Spiritual Midwifery* was one of them. We cuddled a lot during your labor. Touched. When she crowned, you talked me through it, checking for the cord and everything. I caught her and put her on your stomach.''

Numb, she listened to the rest of the details. Delivering the placenta, cutting the cord, nursing Gabriela.

''You nursed her for almost two years. She'd barely stopped when you…disappeared.''

She met his eyes, getting used to his features and the three o'clock shadow on his jaw. Getting used to the idea of telling him what she must. ''What did you think had happened?''

''I didn't know. Your wallet was gone, but I had the car. You never hitched rides. Gabby was with me, at the studio.'' He paused. ''You don't have any idea what happened?''

''Not really.''

''Tell me about your head injury.''

''It's focal retrograde amnesia, basically. I never forgot how to *do* things—which probably explained my becoming a midwife again. But there was a hell of a lot of stuff I didn't know. Presidents, current events. I took some history classes and pop culture, just so I didn't embarrass myself.''

He sat back on his heels. ''What caused it?''

''A blow to the head. I could have fallen. I could have been hit. It could have been an accident. No one knows. And probably no one ever will.'' She gathered herself. ''I was—I was bleeding from a recent miscarriage.'' Her breath hurt. ''Or a failed abortion.''

He was white, his jaw hard.

Cullen wondered how much to say. Now was the time to tell her. He didn't want to. Somehow it was between him and Gina. *But it's her body. Same woman, Cullen. Your wife.*

And now, he'd just learned, she had carried his child.

HARRY S. TRUMAN JUNIOR High School sat on a hillside overlooking Guyandotte. The redbrick walls showed above the trees before her Saab began climbing the hill with Cullen silent at the wheel. It gave Ivy extra minutes in which to be more nervous than she'd ever been.

As they reached the school, following other parents and two school buses, Cullen asked, ''Are you all right?''

At last. He speaks. He'd returned to the darkroom after her revelation—more to be alone, she suspected, than to work. ''I'm just worried she's not going to like me or is going to resent my presence. She doesn't even know me. And you were dating her ballet teacher.''

He pulled into the parking lot and took a spot along the curb to wait for Gabriela. ''You know, she was really a mess when you disappeared. Now she's resisting the idea of you, and it's probably for reasons she doesn't even understand. But I think she needs you.''

No one had ever needed her that she could recall, except women in labor, and there'd never been a situation in which someone else couldn't have attended a birth. ''Thank you. For saying that.''

''I mean it.'' Should he say more? Why not? Part of his rationale in asking her to come home had been the sense that *she* needed *him*. ''Ivy, after the sheriff came last week, I just sat there for ten minutes thinking about Tracy—the ballet teacher—and about you. Sure, a stepmother was beginning to look like a good second option for Gabriela. But you?'' He met her eyes. ''I think you have the magic with her.''

''I lost my personality.''

''I believe love is stronger than that.''

Ivy heard. He wasn't just talking about her and Gabriela.

He was talking about the two of them, husband and wife.

Her answer came from her heart, not from her mind. ''So do I.''

He broke the eye contact, looking past her shoulder. ''Here's Gabby. I'd better get out. She won't know this car.''

Ivy saw the blond girl applying lip gloss as she walked, a boy on each side of her. As Cullen opened his door, she couldn't stop herself.

She opened hers, too.

OH, GOD. THAT'S HER.

Blinking, Gabriela stopped on the sidewalk. "I'll see you guys later. There are…" They would think she was totally weird if she suddenly said "my parents." She'd been going to school with Roger and Jeremy since kindergarten, and everyone knew damn well she had no mother. "There's my dad."

And the most beautiful woman Gabriela had ever seen, drop-dead gorgeous like her photos.

No wonder he wanted her back.

Gabriela swallowed. For a second, for her dad's sake, she wanted this Ivy woman to love him, too. But how could she when they'd been apart so long and she supposedly couldn't remember his face?

Oh, come on. She's not blind.

Gabriela hoped she wasn't stuck up, either.

Her dad had come around to the passenger side of the black car and was waiting for her. As she came near, he put his arm around her. He cast a glance at people nearby and spoke softly. "Gabriela, this is Ivy. Ivy, Gabriela."

Ivy tried to read her daughter's expression. It wasn't hard. *She's terrified. I'm scared, too, Gabriela.*

Once she'd asked Tara, "Aren't you ever afraid to meet people?" Her sister seemed to greet everyone she knew or met with a hug and a grin. Tara had said,

"Of course I am. Why do you think I act this way? It makes me brave."

Ivy had never been able to greet a new acquaintance with an embrace until today.

And only because Cullen had taught her how.

She stepped forward and hugged her daughter. Slender bones. A child turning into a woman. "I'm so glad to see you. I drove across the country most of all to meet you." She tightened the awkward hug for a moment, then released her daughter, who was already as tall as Ivy. "You're beautiful." *Gorgeous.*

"Thanks." Gabriela's voice was low, flat. "So are you."

Her dad had his arm around her again, which made Gabriela feel better. He tugged on her ponytail. "Let's go home, Gabby."

THE PHONE WAS RINGING when they opened the car doors outside the cabin. Cullen sprinted to get it.

Tom said, "Your mom just called us at the store. The judge is missing."

Gabriela and Ivy trailed into the cabin. His daughter wore the face of a death-row inmate.

Ordinarily, he would have left in a second to track down his father. Not today. "Where's Matthew?"

"Atlanta. I'm about to go look, and Shelby said she'd go, too, but he's got the Lincoln. It could take a few of us."

Hanging up the phone, Cullen found Gabriela and Ivy sitting at opposite ends of the couch. "Grandpa's missing." He turned to Ivy. "My father has Alzheimer's."

Her eyes plunged into his, doing something to him. "I'm sorry."

"He was a district judge."

Wincing, she shook her head.

Ivy noticed Gabriela gazing at her as though she were a creature from another realm. When Ivy caught her eye, the twelve-year-old said, "He really has to explain *everything* to you? I thought you grew up in Guyandotte."

"My earliest memories begin ten years ago."

"So, does that make you like a ten-year-old?"

"Gabby." Cullen's voice was stern.

"Sorry." Her apology carried no remorse.

Ivy took the question as asked. "The answer is no. I still have emotional memory and what's called procedural memory. I remembered how to drive, how to tie my shoes and, to some degree, how to attend births. I'm a midwife," she added, in case Cullen hadn't told her.

"You used to be a midwife, too. That's totally weird."

Her honesty made Ivy smile. "Cullen, do you need to look for your dad? If you'd like help, we could take separate cars."

He considered. "All right. He's driving a navy Lincoln Continental with the license plate SALTILL. Samuel Abraham Lincoln Till. Gabby, you go with her. Grandpa knows you, and you can suggest places for Ivy to look. Try the country club. If he's not there, wait for me, and I'll meet you."

GABRIELA CHECKED OUT the interior of the Saab. It was the kind of car she'd always wanted. It really annoyed her that her father still drove the muscle car he'd had in high school, even though all the guys at Truman and at the pool in summer acted like it was a Ferrari or something.

She watched Ivy start the car and thought how beautiful her hands were. *This is so weird. She's my mother, but she's not.*

"Okay, you'll have to direct me."

"Sure." Gabriela couldn't stop herself. "Can you remember how you got here?"

The blond woman turned her head and met Gabriela's eyes. "No problems with recent memory."

Her eyes are like mine.

Also, something about the way this stranger looked at her said she wasn't amused by the question. So much for that conversation.

She drove as if she was used to snow, and Gabriela said, "You live in Colorado?"

"I have been living in Colorado."

Gabriela did not like the sound of that. As they headed out of the hollow, she said, "So, how long are you staying?"

The Saab drew to a halt, although the stop sign was still yards away. Ivy faced her. "How long do you want me to stay?"

Her eyes were too direct, like she was already in

charge. Not in a mean way. She seemed like a person used to finding out what people really wanted. Gabriela watched her key ring swing from the ignition. It was a cluster of diaper pins on a larger pin with a blue wildflower on it and the words "Mountain Midwifery."

How was she supposed to answer a question like that?

"I guess it wasn't a fair question," Ivy said.

No kidding, Gabriela thought rebelliously.

"I'd hoped your dad would be the one to tell you this, but he and I had a chance to talk before we picked you up at school. I'm married to your dad. I'm your mother. And I'm going to stay here and live in the house where my grandmother was born, where my mother was born, where I was born and you were born."

"Don't you have a job somewhere else?"

"People in West Virginia don't have babies?"

"Not with midwives. We're not hillbillies."

"Mmm." Ivy put the car in gear and drove down to the stop sign. "Okay, which way? There's a tape case behind your seat if you want to hear some music."

A MARY CHAPIN CARPENTER album was playing in the country club, where a man in a well-cut suit sat laughing with the barmaid.

"Uncle Matthew!" Gabriela crossed the bar as if she owned the place. "Are you looking for Grandpa, too?"

"Is Grandpa missing?" Shifting on the bar stool, he faced Gabriela, then caught sight of Ivy still in the doorway. His hair was the same shade as Cullen's but more coarse and wiry. When he stood, it was to a good four inches taller than Cullen's six feet. "Well. Well, well, well." He paused long enough to make a statement with his distant inspection, then, confident and deliberate, strode toward Ivy and stopped before her. "I recognize this lady."

Feeling like he was hungry and she was what he wanted to eat, Ivy resisted taking a step back. "Then you have the advantage."

Not to be left behind, Gabriela joined him and Ivy. "She doesn't recognize *anyone,* even my dad."

"How interesting for both of you." Matthew sounded as though he wished he was part of the situation.

Why is this man coming on to me? Obviously, he was some kind of relative. Trying to forget Gabriela's coolness on the way to the country club, Ivy gazed at her until Gabriela waved absently at the man.

"Oh, this is Uncle Matthew."

Matthew was more precise. "Matthew Till."

"My husband's brother?"

A smile played on his lips as he gave a faint nod. His head tilted toward the bar. "Will you join me in a drink?"

They had promised Cullen they'd meet him in this place. Clearly his father wasn't here; there was no navy Lincoln in the parking lot. The last thing Ivy wanted was to sit down to a drink with a man sending out these kinds of signals. Particularly if he wasn't Cullen. *I'm too tired to deal with this.*

Had she imagined it all?

His expression left no hope. Matthew Till was a wolf in wolf's clothing.

She gathered her strength.

"We should hang out," said Gabriela. "We're supposed to meet Dad here anyway."

Matthew's smile showed only delight. "By all means, then. Gabby, what can I get my favorite niece? And nothing alcoholic, please, or I believe Corky *will* kick you out. Otherwise, I think she'll be indulgent." He threw the barmaid an affectionate wink.

The woman's expression was less forgiving. "For you, Matthew, anything."

"Do you have Perrier?" Gabriela asked.

"Absolutely." Corky eyed Ivy coldly. "Gina?"

Ivy stepped up to the bar. "Actually, my name's Ivy now. And you'll have to forgive me—"

"She has brain damage," Gabriela interjected. "She can't remember anything or anyone from when she lived here before."

It sounded like an effort to embarrass masked as an effort to be helpful. Ivy glanced at Gabriela. "Thank you for explaining, Gabriela."

"Anytime." She gave her uncle a saucy smile.

Brat. Ivy looked at the barmaid. "And you are?"

"Corky Stone. We went to school together." Her expression had softened some. She was blond and tiny, with a little scar on her upper lip and a blue-and-white crop top stretching over her full breasts.

"I'm so sorry. Everyone wondered what had happened to you."

"If anyone finds out, I hope they'll tell me. I've been living in Colorado for the past ten or so years. I'm a certified nurse-midwife."

"Good for you. I just can't believe you're back! And you've seen Cully and everything?"

Those eyes and ears were avidly gathering news—like hands snatching up twenty-dollar bills dropped in the street. Did this have to do with the ballet teacher? Ivy took a breath. "Yes."

"So—he's happy?"

A silence. What should she say?

"He's *way* happy." Gabriela's voice drew a line on the spotless bar. "My mother's home. He's happy. And I'm happy."

So that's part of who you are, Ivy mused.

She was defending her father.

No.

Her family.

I like you, Gabriela.

"Your mother's return is something to be happy about." Matthew's large hands settled on Ivy's shoulders. "What can I have Corky pour you?"

Her movement was instinctive. His hands were gone, he was busy regaining his balance, and she had put four feet between them. "Matthew, please don't startle me that way. There was a possibility I lost my memory because of an attacker, and you can imagine how I wouldn't want that to happen again. So I tend to react very quickly to someone touching me without my permission. Please don't do it again.''

Behind the counter, Corky danced to ''I Take My Chances.'' ''What can I get you…Ivy, was it?''

''I'll have what Gabriela's having, please.''

Gabriela had gone motionless. Her eyes started to Ivy's. Slowly, she smiled. A real smile, from her eyes. ''I'll get us a table.''

''Thank you.''

''Tell me,'' Matthew murmured when Gabriela was out of earshot, ''does Cullen find you even more intriguing than before?''

Ivy was thankful for ten years of observing relationships between men and women, often at intimate range. Husbands and wives at the birth of a child. Tara's relationship with her ex-husband. Francesca's with hers, which was something different altogether. And dating had given her practice in discouraging unwanted advances.

Easy to tell Matthew, ''You'll have to ask him that. Is Cullen a member here, Corky?''

''Sure. Want me to run a tab?''

''Thanks. I know he'll pick this up.'' Ivy left the bar to join Gabriela at the table she'd chosen. There was no way of knowing why Matthew had behaved as he had, with such confidence, toward his brother's wife.

But it was possible to guess.

And Ivy didn't like her guess at all.

A HALF INCH OF SNOW had covered the Lincoln. The surrounding landscape was all white, even the woods.

On the judge's cell phone, which he'd stopped at Coalgood to pick up, Cullen dialed his brother-in-law's mobile number.

Tom said, "Yeah?"

"I found him."

"Where are you?"

"State park." His father had taken him hiking here, camping in summer, caving. "To be specific, I found the car and his tracks. I'm going after him now." His father's request—to die—hung in the air.

"The store's closed. Shall I pick up Zeya and bring her to drive the Lincoln back?"

"Thanks." Besides, Daddy might give him an argument about coming home. The judge outweighed him by thirty pounds, and Cullen didn't want to risk hurting him. "Will you please call my mother, too?"

"Of course."

Cullen hung up and opened the door of the Camaro.

He slogged through the snow-covered mud, past the Lincoln frosted with white. The footprints led toward the trail to Soldiers Cave.

How strange to have these thoughts. That he was glad for the chance to be here with the judge one more time.

The judge was only twenty feet up the trail, stopped. Maybe he'd forgotten where he was going. He squinted at Cullen as his younger son climbed to where he was standing.

"Cully." Sam Till felt his own lucidity. *That's my son, Cullen. Where am I? What are we doing here?*

He remembered then. Illness. Old age.

Alzheimer's.

He looked around. *What was this place? Oh, yes, Guyandotte State Park. Why did I come?* "They sent you after me, didn't they?" The snow fell softly, drifting down through the trees.

"Want to come back to the car? I'll drive you home. Tom and Zeya are coming to get the Lincoln."

The world was a blank, a place of mystery, where even the simplest things were withheld from him. Cully talked slower than other people, but it didn't help now. And there was something...something...he wanted Cully to do. Oh, yes.

"I'll drive you to Coalgood," his son offered.

Sam wasn't ready. He wanted to decline, which he could do with a single word that he could not remember.

His eyes leaked tears.

Cullen jammed his hands in the pockets of his red-and-blue alpine shell. His ears hurt from the cold. He pulled the hood over his head, half-waiting for a repeat of the request his father had made just the previous night.

Help me die.

It never came. Maybe the judge was past asking.

And maybe past moving on his own initiative. "Come on. Let's go home. To Coalgood."

The judge didn't move.

"Daddy, I need to get back to my family. Gina has

come home. She goes by Ivy now, but she's come home to live with me and Gabby. I need to go. Will you please come with me?''

Sam heard. *Gina.* Gina. Cullen had a future ahead of him. Still sowing his oats, hiking all over the world, caving, still wandering the hills like some hillbilly, but at least he'd sold some photos. He'd been at the right place at the right time more than once.

But *Gina? Cully, did you have to knock up that girl and marry her?* And then...

Time jumped, forward, then back. ''You should think hard if you really want to marry that...'' What were they, that class of humans? Zeya and Mitzi, his wife. He saw them in droves and tried to think of the word for them. *Woman.* That was it, he thought with a moment's satisfaction. *Woman. Woman.*

The cold seeped into Sam's bones. He saw his own shoes in the snow. Why had he worn these shoes hiking?

Cullen had his arm, was helping him down the trail.

I'm old and sick, and my kids are taking care of me.

Another thought followed. Then evaporated. It was important. What was it?

''You know, Your Honor, you're my favorite judge.''

''Smart-ass kid.''

''I love you.''

Sam's tears froze on his cheeks. ''I hope you find another wife, Cully. You deserve a woman who loves you.''

Cullen steered his father around a snow-covered walk. How was he supposed to answer that one?

Another wife.

A woman to love him.

Well, Daddy, I have the first of those, anyway. "Let's go home to Coalgood. And the woman who loves *you.*"

CHAPTER FOUR

HE STOOD IN THE DOORWAY in his parka, which was purplish blue with bright red lining and trim—good outdoor gear. When she first glimpsed him there, so tall and strong, Ivy felt a trill along her pulse. For ten years, she had tried to feel something for other men and had felt so little that she wondered if her head injury had damaged her emotions, even her attraction to the opposite sex.

Each time she saw Cullen dispelled those doubts. She was attracted to this man. Powerfully.

His eyes barely flickered over her or Gabriela but settled on Matthew, their expression unblinking and cold.

"You must come to Atlanta to see the museum when it's done," Matthew was saying to Ivy, referring to the new Museum of the Confederacy, which he'd designed. "I'll fly you there. In my plane."

"Excuse me." Rising, Ivy caught Cullen's eye. She had to step around Gabriela's chair to go to him.

His slightly parted lips, his hands catching her arms through the wool of her ribbed turtleneck, could have meant anything.

She asked, "Did you find your father?"

"Yes. He's back at Coalgood. I'd gotten him home

before I remembered you haven't slept. How are you holding up?''

"Getting sleepy.''

"We'll leave the Camaro here, and I'll drive you home.''

"Find Daddy?''

Matthew's proximity heated her back. He'd stopped short of touching her, but only just. Ivy's instinct was to slam her elbow into his solar plexus. Instead, she took one long step forward, turning to stand beside Cullen. "Corky ran a tab for the drinks, Cullen. I hope that's all right.''

"I offered to get them, but your lady was very insistent.''

Cullen ignored the remark. "I did find Daddy. I thought you were in Atlanta until I saw your car outside.''

"I only just returned and had the privilege of seeing my favorite niece and this beautiful creature.''

Ivy studied their faces, assessed the energy between them. *This isn't about me at all.* "I'm going to sit down with Gabriela.''

"Sure.''

Cullen watched her legs, her body, her confident walk. She'd always been a good athlete; she probably still was. Maybe this summer he'd take her somewhere instead of going with Tom. For her, he'd shave with ice water.

"She is absolutely the most irresistible woman I have seen in some time.''

Cullen glanced at Matthew. As a teenager, he'd

stopped fighting Matthew. But Matthew had a way of pulling on your shirt, punching and beating on you until you hit back.

Cullen had developed a system for dealing with his brother. Strength through resistance to anger. It worked until human frailty snapped, as it had at Coalgood the other night, when he'd been unable to keep from saying, "With her husband." But Ivy's behavior had met with his complete satisfaction. "She's beautiful," he agreed. "Join us, or are you going home, Matthew?"

"Oh, I'll run along and let you enjoy your wife and Gabriela."

Another subtle dig. One with more dangerous implications—what Matthew knew about Gabriela. Ivy seemed able to take care of herself. Gabriela was a child.

The best protection for her was to pretend indifference to Matthew's insinuations. "Okay. Drive safely. The roads are slick."

"Not as slick as Gina's crotch, I'll bet."

With a sudden intake of breath, Cullen walked away.

At the table, he squeezed Gabriela's shoulders and grabbed a chair beside Ivy. "Does my family want to go home or eat here?"

"Ivy is a black belt in aikido and in tae kwon do. She almost made Uncle Matthew fall down."

"Did she?" He grinned at Ivy, swallowing other feelings. Knowledge. "I'll have to be careful."

"No." Her face was solemn. Honest. "I'd defend you with my life."

He believed her. "It's important to me that you never do that. Defend me in any physical way." Especially from Matthew.

Their eyes held long.

"Do you understand?"

"Not why." A second passed. "But if that's what you want, I won't."

"Thanks."

Gabriela sat up in her chair and all but snapped her fingers for a menu. "Let's eat here."

IT'S HAPPENING, Gabriela thought later that night.

Her dad was totally caught up in Ivy. But the weird thing was, they were both paying a lot of attention to *her,* too.

Like Ivy standing in her room now, checking out her posters. "Okay, tell me who these people are."

"All right, that's Peter Martins. That's—"

"Wait! I know!"

Gabriela couldn't help laughing.

"Baryshnikov." Ivy grinned at her. "Right?"

"That earns you one point out of a hundred as a ballet lover."

Ivy pointed at another poster. "The Alvin Ailey Company?"

"The words kind of give it away, don't you think?"

Ivy laughed, then examined the other posters. "I'm stumped. Educate me."

Jumping off her bed, Gabriela plucked two books from the maple bookcase her dad had made. "Educate yourself."

Ivy read the first title. *Writing Dancing in the Age of Postmodernism.* "Have you read this?"

"Some of it. Tracy—my ballet teacher suggested it. I'm going to be a prima ballerina and then a choreographer. I've got great videos, too. That's what you really need to do. Watch videos." She looked over her shelves again.

"Wait, wait. I want to watch them with you."

"Tonight?"

It was almost ten. "How about tomorrow?"

"Thanksgiving. We'll have to go to Coalgood. That's my grandparents' house. But we could take some videos, and Noel can come over. She's my best friend. I want her to meet you."

Ivy felt her eyes watering. *She likes me.*

"Are you all right?"

"I'm just happy. To be here with you." And Cullen.

Gabriela's whole body seemed to grow light. This was her mother, and it felt good. It felt like it was meant to be. She didn't know what to say, so she said nothing at all.

IVY WAS PRACTICING tae kwon do patterns in Gabriela's dance room when Cullen came in. He sat on a mat by the mirror to do his nightly sit-ups and push-ups. He'd run in the snow that morning, a lifetime ago.

She seemed not to notice him. He watched a few kicks reaching high over her head and decided she was lethal. And she'd dealt with Matthew, though she hadn't managed to discourage him.

He counted sit-ups, keeping his mind empty.

Then push-ups.

When he stopped, she was stretching, and he moved closer. She'd put on some loose black pants and a white long-sleeved T-shirt. He wore sweatpants and a T-shirt.

"Cullen," she said, "I'd like to start a midwifery practice here."

"Sure. You just worked out of the house before. Is that all right?"

"I think so. I'd like to find a backup physician. Anyone you'd recommend?"

"My sister and my sister-in-law like Mata Iyer."

"Is she an OB/GYN?"

"As far as I know. I'm more inclined to notice that she's gorgeous. I think she's Indian."

"Great. I can't wait to meet her." On her back, Ivy stretched a leg over her head. *Matthew. Should she bring it up?* Yes. "Your brother came on to me pretty strong."

Cullen relaxed forward, over his legs, stretching. How direct she was. Not like Gina. Not that Gina would have betrayed him. She just…

He couldn't put it into words.

He'd never wanted to.

"I know." What else could he say? Did one fair turn deserve another?

He got up, checked that Gabriela's door was shut, then shut the door of the dance room. He sat beside Ivy, facing her. "Gabriela is his natural daughter."

The single beat of her heart slammed Ivy's chest.

"You worked part-time in the courthouse. I think he met you there, when he was stopping by to see my dad. You fell in love with him. He was married, you got pregnant."

"Slow down. Please." It obviously wasn't his favorite story to tell, but she needed to know everything. "Was I married to you?"

"No. We were friends from school. I'd...liked you for a long time. You kept guys at a distance, so it seemed easiest to be friends."

"You married me because I was pregnant."

"Wrong. I married you because I was in love with you."

"And I loved your brother."

"Not after the mess he got you into."

Ivy had her doubts. "Gabriela doesn't know?"

"No one knows except Matthew. And it's possible he's told Shelby—his wife—somewhere along the line."

Ivy had noticed Matthew's wedding ring over drinks.

She'd slept with a married man. Borne his child. Married his brother.

Not me. Gina.

How convenient. A blow to the head had changed her into someone who didn't do such things.

No. Francesca and Tara had. Midwifery had. Martial arts had. Most of the ways she'd developed, she'd collected on her own, through the use of her mind, her will, the skills she'd learned.

But she hated this. Hated that Gabriela was Matthew's child instead of Cullen's. Obviously, Cullen was Gabriela's dad in every other way. But...

Could she live with that kind of lie?

It seemed wrong. Maybe Gina would have accepted it from start to finish, to cover her own crimes. But it didn't sit well with Ivy Walcott.

"Cullen, I want her to know. I think it's important."

"Then we disagree."

"But what if your brother tells her?"

Cullen sighed. Matthew was capable of telling her. He hadn't in twelve years, but... "Let's take this up again when you're not tired." He changed the subject. "Think you can sleep now?"

Her limbs were heavy as bags of sand. "I think."

"Why don't you turn in? I'll be up in an hour or two. I have some slides to put in the mail."

Ivy hesitated. "You don't have to. Stay up late, I mean."

She was getting used to his smile lines. "I think we'll both sleep better if I do. Go on up."

LEAVING OFF the overhead light in the loft, Ivy changed into flannel pajamas and left her clothes on the floor beside the dresser. Downstairs, Cullen had put Jackson Browne on the stereo, low.

The tester bed seemed bigger in the dark, the canopy like protection. Gabriela's bed was cast iron; Cullen said it was the bed Ivy had slept in growing up. Both of the beds had been in her family since her grandmother was a child.

This is really my home.

He was her home.

She had put the box in her top drawer. It was just a small white gift box in which she kept all her earrings and a couple of bracelets and necklaces, most of them gifts from Tara and Francesca.

Her rings were there, too. A gold band and another ring, a circle of lapis lazuli stones set in gold.

She'd been wearing the rings when she was brought to the hospital in Boulder. For days, she'd twisted them on her finger, rubbed them like talismans. One nurse after another had said, "What beautiful rings."

Ivy had loved them, too. And wondered who had given them to her.

While she slipped them on her left hand, Jackson Browne sang "Tender is the Night."

The clean flannel sheets on the daybed smelled faintly of pine. The mattress was firm, and to her left the windows reached to the ceiling. Shadows from the moon, far beyond the trees, cast black shapes on the warm wooden walls, just as the moonlight illuminated the trees through all the windows, including those behind the tester bed.

What had he said today? That she could trust him to leave her alone...for a while?

Was Cullen waiting out of kindness? Or to give his

grief over the loss of Gina a chance to heal? Or was it because of Tracy, the ballet teacher?

Who was Gina? Cullen had promised to tell her things—and he was, gradually—but so far she just couldn't picture the person she'd been at twenty, when she'd married him, or at twenty-two, when she'd disappeared.

Today, she'd instantly pegged Matthew Till as a seducer, a womanizer. She'd seen them in all forms in Precipice, and she'd seen them more skillful than Matthew. How old had he been then? He had to be at least forty now. But maybe not.

I slept with him.

It disgusted her. She really couldn't stand the idea of sex with a man who couldn't control his sensuality, a man who saw women as conquests.

But Gabriela... *I love her.*

What if Gabriela was to find out the truth? Would she hate her mother? Would she hate Cullen for lying to her?

The point of change needed to come immediately. Only now would Ivy have the right to explain, to say, *I'm not the same woman I used to be.* But if she conspired with Cullen and Matthew to keep the secret, how was she different?

Suddenly, a fourth party entered the picture.

Matthew's wife. Shelby.

Cullen had said he suspected Shelby knew the truth. But did she? And if she didn't...

Ivy hugged the sheets around her in the dark. As she'd driven across the country, she'd tried to foresee all the possibilities of what she'd find in West Virginia. A husband she didn't like. A daughter with whom she felt no connection. People with different interests. A place where she'd never feel at home.

Instead, she'd discovered a gentle man who seemed to respect her—a man *she* could respect. Her daughter liked her, and Ivy liked and loved Gabriela without trying. The hill country was beautiful, the cabin a place where she could live and die in happiness.

Her imagination had fallen short in assessing the possible problems.

She'd never suspected that the woman she'd been would have left the kind of unfinished business that Gina had.

And I should have guessed. To arrive at a hospital a thousand miles from home, broken and bleeding. Why? What had happened?

Who were you, Gina? Tell me.

Who was I?

SHE SLEPT IN blue flannel pajamas with pictures of appliances on them. Cullen had seen them earlier when she was unpacking, putting her clothes in the dresser he'd cleaned out. She said she'd brought everything she owned but furniture. She didn't have much—of anything.

In the moonlight, he stripped off his T-shirt. Her blond hair sprayed over the pillow, over her pajamas. She'd already kicked off half the covers. The heat from the stove downstairs collected in this loft all day.

Cullen carefully gathered her grandmother's log cabin quilt and folded it over the back of the rocking chair.

When she sighed in her sleep, he started slightly. She rolled to her side, and the top of her pajamas hung loose, showing the curve of her breasts. There must be some of Gina left in her, something to make her trust him so completely. Or else it was simply that she'd lost years of her life and it had made her naive.

She hadn't seemed naive at the country club.

Before he could turn away, to get in the canopy bed they'd once shared, he saw her hand resting on the sheets, on the bed where Gabriela had slept as a three- and four-year-old.

The moonlight was tender.

He opened the drawer where he'd put her photo, found his ring and put it on.

HER EYES OPENED, and the natural light in the room was wonderful despite the gray day. The limbs of the man tugging a T-shirt over his head held the same warmth as the wood. Ivy admired his abs and pecs and the muscles of his arms. What would his chest hair feel like if she touched him? As the white cotton fell down around his body, he saw her eyes and paused beside the tester bed, his head higher than the canopy. "Good morning."

"Good morning." *We spent the night in this room together.* She'd never heard him come in.

His jaw was shadowed, unshaven. "Gabriela and I have a Thanksgiving tradition that she claims to hate.

We snowshoe to Ganfrey's Pond, about a mile away, and go ice-skating. Then, regrettably, there's a command performance at Coalgood. The family home.''

"That sounds really nice, the skating. So I should dress warmly?"

"When you feel like it. The other part of the tradition is a leisurely, healthful breakfast—as Gabriela says, to make up for what Lily will do to us later. Lily's my parents' housekeeper,'' he added quickly. "And a wonderful cook.''

Before Ivy could bring up the issue of telling Gabriela about her natural father, there came a bump on the floor.

Cullen called, "Hold your horses. I'm coming down.''

Gabriela yelled, "I want to get this miserable day on the road!"

"A lover of the holiday, you can see." With a wink at Ivy, Cullen headed for the ladder.

"Cullen." He looked back, and Ivy put thoughts of Matthew and Gabriela aside. "Thank you."

"For what?"

"For welcoming me back."

"Wait to say that until you pass the ultimate ordeal."

"What's that? I can cook,'' she offered.

He laughed. "So can I. That's not what I meant."

His eyes turned momentarily mischievous. "I meant,'' he stage-whispered, "Pass the ultimate ordeal. *Coalgood.*"

CHAPTER FIVE

THROUGH THE CASEMENT windows of the living room and beneath the snowy limbs of the climbing oak, Zeya watched Cullen and Ivy overturn the toboggan in a snowbank. Legs tangled in the snow, they laughed, and Cullen caught her in a one-armed hug before they got to their feet. "I haven't seen Cully that happy in years."

Her elder brother peered over her shoulder for a view. "Gabriela doesn't seem so happy."

"Matthew," his wife called from the couch, "come look at these photos Cullen brought over. He actually got something flattering of me. It's a miracle."

Shelby, Zeya wanted to say, *you're a saint.*

Matthew edged over to the coffee table where his stepmother and Shelby were passing photos back and forth, Mitzi sharing each one with the judge. Scrutinizing the photo of Shelby and Scout, Matthew finally bent over and kissed his wife. "You are a beautiful subject." He tugged absently on a red curl, then returned to the window. "Well, I think I'll go join the lovebirds and my nieces and Tom."

Matthew was not usually a sledder, and Zeya exclaimed, "Good grief, Matthew, why don't you give him some peace to be with his family?"

"Why, Zeya, are you suggesting that I would choose this joyful moment in my brother's life to torment him?"

"Matthew," the judge barked abruptly, "leave your brother alone. Let him play in peace."

As Matthew gritted his teeth, the three women smiled at the judge's twenty-five-year time leap.

Matthew finally smiled. "He's not playing, Daddy. He's outside with Gina."

Rising from the couch, Shelby stretched languorously. "Feeling like going upstairs for a while, Matthew?"

Definitely a holy woman, thought Zeya. No other being in the universe would have so much patience with Matthew or so much compassion for him.

"Gina?" The judge walked to the window.

His wife followed. "She's different now, Sam. This is Ivy."

"That's not Gina. Why the hell did you say Gina was out there?" Before anyone could answer, the judge exclaimed, "By God, there she is, after Tom now, it looks like. Matthew, tell her to go home."

Zeya, her mother and Matthew saw in astonishment what the judge had noticed. Gabriela and Scout climbing off a sled at the bottom of the hill, where Tom had met them. Gabriela.

No one spoke for seconds.

Then, abruptly, Matthew threw back his head and howled with laughter.

CULLEN DRAGGED Gabriela's sled back toward the top of the long run, alongside the sunken garden behind the house.

"Uncle Cullen, take me. No, Daddy's going down. Daddy, wait!"

As Scout ran to join Tom on a toboggan, Cullen gave Gabriela's shoulders a squeeze. "How are you doing?"

"Fine."

Something was amiss, but Cullen had no idea what until Ivy hauled the other toboggan over the snow toward them. "Gabriela," she asked, "when can we watch those videos?"

"Now, probably. If you want."

"I do."

Like that, the sparkle returned to Gabriela's eyes. Cullen debated if he should volunteer to join them, then decided Gabriela wanted Ivy to herself.

Know just how you feel, Gabs.

"Come on." Gabriela abandoned her sled. "Let's go in the back way. Then we won't get the snow-on-the-floor lecture from Grandma and Lily."

A figure in a fisherman-knit sweater and flannel-lined khaki pants trudged around the corner of the house and up the hill toward them, looking like an advertisement for L.L. Bean.

Catching sight of Matthew, Ivy said, "Great, let's go. I'll race you," and sprinted over the snow to the back patio.

Gabriela passed her and wheeled, throwing up both hands to stop her so that Ivy ran into her, and they both stumbled, laughing. "Slow down," Cullen called out. "The patio's slick."

"Mother and daughter," Matthew remarked softly. "Anywhere on earth, a person could see that Ivy is that child's mother. And that Gabriela is her daughter."

Ignoring him, Cullen chose the fastest sled and continued up the hill that rose alongside the sunken garden.

Helping himself to the toboggan, Matthew followed. "Except, of course, the judge. Our father, get this, mistook Gabriela for Gina. 'By God, there she is, after Tom now, it looks like. Matthew, tell her to go home.'" He shouted a laugh. "Let's go to the top, Cullen. I'll race you. Course, you have the faster sled."

Cullen offered his brother the rope.

"No, thanks. I just wanted to point out that you have the superior equipment so you'll feel a greater sting of humiliation when you lose."

They found the launching point, the highest launching point on the property, too high for Scout—and Gabriela was too aware of her future as a dancer to risk a sledding accident. Cullen settled on the sled, using one foot behind him as a brake. "You say when."

"Now." Matthew caught Cullen's arm and yanked him along.

Cullen had intended to give his brother a solid head start. Now he was ahead, though Matthew's heavier weight evened the contest some.

The snow had crusted to ice in places. Through the clatter of the runners, he heard Matthew's words, the judge's words. *There she is, after Tom now, it looks like.* His thoughts pulsed red. White flew at his eyes.

"Get over!" Cullen yelled.

Matthew nudged the side of the sled with the toboggan.

They were at the right edge of the run. They needed to move left, not right, to avoid the cluster of oaks separating Coalgood from the Nathans' place next door.

Cullen gave the sled a sharp jerk all the way to the right and rolled off it to the left, coming to within a foot of the second oak.

"Yee-haw!" Matthew yelled, lifting a fist as he rode the rest of the way down the run. "You're a chicken, Cullen! You always were."

Cullen dragged the sled to the house, then walked down the hill to meet Matthew.

Getting up from the toboggan, his brother reached out and patted his cheek with a snowy wool glove. "Still Daddy's little puppy, aren't you, Cully?"

"Why would Daddy think Gina was hitting on Tom?"

Matthew's face changed, became overly concerned with the question. "Now, why *would* he think that— when she was always so faithful to you?" He tossed wiry, gray-flecked golden hair back from his eyes. A second later, he grinned and slammed Cullen on the back. "You're so *easy*, Cully. You're easy to bait."

He hugged Cullen and kissed his cheek loudly, then whispered, "He never said it. Ha-ha-ha!"

Staying behind, Cullen watched Matthew drag the toboggan back up to the house.

Tom came up behind him. "I recommend a padded cell for that man."

"Uncle Cullen." Scout tugged on his coat. "Will you take me down the big hill?"

The front door shut behind Matthew. "Sure, Scout. Let's go."

"Can you pull me up on the sled?"

"Dream on."

Tom laughed. "Start walking, kid."

"I'll beat you both!" she yelled and ran.

"I never met Gina, but Ivy seems nice."

"She is."

"Not exactly a dog, either."

"Not exactly." Cullen was glad when Tom continued up the hill after his daughter, leaving him to grab a sled, to be alone.

There she is, after Tom now, it looks like.

The judge's words.

Matthew was mean, but he just wasn't that clever.

"OH, WHAT WOULD YOU GIVE?" Noel exclaimed. "Did you *see* that?"

Gabriela had invited her friend over to watch the ballet videos, and two hours ago Noel had arrived with the news that Zeya and Tom had gone to the toy store to prepare for the start of the Christmas season tomorrow, and Cullen was building "snow creatures" with Scout.

In Coalgood's rec room in the basement, Ivy listened to the two girls' ballet dreams and watched some of the most phenomenal dance she'd ever seen. Postmodern ballet and more.

She wanted to encourage Gabriela's dreams, but she wished they were less tied to the prospect of fame.

"Look at all those flowers," Gabriela said. The ballerina's arms were overflowing.

Ivy asked, "How would it make you feel to get so many flowers?"

"Great!"

Ivy wanted to help her through this adolescence, help her make the transition to womanhood. From needing to be loved, from needing approval, to loving and nurturing.

But for now, her immediate concern was that Gabriela be told Matthew was her natural father—before Matthew decided to tell her. That meant first convincing Cullen, then telling Matthew and Shelby their intention. One meeting with Shelby had made Ivy suspect that Matthew's wife did know the truth. It had also made her admire Shelby, who was an unlikely partner for Matthew Till.

But she really hadn't had a second alone with Cullen since that morning. When she'd come downstairs, she'd found him cooking breakfast while Gabriela photographed him with his camera and begged him to let her go away to New York City to ballet school. Ivy had the feeling that it was the continuation of a long conversation on the subject because they both did a lot of laughing.

And who, Miss Gabriela Till, would steal all the hot water in the morning if you were gone?

Ivy.

And who would talk back to me?

I'll teach Ivy how.

They ended the conversation with a hug and Gabriela saying, *Okay, I'll stay and torment you for one more year.*

He was a good father, and Gabriela was a wonderful girl. *How did I get so lucky?*

"Hello, ballet fans. We've been summoned to dinner."

Noel and Gabriela perked up at Cullen's entrance.

"Dad, can I sleep over at Noel's? Her mom said it's okay."

His hesitation lasted no more than a moment. "Yes."

"Hooray!" The girls sent up a cheer, and Noel jumped to her feet.

"Okay, I'm going home. Come over as soon as you can. We've got a toothbrush and everything, Mr. Till. It's nice meeting you…Mrs. Till."

As Gabriela shut off the VCR, Noel went through the big arched doorway of the rec room. Instead of heading up the stairs, she turned down the hall to the right. Leaving the room with Gabriela and Cullen half a minute later, Ivy peered down the hallway. Noel had disappeared.

"There's a mudroom down there—and stairs up to the sunken garden," Cullen explained.

"The laundry room's in there and the dumbwaiter," Gabriela added. "Once, Uncle Matthew pulled my dad partway to the second floor in the dumbwaiter and just left him for a whole afternoon. Can you believe it?"

Ivy couldn't tell how Gabriela felt about the event. Perhaps she viewed it as an amusing family anecdote. Or maybe she was alarmed on behalf of the boy trapped in the dumbwaiter.

"How old were you?"

"Three." Cullen nodded toward the stairs. "Let's go up. You can see my family in full color now."

"It's always *so weird,*" Gabriela confided.

Ivy wondered if that was why Cullen hadn't met her eyes once since he'd come downstairs.

SHE SAT ON the judge's right.

He said, "You aren't a vegetarian, are you?"

"No."

"Good. Glad Cullen's met a nice girl."

Gina wasn't?

Mitzi Till threw Ivy an apologetic look and shook her head, a sign to pay no attention to the things he said.

On Ivy's right, Cullen ate silently, never looking up at her.

What was wrong? She couldn't escape the feeling that something had changed for him since they were last together on the sledding hill.

"Ivy *is* a nice girl," remarked Matthew. "Incorruptible, I'd say."

"You would know," the judge muttered.

"Daddy!" Mitzi Till shook her head. "Please be nice. This is Thanksgiving. Matthew, help him with his turkey."

But Lily had appeared over the judge's shoulder. "Let me help you, Judge Till."

"I can cut my own food!"

Cullen's arm went across Ivy, keeping her back from the brandished steak knife. "Easy, Daddy."

Ivy trembled, and Cullen rose. "Switch seats with me," he said.

She did, without a word, and found herself next to Scout.

"How gallant of you, Cullen," Matthew murmured.

Scout nudged Ivy's leg. She held up a small plastic figure. "Aunt Ivy, watch out. *An alien!* He wants to steal your heart."

Ivy started to giggle at the idea when Matthew's smooth voice overrode her laughter. "I'm sure he's not the only one."

Courtesy kept Ivy from casting a look at Shelby, on Matthew's left, to see how she was taking this behavior, the incessant digs at his younger brother.

"Zeya, take the toys away from Scout, *please.* Scout, honey, it's not good manners to have toys at the table. Grandma says please put the alien away. Honey, don't you want some turkey? It's so good."

"Did you take my bread?"

Matthew sat back from the judge. "No, Daddy, I most certainly did not take your bread."

"Mitzi." The look the judge threw his wife was suspicious.

"Daddy, you *ate* it." Zeya passed Ivy a bowl. "Ivy, try this rice pilaf."

"I did *not* eat it."

Cullen lifted his chair and set it back on the patterned Karastan, then retrieved his camera. "Daddy, sit next to Matthew. Let's have a photo."

IN THE FRONT SEAT of the Saab, he started the car without a word.

Instinctively, she touched his hand. "Cullen."

His glance was a snake's bite, that quick and sharp.

She never flinched. "What is it?"

He switched off the ignition, sat back in his seat and watched snow falling in the headlights. In a row along the curb, the snow bandits and snow Martians he and Scout had built were losing their shape. Should he share what Matthew had told him, what the judge had said? Pride rebelled against letting Ivy know... know what?

It was all guesses. A suspicion Matthew had raised, preying on his own insecurity. An insecurity with powerful reason behind it. The most powerful reason of all. And even if the judge had said it, what did that mean? He could have just confused times. Perhaps he'd seen Matthew with Gina before she was pregnant with Gabriela....

Though he'd never said so.

The judge didn't know about Gabriela.

Cullen finally answered, "Too much Coalgood. Let's go home."

She stopped him before he could start the car again. "Cullen, please don't keep things from me."

"All right. My brother said something that led me to think my wife—that would be you—may have betrayed me with him after our marriage." With a bright, mirthless smile, he started the car.

"I'm sorry. If it's true. I'm not that kind of person now."

"If it's true, your apology is inadequate. Keep it." He drew the Saab away from the curb and into the road, making the first tire tracks on a blanket of white.

Ivy shut her mouth, opened it to argue, then closed it again. Who else, after all, should be expected to suffer for Gina's wrongs?

The Saab made its way around the island, and Cullen glanced toward a house on the left where a light burned. Ivy had learned from Noel and Gabriela that Tracy lived on this street. "Was that Tracy's house?"

"Yes."

Ivy changed the subject. "Have you given any more thought to telling Gabriela the truth about Matthew?"

"About Matthew and you, do you mean?"

There was no point in saying he had no proof. The signs were there. "Yes. About who her natural father is."

"Her natural father." His tone was bitter.

She winced. *Don't do this, Cullen.*

Still, to have taken blame for the unplanned pregnancy, to have married her and then been betrayed…

He was right. Sorry would never be enough.

The wipers crossed back and forth on the windshield in sweeping arcs. Dark miles passed on the highway before he turned up the road that led toward the hollows.

They didn't speak again until the cabin.

Shutting off the engine, Cullen said, "It's better for her not to know. You have to understand this about Matthew. He has limits. He wants to hurt me, not Gabriela."

"I don't think he'd hesitate for a second to hurt me, Cullen. Or any other woman he wanted. Obviously, he doesn't mind hurting his own wife. What makes you think he'd be more sensitive to his niece's feelings, especially since she's your daughter?"

"His daughter, you mean."

"And since you brought it up, what is it with you two?"

Cullen released his seat belt, tried to get comfortable with his back to the door, his knee behind the gearshift. "He's fourteen years older than me. His mom died when he was Gabriela's age."

"Ouch."

"And Daddy remarried pretty fast. Also…"

When he didn't finish, Ivy guessed. "You're Daddy's favorite?"

His silence was no denial.

She made a face. "He'll tell her, Cullen. And I don't want him to be the one to do it."

Cullen shifted in his seat, opened the door. "Let's continue this discussion inside."

EIGHT HOURS EARLIER, if someone had told him Gabriela would be spending the night at a friend's, he would have rejoiced. Now the last thing he wanted was time alone with Ivy.

Gina.

Building the fire in the woodstove, he contemplated nature and nurture. Ivy must still possess Gina's nature. Was it a lack of nurture that had made her unfaithful? He wanted to believe it—and didn't.

"Care if I put on a CD?"

He glanced up. She was picking over his collection of CDs and the few of Gabriela's that were jumbled in with them. "Go ahead."

She chose Neil Young, keeping it low so they could talk.

For a second, in the car, she'd almost convinced him about Gabriela. "Ivy, my name's on her birth certificate."

She digested that. "I can see your point, Cullen. I just—don't feel at ease with it."

Sitting on the rag rug, Cullen felt a little of his rancor fading. How many nights would they sleep in separate beds? He stood and turned up the stereo. Not sure it was what he wanted, sure only that he needed to start somewhere, Cullen beckoned her from the couch.

"What?"

"You'll see."

Slowly, she rose in her socks and jeans and white turtleneck with diamonds on it. When she neared him, he took her left hand in his right and lightly wrapped his free arm around her as Neil Young sang "From Hank to Hendrix."

Cullen sang to her, and she couldn't help smiling.

Their smiles faded simultaneously, changing into something else.

He angled his head down, and she brought hers up.

Their lips touched, trying to answer the questions, trying to figure out if they could travel the long road together as they'd promised thirteen years ago—and the day before.

His lips were warm. Nothing familiar in them, but she liked his scent, liked his taste, liked the gentle pressure on her mouth. But his body was so big, so hard. Her other contact with men had been…different. More like the encounter with Matthew at the country club. Touches she didn't want. Dancing with Cullen, kissing him, was like skiing the backcountry, like snowshoeing in solitude through the forest, like the speed of skates on the ice of Ganfrey's Pond that morning.

"I've never…liked a man before."

He drew back, to study her face. Her eyes.

Slowly he smiled, but not with trust. "Lucky me."

Cullen released her, mostly so he wouldn't tell her his thoughts, which were bitter. *Unfortunately, I loved you. And you broke your vows.*

He told himself again not to leap to conclusions,

but it was too late.

In his heart, he had always known.

THERE WERE NO MORE KISSES that night. He settled down with some slides, she phoned Tara for the least candid conversation she'd ever shared with her sister, and finally, sensing he wanted her to turn in first, like the night before, Ivy did.

This time, sleep came slowly, and she was still awake when Cullen came up. Not wanting to surprise him, she said, "Hi."

He glanced toward the daybed. "Can't sleep?"

"No."

He indicated the canopy bed. "Want to get in here?"

She'd have to sometime, unforgiving husband or not. This wasn't the way she'd imagined it. *It probably isn't the way he wanted it, either.*

"I'd prefer to wait until you want me there."

"Oh." He unbuttoned his flannel shirt and hung it on the rod in the small closet. "Then don't let me disturb your insomnia."

Beside his bed, he stripped off his pants and underwear, and she knew it was his way of saying he was through giving her special treatment.

Starting with his discovery that day. Which had nothing to do with Ivy—and everything to do with Gina.

She closed her eyes, listened to the bed creak as he climbed in.

He sighed, expressing that his was the more comfortable bed. "Good night, Ivy."

"Good night, Cullen."

"Let's see," he muttered. "Gabriela will probably spend the night with Noel again in…May."

She knew what he meant, but…

"Those aren't the magic words."

"If only I knew them. Like—like *Matthew* does."

His bitterness chilled Ivy. Maybe he'd always doubt her, even knowing how much she'd changed with the loss of her former personality.

She was the one who needed magic words, and there were none.

She did the best she could.

Abruptly, she got out of bed, went to the far side of his and lifted the covers, remembering belatedly that he was naked beneath. The sudden realization made her sway on her feet. *What was she doing?*

Too late to back out.

It had been too late yesterday, when he'd met her with an embrace.

It was too late a week ago, when she'd promised to come home.

She got into bed and prepared her apology, while he eyed her as one might an affectionate coyote.

"My unfaithfulness to you was abominable. I'm sorry for hurting you. You can rest assured that the woman in your bed tonight would never do such a thing."

He didn't blink.

"I'm really sorry, Cullen."

"More sorry. Be more sorry."

"How can I be more sorry for something I don't remember doing?"

"So who did it? Where did she go? She looked a lot like you, and she called herself my wife, the way you do." He had sat up.

Cowering against a second pillow that smelled faintly of him, Ivy wondered how he expected either of them to get any sleep in this bed.

"I apologized. What else do you want me to do? Wear sackcloth and ashes for a year?"

"That would be a start. But you know what? You're right. There's nothing you can do. Except wait."

"For what?"

"For me to pay you the compliment of sharing my heart with you again."

"Well, don't expect to share my body in the meantime!"

"Tonight, it would be a chore." He fell back on the bed to stare at the canopy. "Good night."

She started to climb out of bed, but his hand locked on her wrist. "Oh, no, you don't."

"What?"

"I think it's time for you to start sharing your husband's bed—if nothing else."

This is ridiculous. What does he want? Irritated, Ivy eased herself back into the bed, careful not to touch him.

Slowly, he released her wrist. "Sackcloth and ashes for a year, did you say?"

"I want to go to sleep now, if you don't mind."

He ignored her. "A year... And what else did you say earlier tonight? I remember! 'I've never liked a man before.'"

Ivy shut her eyes and put her hands over her ears.

He moved them, pressing them to the pillow on either side of her, and when she opened her eyes, his gazed down at her and just enough of his weight covered her to make her want to feel the rest of him.

"Sleep well, *Gina*." He didn't kiss her but released her and turned away.

BEFORE AN HOUR HAD PASSED, Cullen realized that her penance was going to be his hell. He wished he'd accepted her apology and left it at that.

The only problem—he didn't forgive her.

He didn't forgive *Gina*.

Ivy had had the last word, then drifted off to the sleep of the innocent. *I'm not Gina.*

In the night, he massaged his forehead. He'd been a jerk, and he was going to suffer unless he took back the things he'd said.

Suffering seemed more appealing.

She shifted in her sleep, her face resting against his upper arm. He didn't want to push her away but didn't want her close. She smelled so good. The scent hurt.

Gina, how could you? With a baby?

She'd had opportunity galore. She and Matthew could have met in this bed while he was at work.

And it explained...things he'd never wanted explained.

His eyes stung.

It was Gina's scent doing this to him, the familiarity.

But Gina had never slept with her head against his arm.

Gently, he moved, turning his back to her.

She slipped toward him, filling in the part of the bed he'd vacated.

Cullen flipped back and lifted her to move her over.

She jerked awake, eyes wide and mouth open in a cry, terrified, and her hands began to react. Not wanting to know what they could do, these hands, he caught her arms gently. "It's just me."

She relaxed.

A woman who had not slept with a man.

When he moved her over in the bed, she allowed it, like a sleepy child. *No one's going to hurt you again.*

The darkness reminded him that whatever wrong she had done him, something much worse might have been done to her.

To both of them.

She'd lost herself—and their child.

It hit him for the first time.

Gina had been pregnant when she was hurt. Pregnant with whose child?

To suspect Gina of sleeping with Matthew was one thing. But the other...

She wouldn't do it. Not that.

If only he knew.

Ivy's eyes, gazing at him, made Cullen realize that

he was propped on his arm, staring. At her. He lay down again.

"What were you thinking?"

"Wishing I could get your memory back for you. Every bit of it."

She didn't ask why. But after a long time, she said, "I don't want it so badly anymore."

CHAPTER SIX

SHE AWOKE SOMETIME in the night with her face on his skin and remembered his anger. Carefully, she shifted away, and he turned in his sleep, his head nearing hers.

Who's he dreaming of? Tracy?

Or Gina.

I don't want Gina to have done what she did.

I don't want to have done it.

Maybe she hadn't. Undoubtedly, that was why Cullen wished her memory would return. So that he could learn the truth.

She'd spent nights yearning to regain her memory the way Cinderella must have yearned to go to the ball. But her memory would never return. If Cullen wanted the truth, he should ask Matthew.

And what kind of answer would Matthew give?

Whatever answers would pain Cullen most.

But there was another solution. *What if I asked?*

"DON'T FEEL TOO SPECIAL. It happens every morning."

Ivy knew she'd been staring. She'd tried not to, but she found him beautiful.

Quelling an inner flush, she averted her eyes as he pulled on his sweatpants.

Cullen remembered, too late, that his was probably the first erection she'd ever seen—that she could recall. Anger over infidelity warred with other things, feelings that had more to do with Ivy than with Gina.

Anger won.

Taking clothes for the day out of his closet, he said, "I'm photographing kids with Santa Claus at Zeya and Tom's store from ten until two. I need to head downtown soon, get ready. Noel's mom said she'd bring Gabriela by the store after lunch. So the day is yours." *Invite Matthew over, if you like.*

"Is there anything I can do to help you?"

"Nothing," he lied.

Then she could run some errands, start advertising her midwifery practice. Only one thing troubled her. She sat up in bed but had to duck down again to see his face, he was so tall. "Cullen, I need to know something. I understand you're angry, but do you still want me to stay?"

His eyebrows lifted. "Thinking of leaving your husband and daughter already? Two days—"

"I'm not thinking of leaving. I'm asking if you wish I would."

"I wish you'd never screwed my brother."

I didn't.

The protest died inside her for the hundredth time. "Me, too. Though I can't regret our beautiful daughter."

He was silent. When he shut the closet door, it was

one degree short of a slam. He went downstairs without another word.

CLOTHES FOR SALE.

The table sat by the edge of the road, behind an old mini pickup with a camper shell, and the woman beside it wore exhaustion in her skin and her bones. It was the exhaustion of poverty, apparent in her gauntness and the slump of her shoulders. Ivy drew the Saab to the side of the road and got out, just as another woman came from the snowy woods, carrying a bag of dried vines. For ornamental wreaths, perhaps?

The woman who had emerged from the woods was pregnant, and Ivy instinctively assessed the size of her abdomen, how she was carrying. Was she getting prenatal care—or would her family do it the old way, at home?

Remembering Gabriela's reaction—"We're not hillbillies"—Ivy bet on a hospital birth.

Trudging through the snow from the car, Ivy called, "Good morning."

"Morning."

Ivy stopped at the table. The clothes on it were faded and tattered, with the exception of a satin affair that looked like a prom gown. But one of the older dresses was quite pretty, a blue calico, and there was a gorgeous quilt, too, a wedding-ring pattern.

"Can I help you?" The heavy mountain twang resonated in the older woman's voice. Her cigarette puffed clouds into the cold as she eyed the Saab distantly. Clearly, Ivy couldn't have appeared more foreign had she arrived on a camel.

"This dress is lovely. And the quilt." Ivy considered. The quilt looked newly made, albeit from well-worn fabric. There were plenty of quilts at the cabin—quilts Cullen said she and her grandmother had made—but the wedding-ring quilt would make the perfect Christmas gift for Francesca.

How much should she offer? She wanted to help, yet the last thing she needed was to appear too different from her client pool. And truthfully, she would earn less money working as a midwife here in Guyandotte.

The midwife in Morgantown to whom she'd spoken on the phone had said, "Get used to the idea of working for barter. A lot of these people won't even take public assistance, so there goes any possibility of medical insurance. More than half the time, you'll be paid in quilts and curtains and jars of Grandma's blackberry preserves. Be sure to find out who the people with money are and socialize some. You'll need at least a few paying clients."

Ivy asked, "Would you take ten for the dress and sixty for the quilt?"

"These quilts sell for two hundred in Morgantown."

It was worth that, at least, but Ivy couldn't pay it, and the woman didn't expect it. "The most I can give you is ninety for the quilt and ten for the dress."

"That'll do."

Ivy fished in her bag for her wallet, glad she had

the cash. The woman had hidden the hunger in her eyes, but...

"By the way, I'm Ivy Walcott." She held out her hand, and the woman could do nothing but take it—warily. In the frigid day, Ivy felt the calluses, the veins and wrinkles, of her hand. "I'm a midwife, and I'm just starting a practice here." She started to address the younger woman and faltered for a moment. *She's just a child...* Fifteen, perhaps, but *still.*

The older woman stared as though Ivy's profession had nothing to do with her.

"I know you've probably established a relationship with a doctor, but I just want to let you know in case you haven't. I grew up around here. My grandmother and mother were midwives, too."

"You don't say. Who was your grandmother?"

"Mrs. Naggy. I was Gina Naggy. I'm married to Cullen Till."

The woman squinted at her oddly. She stuck her cigarette back in her mouth. Ivy's hundred dollars had found their way into the pocket of the woman's quilted coat. "I thought that was you, but I was afraid to hazard a guess. I don't suppose you remember me. Emma Workman."

She thrust out her hand, and Ivy shook it again and hastily explained about her memory loss.

"That explains it. We were never close, but you would have seen me four or five thousand times in your life."

Emma swiftly changed topics. "Actually, Devon's not seeing a doctor. I've had four children and six grandchildren, including Devon. The doctors just want to run all kinds of tests, and we're keeping this baby. Doesn't seem a need for tests.'' She paused. "How much do you charge?''

"I have a sliding scale. It depends on what you can pay.''

Emma sucked on her cigarette. "Say we give you back fifty dollars of your money. Would that be enough?''

"Yes.'' Devon was far along. Thirty-two weeks? Thirty-three? *I have to get a backup physician.* But surely that wouldn't be a problem here, where poverty was rampant; any physician with a lick of sense could see that a midwife's services could only help. "Do you have a phone at your house?''

"No. But we live up Missing Girl Hollow, too. I know your place.''

The girl should be seen without delay, and Ivy told Emma so. "I need to know what to expect.''

"Our family births easy.''

"Nonetheless. May I visit with Devon for a bit?''

She retrieved her midwifery kit from her car—she always kept it there for emergencies—and took Devon's history on the rear bumper of the pickup, writing with her wool gloves on. Devon was sixteen, and the father was her boyfriend, Rowdy.

Ivy listened patiently, glad that Mrs. Workman stayed at a distance, allowing them to talk privately.

"Are you sure you want to keep this baby, Devon? You're young. A baby changes your whole life.''

"I want her. I think it's a girl. Rowdy and I are

probably going to get married anyway, but if we don't, there's always Gran to help.''

"Do you live with your grandmother?"

"Yeah. My mom has to work up in Morgantown. It's the only place she could get a job.''

"Well, I'll need to do a home visit in the next few days. Do you mind if I feel your abdomen, to see how your baby's lying? That way, I can also start to assess how many weeks pregnant you are.'' Devon didn't know the date of her last menstrual period.

"All right.''

IVY LEFT THE ROADSIDE a half hour later, excited at the prospect of an upcoming birth yet uneasy about Devon's future. Undoubtedly, she would spend the weeks up until the girl's delivery and through the postpartum period dealing with those emotions. She'd never expected that her first client in Guyandotte would be sixteen years old and pay her fifty dollars for all prenatal services and the birth, but at least she *had* a client.

She needed to talk to Cullen about money. In Precipice, she'd been paid two thousand dollars for each birth, including prenatal services, and nearly everyone could pay. Did Cullen mind another mouth to feed?

Judging from the country-club membership and Gabriela's ballet lessons, he was doing well, and it was possible he had family money, too. She wasn't going to worry about it right now.

After parking near Guyandotte Toyland, three spaces from Cullen's Camaro, Ivy consulted her list of errands. "Backup physician" was at the head of the list, followed by a Yellow Pages listing, flyers, finding an answering service. Mata Iyer's office was at the medical clinic on First Street. She was on Main now.

Ivy struck out walking, turning down Cardinal. Yes, there was First Street. It began to snow as she peered down the block at an official-looking building with a wheelchair ramp in front. Clinic or post office? She gambled and hurried toward it.

The medical clinic. Mata Iyer, M.D., was listed with several other doctors.

An Oldsmobile idled at the curb in front of the clinic, and an unshaven man with unkempt gray hair stood before the building, staring vacantly toward the street. His fly was open, and he was masturbating.

Ill.

Wondering if he belonged inside, Ivy started up the stairs to the clinic just as a woman emerged from within. "Sam!" She clutched the man's arm, and as she turned to lead him toward the automobile parked at the curb, Ivy recognized both her and the man. Cullen's parents. "Come get in the car, Sam."

The man seemed to recall himself but couldn't get zipped.

"Just get in the car."

"No!" Querulous, he started back to the clinic. "'Pointment."

"We already went."

The judge opened the glass door, preparing to walk inside.

Ivy hurried over. "Your Honor." She grasped his arm.

His eyes did not recognize her.

"Please get in the car. Your appointment is over. This way." She tried to lead him down the steps. His wife took his other arm.

In increments, he allowed himself to be led. He folded himself into the automobile, sat down, then began playing with himself again.

Mitzi Till shut the door. "Thank you, Ivy." There was no gratitude in the words. "You must excuse me." She hurried around to the driver's side and got into the car.

The Oldsmobile left Ivy in low clouds of steam and exhaust.

Should she walk to the toy store and tell Cullen?

His mother just wasn't big enough to handle the uncooperative judge. She would've gone to Coalgood herself, make sure they were all right, if not for Mitzi's coolness, the message that Ivy should really mind her own business.

In that case, she'd make an appointment with Mata Iyer, then hurry to the toy store. She'd find three family members there. Surely someone could get away.

A BLACK-HAIRED MOPPET planted herself at Ivy's feet before she'd progressed a yard inside Toyland. "Santa Claus is going to bring me a flying saucer with aliens."

It took Ivy a second to realize who was addressing her. "Scout! Hello."

A sea of bodies, parents and children playing with toys, banging shopping bags, separated her from both the dais in the center of the store and the ringing cash register. While a mechanical unicyclist pedalled on a wire overhead, Scout held up the alien of the night before. "This alien wants to steal your heart, Aunt Ivy."

Ivy lifted the five-year-old to hug her. "I think you've stolen it for him." It was a madhouse in here. Would Cullen really want to know about his father right now, in the midst of this chaos?

Yes. She would offer to go over to Coalgood and check on things. With Cullen's blessing, Mitzi might be more receptive.

"Will you take me to the ice-cream store?" Scout asked.

How could Zeya and Tom keep track of her in here? "If your mom and dad say it's okay."

"Hooray!" Scout squirmed out of her arms and zigzagged through the shoppers to the cash register.

A foam football sailed over Ivy's head, almost colliding with a mobile, as she made her way around the Santa Claus line to the place she'd seen Cullen's flash.

When she saw him, she sighed. He'd told her this morning he didn't need help. It would have been true if he were an octopus. Forms and pens and a camera on a tripod. While he worked, a mother leaned toward him and yelled, "Excuse me! Excuse me! Can you tell me how long it's going to be?"

Santa Claus addressed the girl on his lap. "A bunny! Did you see the bunnies over in the corner?"

Ivy found herself standing between Cullen and the mother. "Can I help you?"

"Yes. I want to know how long the line will take."

The girl scooted off Santa Claus's knee.

"Well, it looks like Santa Claus is taking about two minutes with each child. And I see, oh, eight children in line. Fifteen or twenty minutes?"

The mother eyed her watch, which had a water-color palette on the face. "All right, Amy. Get in line. And thank you."

"You're welcome. I'm Ivy Walcott, by the way." A woman with two toddlers in tow might have more children in the future. "I'm a nurse-midwife, and the photographer is my husband."

"Oh, nice to meet you. Karen Beck." They shook hands. "Well, time to deal with this line."

"I think you need to fill out one of the envelopes on the table."

Shortly after, she had a second to speak to Cullen as he paused to change film. She spoke quietly, under the happy din of the store.

"I just saw your mother and father outside the medical clinic. He was masturbating, and she had trouble getting him in the car. Would you like me to go to Coalgood and make sure they're all right?"

His glance told her nothing. Eyes on his camera again, he said, "Matthew should be there." His gaze shot up. "You'd like that, though."

"I don't deserve that."

He finished loading the camera. "Please tell Zeya or Tom what you just told me and ask one of them to call Coalgood. If my mother needs help, you can go over. Otherwise, you can help me, if you want."

The words—and his tone—said her help was immaterial to him.

Ivy kept calm. "Thank you. I'm happy to help. If you can refrain from insulting me."

"Has anyone made you wear a scarlet *A?*"

Someone played a musical toy so loudly all the parents in the store winced or covered their ears. *That one won't be selling well.*

"Bitterness doesn't become you," she murmured.

"Or infidelity, you."

"You're talking to the wrong person."

He stepped back, looked her up and down, met her eyes. *I am?*

She turned away. "I'll tell Zeya and Tom."

ALL RIGHT, HE WAS BEING a jerk. But how much of the past was changed by the fact that she'd hit her head? She'd been unfaithful, she'd hit her head. Now, she was suddenly both trustworthy and unblemished? He didn't buy it.

Little Penny Jones tugged hard on Santa's beard. Cullen caught it on film.

"Your beard's real, but I don't believe you're Santa Claus at all!"

"Well, Penny, we'll have to see about *that* on Christmas morning, won't we?"

Tom shouldered his way alongside Cullen. "Matthew's at home. An interesting conversation, as always."

"What did he say?"

"Among other things, to give the puppy a pat on the head and tell him everything's all right."

Cullen made an indifferent sound. "Thanks. For checking on them."

"He also suggested a family forum to convince your mother to hire an attendant."

"Good luck."

"Tomorrow night at eight."

After dinner at least. He could digest his food at home. *An attendant.* This was what his father had dreaded. Just two days ago, he'd been able to talk about his illness and death. Now he was masturbating in public.

It was almost as though some stress had caused the sudden deterioration. *Gina's return?* But his father hadn't recognized Gina. Instead, he'd mistaken Gabriela…

"And by the way, Ivy's taken Scout for ice cream. She said to tell you she'd be back soon. I told her you like mint chip."

"Thanks," Cullen repeated. He took another envelope from a parent, made a notation.

"She's pretty special. I can see why you waited so long."

Cullen stared at him.

Tom exclaimed, "Don't look at *me* like that. I was merely celebrating your good fortune. And now I think I'll go celebrate mine." He rubbed his hands together, scanned the floor-to-ceiling toys, the store packed with shoppers, and hurried back to the cash register.

THE FOLLOWING MORNING, Saturday, Gabriela had ballet class, and Cullen drove her into town, then went to the studio. He had sittings from ten until two, so Ivy was supposed to pick her up.

Not wanting to think about the inevitable meeting with the ballet teacher, Ivy used her free time to phone Tara in Sagrado, Texas, for a heart-to-heart.

She tracked her down in the communal housing at the clinic and for half an hour did most of the talking.

"Let me get this straight," Tara summarized. "Your former persona was unfaithful—with this brother—and he's treating you like a murderer who's found God on Death Row."

"An exaggeration, but you have the gist of it."

"And you're sleeping in the same bed, where he treats you like a leper."

"That's a bit of a contradiction, but yes. He knows I'm interested in him, and this is some kind of repayment. I don't know how *he's* sleeping, but it's been lousy for me."

"You're in some kind of narrow Victorian bed, and you don't know how he's sleeping?"

"I think he fakes. Sleeping."

"I'll bet he does. You know, I can solve your problem with the unaffectionate spouse."

"I'm not sure I want to hear this."

"Well, listen anyhow. I know you and I don't own

armloads of the stuff, but I've *never* met a man who wasn't fascinated by lingerie.''

In spite of herself, Ivy began laughing. "I needed to talk to you. Just for this laugh.''

"Imagine it. You, Ivy Walcott, in a clingy... Okay, Victoria's Secret isn't really you—''

"And I refuse to wear a red teddy with black lace.''

"Okay, anyhow, you put on some gorgeous ivory silk number and come downstairs to say good-night. I guarantee his eyes will pop out of his head. You did say, the other night, that he's cute?''

"You asked if he's cute, and I said yes. The truth is, he's the only man I've ever found attractive in my life.''

"As Ivy Walcott.''

With a sudden vision of Matthew Till, Ivy whispered, "Shit.''

"Is the brother cute?''

"If you like the type.''

"Which is?''

"Okay, the *Anne of Green Gables* movie. The second one. The captain?''

"Mmm. Interesting. He was an appealing guy.''

"A cross between that and, you know, Gregory Peck—but he acts like he's on a soap opera.''

Together, they went into peals of giggles.

Ivy sobered first. "It would be funny, except he's married. His wife is a public defender. Nice. With the most beautiful red hair you ever saw.''

"Anne of Green Gables?''

"Shelby of Coalgood. She's really lovely. And you

get the idea that she knows he's unfaithful and yet she loves him.''

"I've seen it before. Didn't work for me."

Ivy flinched. For a moment, she'd forgotten that Tara's husband had left her for her former midwifery partner just two years ago. *That swine.* It didn't help that he and Solange hadn't consummated their relationship until they'd told Tara they were in love.

In some ways, that had probably made it worse.

Ivy hunted for something to fill the silence and found it quickly. "I almost forgot!" She told Tara about Devon. "We have our first prenatal on Monday. I also have an appointment with a woman who I hope is going to be my backup physician."

"Good luck." Tara's experiences with the medical community had made her pessimistic about dealing with physicians. "But I'm glad you've got a practice going, Ivy. What are you going to call it?"

"I don't know." She squinted, thinking.

"Oh, come on, it's so obvious. And Mom won't mind. She'll love it."

Suddenly, Ivy laughed. "Okay. Mountain Midwifery it is."

LINGERIE.

She had an hour before she was supposed to meet Gabriela. Surely that was time enough to find something pretty in Guyandotte. Biting down a grin, Ivy grabbed her coat and purse and headed for the door.

Downtown, she visited Regina's Dress Shop. She was going through the racks in the back when she noticed another woman browsing nearby. She would've recognized those red curls anywhere.

"Shelby. Hi."

Matthew's wife glanced up. "Oh. Ivy. I didn't see you. I was in a pre-court trance."

Had Ivy imagined it, or did her eyes turn wary when she saw the rack Ivy had been studying, full of satin and lace? *If something was going on before, she has to be at least a little worried it'll start up again.*

"Shelby, do you have a minute?"

The wariness became tangible.

"I'm trying to figure out something to interest Cullen, and I need someone whose taste I can trust."

Shelby pushed between two circular racks. "*You* need something to interest Cullen?"

Ivy grimaced. "Believe it or not."

Lifting her eyebrows, Shelby turned her attention to the racks, but Ivy could see her mind wasn't on shopping. Maybe she'd start talking if Ivy waited.

Ivy flipped aimlessly through long gowns. Not what she wanted. "Think...think irresistible. I want something that'll make me irresistible to him."

"Ivy."

Shelby's sober tone drew her attention, but Ivy saw that the other woman was still fingering garments.

"Did you really lose *all* your memory?"

Let's get this on the table. If Shelby didn't know about Gabriela, Ivy didn't want to be the one to tell her. That was Matthew's burden. But she did want to reassure Shelby, make sure she knew the past was done.

"Yes." Ivy found a place close enough to Shelby that no one else in the store could overhear their conversation. "And I've come home to some unpleasant surprises that don't reflect the person I've thought I was for the past ten years."

The lenses of Shelby's glasses winked at her. Behind them, she assessed Ivy with pale eyes, as she might a person she was expected to defend in court. "I'm forgiving," she said at last.

Ivy bet she'd had lots of practice. "And I'm sorry."

Unexpectedly, Shelby took her hand. "Don't be sorry for Gabs. She's a great girl."

She knows. A huge feeling of relief went through Ivy—and wonder at the kind of person she was dealing with. She couldn't stop herself from reaching out and embracing her. The arms that hugged her back were surprisingly strong, firm and sure.

"Changing the subject—" Shelby straightened her glasses "—I wanted to ask if you know any natural fertility treatments. I'm not big on fertility drugs." She was blushing.

"Sure. There's a lot to talk about. Do you want to get together at the cabin some day?"

"Tomorrow works for me."

"Cullen and Gabriela will be around, but we can go up to the loft and talk."

Shelby smiled. "I'd like that. And I'll pay you."

Ivy waved her hand, dismissing it.

"Hey, sister, let me give you a clue about working in Guyandotte County." Shelby lowered her voice conspiratorially. "When someone offers you cold hard cash, *take it.*"

A few minutes later, her voice distracted Ivy from two lukewarm lingerie possibilities.

"Hey, Ivy."

She glanced over.

With an elfin grin, Shelby held a scrap of cream-colored stretch cotton lace against her blazer. "Yes?"

"That's not clothing. That's a Kleenex!"

But Regina herself chose that moment to appear, and Shelby pointed from the garment to Ivy as though to say, *What do you think?*

The shop owner looked Ivy up and down. "For you?" In a heartbeat, she pronounced her judgment. *"Perfect."*

CHAPTER SEVEN

MATTHEW WAS LEAVING the dance studio as Ivy arrived. Since she was still two doors down and he was going the other way, he didn't notice her. Her mind leaped through questions. What had he been doing at the studio?

Not talking to Gabriela?

Well, he's going to talk to me now.

"Matthew."

His eyes showed interest if not pleasure. "Why, hello, Ivy."

She reminded herself that he'd lost his mother young, that he behaved as he did because something inside him was broken. "Matthew, I'd like to ask you some questions."

He raised his eyebrows.

They had the cold sidewalk to themselves. She plunged in. "Did you and I have an affair after I married Cullen?"

"You really can't remember?"

He wanted to play with her, she could see.

She didn't play. "True."

He smiled. "Then I suppose that's for me to know."

No, Matthew, this isn't how it's going to be. "Matthew, the sheriff may not feel that way. I suffered an injury. If I suspected you—''

''My dear girl, whatever *your* suspicions, the sheriff would not suspect me. He would suspect Cullen. And surely you don't want him to know about Gabriela?''

Matthew was fishing. He couldn't possibly know whether or not Cullen had told her the truth. ''What earthly advantage,'' she asked, ''do you see in not telling me the truth?''

He seemed to consider, then smiled. ''I simply like the idea that there's something I have that you want. It promotes a certain intimacy between us.''

''On your side, maybe. Not on mine. And there's something else I want to know. I was pregnant around the time I left Guyandotte. Do you know whose child it was?''

He stared unblinking. ''In fact, this is news to me, Ivy. You don't say!'' He seemed delighted with himself.

Oh, shit.

''Does Cullen know?''

''Of course. We have no secrets.''

Matthew smiled. ''But I do. I like this. Let's be friends, Ivy.'' He offered his hand.

She didn't take it. ''I'm going to think very hard about speaking to the sheriff, Matthew.''

''Suit yourself. I think you'll decide it's not such a good idea after all. What if the truth should get back to Gabriela?''

"That may be for the best." *You are not going to hold one card over me, Matthew Till.*

"Cullen surely doesn't agree with you. This is his virility on the line."

"Somehow I can't help thinking *you're* the one with your virility on the line, Matthew. Why else would you persist in harassing your younger brother?" She'd gone too far and wished she could retract the words.

"It so happens," he answered calmly, "that you're wrong. And now I'll leave you to pick up our daughter." The last word firmly in his favor, he began walking away.

Ivy rubbed her forehead, her face. Matthew had won that round. She'd given him a feeling of power. Still, she didn't regret it. She'd been straight with him, which was the only way to deal with people. Maybe the answer was to see the sheriff. But what crime had been committed?

Did someone hit me on the head?

She tried to imagine Matthew becoming violent with a woman. It wasn't out of the realm of possibility. But he'd been right. If she started raising questions about how her head injury had occurred and in the process revealed the suspected affair, Cullen would become the primary suspect. That was the last thing they needed.

Only when she turned to enter the dance studio did she remember one question she'd neglected to ask Matthew. What had he been doing in there? At the doors, she checked quickly to see if the building contained any other businesses. No. Then why had he come?

Ivy pulled open a glass door and went in, entering a world of sweaty adolescents removing pointe shoes and heading for the lockers. She spotted Noel and Gabriela and waved, and Gabriela beckoned.

There was a sign about shoes at the arch into the dancing room, so Ivy removed her hiking boots and ventured inside in her socks. She saw Tracy Kennedy.

She's beautiful. Her less classic features, like her nose and prominent chin, only made her face more arresting. Ivy swallowed, remembering Cullen glancing at her house the other night.

The dance teacher walked toward her, regal and graceful.

That skin.

The possessiveness and jealousy gripping her stomach surprised Ivy. This woman had made love with Cullen. *I don't like this feeling.*

It gave her more sympathy for Cullen's recent behavior.

"Hello, Gina. I understand you probably won't remember me. I'm Tracy Kennedy."

"It's Ivy." She'd never felt anything like the tightness inside her now. She tried to remember Shelby's graciousness and use it as her model, then told herself there was a big difference between a woman who'd slept with your husband ten years before and one who'd done it a few weeks ago.

No, there's not that much difference. And you bore Matthew's child. Grow up, Ivy. She'd never be as gracious as Shelby, but she could behave like a civilized adult.

"I changed my name," she explained to Tracy, then changed the subject. "Gabriela is very excited about your class."

"She's a good student."

There was a pause; Tracy didn't attempt to fill it. Instead, she took a breath and looked quickly around the emptying studio. "Well, it looks like Gabriela's ready to go."

She's not over him.

Maybe Cullen wasn't over Tracy, either. Was that why he was able to sleep beside Ivy without touching her?

Maybe the lingerie was for nothing.

Her daughter approached them both. "Tracy, this is my mom, Ivy."

"We were just meeting. Gabriela, your pas de bourrées are much better today."

"Thanks to you. Oh, wait. Ivy, Tracy's taking a group of us up to Morgantown to see *Nutcracker* in two weeks. It's at the university. Can I go?"

"Need to ask your dad." Morgantown was a long way. The capital, Charleston, was far closer. But clearly, Gabriela was eager to spend time with her teacher. "Do you have a permission slip?" she asked Tracy.

"Gabriela has one."

The comment seemed to suggest things were taken care of between the two of them, that Ivy was an afterthought. Her own insecurity talking. She told Tracy, "I'll ask Cullen."

"Of course. Bye, Gabriela. Goodbye, Ivy."

Ivy's legs were rubber as she and Gabriela walked to the car. She wished she could say something both sincere and gracious. *Your teacher seems nice.* But the more accurate assessment was, *Your teacher is ladylike.*

Think about her feelings, Ivy. You just met Cullen three days ago. She dated him for a year.

But that was it. It didn't *feel* like days since she'd met Cullen. He seemed familiar already, and she couldn't help believing it was emotional memory kicking in from long ago.

Suddenly remembering, Ivy asked, "Did Uncle Matthew come into the studio to talk to you?"

"No. To Tracy. I don't know what he wanted.

"Hey, Ivy, will you take me shopping in Charleston? I get my clothing allowance today, and I want something cool for *Nutcracker* and the Christmas dance."

A dance? Well, she was in junior high. "You're pretty sure you're going to *Nutcracker*."

"Oh, Dad'll let me. He trusts Tracy." Her face suddenly froze, and her eyes shot up at Ivy's.

Ivy smiled patiently.

Gabriela said, "You know…?"

"I know."

"Sorry for mentioning it."

She really was a sweet girl. Thinking uneasily of Matthew and wondering if Gabriela would stay sweet, knowing the truth, Ivy said, "Let's walk over to the studio and ask your dad if he minds our going to Charleston."

THE FAMILY GATHERED in the living room of Coalgood that night. Cullen had left Ivy and Gabriela at home, listening to Jewel, making popcorn and getting ready for a movie. Matthew's "family forum" began half an hour late, after Tom and Zeya had struggled to get a wound-up Scout to bed.

Shelby was upstairs with the judge, interesting him in a computer game. The rest of them clustered around on various pieces of spotless furniture.

"No fair bride tonight, Cullen?"

"No, Matthew."

Matthew sat back against the couch, then moved suddenly. Produced a lemon from behind him.

Mother held out her hand for it. Shaking her head, she explained, "The judge hid it there. He thinks I'm stealing his food. Can you imagine? Now, I don't understand the nature of this meeting. Daddy and I do fine together. I want to care for him."

Matthew surrendered the lemon. "That's commendable, Mitzi. But eventually, he'll require lifting. I think it's time to look at a full-time attendant."

"He's nowhere close to needing lifting, and he's certainly not dangerous."

Cullen, half-lost in the quagmire of his father's request to die, waited for someone else to say it. The judge yelled at all of them. He threw things in the kitchen when people didn't understand what he wanted to eat because he couldn't remember the word for bananas or steak. Not to mention that he suspected his wife of stealing his food. "Let's take shifts," Cullen suggested. "The men. Do you mind, Tom?"

"Does it matter if *I* mind?" Matthew asked.

Cullen stared at him.

"This is unnecessary, Cullen. *And* Matthew. Daddy and I get along fine. There is absolutely no reason for my children to act as bodyguards. Or to hire an attendant."

"Not bodyguards," Zeya said, "but, Mother, wouldn't you like help?"

"You children have your lives and your work."

"Cullen has flexible hours." Matthew worked on a glass of Merlot. "He's Daddy's puppy anyhow."

"Matthew, I wish you wouldn't say that. Heaven knows what you mean," exclaimed his stepmother.

"It's affectionate. When he was little, don't you remember Daddy putting out his arms to get Cully to run to his chair?"

The recollection brought sudden tears to Mitzi Till's eyes.

Matthew's look was sardonic.

"Affectionate?" Cullen asked.

Matthew blew him a loud kiss.

"Not now, you two," Zeya snapped.

Mother stood up. "None of you need put yourself out. Cullen's wife will want him at home, and the rest of you arc busy. Now, I'm going up to the judge. Shall I have Lily bring coffee?"

The subject was closed.

When she left the room, Tom murmured, "I think we're in denial."

"Speak for yourself," Matthew muttered, as though not understanding the remark. Setting down his wineglass, he rose. "Tell Shelby I've gone for a walk. I'll be a while." He smiled at Cullen in particular. "Doctor's orders."

He left, and Tom and Zeya and Cullen stared at each other glumly.

Zeya shook her head. "This is crazy. He *is* too big for Mother to deal with. What are we going to do?"

Cullen and Tom exchanged looks.

"Okay, I know it's the coveted shift, but I'll volunteer to take the evenings. Zeya and I are really going to be swamped until Christmas and for at least a week afterward. I'll sit with the judge every evening, even Christmas Eve."

"Thanks, Tom." Cullen shook his head. "But Matthew was right. My plan was bad. I need to work. You need to work. He needs to work. And someone has to be with Daddy during the day."

"An attendant," Zeya said. "It has to happen, whether she likes it or not. You know it's not the money that's stopping her. Want me to start asking around on Monday?"

"Okay. Let me know if you want to do it together." He got up. "I think I'll head home."

Zeya's eyes, the same green as his own under hair the same shade as his, sparkled up at him. "Ivy's sweet, Cully. Sweeter than she used to be."

For just a second, Cullen was tempted to ask his

sister if she'd ever noticed anything between Matthew and Gina. But he couldn't expose Ivy that way. And Matthew was the one to ask.

But Cullen wouldn't waste his breath.

HE DROVE SLOWLY around the island, half-dreading his return home. After Gabriela went to bed, there would be an awkward hour, at least, when just he and Ivy were awake. Every attraction he felt toward her would rouse his anger and distrust. If he was cold, she would be calm. If he was rude, she would be fair. Then, finally, she'd retreat to bed, and when he came up, the cycle would begin inside him all over again.

Also, the more time he spent around her, the more he noticed ways she *hadn't* changed. Many of her gestures. The way she brushed her hair. Cooking, dishwashing and laundry rituals.

She was the errant wife who swore she'd reformed.

What if he was wrong? What if she'd never slept with Matthew once she was married? What if his whole reaction had grown out of possessiveness and insecurity?

He couldn't believe it anymore. He knew how little passion there had been between him and Gina.

If Ivy would just keep to her own side of the bed at night!

But it was her habit to lie on her side, facing him, with a bundle of covers tucked under one knee. When he came to bed and moved the covers, she rested her knee on him instead.

There was Tracy's house, her porch light on. Her

door was open, and she was letting a man inside, and the man was Matthew.

Neither of them noticed the car passing.

The front door shut.

Cullen drove thoughtfully to the bridge. Tracy knew Matthew was married. She'd invited him inside in innocence, Cullen was sure, and Matthew wouldn't get far with her.

Did Matthew really think this would hurt him?

Cullen still felt protective of her, but other tender feelings had disintegrated. Now their memory was lukewarm.

Only one woman in his life had ever awakened his deepest feelings, good and bad. He'd given her his heart, promised her his life, raised her child.

Her betrayal had cost her his respect. And Cullen didn't see how she would ever earn it back. The only answer was time.

As GABRIELA SAID good-night and went off to her room, Ivy tried to quiet her nerves. What was the worst that could happen? She'd put on the silly teddy, and he would lift his eyebrows once and proceed to ignore her.

No, I'll put it on and go to bed. He can notice when he gets into bed. She absolutely could not parade in front of him in that thing.

She spent some time stretching in the dance room before she went up to bed. As she was leaving, Cullen came in to do his usual sit-ups and push-ups. "Good night," she told him.

"Good night."

Indifferent. She headed through the living room to the sunroom and the ladder to the loft, her eyes burning. He'd loved her once. She couldn't remember those days, but she'd seen evidence of that old, never really extinguished love when she'd first arrived in Guyandotte. Seen it in a dozen different ways.

But now… This discovery he'd made had killed it.

I killed it. More than ten years ago.

The worst part was what she felt for Cullen. As Gina, she must have loved him, too, or how could she feel something so strong now, in such a short time?

Why did she do it?

Why did I make love with his brother?

If only she knew at least that much, could somehow understand. Did Cullen have any idea why she'd done it?

In the loft, she undressed and put on the teddy she'd bought that day with Shelby's help. She'd bought it with such hope, and now she couldn't help thinking that hope was doomed to failure.

She glanced in the mirror.

She looked beautiful, long-legged and lithe, the lace creamy against her flushed skin.

But Cullen's rejection wasn't about her looks.

She should tear the thing off and put on her flannel pajamas again.

Oh, come on, Ivy. Think what it might do if the two of you could just touch tenderly. He loved you once.

He'd loved Gina.

No, if she was to be blamed for Gina's crimes, she

would take the good, too. Nursing her child, being loved by Cullen, making quilts with her grandmother.

I should teach Gabriela. I should pass on this tradition.

She climbed into the old bed, comforted by its creaks. This cabin, these mountains, were her home and her birthright. Her thoughts wandered—from planning her rural midwifery practice, to sewing a quilt with Gabriela, the carrying on of tradition. She tried to blot out the simple human want so keen inside her.

To know her husband's love.

CULLEN CAREFULLY drew back the covers. She stirred, and as the covers fell from her, he saw her bare arms. It took a second to register. No flannel pajamas.

Uneasy, he tried to see what she was wearing, and as he did, her moonlit eyes opened and blinked at his.

From where he sat on his side of the bed, naked, he glimpsed lace. A bodysuit or something?

Unable to resist his curiosity, even though her eyes still watched him, he lifted the covers.

Oh.

He let the sheet and blanket fall and got into bed, turning his back to her.

Ivy couldn't bear it. Maybe he really was in love with Tracy Kennedy. If so, what was she going to do? *I can't lie here in this thing while he ignores me.*

He might have loved Gina, but obviously he didn't love Ivy Walcott. Or maybe it was because she'd *been*

Gina. She couldn't sort it out anymore—who she really was, who he was really married to.

But she was through sharing a bed with a man who didn't want her.

She sat up, climbed out of bed and retrieved her pajamas from her drawer. And damned if she was going downstairs to change at this hour.

"What are you doing?"

"Putting on my pajamas. You don't have to watch."

But he had sat up, too, his hair mussed, to squint at her in the dark as she tugged down one strap and began to maneuver her arm out of it.

Tracy had taught him about teddies.

Ivy had never worn one before, or she wouldn't be struggling with shoulder straps. Gina had never worn one, either. Something inside him cracked gently, starting a slow melt that wasn't about sex but about tenderness.

"Stop."

"What?" She glared at him. "I *said* you don't have to watch."

"Was that for me?"

"No. Actually, it's for Gabriela. In fact, maybe I'll give it to her. Just leave me alone. I can't deal with nasty remarks right now. And I'm—"

He was getting out of bed, standing before her, naked and tall.

Male.

His hand gently caught hers, to guide it back through the arm loop. He eased up both straps, then rubbed her shoulders. She shivered, afraid to look at his hands, afraid to look anywhere but at his chest.

He said, "Come back to bed."

She squeezed her eyes shut. "I need to be loved. I deserve to be loved. I'm *good.* I'm not what you think."

Cullen wished he could agree. "Come back to bed."

Ivy opened her eyes. "No." She tugged down the straps again.

"It snaps at the crotch." He remained where he was.

Stanching tears, she undressed, and Cullen watched, aware of a dark force inside the room, inside himself. Failure to forgive. He was hurting their chances now and couldn't stop. He wanted to wound her as she'd wounded him.

He wished he didn't feel like this.

Ivy pulled on her pajamas, aware of the new barrier between them, of the way things had changed.

Cullen said, "Come back to bed."

Maybe, Ivy reasoned, that was as far as he could go.

And she would have to take a small step, too.

She did. Back to the tester bed.

IN BED, CULLEN EMBRACED her, holding her tight. He couldn't speak, but he could do this. Gather her close and closer.

Ivy had never felt anything so wonderful as this man keeping her against his body, surrounding her with his body. And when she looked up, he kissed her, slowly.

Their mouths opened gradually, and she felt his tongue. It was a match to the never-lit tinder inside her. The strongest force she'd ever known urged her closer to him, directed her hands to his bare shoulders, directed her arms to clasp him around the neck.

Cullen kissed her cheek, her jaw, her throat. "I love you."

He spoke so softly she wasn't sure she'd heard him right. She was still wondering when his mouth covered hers, when their tongues touched again, a prelude to greater intimacy, like the erection she felt against her leg, like his hands on her arms. Her body simmered. She writhed as he unbuttoned her pajama top and lowered his mouth to her breast.

This is making love. This is what it's like.

He drew down the bottoms, tossed them out of the bed. His touch was tender, in her wetness.

"Cullen."

He kissed her again as he stroked her, teased her. He'd never seen Gina like this, and he knew what he was seeing in Ivy.

Innocence.

Gina had somehow never been innocent, not even in high school, before she'd met Matthew.

"Open your eyes."

She did, and could hardly meet his. He kissed her more and embraced her, feeling her hair against his cheek. She was tremulous heat, and his hands memorized her. *Lover.*

Tracy had never been...

He cleared his mind, but it was too late. His penis grew limp.

He kissed Ivy and remembered Gina and Matthew. *This woman is different. This woman is mine.*

His body would not obey him.

What in hell? He needed, wanted, to make love to Ivy. *Now.*

Cullen drew back the covers to see her body, and she trembled, opening herself to him slightly, obviously wanting to give. He turned her, to put his mouth to her. His erection was back. She moaned, and he gently stroked her legs. She invited him to deepen the intimate kiss, and he did and had to hold her still.

"Cullen." She dragged his head up.

Kisses, her body beneath his. "I'll be right back," he promised, and left the bed to find condoms. He saw her teddy.

Tracy's had been purple and black, another turquoise and black. *Don't think about her.*

By the time he returned to bed, he'd lost his erection.

Ivy knew. His kisses were the same as before, but—

"Are you in love with Tracy?"

Was she psychic, to know he'd been thinking of Tracy? "I am not in love with Tracy," he said quietly. It was the truth.

Then is it because of my head injury? Am I not human enough?

His lips lowered to hers again, and she kissed him

back, trying to infuse him with the passion they'd shared moments earlier. But there was no awakening in him, no change at all.

Cullen could imagine fifty bad scenarios that would be better than this. Even Matthew telling Gabriela he was her father...

Was it discovering he'd been made a cuckold that had done this to him? Was it something about her, or about the two of them?

Forcing himself to relax, Cullen rolled onto his back and drew her against his chest. She settled with her head on his shoulder, her hand in the hair on his chest. Her hand reached down.

This should do it. Cullen felt her tentativeness, her nervousness. It coaxed desire from him.

He was unprepared for her mouth.

He hardened immediately. "Ivy."

Her hands were healing hands, honest hands. She was giving herself to him, and he gave himself back.

"WELL, DID THE TEDDY WORK?" Shelby asked that afternoon, when she and Ivy had gone up to the loft to talk fertility. "You look sort of...pink and glowing—if you'll pardon the cliché."

She'd felt flushed all day, and happy. She and Cullen had made love again this morning, and this time he'd had no trouble keeping an erection. "Yes, it worked. Thank you for your help yesterday. Now tell me how I can help you." She sat on the edge of the tester bed, and Shelby took the rocking chair.

"I want a baby. We've been trying for maybe... two years?"

"Have you had any tests at a fertility clinic?"

"Yes. Everything indicates we should be able to get pregnant. And we've been given the whole scoop about what position is best, things like that. What I want to know is, are there any herbs that could help?"

"Sure. I can set you up that way. In fact, I have some on hand." She made another mental note; in the spring she should begin gathering herbs. She could take Gabriela with her and teach her.

But Gabriela didn't care about herbs or midwifery. She wanted to be a dancer.

"Also, I've got a book to lend you." She handed Shelby *Conscious Conception*. "It's...different, but it can be fun to read about different perspectives on fertility."

"I'll enjoy that. Thanks."

"Now, let's talk herbs and diet."

For half an hour, they visited together, discussing fertility-promoting foods and herbs. As they finished, Shelby fingered one of the quilts folded at the foot of the tester bed. "This is beautiful. I've always wanted to know how to do it. It seems like such a West Virginia thing. I don't know if I can get my New York fingers around a needle."

"Sure you can. I want to start one with Gabriela. Want to join us?"

"Oh, it would be an intrusion. It's a mother-daughter thing."

"The more hands the better. Let's go ask her."

They went downstairs and found Gabriela practicing dance.

Ivy wasn't one to foresee disasters around every corner, but it still troubled her some to see Gabriela focusing all her hopes and dreams on what seemed like a fickle profession. And the idea of fame. Those dreams should be part of childhood, but Gabriela was on the cusp of womanhood.

I want her to know other things, to understand how to nurture.

The onset of menstruation was a special time. Perhaps some special initiation into womanhood was in order, to help Gabriela celebrate becoming a woman.

She asked Gabriela if she was interested in starting a quilt with her and Shelby.

Gabriela paused in a movement. "Oh, sure. I guess. You mean, like, now?"

"As soon as you finish practicing."

"Okay. I'm almost done."

Cullen was out of the house photographing a wedding, but Ivy knew there was a cedar chest full of fabric scraps in the day room, enough to start with. When she'd first seen them, she'd known they must have been hers or maybe her grandmother's. "I've seen a book around here, Shelby. I'll let you and Gabriela choose the pattern." Ivy searched the living-room bookcase and plucked out the book of patterns, then collected fabric scraps from the cedar chest. A decent pair of scissors was harder to come by, but she found a ruler, pencil and paper for drawing patterns.

"Mom—Ivy." From the door of the dance room, Gabriela blushed.

Ivy hurried to her side and put an arm around her. Low, she said, "You can call me Mom. I'd love that."

Gabriela's eyes watered, and she suddenly hugged Ivy.

Hugging back, Ivy blotted the specter of Matthew from her mind. *Don't let anyone destroy this happiness.*

"What I wanted to say—" Gabriela wiped her eyes "—is that I know where your sewing box is. Dad sort of said I can have it."

"Then it's yours. But go get it, okay? Because we'll need it."

Gabriela and Shelby sat on the couch to look through quilt patterns and finally decided on the Variable Star.

"Good choice. Okay, let's get started."

It was five before Shelby left, with a bagful of scraps to work on at home. As she drove away and Ivy went to the kitchen to begin making dinner, Gabriela said, "You know, I think we should let Shelby keep the quilt. What do you think?"

Ivy smiled, terribly proud of her. "I think that's a great idea." She gave Gabriela another hug. She'd never imagined such a wonderful relationship with her daughter.

But an aura of darkness hovered around them. The secret Gabriela did not know.

CHAPTER EIGHT

THE BLACK CURLS THAT FELL past Mata Iyer's shoulders sprang slightly as she moved. "Ivy, I'm so glad you came in. I'd be happy to provide physician backup for you. This community desperately needs a way to reach out to low-income women, and I've often thought that a certified nurse-midwife might be the answer, might help reduce poor outcomes. I see so many fifteen-year-olds coming into the ER with no prenatal care behind them. These teenagers really have a difficult time, both before and after the births."

It was the perfect opportunity to bring up Devon—and the family's concern about finances.

"You know, Ivy, we're always willing to work with low-income families, but people are just afraid. They really don't know the situation. Anyhow, I'm happy to see Devon. Check with the receptionist on the way out for an appointment."

Before Ivy left, Mata shook her hand warmly. "I'm so glad you're here. If you don't mind, I'll start spreading the word about your services."

"I feel blessed," Ivy answered sincerely. "Thank you so much for your help."

THAT AFTERNOON was Ivy's first prenatal with Devon Workman. Ivy put her midwifery kit in her mountaineering pack and hiked down the hollow to the Workmans' trailer. Gabriela had ballet class, and Ivy had asked Cullen to pick her up. The thought of his seeing Tracy troubled her—but that was why she'd wanted him to get Gabriela. *We have to walk through these things.*

The Workmans' was the place closest to the main road, a single-wide trailer that had been patched and added to with a hodgepodge of building materials. Seeing homemade curtains in the windows, a collection of antique bottles along one sill, Ivy felt a renewal of pride in her heritage, pride in people who kept things clean and well repaired even in the face of poverty. Remembering the quilt she and Gabriela and Shelby had started, she thought again of planning an initiation ceremony for Gabriela.

But how could she honestly participate in that if Gabriela didn't know the name of her natural father?

She needs to be told.

Ivy could imagine nothing worse than Matthew insensitively telling her. She probably wouldn't even believe him.

That thought made it easier to accept the lie.

And more difficult to accept herself.

THE TRAILER WAS CLEAN inside, and Emma Workman gave her a tour through the rooms, hers and Devon's. "There's space for the baby in Devon's room."

"Devon, are you still in school?"

She shook her head. "Not just now. But I'm going back after the baby comes."

Ivy hoped so. She wanted to mother this girl and wished for Devon that her mother was there. "Will your mom be able to come down for the birth?"

She shrugged.

Emma looked faintly disapproving.

So Mom's not involved with her daughter's life anymore.

Devon had said she'd needed to go to Morgantown to work. What kind of world made such a thing necessary?

"Where's your father?"

"Oh, he lives in South Carolina with his girlfriend."

Emma refrained from sighing, from uttering a disapproving word. But Ivy could see her eyes over Devon's shoulder and guessed her feelings. She made a wordless promise to Emma Workman. She, as midwife, would be present for this girl, too, would help her on the rocky road ahead. She made a mental note to stop by two or three times a week until the birth and more often afterward.

"Okay, why don't we go sit down in your bedroom, Devon, and we can talk about the kind of birth experience you'd like to have."

THE LAST PERSON CULLEN wanted to see was Tracy Kennedy. He resented her intrusion into his thoughts when he was making love with Ivy. He keenly regretted ever having asked her out.

And when he entered her studio that afternoon, he immediately saw his brother. Tracy lounged in the arched doorway between the foyer and the dance room, smiling up at Matthew, while he stood with one hand braced against the arch over her head. On the make.

Cullen considered walking outside and waiting there for Gabriela, but Tracy spotted him.

What are you doing with Matthew, Tracy?

Could she switch that easily from him to his brother? Did she *want* to?

Matthew turned his head and caught sight of Cullen. ''Well, look who's here. How's my baby brother?'' He hooked his arm around Cullen's neck, tight, and rubbed his knuckles against his scalp. Hard.

Cullen escaped the headlock. ''Hello, Matthew. Nice to see you.''

''Dad, can I go to Morgantown with everyone to see *Nutcracker?* Tracy's driving.''

''Yes, Gabs.''

''Morgantown,'' remarked Matthew. He gave Tracy a quizzing glance.

''Field trip.'' Her smile tilted wryly at Matthew.

She does like him. How can she like him? Cullen experienced a pang on Shelby's behalf. Matthew was an idiot.

''Ready to go, Gabriela?''

''Yes. Where's Ivy?''

''She has a prenatal appointment.''

''Pregnant?'' Matthew asked. ''Already? After only a dozen years of marriage?''

"She's taking care of a midwifery client," Cullen clarified, hyperaware of the unspoken—that he and Ivy had never conceived a child together. Unless... "Bye, folks."

"CULLEN?" IT WAS the second night they'd gone up to the loft at the same time.

He slid between the sheets. "Mmm?"

"I have a strong need to tell Gabriela the truth. I think it's wrong not to."

"As I said before, we disagree. It might be easiest for you to tell her—to get it off your chest—but the greatest gift you can give her at this point is to maintain the lie. She believes I'm her father. Do you think this secret has been easy for me?"

Ivy didn't answer right away. "I guess not."

"It's truly for her, Ivy. She has a strong identity, and part of it is that she's your child and mine."

"It's a lie."

"I don't believe all lies are bad. This one is best for her."

"What if Matthew tells her?"

"We deal with it then and explain why we kept the truth from her."

"That frightens me. Can you imagine what it would do to her to learn it from him?"

Cullen echoed her own thought of earlier that day. "Frankly, I doubt she'd even believe him."

"Would we then tell her more lies?"

"Maybe. It's protecting her, Ivy. I don't fear Gabriela's anger. Revealing the truth would be a load off for you and for me, but I can see no way it would benefit her. She's not going to get a father-daughter relationship out of Matthew.''

''Maybe that's what *he* needs.''

Dead silence.

''What?'' she asked.

''Why are you concerning yourself with what Matthew needs?''

She'd better get out of this conversation fast. ''Because I like his wife.'' She changed the subject. ''Cullen, at the country club, you asked me never to defend you physically. Why is that?''

''If Gabriela hadn't been there, I would have been more specific. Sure, if someone threatened this family, I would welcome your help in a fight. Matthew was on my mind. I decided long ago not to rise to the bait, not to fight him. And I'd hate it if you did my fighting for me.''

Ivy remembered her conversation with Matthew outside the dance studio. ''Is he violent?''

''He can be.''

Did she dare bring it up? She must. ''Cullen, do you think there's any chance he hurt me?''

He was quiet so long, she said, ''It just occurred to me for the first time the other day.''

''I don't think he'd hurt you. I can't picture it. Me, yes. But a woman? I don't think so.''

''Why won't you fight with him? Even to defend yourself?''

Cullen hesitated. Describing the things Matthew had done would make him sound like a psychopath, a maniac. Cullen couldn't say why, but he loved his brother and felt a need to protect him. There were things about Matthew that people outside the family would never understand. He wasn't sure he could make Ivy see them, either.

"Because I did once."

"Fight with him?"

"Yes."

"Did you lose?"

"No. I won."

Ivy rolled over to face him. "What would you do if he seduced me now? Some things are worth fighting for."

"Seduced *you?* What makes you think you were so innocent? What makes you think you didn't play a role?"

Chagrined, Ivy fell quiet.

"Yes, some things are worth fighting for," he said quietly. "But have you ever noticed that as a culture we almost never consider *not fighting?* Being able to kill makes people feel powerful."

Ivy swallowed. Being able to kill did make her feel powerful. It was a need for that power that had led her, in part, to tae kwon do. She thought he could teach her something, yet it was just out of her reach, unspeakable and unexplainable. "Didn't defeating Matthew give you a sense of personal...strength?"

"Truthfully, when it was all over, I felt slightly foolish. It was only fighting. It didn't make me stronger or better." He kissed her, drawing her close. His hands cupped her bottom, and his penis stirred, but he was distracted. She thought Matthew might have hurt her. Cullen was sure he hadn't.

But *had* someone hurt her?

ON HIS WAY HOME FROM WORK the following day, Cullen stopped at Coalgood. Zeya's search for an attendant had so far yielded nothing they liked, and the judge's unruliness made Cullen uneasy. When he entered the kitchen that afternoon, his father had just knocked a bowl of macaroni and cheese to the floor. Lily was cleaning it up while his mother tried to find something to placate him.

"White!" he yelled at Mitzi. "White."

Cullen's mother showed him a box of spaghetti from the cupboard. Lily took out the Swiss cheese. Milk. Cottage cheese. Yogurt.

The judge yelled again and swept everything that was on the table—salt and pepper shakers, butter plate, coffee cup—to the floor.

Cullen helped pick things up. "Where's Matthew?"

"Atlanta, working."

And Tom was at the store.

Standing suddenly, the judge knocked over his chair.

"Daddy." Cullen touched his arm, and his father slammed into his face with the back of his arm. Blood spurted over the table.

"Oh, Cully. Daddy. Sam, sit down."

His father seemed surprised by the blood.

Cullen grabbed a dish towel and held it to his face. "Sorry, Lily."

"It's all right, honey. You just don't touch him when he's like that, you hear?"

Cullen heard. And saw. These two women were alone with a big man who could turn violent over being offered the wrong food.

"White!" yelled the judge.

Opening the refrigerator, Cullen searched the shelves, the drawers, the door, for anything white. Still holding the towel to his bloody nose, he held up an egg.

His father grunted.

Cullen set a couple of eggs on the counter and pulled a skillet from under the sink. His father liked them scrambled.

"I'll do that. You just sit down." Lily took over.

Mother tried tucking a napkin under his father's neck, and the judge pulled it out.

Bad. Daddy didn't know his own strength, and he was querulous, his faculties impaired.

Cullen stayed while his father ate, then helped him upstairs. His mother got out the judge's medications, and her husband took them with a glass of water while Cullen examined the bottles.

He's just getting sicker and sicker.

The judge hadn't wanted this to happen. He'd asked his son to keep it from happening. Cullen pictured it for a moment, losing his father somewhere dangerous, letting him die in the cold and the snow.

He could sit with him and let him die of exposure, for instance.

And bear the weight of the secret.

I should do it. It's what he wanted. It can be my last gift to him.

"When's Matthew going to be back?"

"Dinnertime."

"I'll stay till he comes home."

The judge spoke up. "They're all ungrateful, Mitzi. Where are they? Our children don't give a shit. Spending our money and never coming around." He seemed to see Cullen. "Except you. You get everything, Cullen, when I die."

"That is not true!" his wife exclaimed. "I don't know where he gets these ideas. Cully, will you sit with him a minute? I just have to call Joanne." Her sister. "She called last night, and I haven't had a chance to phone her back."

"Sure."

"You get everything, Cully. Everything I've done, I've done for you."

Cullen entertained a notion of the judge taking up this train of thought at dinner. It was fleeting. "Daddy, you still want me to help you die?"

"What?"

His mother returned to the room, and Cullen decided not to repeat the question. She put one of her sweaters in a drawer.

"You get everything. Your brother's worthless. He screwed your wife. You know that? Walked in on 'em."

Mitzi had straightened up. She stared at the judge. "Is that true?" she demanded, turning to her son.

Cullen shook his head. "Of course not." The judge had walked in on Gina and Matthew? Where? When? It must have happened at Coalgood. It explained his father's comment about Gina being after Tom.

His mother slanted a look at him but didn't challenge his answer, and Cullen was glad when she left the room.

He was alone with the judge. And the truth.

It was no longer a suspicion. It was a fact.

His wife had committed adultery.

WHEN HE GOT HOME, Ivy had cooked dinner. He ate it in silence while Gabriela talked about ballet and Ivy cast questioning glances toward him. They were just finishing when the phone rang.

Ivy picked it up. "Hello?"

"Hello, is Gabriela there?"

A boy. A boy with a deep voice. Ivy said, "Who's calling?"

"Brad. Sorry."

Ivy bit her bottom lip and at last said, "One moment. Gabriela, it's Brad."

She leaped up, wiping her mouth. "Oh, thanks. I'll take it on the cordless." It took her three seconds to locate the phone, carry it to her room and shut the door.

Ivy shook her head and checked Cullen's reaction.

Something in his expression went beyond Gabriela

and Brad. It had to do with her. *Is he angry?* If so, he could tell her later. "How old is that guy?"

"Ninth grade."

"Have you met him?"

"Only on the phone."

"And you didn't say, 'Excuse me, my daughter will call you back in a few years?'"

"No, I didn't. She's not dating him. She swears they're just friends."

"That was not the reaction of one friend to another."

"She does the same thing when Noel calls."

"Oh, come on, Cullen. You were fourteen once."

He didn't answer except to say, "Let's go for a walk."

And leave her alone with that guy?

Relenting, Ivy helped him clear the dishes from the table, then put on her boots and her coat and stocking cap.

They went out into the snow, and she let him choose the path, back through the woods behind the cabin.

"You screwed my brother."

"What?" Not this again.

"My father confirmed it. He walked in on you two, apparently."

Oh. So the imagined was now reality.

She felt the ridges of a scar inside her, the scar of who she'd been, the sins she must carry. The cold numbed her face, made her slur her words. "Cullen, do you have any idea what might have made me behave like that?''

"It's behavior I don't understand at all, Gina. Ivy,'' he corrected.

"Truly?''

Cullen obviously didn't have the patience to psychoanalyze an unfaithful wife. "Lack of character?''

"No father in the house?''

"It's no excuse.'' Abruptly, he grabbed her, and she found herself pinned against a tree. "I want to kill that bastard!'' It was a guttural confession, hissing and lethal. His breath warmed her face. His hands on her arms hurt.

"Take your hands off me *now*.''

"No.'' He grabbed the waistband of her jeans.

"Don't do this,'' she warned.

"You know how to stop me.''

She didn't stop him, and he thrust inside her there against the tree. It felt good, and she clung to him, her arms around his neck, wanting an orgasm he didn't allow. Only his.

Warmth dripped on her legs. She drew up her pants as he closed his fly.

"What was that about?'' she asked. "It wasn't love.''

"You have to ask what that was about?''

No. She didn't. It had been a primal assertion, a statement of possession, of maleness. Proof of the power men had over women—and women had over men.

She wanted to touch him, to soften edges that had grown hard.

She chose not to.

He led the way onward in the snowy woods, away from the cabin, into cold and darkness. She followed, like Enid following Gereint in the old story from *Mabinogion*.

Except Enid had been innocent.

So am I.

No, she wasn't.

She grew cold. She tripped over a root.

He continued walking, never slowing his pace until he stopped suddenly, eased her against another tree, more gently this time. Unzipping her jeans, tugging them down. The bark was cold behind her. Snow dripped on her legs.

He filled her, and she squeezed back.

"Come," he said. He kissed her, stroked her tongue with his, whispered words. "You're going to come on me, and I'm going to come inside you again. And again tonight. And maybe again."

She shuddered over him and was limp.

WHEN THEY GOT HOME, Gabriela was off the phone. "Brad asked me to the Christmas dance." She beamed.

Ivy gave Cullen a look of superior knowledge.

He said, "Good for Brad. I'm sure he won't mind if your mother and I accompany you."

"Dad!" Gabriela moaned. "No way. I mean, you can drive us, but I think his brother's going to."

"Oh, no, he's not."

"Why not?"

"You're twelve years old. That's why not."

"Oh, please. I'll be thirteen in May."

"Talk to me about that in May. If you're going to the Christmas dance with Brad, the two of you ride in the Saab with us."

She shut her eyes and reopened them. "That's *mortifying*. I'm not a child."

"Could Brad's father drive them?" Ivy suggested.

"He doesn't have a father," Gabriela answered.

Cullen didn't like that at all. He felt for Brad, but Brad's older brother would not be the one driving them to this dance. "You tell Brad that I'm going to drive."

"It's too embarrassing. Everyone'll laugh if we drive up to the dance with my parents."

"Brad won't. I guarantee he'll understand perfectly."

"How do you know?"

"Because I'm a man. Tell him I look forward to meeting him."

"I won't go." It sounded like a threat.

"Have you already accepted?" Ivy asked.

"Yes."

"Then you're going."

"Oh, you'll *make* me go to the Christmas dance?"

"We'll make you keep your promise, yes."

"I'll get the flu."

Ivy had been wondering when she'd see this side of Gabriela. "You will not get the flu."

"Stop me."

Cullen had been hanging up his coat and Ivy's. "Apologize."

"For what?"

"For being rude to your mother."

"I'm being *honest*."

His eyes nailed her. She stared defiantly back. He said, "I'm waiting."

"Oh, I'm really scared."

Ivy knew she should say something. But what? What would make an impact on this child? Then, she knew. "No *Nutcracker*."

Gabriela stared as though Ivy had betrayed her. "Since when are you making the rules?" she exclaimed.

"I'm sure your father agrees with me."

Gabriela shook her head. "Uh-uh. He totally supports me about ballet."

"Gabriela."

She looked at him.

"I agree with her. Get used to the idea that when it comes to you, sooner or later we agree about *everything*."

Gabriela addressed Ivy. "Why don't you go back to Colorado?"

Cullen gritted his teeth.

Ivy seemed unfazed. "Because this is my home. I love your father, and I love you, and I'm here to stay."

Something changed in Gabriela's eyes. They no longer met those of her parents. Abruptly, she turned

on her heel and walked to her room. The door shut
behind her with a firm, calm click.

WHEN SHELBY CAME BY the following weekend to
work on the quilt, Gabriela claimed to have too much
homework to join them. Ivy and Cullen were both
getting the silent treatment. Gabriela remained cold
and unfriendly when her mother picked her up from
ballet or school. At home, she practiced ballet and
spent the remainder of her time in her room with the
door shut.

Ivy could see that Cullen was hurt by it, but he
didn't suggest relenting about the trip to Morgantown.
When Ivy mentioned it, he'd said, "I'm not really
crazy about Tracy as a role model at the moment."

Probably he was talking about the time Ivy had met
him for lunch downtown, and the two of them had
seen Matthew drive past with Tracy in his car.

Now Ivy found it hard to be with Shelby and not
mention what was going on. *If Cullen was driving
around town with another woman, would I want to
know?* The answer was a definite yes. Did that make
it right to tell Shelby?

"Let's go up in the loft and work," she suggested.

Ivy sat on the daybed, leaving the rocker for
Shelby, and they took out their needlework. Ivy admired the two squares Shelby had stitched at Coalgood. "They're beautiful."

They set to work in silence.

Ivy said, "I think Matthew's seeing Gabriela's ballet teacher."

Shelby slowly laid down the piece she was sewing. Her lips were tight. She met Ivy's eyes. Finally, she said, "No one's told me about that one yet."

Why do you let him get away with it?

And Tracy... Ivy gritted her teeth. She knew better than to let jealousy color her impression of someone. But... She closed her eyes. "I really want to trash that woman just now, and I know it's partly because of Cullen. However, I think it's more than that. As a culture, we need to criticize that kind of behavior in order to protect the social order. I mean, if it's okay for one woman to sleep with someone else's husband, that seems to make it okay for the rest of us—even though we know it's not."

Shelby resumed stitching, then laid down her work again.

Ivy wished she'd kept her mouth shut.

"It'll burn out," Shelby said. "And in this case, I'm sure it's not about Tracy. It's about Cullen."

Parts of Ivy's body hurt, as though they'd been stretched too hard. "As it must have been with me."

"Yes." Shelby was so calm. She must be enraged beneath the surface.

"Do you ever confront him?"

"Sure. It's always nasty."

"Do you ever confront the woman?"

"And say what? 'My husband can't keep his pants zipped. I'd appreciate if you could help him with his problem by not sleeping with him.'"

"Well, it's a start. It might make you feel better to take a part in stopping it."

"Nothing's going to make me feel better at this point but a child. *That* would make me feel better. And fortunately, Matthew's with me, as far as it goes."

Ivy thought of Cullen. He obviously wanted a child, and she wanted to have one with him. After their walk through the woods a week ago, he'd ceremoniously dropped the condoms in the trash without asking her opinion. They were of one mind. She wanted to carry his child as badly as he seemed to want it.

He made love to her at least twice a day, once in the morning and once at night.

But Matthew was the subject here. "You've never considered divorcing him?"

Shelby smiled ruefully. "A very long time ago. But you know the sad part?"

She was crying, and Ivy set down her own work to go to her and embrace her. She knew what Shelby was going to say.

"I love the jerk. I understand why he does the things he does, and I just want to keep him."

GABRIELA WAS PISSED OFF. The *Nutcracker* field trip was next weekend, and she wanted to go. Good grief, she hadn't been *that* rude to her mother. Did they want her just to sit there and do nothing when they made up some totally stupid rule? Her father absolutely had to back down about driving her to the dance. She was afraid to mention it to Brad; he might not want to go with her anymore.

How am I going to make them listen?

The dilemma sucked all her concentration from ballet practice, and she finally quit her workout in frustration and stood in front of the mirror, checking out her body, looking for cellulite. She had pretty good muscles, and Tracy said thin wasn't necessarily in; healthy bodies were. *Well, I look healthy.*

In fact, when she looked in the mirror, she liked what she saw. And Brad Petersen had asked *her* to the Christmas dance.

Brad was not going to ride to the dance with her parents, Gabriela just knew it. She fought for other solutions. Maybe if Noel had a date and went with them?

No. They wouldn't go for that, either.

Ivy sure had a nerve. If she hadn't started butting in, her dad would've let her go with Brad and his brother. Gabriela was sure she could have talked him into it, but now there was no way.

Whatever I do, I don't want to grow up to be like her.

A midwife. It sounded so gross. Every time Gabriela saw something being born on the Discovery Channel, she changed the station.

Also, the quilt... Part of her thought it was neat, but another part thought it was embarrassing that her mother was so into these hillbilly things. Midwifery, quilting. Bad enough they lived up in this hollow. She'd much rather live over by Noel, even at Coalgood.

A horrible thought came to her. If Brad's brother

drove, they'd have to come to the house to pick her up!

Oh, well, I'll show them this room. They might even think the cabin was kind of cool when she told them it was a hundred years old.

Except *they* wouldn't be coming up here.

Frustrated, she tapped her foot in rhythm with Michael Torke's music, a CD Tracy had suggested. There had to be some solution.

But she couldn't find one.

She could feign illness the night of the dance.

Or she could tell Brad.

She had a feeling her parents wouldn't let her be sick. In fact, at this point, even if she had pneumonia, they'd probably make her go.

She shut her eyes. Well, Ivy wasn't coming. If her dad had to drive, so be it, but for her mom to be there would be the ultimate in gross.

I'll tell Brad tomorrow.

It was going to be the worst day of her life.

SHELBY TILL RARELY TOOK walks at night, but no one had blinked when she'd said she was going out. Matthew had said, "Want company?" And she'd considered it.

Maybe the best thing was to be close to him, to show her love for him. But in the end, she'd said, "No, thanks. I won't be long."

And now she stood on the snowy sidewalk outside Tracy Kennedy's house. The porch light was on. *Expecting company, Tracy?*

Damn Ivy anyhow. But once Ivy had put the idea of confronting Tracy in her head, Shelby began to derive some satisfaction from the prospect of telling this woman to keep her hands off Matthew.

And after she told Tracy, she'd go home and tell Matthew.

She hesitated.

He'd be sardonic. She'd be a bitch.

So be it.

She walked up the flagstone steps to the front door and pressed the bell.

"STILL NOT TALKING TO US."

"She's strong-willed." Ivy studied the underside of the bed's canopy. It could stand a new cover. That would be fun to sew. "I think that's good."

Cullen sighed. "I'd practically forgotten who I was living with before you came back. Meet Gabriela."

"I think it's normal." Ivy thought of Devon. Did Emma quell her rebellions?

"She hasn't told Brad yet. I know she hasn't. He's called twice. She would've said something if she'd told him."

"The only person whose opinion matters to her is Brad, and I think you were right. I think he probably expects it."

"Maybe. You never can tell. I'm just glad I'm going to have the chance to meet him."

"Were you serious about chaperoning the dance?"

"Why not? It beats bringing cupcakes to class parties."

He had done all that, she realized. Reaching for him, wanting to love him for all his gifts of love, she thought of something else. ''Is she menstruating yet?''

''For a year and a half now.''

''How did you handle that?''

''Carefully. Actually, I asked Shelby to talk to her before it happened.''

''Why Shelby? Why not your sister or your mother?''

He considered. ''I don't really know. There's something real about Shelby.''

''I like her.'' Ivy liked her enough not to talk about her tears over Matthew. Instead, she shut her eyes and envisioned Shelby wonderfully pregnant—and Matthew miraculously reformed.

But Cullen's hands found her, and thoughts of conception came closer to home.

TRACY'S SMILE DIED when she saw who was at the door.

A rude comment sprang to mind, but Shelby didn't utter it. She felt too sorry for the other woman. *He doesn't love you. He'll never leave me and marry you.*

Maybe the favor she should do Tracy was to tell her so. ''May I come in?''

Tracy drew back to allow her inside, then shut the door.

Shelby checked out her surroundings. She hated the decor too much to say anything complimentary. It tried for the elegance of Coalgood and failed, and

Shelby would have preferred a tattered sofa and worn rug. *Matthew must hate it, too.*

She wandered into the living room and sat on the mauve velveteen couch.

Tracy asked, "Can I get you something to drink?"

"No, thanks."

Tracy did not sit but stood poised beside a wing chair as though waiting for Shelby to explain her presence.

Shelby decided to keep it as short—and dignified— as possible. "You may find this hard to believe, but my husband loves me deeply."

Tracy's jaw was tight.

"I'm the big love in his life." Shelby got up and managed to smile at Tracy. "I just thought you'd like to know." She showed herself to the door.

Tracy stayed silent. But just as Shelby reached for the door handle, she said, "I apologize. Obviously, you're staking your territory, and I can respect that."

If you respected my territory, you would have told my husband to kiss off the first time he approached you. "Actually, that's not it at all."

No smiles from the other quarter. Just cold eyes.

"I'm trying to keep you from getting hurt."

"I don't believe that for a minute."

Shelby shrugged. "What can I say? Good night." She grasped the door handle.

"I don't care about Matthew."

Oh, she cared about someone else. Shelby could hardly blame Tracy for being embittered about Cullen. He'd seemed free when he and Tracy had dated. *But he's sure not now.*

Shelby wished she hadn't come over. Tracy made her sad. Here was a beautiful woman, teaching kids, and... *What made her like this?* Shelby said, ''I hope you meet the right man soon.''

Tracy's eyes were cool, and she didn't answer.

Feeling like a jerk, Shelby left. She'd never been anyplace so sad.

CHAPTER NINE

BRAD HAD STARTED ASKING her to eat lunch with Tyler and Jim and Ellen Watts. Gabriela was going to have to catch him alone in the hall to give him the grim news. She usually saw him as she was leaving math, and sure enough, he was at his locker, alone.

When he saw her, he smiled. "Hi!"

"Hi." She moved closer to the lockers. If anyone overheard this, she would die. "I have to talk to you about the dance, and, I'm warning you, it's bleak news."

"What?" He wasn't smiling anymore.

"My dad has insisted on driving us."

Brad made a face. "No way."

"It's true. I'm sorry. You don't have to go with me if you don't want. I guess these are the perils of seventh grade."

She felt him glancing at her, considering.

"I thought Ben could drive us."

"I told him that. But I'm his little girl." She batted her eyelashes to make clear to Brad that she was *not* a little girl. Then something occurred to her. This guy really didn't want to go to the dance with her because her father would be driving them? Her father wasn't some nerd. Impatient, she said, "So, make up your mind. If you don't want to go with me, I want to find another date.''

Brad tossed back his dark bangs. His lips were full and expressive, and he had some hair on his upper lip, which Gabriela found interesting. "No, I want to go with you." He made a face. "It would've been cool to go with Ben, but oh, well."

"Oh, well," Gabriela agreed.

Surely her dad had been kidding about actually coming to the dance.

THE QUILT WAS GROWING. Gabriela joined in again and actually sewed some squares with Ivy in front of the television, usually watching ballet videos. Ivy was impressed with Gabriela's discipline in ballet, how she chose to dance every day on her own initiative. And she was beautiful when she danced.

Tracy Kennedy deserved some credit, and when Ivy picked Gabriela up from her last class before winter vacation, she decided to tell her. Shelby had told her about going to Tracy's house, and Ivy somewhat regretted butting in—except that apparently Matthew's affair with Tracy had ended.

While Gabriela gathered her belongings after class, Ivy watched Tracy smile at parents and encourage students. But whenever she turned away, her features were etched with exhaustion, her eyes lifeless.

Ivy took off her boots and wandered out onto the floor.

Tracy looked surprised.

"I just wanted to tell you how much pleasure it

gives me to see Gabriela dancing. You must be a very good teacher to inspire the habits she has.''

"She loves ballet.'' Tracy seemed to hesitate, then plunged in. "I know this is hard for parents to hear, but you and Cullen might want to think about letting her go away to a performing arts school. I enjoy teaching her, but she really has something, and she could use more than I can give her in a two-hour class a few times a week.''

Go away to school? The suggestion tore at her. But if Gabriela loved dance so much... "Tracy, will it hurt her chances in the future if she continues as she has been, taking classes from you?''

Tracy didn't answer at once. Slowly, she said, "To do what she wants to do, yes. She's more committed to excellence than...'' She left the sentence unfinished.

There had to be another solution. *I just found my daughter. I don't want to lose her again.*

"Would private lessons help? And would you consider doing that?''

"I'd do it. It would help, but frankly, I'm not that good—as a dancer or a teacher. I wouldn't be saying this if she wasn't so serious about dance.''

"Saying what?'' Gabriela had suddenly appeared, standing at her shoulder.

Ivy needed to talk to Cullen, but she saw no point in keeping this conversation from Gabriela. "Tracy just suggested that you go away to a performing arts school. How do you feel about that?''

Gabriela's eyes shone. "Yes.''

"Yes, you want to?"

"Yes."

Ivy chewed her bottom lip. *I can't stand this. What's the right thing to do?* She turned to Tracy. "Thank you for mentioning this, and thanks, also, for all you do for Gabriela."

"It's my job." The smile in Tracy's eyes was bittersweet. "And she's a wonderful girl."

You wanted to be her stepmother.

The thought was useless. Understanding Tracy could not change what was.

"No," CULLEN SAID.

"Just like that?"

Gabriela was in bed, and her parents were using the dance room, both stretching after their workouts.

"Just like that."

"Why not?"

"Being part of a family is more important than ballet."

"Tell that to Baryshnikov."

"A perfect illustration of my point."

Ivy understood, but he needed to see the other side. "Cullen, the world needs great artists, and Gabriela wants to be one. It's not just wanting fame. At first, I thought it was. But she cares about dance. She loves it. I think this might be a time to give her what she wants."

Cullen quit stretching. "I can't believe I'm hearing this. From you, who visits the sixteen-year-old down the road practically every day."

The phone rang, and he got up to answer it. Ivy heard him speaking but couldn't tell who it was. Finally, he came to get her. "Your mom."

Ivy raised her eyebrows. Though she spoke with both Francesca and Tara once a week, until tonight neither of them had even heard Cullen's voice. After she finished talking to Francesca, she would ask Cullen what had been said.

Francesca said, "Hi, Ivy. I just finished a birth, and I'm exhilarated, but it made me miss you so much."

"I miss you, too. Hey, I think I might have another client on the way. Emma Workman, the grandmother of the girl I told you about, said her sister's daughter is pregnant. She was going to give her my name. Emma was nearly certain she'd be interested."

"Wonderful!" Francesca sighed. "You know, Ivy, however much I miss you, you have to know that my heart just feels *full* that you've found your family and your roots and that you're practicing midwifery where your mother and grandmother did. Sometimes I cry about it," she admitted.

"Me, too."

A slight pause. "Cullen seems very nice."

"He's a wonderful man. Good inside."

"I'm eager to meet him in person. In fact, that's part of why I'm calling. How would you feel about a couple of visitors for a few days at Christmas? We don't want to intrude—we'd stay at a hotel—"

"Just a minute." Ivy put down the phone and hurried back to the dance room.

Cullen was doing extra push-ups. He stopped in the middle of one, then quit to give her his attention.

"Do you mind if Francesca and Tara come for Christmas?"

"I'd like it."

"She plans to stay in a hotel—"

He shook his head. "If they really want to. But they're welcome here. We can put mattresses in the sunroom—or in here. Or someone can sleep on the couch."

Ivy walked over to him and kissed him on the mouth. He responded so earnestly that she had to pry herself away to return to the phone.

Cullen watched her leave, listened to the tones of her voice and used his T-shirt to wipe the sweat from his body. He wandered out to the living room just as she was hanging up.

Ivy said, "So you talked with her. What did the two of you say?"

"She said she was eager to meet me and Gabriela, and I said likewise. She asked about the weather, and I told her."

Gabriela. Ivy remembered what they'd been discussing before the phone rang.

"Want a shower?" Cullen asked.

They wouldn't get any talking done in there.

"I'd like to go upstairs for a bit. And finish our conversation."

"It is finished."

"Cullen, that's not fair."

He gestured elaborately for her to precede him into the sunroom and up to the loft.

She sat in the rocking chair.

Cullen imagined her rocking their child there, and he remembered her rocking Gabriela—and remembered that during the same period she'd been sleeping with his brother. He sat on the edge of the tester bed closest to her. "Do I need to explain myself further?"

"Yes."

"I hope the world always has great artists. I hope, if Gabriela wants to become one, she will. But it's also important to me that she become a great adult."

"There's probably a performing arts school in Charleston. It's not that far. We could see her frequently."

"Tracy and I have discussed this before. I understand from her that Gabriela should go to New York."

New York?

"But I want to see her every morning and every night," Cullen added. "Right now, she's the sun and all the rest of us are planets spinning around her, and she never notices unless we displease her. She needs us more than she needs to attend a ballet academy."

"Even so, I can't help thinking that we may be standing in the way of her dreams."

Cullen touched his chest. "Great is inside."

Ivy got up from the rocker and went to embrace him. "And you're pretty great, Cullen."

"DAD, CAN I ASK A FAVOR?"

Saturday morning. The dance was that night. Ivy

had gone down the hill to see Devon. Cullen scraped an omelette onto Gabriela's plate. "You can ask."

Gabriela's expression reminded him of Ivy with a dilemma or with bad news. "Can you drive us to the dance by yourself?"

He turned off the stove and took his own plate to the table. He knew his answer, but he wanted to hear her reasons. "Why?"

"It just seems more dignified than having both my parents in the car."

He cut into his omelette. "Eat," he suggested.

She sat down across from him and didn't touch her silverware. "Please?"

"Can't do it."

"Why?"

"Because your mom is my date, and it would be rude."

"Your date?"

"Chaperons for the dance."

Her eyes went wide. "No. No. Please, no. I really couldn't handle it. It's more than I can bear."

"We won't look at you. In fact, once we get inside, we'll pretend to be someone else's parents if you like. We'll even take assumed names."

She didn't laugh. "I will never forgive you if you do this to me."

"Never's a long time."

Desolately, she regarded her meal. "I can't eat."

He swallowed another bite. "What's bugging you? We clean up good."

Her eyes slanted away from him. "You wouldn't understand."

"Try me."

"I'm going to this dance with a *ninth grader,* and you're treating me like I'm in grade school."

"Actually, I'm treating you like you're extraordinary and special, which you are. The chances that your future is with Brad Petersen are slim, and you're twelve years old—"

"Stop saying that!"

"You are not yet thirteen."

She glared at him. "I want to go away to school."

"I know."

She softened. "Did Mom tell you what Tracy said?"

"Your mother and I don't agree with Tracy. But…"

She hung on his every word.

"We reached a compromise. Tracy has said she'll work with you privately, in addition to your regular class. And we think you can go away for the whole summer next year, instead of just three weeks."

Her eyes glowed, and she leaped up from the table and hugged him around the neck.

"Thank your mom. She talked me into it."

"I will, I will." She turned a pirouette there on the floor, and she shone.

His heart twisted. He never wanted anything to go wrong for her.

He resumed eating his omelette, and she sat down and began eating hers. After a moment, she stopped.

"You know, Brad's going to hate me for you guys being chaperons, but I guess I don't care. I have cool parents. It's not like you're nerds."

Cullen quirked his eyebrows. "Thanks."

"But I have final approval on your clothes."

He could live with that and imagined Ivy could, too. "Deal."

GABRIELA WAS SO GLAD her mother had taken her shopping. She never would have found this dress otherwise.

It was ivory and long and totally elegant, and Ivy had suggested these incredible long gloves, too, and helped pin her hair up. She felt like Audrey Hepburn in *My Fair Lady*.

"Okay," she told the mirror, "it's time to check *them* out."

They were sitting on the couch together, going through their wedding pictures. They looked kind of cute, except for... "Dad. The tie." When he glanced up, Gabriela made a slicing motion across her throat. "No patterns. Wear your red tie." She contemplated her mother. "Stand up."

The two of them exchanged a look that meant they were *letting* her boss them around. So what? The most important thing was that they not embarrass her tonight.

Her mother's dress was retro, a flapper look in purplish blue, and it looked suspiciously like she'd bought it at a used clothing store. Well, retro was cool. And Gabriela supposed she could live with the ballet-slipper shoes. Her hair should be up, but then it would all seem too planned.

"Just a minute." Gabriela sped into her room. Her dad had come downstairs with a better tie, the narrow red cotton one. She flashed him the okay sign and told her mother, "Turn around."

Ivy obeyed, and Gabriela moved her hair and fastened something around her neck. Ivy reached up to touch it.

"It's my locket, and it has Dad's picture inside, so everyone should be happy. Don't lose it."

"I'll certainly try not to. Thank you for lending it."

"Okay, get your coats."

"Can you get mine?" Ivy asked. "It's in our closet upstairs."

"Not the sheepskin." Gabriela seemed alarmed.

"No."

"Vintage?"

"Yes."

With a satisfied nod, Gabriela headed for her own room to get her wrap.

"WANT TO GO UP in the bleachers?"

Yes. Oh, yes. She wanted to go up in the bleachers with Brad, but where were her parents?

"They just went out to the front area." Brad must have read her mind.

"What lousy chaperons." Gabriela laughed. "Sure. Let's go."

She kept one eye on the doors as they reached the

bleacher level and climbed up into the darkness. Then she had to concentrate on keeping her dress out of the garbage scattered everywhere.

She remembered reading in one of her dance books that one thing you didn't want to do in a dancing career was kiss strangers on the mouth. You would catch their colds and their cold sores.

Brad wasn't a stranger.

"They can't see us up here," he said, holding her hand as she sat down. He put his arm around her and kissed her, like that.

Oh, wow. Kissed by Brad Petersen. Then she felt his tongue and just about gagged. French kissing was supposed to be cool, but why had no one ever said it was gross? She pulled away.

He looked irritated.

Okay, she'd try again. Nervously, she scanned the area below one more time for her parents. Oh, shit, they were back.

And they were staring right up at her and Brad.

"They're looking at us," she said. "I'm going to the girls' room. Meet me by the pop stand."

She would absolutely die if her mother followed her into the rest room.

As soon as Brad saw Gabriela's dad appear by the bleachers, he knew he was going to have to go through some real bullshit. This girl was turning out to be too much trouble. *Friends. We'll be friends.* He'd find someone else to ask out.

He started to get up, but Gabriela's dad sat down beside him.

If he starts lecturing, I'll just leave. I don't need some father breathing down my neck.

"You like to take photographs?"

What was this? Brad smelled a big-brother act coming on, and that was worse than the cop routine. He wasn't going to put up with it. "Look. I just kissed her. Okay? No hard feelings. I'm not trying to lay your daughter. Frankly, she's not my type."

The man beside him didn't say a word, just looked at him.

"And I'm not going to be your little photographer's apprentice. I don't want your help or your guidance or your mentoring. I don't *need* it. My brother and I take care of my mom, and you probably don't understand it because you grew up in your big house with your big happy family. Well, I don't need your shit." Brad wanted to punch him.

"Okay." He stood. "What you need is to come down from the bleachers."

Brad watched him spot another couple several sections down. They were already leaving in a hurry. Stupid rule.

"I can make a camera from an oatmeal box," Gabriela's father said.

That was a load of shit.

"I can even make a camera from a bus."

"You're multitalented. What can I say?"

"Would *you* like to make a camera from an oatmeal box?"

"Kindergarten." But Brad had a flash, a great flash that would prove once and for all that this guy was full of shit. "Your car. I want to make a camera out of your car."

SHELBY CAME OVER THE DAY after the dance to work on the quilt. "I'm pregnant."

"Shelby!" Ivy hugged her.

Gabriela blinked back and forth between the two of them. What was the big deal? She never wanted children. They were so *loud*. Whenever she was around them in restaurants, she wanted to leave.

She stood up and went to the loft window to look out. Ben was supposed to drop Brad off so he and her dad could make a camera out of the Camaro, which was about the stupidest thing she'd ever heard in her life. She really wanted to kiss him again.

"Do you know your due date?"

Gabriela tuned them out and went back to sewing. As soon as she heard them coming up the road, she was going to put on her workout clothes and start practice. She would totally ignore Brad.

Restless, she returned to her seat on the bed, relieved her mother wasn't the kind of person who would follow her into the rest room at a dance.

"OKAY," CULLEN EXPLAINED to Brad. "I've got this worked out *perfectly*. The thing we want to avoid is dumping chemicals in the car, so we've got to be careful of the tubs."

Brad really couldn't believe it. They were going to

make a camera from a Camaro? "I guess the photos won't be that great."

"Oh, yes, they will. Provided the people do well."

Brad looked from the Camaro to the bins and rolls of paper and tape, to the red light and timer and a five-gallon container of water, all amassed in the passenger seat of the car. "What do we do first?"

"Black out every inch of light inside the car."

GABRIELA FINISHED her workout. Brad had barely said hi, the jerk. *He was friendlier when we were just friends.*

She heard the screen door. "Gabriela! Ivy! Shelby! We need bodies."

She rushed out of the dance room to see her father in the doorway. "You did it?" She knew he'd made a camera from a school bus once. There were huge photos at his studio of miners at MinCo.

Her father nodded. "Put on something warm. You'll be standing out there a while. The exposures are long."

IVY, SHELBY AND GABRIELA stood against a tree, each with her back to it, Gabriela in the center. Cullen moved Shelby over some, closer to Gabriela, then did the same with Ivy.

Ivy whispered, "I love you."

He kissed her. "Okay. Ten minutes. If you decide to move, be sure to hold each pose for a *long* time. No more than, say, three poses."

"It's cold out here!" Gabriela said. "Hurry."

He jogged back to the car.

EVERYTHING THEY NEEDED barely fitted inside the car, with the thin black hose for water reaching in through careful taping. Cullen made a quick check for light, double-checking the rusty section on the floor, making sure no chemicals were slopping onto the back seat, where they'd set up a developing station.

He said, "Ready?"

Brad held the electrical tape on the window, prepared to remove it from the windshield.

Cullen set the timer. "Go for it."

Brad peeled off the tape, and light came through the windshield onto the photographic paper. *It's going to work,* he thought. The test strips had blown him away. Cullen had explained how it all happened, but he hadn't really gotten it. Well, they had to do something for the next ten minutes. "Okay, tell me again how all this works."

"WOW!" IVY AND SHELBY shouted in unison.

Gabriela's mouth hung open. "You took that with the *car?*"

The three women looked both ancient and lovely. *Women.* Cullen realized he'd thought of Gabriela that way, too. Young woman.

Brad shook his head. "That's incredible." He shot a glance at Cullen. "Can we do it again?"

"Oh, yeah. We can do it till it gets dark. Let's not waste this light. Okay, what are we doing this time?"

Ivy, Shelby and Gabriela were still checking out

the photo, and Brad edged away from the group. Sensing he wanted to say something, Cullen followed.

"Tell me if this is too much of a favor. But would you mind if I asked my mom and brother to come over so we could take a picture of them? I'd pay you for the paper."

"You don't have to do that. Sure, go call them." Cullen smiled and whispered loudly, "This group is going to start whining about the cold in a minute."

IVY ROLLED OVER SLEEPILY to hug Cullen. Brad had gone home with pictures of himself and his family, and him and Gabriela. About five pictures in all. "You're great, Cullen."

"No. I'm just lucky." But he thought of his father and of Matthew. Zeya had finally found an attendant, a black man named George, and he would be at Coalgood every day except Christmas Eve and Christmas Day. Cullen had liked him but was glad to avoid the family during their period of adjustment to the change.

"I'm so happy Shelby's pregnant. I'm really hopeful this will change Matthew."

"Don't hold your breath."

"Shelby says he wants a baby."

Cullen changed the subject. "When are Tara and Francesca arriving?"

"Wednesday. That's the twenty-third. They're leaving on the twenty-sixth."

"You know, if I borrow one of my parents' cars we can all go to the airport."

"The Saab would get kind of crowded. Let's do that. Thank you!" In the dark, she worried her bottom lip. "But you know, Cullen, I'm a little concerned about the possibility of Devon going into labor. I'm not sure I want to be that far from town." She'd hired an answering service and now wore her pager everywhere.

"I thought she wasn't due for weeks. January tenth? And you've got a backup physician."

"That's less than a month away."

"And you're particularly attached to this client."

"I care about *every* client."

"How about if just Gabby and I go to the airport?"

"Would you mind?"

"If you don't think they would."

"You don't know these women."

He had the feeling he was going to be descended on by witches. "Tell me."

"Well, Tara will give you this big hug, and I'm warning you, she's—"

"What?"

"Exciting."

"Oh." He made a sound through his teeth. "Maybe you *should* come to the airport."

"Oh, no. She's very loyal. I trust her completely. Anyhow, Mom—she'll smile and shake your hand and be kind of reserved, and on the way home she'll ask you ladylike questions about your work, and after a while you'll realize you've told her your most interesting secrets."

Witches. Just like he'd thought. Well, he'd meet

them at the airport with Gabriela, and she could absorb some of the conversation. He reached for Ivy. "Guess who else wants a baby."

She shaped her body against him. "Me."

CHAPTER TEN

ON MONDAY, IVY GATHERED her midwifery kit to take out to the Saab. She would stop briefly at Devon's before heading up to Thousandsnakes Hollow to see Emma's niece, who was expecting her third.

Gabriela, who had been drooping a little since the day Brad came over, asked, "Can I come with you?"

"Sure. Get your coat."

Surprised by the quick decision, Gabriela hurried to get her coat. *I can't believe she's letting me do this.* It had just been a whim, asking to come along, but she did have some curiosity about what her mom did for these pregnant women. And she knew she'd been born at home, with just her mom and dad there.

Climbing into the Saab and shutting the door, she said, "I just don't want to see anything born. It grosses me out on TV."

Ivy contemplated that. It was the third time Gabriela had mentioned being disgusted by birth. It almost seemed as though she wanted someone to convince her that birth *wasn't* gross. Ivy didn't argue with her. She started the car. "Okay, I'm taking you with me because you're my daughter, and my grandmother took me with her when I was your age. But there are some rules, and if you're going to have trouble with any of them, you need to stay home.''

That sounded both interesting and serious. What rules could be so important?

"First, we care for the pregnant woman and her family. That's why we're there. Second, if you want to tell your friends at school that you went to work with your mom or that you helped a pregnant lady, that's fine. But gossip has no place in this profession. We're there to support and nurture each pregnant woman, to celebrate her strength. You're no better or worse than she is, and she's no better or worse than you.''

Gabriela waited. "That's it?''

Ivy smiled. "That's enough for now.''

"Okay. I agree.''

Her mother's smile came from her eyes now, a smile that said she, Gabriela, was special and wonderful.

They pulled up in front of the Workmans' trailer, and Gabriela couldn't help staring. *We're going in here?* These people were poor, really poor, and pretty tacky.

Well, I'm not here to be friends.

But what had her mom said? "You're no better or worse than she is…''

Do I really believe that? Gabriela wondered.

Her mother was opening the driver's door, and Gabriela opened hers to get out.

"GABRIELA, I'M MEASURING the fundal height. This tells how much the baby has grown since the last time we measured. It also helps tell us how many weeks pregnant Devon is.''

Gabriela found the place on the chart for fundal height. So far, she'd written down a lot. The results of the glucose test, Devon's and the baby's heart rates, blood pressure... Her mother told her what she was doing in each case, and Gabriela's head was spinning. At first, she'd sort of tuned out the explanations. But it was actually pretty interesting.

''Thirty-seven centimeters.''

Gabriela wrote it down.

''Now, let's see what baby's up to.'' Ivy smiled at Devon. She'd accepted Gabriela's presence when Ivy had said, ''This is my daughter, Gabriela. She's going to help me today.'' Now Devon was relaxed, smiling a little. Good. Ivy knew what the baby was doing. The baby was breech, but the presenting part wasn't engaged. With Devon relaxed, she should be able to turn her. Where was that heartbeat? She found it, measured. One hundred and thirty beats per minute. *Okay, kiddo, let's see if you want to turn around.*

Gabriela watched her mother's hands. What would it be like to be able to feel someone's stomach and know which way the baby was lying inside her, know what was the head or a foot or anything? It seemed almost magical.

Her mom was listening to the heart again. ''Oh, baby, you're doing so well.''

When her mother smiled at Devon, Devon's whole face brightened. *She's excited about having a baby.*

Only a real loser would get— Gabriela heard her mother's voice, telling her she was no better or worse than anyone else. *Okay, she's not a loser. She did something dumb, but she's not worse than me.*

Support and nurture? How was she supposed to do that?

Forget this stuff, Gabs. You're just an observer.

IVY SHUT THE CAR DOOR and resisted asking Gabriela how she'd enjoyed the experience. In her heart, she longed for Gabriela to become a midwife. But Gabriela's passion was dance, and she absolutely must follow her own heart, no one else's.

Her daughter was silent as Ivy started the Saab. But when they reached the stop sign at the foot of the road, Gabriela asked, "Where are we going now?"

"Thousandsnakes Hollow. I have directions, but maybe you can help. Do you know where it is?"

Gabriela shook her head.

Ivy handed her the map Emma had drawn for her. "This lady is Emma's niece, and she already has two toddlers. It would probably be helpful if you played with them and kept them out of our hair while Rhonda and I visit. This is a first visit, so we won't be doing much more than talking, getting to know each other."

"Okay." Gabriela sounded grim, but she said nothing else.

"CULLEN, THEIR *HOUSE*. I've never seen anything like it. It was hardly more than a tar-paper shack, and her boyfriend was drinking from a bottle, and the kids, neither of whom are his, were dirty, and one of them was still in diapers, and...it was despair. They have no car, no phone, no utilities. Their water isn't potable, and they're boiling it to drink."

"How did Gabriela take it?"

Ivy stared. "That's all you can say?" They were talking in the dance room again.

Cullen kept his head down. "I guess I'm not shocked by it anymore."

"Have you ever been in one of those places deep up in the hollows? Ours is practically a neighborhood in comparison."

"No. I haven't." *It's not that I don't feel, Ivy.* It was just that he didn't *know* any of these people. And people were touchy about charity around here. He thought a minute. "What were they doing for heat?"

"A homemade stove that didn't look safe."

"What are they burning?"

"Coal."

"I take it you'd like to change this situation."

"I can't in good conscience *not* change it. Or try to."

"How are you going to get them to let you do that?"

"What do you mean?"

"You don't know the people here, Ivy. They're proud."

"She's not of that generation."

He cocked an eyebrow.

"So you're saying I should do nothing?"

"No." He rubbed a hand through his hair, getting

sweaty bangs off his forehead. "Okay, so this is what we need to do. We go up there, and you say, 'You know, I'm really concerned about how you're going to get along after the baby's born, Rhonda. As your midwife, I really need to make some provisions for you and the baby, so I brought my husband along to see if he can look at your stove and check out your water.' Then I go to work and use whatever I can find on their property to fix things."

"But the water—"

"I'll take care of it if I can. Is her boyfriend violent or just drunk?"

Ivy drew in a breath. "He seemed like a hell-raiser to me, so the answer is...possibly violent."

"I'm coming with you on these visits. All of them."

She didn't object.

He repeated his first question. "How did Gabriela take it?"

"Total shock. You saw her tonight."

"Probably didn't hurt her a bit." Cullen smiled at Ivy and touched her arm. "Ready for bed?"

TWO DAYS LATER, he and Gabriela drove to the airport in Charleston to pick up Tara and Francesca. They planned to spend some time Christmas shopping before the plane arrived. He and Ivy had already planned Gabriela's big gift, and they both had a few smaller things for her. And Cullen had one gift for Ivy—a photo of the three of them that Brad had taken with the Camaro. Ivy had seen it, but he'd framed it for her. Still, the incident of the lingerie continued to bother him. He'd like to buy her a pretty nightgown, and Gabriela could help with that.

It was a two-hour drive, and after half an hour of silence, Cullen said, "You sure haven't had much to say the past couple of days."

More silence.

"Are you upset about going with your mom on Monday? She said the place was pretty bad."

"I don't want to talk about it."

He had to accept that. The experience was changing her, and he had to let that take its own course.

"Mom is like…like Mother Teresa or something. It makes me feel guilty."

"What do you have to feel guilty for?"

"Caring about clothes and ballet. I feel like I should be doing what *she's* doing."

"You're twelve years old, and she would not want you to feel that way. Guilt is totally useless. It doesn't make anyone a good person. Whenever you start to feel it, stop thinking until the feeling goes away. Because when you stop thinking about what you should do, you do the right thing."

"I don't believe you."

"Try it. Anyhow, Ivy told me you did a great job looking after the kids while she talked with their mom. You really helped."

Gabriela began to cry.

He saw a gas station with a convenience store up ahead and prepared to pull in.

"I'm fine." She dug a tissue out of her backpack,

which she'd brought with her. "You don't have to stop."

"Yes, I do. We need gas." He turned into the lot and pulled up to the pumps. But before he got out, he asked, "Can I do anything?"

"No."

He smiled at her. "Don't think."

Through her tears, she giggled.

"DAD, WHAT ABOUT THIS ONE? I know it's flannel, but she's kind of old-fashioned."

The nightgown was blue with white flowers and white ruffled trim and flower-shaped buttons. He pictured Ivy in it. "I like it. Let's get it. It'll be from both of us."

Gabriela frowned. "What can I get her? She doesn't seem to want anything. When we went shopping for my dress for the dance, she just didn't look twice at the stuff in the stores."

Cullen took a moment to consider. "I think she liked wearing your locket to the dance."

"But *you* should give her that."

"Why not put your picture in it, Gabriela? She'd probably treasure that the most."

Gabriela stared up at him for only a moment, then exclaimed, "Okay. Let's find a really cool one." A second later, she thought, *My dad's the best.*

THIS WAS SO WEIRD, standing in the airport waiting for total strangers. Her mom called them her mother and her sister, but they weren't related to her by blood or… It made Gabriela's head spin, and she felt totally conspicuous carrying a sign that read, "HI, TARA" followed by a big exclamation point with a heart at the bottom. And her dad had one just like it for Francesca.

The passengers were coming out of the gate. Ivy had told them what to look for. Tara was tall and beautiful with long, dark hair, and Francesca had longish, curly, dark auburn hair. Tara would be bursting with energy, and Francesca would seem aloof.

They were midwives. Gabriela sort of hoped they'd talk about it on the way home in the car. But it probably wouldn't be like that.

"Ah! There they are."

The voice came from a tall woman with long, walnut-colored hair and a huge grin. You almost couldn't notice anyone else around her because she was so…dynamic?

"Let's see—Gabriela, right?" Her brown eyes were bright, and she really had the friendliest smile Gabriela had ever seen.

Gabriela said, "Tara, right?"

Tara laughed, drew the sign toward her to examine it, then set it down beside her and gave Gabriela a hug. A second later, she drew back. "You probably get sick to death of hearing this, but you look just like your mom."

"I have my dad's chin."

"Let's see." Tara compared the two of them.

The other woman who'd been speaking to her dad now turned to her. "Hello, Gabriela. I'm Francesca."

While she shook hands with Francesca, Tara grabbed her dad in a huge hug. He smiled, returned the embrace and took a step back from her.

No kidding, Gabriela thought.

He asked them, "The baggage claim?"

"Nope," Tara said. "We've got everything with us." She wore a backpack, and Francesca had a big garment bag. "We're yours."

GABRIELA HAD ANSWERED all the questions about school and ballet, and Tara was busy exclaiming over things outside the window. Everything out there seemed to excite her. "No way! Look at those trees!" Gabriela actually thought they were both nice, although Francesca didn't say very much.

How could she get them to talk about midwifery?

"I went with my mom to see a pregnant girl the other day."

Both midwives immediately looked at her.

"So…" Tara's grin was coming back up. "Tell us about it."

"Actually, there were two." What should she say? She wasn't supposed to gossip. Gabriela searched her mind. "She turned this baby who was…upside-down?"

"Breech," they both said at once.

"She didn't even say she was doing it. She told us all about it after it was done, and then she had Devon go for a little walk, told her to stand up for a while so the head would stay down."

"Become engaged," Tara said. "It means the wid-

est part of the baby's head, or its butt if it's breech—
the presenting part—has passed through the mom's
pelvic inlet. It's exciting for the mom because it
means the big day is getting pretty close. So, anything
else?"

Gabriela thought. "I wrote down stuff for her.
That's about it."

"And then you saw another lady?" Tara was asking the questions, but Francesca was still turned
around from the front seat. These two acted like people having babies was the most exciting thing on
earth.

Another lady. "Yes. She had two little kids, and I
took care of them."

"That must have been a big help to your mother!"
Francesca said. "If you want to come to Colorado, I
have a job for you."

Gabriela admitted, "It's not my favorite thing."

The women laughed.

"Gabby." It was her dad. She could see his eyes
in the rearview mirror, and they were smiling.
"You're a million-dollar girl."

Her mom had told him how hard things were for
that lady, Rhonda. *He's glad I didn't gossip.* Warmth
spread inside her.

Tara said, "Okay, now. Tell me every little detail
about your dancing. I don't know squat about ballet,
except that it's really, really hard."

This was going to be fun, having her mom's...well,
family visit.

IVY HUGGED TARA, then Francesca. "It's so great to have you here, to see your faces."

"And yours!"

"Look at this incredible place," said Tara.

"I grew up here, when there was only this cabin. Or so Cullen tells me. Let me give you the tour."

While Cullen carried in their bags, Ivy and Gabriela showed them around the house. Ivy was surprised how much Gabriela knew of the history of things in the cabin. Cullen must have told her all he knew.

"We thought you'd like to sleep in the sunroom. It stays surprisingly warm in here at night, and we've got these foam futons."

"It's lovely, Ivy." Francesca embraced her again. "And your family's so nice. Gabriela said she went with you to see two clients."

Ivy met her daughter's eyes. "She really helped out."

The look on Gabriela's face was full of feeling, recollection of their visit to Rhonda's house and perhaps other things. Ivy would try to talk with her alone before she went to bed.

She caught up on all the latest with Francesca and Tara as they were preparing dinner together, the way they'd done so many times in Precipice. Tara was planning to leave Maternity House soon. "I'd like to hook up with IHS or else go back to Chile or Mexico."

Francesca sliced a carrot. "I wish you'd stay in the United States where it's safe."

"You don't want me to come to Precipice and work with you."

"You're not legal in Colorado."

"So what?" Tara grinned. "I'm good."

"Your total disregard for the law floors me."

"I don't disregard the law. I hate it. I fight it. And I am *not* caving in."

Ivy had heard this conversation, in different versions, a hundred times. Francesca felt Tara should go to school to become a certified nurse-midwife. Tara said she already had tremendous experience and would learn very little in school that she didn't already know; becoming certified would be no more than caving in to the medical establishment. Ivy tended to agree with her. Tara's decision was born out of integrity, out of her objection to the profession of midwifery being regulated by physicians instead of midwives.

Francesca tensed. "Alex is moving to Hawaii, Ivy. He's selling his house and the Victorian."

The place she rented in Precipice. Either a family might buy it to live in, or a new landlord might raise the rent. In either case, Francesca would be looking for a new home in a town where rents were already high. It was entirely possible she'd have to move her practice somewhere else.

"Any offers yet?" Ivy asked.

"A lot of people looking. It's out of my control."

"Which you can't stand," Tara tossed over her shoulder. "In general."

"Of course I can stand it. Birth is never within my control."

"Which is why you'll do anything for the physicians—so you don't lose hospital privileges."

"Let's drop this, Tara."

Ivy caught the look on her mother's face. "Is something happening?"

"Dr. Henry is retiring," Tara answered. "And guess who wants to do physician backup for home births."

"No one?"

"Bingo."

"What are you going to do, Mom?"

"I haven't decided."

Ivy hugged her. To try to put her mother in a better frame of mind, she told them both about Mata Iyer. Ivy's good fortune seemed to encourage Francesca, but Ivy knew that her mother was going to have to make some choices she herself wouldn't want to make.

"You should have *me* come to Precipice," Tara volunteered. "You can do the hospital thing. I'll do the home births and take the fall if we need to bring someone to the hospital. In fact, I might come up there anyway."

Francesca tensed but fell silent, and Ivy said, "Okay, let's get this dinner on. Tara, how's the rice coming?"

WHEN GABRIELA WENT to her room to turn in, Ivy went with her. She shut the door and came over to sit on the bed, which had become an evening ritual. "How's everything?"

Gabriela shrugged.

Ivy waited to see if she'd speak.

"I'm just confused. I want to be a ballet dancer, but I liked helping you."

"Can you do both?"

"Well..." Her shoulders slumped. "What you do is so important. I wouldn't want to make any mistakes."

Ivy smiled gently, trying to reassure her. "What kind of mistakes?"

"Well, say if you let me hand you things, and I gave you the wrong thing."

What's behind this? Obviously, Gabriela wanted to explore midwifery, but she seemed almost afraid to. "Gabriela, are you afraid that if you help me, I'll think you want to become a midwife?"

"Kind of."

Yes. "I know where your heart is, Gabriela. I would only be disappointed if you ever gave up your dreams, whatever they are. Those are for you to choose. And I'll always be happy to have you help me and to let you learn, if you want. If you think midwifery is interesting, you can learn about it as much or as little as you like. And continue reaching for your dreams."

Gabriela searched her face. "Are you sure?"

"Of course I'm sure. And I had another idea. You're really at the age where you're beginning to turn from a girl to a woman. I think it would be fun if you and I did something special to celebrate your becoming a woman.''

''Like what?''

''Perhaps go on a camping trip where you'd spend part of the time alone, thinking about what it means to you to be a woman, the kinds of qualities you want to develop.''

Gabriela squinted. ''That sounds cool. After, maybe I could help you more. Learn to feel where the baby is, which direction it's turned.''

''That's called the lie. The lie of the baby.'' Ivy smiled. ''Let's take one day at a time. It's cold out. Wouldn't you like to wait till it warms up?''

''My dad—Dad's taken me snow camping before. We could go during vacation. We could just go out here somewhere, on the property.''

''Let me think about it. We can decide after Christmas. For now, we have guests, and tomorrow we're all going to Coalgood for dinner.'' She hugged Gabriela. ''Good night.''

''Good night, Mom.''

''I love you.''

''Love you, too.''

Happy in this experience that she'd never known— to remember—before returning to West Virginia, Ivy stood to leave. *If only Matthew never tells her the truth.*

It didn't seem like a secret Cullen's brother would trouble to carry to his grave. It seemed like a secret he'd use whenever and wherever it would hurt Cullen the most.

"ARE SHELBY AND MATTHEW here?" Cullen had just made introductions, and Francesca and Tara had met everyone but Shelby, Matthew and the judge.

"It's George's day off," Zeya reminded him. The attendant. "Shelby and Matthew are upstairs with Daddy."

Cullen nodded and made no move to go find them. Neither did Ivy, although the whole group, assembled in the main hall at the center of the house, peered up the long grand staircase to the balcony overlooking the hall.

As if on cue, Matthew appeared at the top of the stairs and started down. Seeing the group gathered, he lifted his eyebrows but seemed preoccupied.

The judge and Shelby walked slowly behind him. Mitzi Till said to Tara and Francesca, "Why don't you all come into the living room? We'll have some Christmas cheer, and I know everyone will join us."

The two midwives took the initiative and followed her lead, with Zeya, Tom and Scout in tow, Scout chattering eagerly to Tara.

Ivy lingered to speak with Shelby, and Cullen and Gabriela started haltingly for the living room.

"Here, Your Honor, take my arm." Shelby offered it to him.

They were on the third or fourth step from the top, and the judge hesitated.

"Come on, Daddy," Matthew coaxed wearily from the foot of the stairs.

Shelby caught his arm gently, and the judge jerked

away. She began walking down the stairs alone. Suddenly, the judge pushed her hard from behind.

She fell, in slow motion.

Ivy reached up and stepped forward as though to catch her. But Shelby tumbled down, and her head struck a stair, and she lay still.

"Shelby!" Matthew's hoarse cry echoed through the hall. He ran, taking the stairs three at a time and gathered his wife in his arms. "Shelby. Oh, God, Shelby."

Ivy and Cullen both charged up the stairs, and Cullen said, "Gabby, call 911."

"Matthew, don't move her. She might have a spinal cord injury."

Shelby's eyelids fluttered, and she gave a slight moan.

"Shelby, try not to move," Ivy said calmly. "We're right here with you. You fell down the stairs."

"The baby." Her eyes reached into Ivy's, begging reassurance.

"We'll just have to see."

Matthew said, "Please don't move, Shelby. I picked you up, and I shouldn't have. Now we need to wait for the paramedics."

Cullen had stood, and he climbed slowly toward the top of the stairs.

Behind him, Ivy said, "Shelby, I'm going to hold your head to help keep you from moving it."

"Shelby! Oh, Shelby," cried Mitzi.

Cullen glanced back at the others and continued up

the steps. His father stood near the top, confused. When he recognized Cullen, his eyes cleared some. "Cully. Cully, she was no good." His mouth was open and words deserted him.

Cully, she was no good.

His first instinct was that Gabriela must not hear any of what his father was saying. Only as he guided the judge back up the stairs did the past suggest itself to him.

Patient. If he wasn't patient, he'd never learn the truth.

He might not anyhow.

As they entered the bedroom, he asked, "Did Gina fall on the stairs, Daddy?" *Did you push her?*

In his new, slow, slurring voice, the judge said, "Forget her, Cully. Whore."

"Did you push her down the stairs?"

The judge blinked, suddenly lost.

Cullen nearly grabbed him, shook him. He wanted to break his hand, choke him until he got the truth. He stood in front of his father. "My wife, Gina. Where is she?"

The judge's look had turned vacant.

"Did you take her to Colorado?"

No answer.

"My wife. Did you push her down the stairs?"

"A..." His voice trailed away.

"Daddy, please answer." Cullen spoke more slowly. "Did Gina fall down the stairs?"

His father shoved him.

He should be in a nursing home. He can't be trusted not to hurt Mother.

Some people kept their parents with Alzheimer's at home for years. But the judge was big and violent. The doctor had said to do whatever was necessary to keep him calm. But he'd just pushed Shelby down the staircase.

Cullen picked up the judge's stuffed tiger from the bed and handed it to him.

I have to know.

He tried a new tactic. "I'm angry you pushed Gina down the stairs."

"She fell."

Cullen's chest twisted tight. Now he was losing the power of speech. "You shouldn't have grabbed her that way."

"No one hurts Cully. Cully gets everything."

Cullen sat, trapped in the room with his father. He'd discovered a man in his family who could hurt a woman.

He'd discovered who had hurt his wife, accidentally or on purpose. The judge had concealed the truth, and he must have taken her somewhere and left her. Maybe all the way to the Rockies.

The minutes dragged by. The judge held his tiger. "Checkers."

I am not going to play checkers with you. "No."

No one hurts Cully. What about Matthew? Ivy in lingerie; no wonder he hadn't been able to keep an erection. His brother and his father had stolen from him.

You hurt my wife and lied to me. You lied to me. You lied to me about my wife, Gabriela's mother. I hate you. I'll never forgive you.

He could not utter the words. He never would. It wasn't in him to strike back at a sick old man.

And Mother had never known, or she wouldn't have been so shocked when the judge said what he had about Matthew and Gina.

Gina.

That he loved Ivy more and was loved more in return did not subdue his anger.

"Ivy went with Matthew to the hospital. She wanted to be there for Shelby in case she has a miscarriage."

It was Tom.

Ivy with Matthew? Were they alone? His trust trembled.

"Where's Gabriela?"

"Downstairs with Tara and Francesca. That's why I came to relieve you. She's pretty shaken up and worried. She wanted to go to the hospital."

"Thanks, Tom." He started to leave the room. "He wants to play checkers."

MATTHEW DROVE SILENTLY, occasionally wiping his eyes. Ivy had offered to drive, but he had taken the wheel.

Within a block of the hospital, he said brokenly, "She wants that baby."

Ivy didn't answer. She could have told him to show

Shelby lots of love, but there was no need.

Matthew was in love with his wife.

"HOW COULD GRANDPA *do* that?"

Tara and Francesca had suggested they go back to the cabin, and Cullen and Gabriela had just dropped them off there.

"He's sick. His brain is sick." The effort to speak was Herculean. Why had Ivy gone with Matthew?

He pictured her comforting him in one of Matthew's genuine moments, which were intense when they came. *Where is my wife?*

"Is Shelby going to lose the baby?"

"I don't know." His father's face and body, his confusion, flashed through Cullen's mind. His decision was immediate and final. It wasn't revenge or fury. It was prevention. The judge was serving no one anymore. He was hurting people instead.

I'm going to help him die.

The only question was how.

He parked the Saab near Matthew's XKE. *Did you like the car, Ivy?* Where was she? He unfastened his seat belt.

"There's Uncle Matthew."

Matthew was standing in the snow among trees strung with lights in front of the door. He had seen the Saab, and he strode toward it. His eyes were wild as he flung open the driver's door and grabbed Cullen by his parka, yanking him from his seat. "You little piss."

Cullen stood, and his brother slammed a fist in his face.

"Daddy!" Gabriela opened her door and ran around the car. Her uncle hit her father again. "Stop it, Uncle Matthew! Stop it!"

"Hit back! Hit me, Cully. You can do it."

Cullen drew up his throbbing head and met his brother's eyes. "No."

Matthew smashed his groin.

"Daddy!"

His face. Everything was red.

Gabriela ran for the hospital doors. Her mother was coming out. "Mom! Uncle Matthew's hurting Dad!"

Cullen had walked away from his brother, moving amongst the trees, dripping blood on the snow. Matthew stalked him, and Ivy and Gabriela hurried after them.

"Stop him! Stop him!" Gabriela cried.

"I can't."

Gabriela stared at her mother. "Help him!"

"Yes, help him, Gina. He needs help. Don't you, Cully? You better hit back, or your wife is going to do it for you."

"No, she won't."

Matthew punched him again.

Gabriela ran toward her uncle and punched him ineffectually.

"Now your daughter's defending you." Matthew pushed Gabriela out of the way with little force.

Your daughter. Ivy heard the words with a strange disbelief. Even at this moment, when Matthew plainly wanted to hurt Cullen, he'd chosen not to reveal the truth to Gabriela. And he must know the truth was his most potent weapon.

"Stop hitting him!" Gabriela screamed. "Are you crazy? He's your brother."

"Defended by your little girl, Cully?"

Your little girl.

"Daddy, hit him back!"

"Yes, hit me back, Cullen, or you'll lose face in front of your family."

Your family.

Ivy had moved closer. *I can't do anything. How can I let Matthew do this to him in front of Gabriela? How can Cullen let it happen?*

She knew then. This was the competition. Not to lose control. To win over Matthew again by never hitting back.

Cullen, don't do this to us.

"You're Daddy's little piece of shit, you know that?" His brother shoved him to the ground and kicked his ribs.

Cullen wondered if Matthew would actually kill him. *I can't die. Gabby would never get over it.* He lay on his back in the snow, seeing the trees overhead, his face sticky and cold. He saw his own stupidity in red. He was no better than Matthew. "You win, Matthew. If you come down here where I can reach, I'll hit you back."

"Get up and fight like a man, Cully."

"Daddy." His daughter was crying.

"I'm okay, Gabby." He sat up, battered, and gathered handfuls of snow to wash his face.

Ivy could not bring herself to move, to help.

As Cullen got to his feet, Matthew came over and put his arm around his brother. "I'll help you inside, puppy."

Cullen lightly punched him in the stomach and leaned on his brother.

Ivy and Gabriela slowly followed them to the hospital doors. While Cullen and Matthew went into the men's room, Ivy and Gabriela sat on a bench outside.

Gabriela asked, "What if he kills him in there?"

"I don't think he will. I think they're done."

"Uncle Matthew's insane."

A nurse stopped in the hall and saw the trail of blood into the bathroom.

"It's all right," Ivy said.

"What happened?"

"Christmas tension."

How can you make me part of this, Cullen? She was torn between the need to wait outside the door and the desire to return to Shelby. Shelby, grieving.

Ivy hugged Gabriela. "I love you, Gabriela."

"Why didn't you stop Uncle Matthew?"

"Your dad asked me not to, and I said I wouldn't."

"He could have killed him. Would you have let him kill him?"

"No." *But I basically did. Matthew could have killed him.*

"Why didn't he hit him back? He didn't even try."

"You'll have to ask him."

CULLEN'S HEAD WAS over the sink. Again and again, he pressed water to his face. Matthew stood beside him, and Cullen didn't ask about Shelby's condition because he knew why Matthew must have attacked him.

He dried his face, then turned and hugged his brother, hugged him around his arms, stretching because Matthew was bigger, and Matthew cried. "She wanted the baby."

THEY LEFT MATTHEW at Shelby's bedside and started home. Ivy drove, and neither she nor Gabriela spoke. Cullen's face was cut, his jaw and eye swollen, but nothing broken. She would make a poultice for him when they got home. But what was she going to say to Tara and Francesca?

When they parked in front of the cabin, Ivy said, "Gabriela, will you please go on in? We'll be there soon. You don't have to tell them anything. I'll take care of it."

The door closed behind Gabriela.

Cullen said, "I'm sorry."

Ivy hardly knew what to say. That he should have defended himself against Matthew? Then two people would have been hurt instead of one. *Tough.* "I will defend you next time. I am not going to stand there and watch anyone do that to you. What are you going to say to Gabriela?"

"That I didn't want to fight my brother."

"You were fighting him by not fighting him. You wanted to win, and the price you asked us to pay was too high."

"I recall telling him he won."

"Nobody won. You two better sort out your differences or this will continue until one of you dies, and then the other one will be left with things he wished he'd said or done."

Until one of you dies...

Cullen remembered. The judge. The stairs. *Tell her. You can't keep this from her.*

But if the judge died, would it matter anymore?

Protecting your father who hurt your wife?

His head spun. He knew right, saw it before him.

"You fell down the stairs." He repeated every uncertain word of his conversation with the judge.

Ivy saw Shelby falling.

Cullen played the rest through his mind. Helping the judge wander off. *Whatever happens, I mustn't go to jail for this.* He needed to know the law. In this case, he didn't care about the spirit of the law. Only the question would he or would he not go to jail?

But the life insurance...

His mind cleared slowly. A nursing home. The judge had to go to a nursing home. He tried to avoid the thought that it would be the perfect punishment. *I don't want to punish him. I love him.*

But he might have hurt Ivy—Gina. And he'd concealed her fall down the stairs. What had he done with her once she fell?

The same questions raced through Ivy's mind. Had she fallen? Or had the judge pushed her? In any case, why hadn't he helped her, called 911? If he'd done that, she would have been with her husband and child all this time.

And might never have known Tara and Francesca.

She'd read somewhere that trying to change the future was like trying to handle a master carpenter's tools; she would cut herself.

The judge had chosen her future.

And now he was losing his mind, his memory.

She didn't believe one had caused the other. Still, it was ironic. But the greatest irony was that the justice offered by the law would be useless now. The man was dying; his existence was sad.

He's my father-in-law. I don't remember what he was like when he was well. But he's Cullen's father. Without him, there would have been no Cullen.

Cullen said, "Ready to go in?"

SHE MADE A POULTICE for his face, explaining to Tara and Francesca, "Matthew has some unresolved rage."

Neither of them commented. Cullen suggested, "Why don't you let Gabriela and me make dinner? You three could take a walk or go out on snowshoes."

Ivy accepted the suggestion.

She and Tara and Francesca wrapped up in coats and hats and mittens and went out to the woods. Outside, as Ivy double-checked her pager to make sure it was working, Francesca and Tara studied her.

Each walked on one side of her, put an arm around her.

She needed to reassure them somehow. But what confidence could she offer? What she'd told Cullen was true. Unless something changed, Matthew would hound him until one of them died.

"It's sibling rivalry. Matthew's mother died when he was twelve or so, and his father remarried. When Cullen came along, the judge was crazy about him, the way people are about babies. He's always favored him, I guess."

"It sounds as though Matthew needs counseling," Tara said.

"I think the chances of anyone talking him into that are slim." Although Ivy had told Tara about her long-ago affair with Matthew, she hadn't confided that Matthew was Gabriela's natural father. She wouldn't now, either. Today had convinced her that Matthew would never tell. Nor would Shelby. Only this total sense of allegiance, of shared love for Gabriela, could erase her doubts about keeping something so important from her daughter. Everyone cared about Gabriela. As far as each one of them was concerned, Cullen was her father.

Ivy knew in her heart that unburdening herself of this secret would only relieve her own conscience, not help her daughter. She would be a keeper of the secret, too. She would adopt with heart and soul the knowledge that Cullen and Cullen alone was Gabriela's father.

And no one would ever hurt Gabriela with the truth.

"I think he and Cullen are going to have to work

it out together. To actually talk to each other about this. Cullen looks innocent, but he's not. I think he has his own ways of getting to Matthew.''

''He has some legitimate gripes,'' Tara said quietly.

''Of course.'' Ivy flushed, remembering what she had done years ago. *And the judge caught us together, and when I fell down the stairs, he...* Who could guess what he'd done? No one would ever know.

She wasn't going to talk about that. There was no point.

''How is Shelby doing?'' Gabriela had told them about the baby.

''Physically she's recovering from the miscarriage. She's badly bruised, but no serious injuries. She's really depressed, though. At least no one suggested putting her on the maternity floor.''

They'd all seen it before with miscarriages. Part of caring for a mother who miscarried or had a stillbirth was making absolutely sure that didn't happen.

Ivy took a deep breath, and so did Tara and Francesca. They held each other, leaned on each other. They would open no presents till tomorrow, and perhaps by then some of the pall of this day would have lifted.

''I'M SORRY, GABRIELA. I shouldn't have let your uncle do that,'' Cullen said.

Her eyes were miserable.

''You know, he was upset about Shelby and the baby.''

"Why pick on you? What did you do?"

I've raised his only child.

"It has to do with Grandpa, I think. Matthew had a hard time when his mom died."

Gabriela frowned and resumed tearing up lettuce for the salad. "He tried to kill you."

"No. He didn't want to kill me."

"What *did* he want?"

"You got me." What did Matthew ever want? Did he want a different past? A different future?

He wants Daddy's love. He had it, but Matthew probably didn't believe that.

A memory flashed in his mind. *Cully gets everything.*

Had his father said that to Matthew? It was possible. Matthew had looked depressed when he came down the stairs.

He remembered what Ivy had said, that he and Matthew needed to work things out. She was right, but how could he do it without his brother's help?

"I'm sorry I didn't hit him back, Gabriela. I wish you hadn't seen any of that. I didn't want to fight him, but I have an obligation to you and your mom. It won't go that way again."

Gabriela met his eyes, and he sensed her measuring the weight of his promise.

He smiled, though it hurt his face.

She said, "You need to put that poultice back on. Go sit down. I'll ask if I need you."

Cullen felt worse than ever. For her and for Ivy, he would try to talk to Matthew.

CHAPTER ELEVEN

"YOU'RE KIDDING!" Gabriela stared at the ballet tick-ets in her hands. "We're going to New York? And we're going to see two ballets?"

"And visit two dance schools," Ivy added, smil-ing.

Her scream of delight set Tara and Francesca laughing, while Gabriela embraced each parent in turn.

"February. It's a million years away," Gabriela moaned. She collapsed on the couch.

The ballet tickets were the last gift to be opened. Tara had given Gabriela a friendship bracelet. Fran-cesca had given her a pendant similar to the ones she and Ivy and Tara wore, not of a birthing woman, but of an ancient female figure. Ivy had given Francesca the wedding-ring quilt she'd bought from Emma Workman; for Tara she'd made a quilted wall hang-ing, designing the pattern—images of birth—herself.

Cullen had been the hardest to plan a gift for. What they shared seemed beyond ordinary gifts. He seemed to have the things he needed and he'd claimed not to want anything in particular. Finally, she'd settled on a good pair of binoculars. She treasured her gifts from him and Gabriela.

"Cullen and I need to go over to Coalgood briefly and exchange gifts with his family. Do you want to come, Gabriela?"

"I'd rather stay here."

Tara and Francesca cast looks of concern at Ivy and at Cullen, with his black eye and bruised face.

He said, "No fights today." In fact, Christmas was a good day for healing, for trying to mend his relationship with his brother.

"CULLEN, WHAT HAPPENED to your face?" Mitzi didn't wait for an answer. "It was Matthew, wasn't it?"

"I'm fine."

His mother frowned. Ivy watched the two of them, wondering about Mitzi's thoughts, wondering if she, too, felt helpless in the midst of her son's and her stepson's behavior.

Mitzi was arranging cookies on a platter. Everyone at Coalgood had opened presents this morning, but Ivy and Cullen still had gifts for everyone and gifts to open and others to take home to Gabriela.

"Can I help you, Mitzi?" Ivy asked.

"No, thank you."

Her mother-in-law's distance hurt, but Ivy understood. She was probably a prisoner of pain over the judge's illness. *I wish she would talk to me.* But it seemed as though it wasn't to be.

She tried again. "How is the judge?"

Mitzi shook her head. "I can't get over what happened yesterday."

What happened ten years ago, too.

"I had a miscarriage before Zeya was born."

The revelation surprised Ivy.

"It was so devastating. I wish I could do something for Shelby. She's so sweet, and there's just nothing to do."

Cullen kissed his mother, then Ivy, and excused himself, probably to go find Matthew.

Mitzi seemed to be almost talking to herself. "You know, when I had that miscarriage, my mother gave me a beautiful lace handkerchief that her mother had given her. I'd really like to give that to Shelby, but she's not a lace kind of person."

"I think she'd treasure it."

"Do you?" Mitzi glanced at Ivy but hid her own thoughts, whatever they were. "Then I think I will. Perhaps tonight."

Ivy took Shelby's Christmas gift up to her room. "I brought you something, Shelby."

Shelby was in bed upstairs. The room was filled with flowers from Matthew—even its own Christmas tree. Shelby had said he'd hardly left the room since they'd come home from the hospital, but now he'd gone out to leave Ivy and Shelby alone together.

Ivy handed her a soft, gift-wrapped package.

"Oh, Ivy, thank you."

She'd shed some tears when Ivy first embraced her, but now her eyes were clear. She opened the blue tissue paper and unfolded the garment inside. It was a white cotton sweatshirt painted with a picture of a dragon toasting a marshmallow with his fiery breath.

"It's beautiful." Shelby smiled. "He's cute, and I love him."

Ivy felt something tugging at her, some reason she'd ordered the sweatshirt for Shelby. She couldn't pinpoint it.

They hugged again, and Ivy contemplated that this woman had forgiven her for her past. *I'm so lucky.*

"Is there anything I can do? Are you still bleeding?"

"No, it's stopped. I'm just afraid this was an omen. That we'll never have a baby."

I fell down the stairs, too, or else the judge pushed me.

Suddenly, she remembered. She'd lost a baby. Cullen's? Matthew's? She didn't want to tell Shelby about the stairs. But she said, "When I hit my head, I lost a baby, too. It wasn't the same. I didn't know who I was. I didn't know..." Whose baby it was. She still didn't. "Who my family was, where I'd come from. But I mourned the loss. And Cullen really had trouble with it when I told him." She met Shelby's eyes. "But, Shelby, take it as a good sign that you became pregnant."

"I had an abortion when I was eighteen."

That was new information. "Any problems from it?" Shelby would have found out at the fertility clinic.

"No. But I can't help thinking this is some kind

of retribution. At the time, I felt I had no other choice. As I got older, I realized I did.''

She was crying again, and Ivy held her, wishing a baby for her and Matthew. She'd had many clients who'd had abortions. Emotions nearly always surfaced with pregnancy and birth, and usually the entire process helped with healing, with the stigma and silence and pain surrounding the issue. "You're a wonderful mother, Shelby. You took such good care of yourself through these early weeks. You were wonderful to your child.''

Shelby continued to cry. "What about the baby I aborted? Was I a mother then?''

"What do you think? That's what matters.''

"I suppose I wasn't ready to be.'' She took slow breaths. "Someone told me that in France, a midwife is called a *sage-femme,* a wise woman. You've shown me why, Ivy.''

Ivy shook her head. She tried to find the best course of action in any situation, but sometimes her choices had unexpected consequences. If birth had begun to teach her anything, it was to try not to shape the future but instead face the present.

She found it the hardest lesson of all.

TOM WAS WITH THE JUDGE, and Cullen caught Matthew emerging from his and Shelby's room. "Hi. How are you?''

He shrugged, avoiding Cullen's eyes.

"I'd like to talk.''

Matthew looked at him. "All right.''

"Want to go for a drive?"

"I need to stay here. For Shelby."

They sat on the couch in the rec room. Cullen hadn't planned to say anything in particular, except a general suggestion that he'd like a better relationship with Matthew. "So. I'm tired of fighting."

"You don't fight."

"I do. In other ways. I ignore you. I act like nothing's wrong when you've totally pissed me off. That's my way of fighting."

Matthew remained silent, but only for a moment. "He says he's giving you everything. Which is what he's always done."

Cullen didn't smile. "He has Alzheimer's. It's not true."

"He says to me, 'Cully gets everything.' He wants you to have everything."

"He doesn't know what he's saying. And by the way, we need to convince Mother that he belongs in a nursing home."

Matthew said nothing.

The conversation was going nowhere. Whatever made Matthew behave the way he did wasn't something Cullen could fix. He stood up, made a last try. "I just wanted to say that I'd like to replace the sibling rivalry with a real relationship." *Even though you slept with my wife, and I'll never forget it and maybe never forgive you.*

Matthew didn't reply.

"Do you want to talk to Mother about the nursing home, or shall I?"

"George will be back tomorrow."

I don't live in this house. All of them do. Cullen backed away from the subject. "It's up to you."

IVY DROVE FRANCESCA and Tara to the airport the following day, and that evening Gabriela brought up the idea of snow camping. "We could do it tomorrow night."

Ivy had discussed her suggestion with Cullen, and now he left them alone up in the loft to talk about it.

Sitting on the tester bed with Gabriela, Ivy asked, "What kinds of things would you like to do?"

"Well, if we had two tents, I could pitch mine a little ways from yours."

"How about a long way from mine? No one should come around. This is our property."

"Okay."

"How would you feel about keeping a journal of that time? Just for yourself, not to share with anyone else. You could think about being a woman and explore your real feelings and the kind of person you want to be."

"Okay. I'd like that."

"Can you think of anything else?"

"Well, I've decided I probably have time even with ballet and school. I want to learn more about midwifery. Could you teach me to be your assistant?"

Ivy considered. "I'm happy to teach you anything I know about midwifery, but being an apprentice implies a commitment. You're just twelve, and I think you have plenty of commitments just now. How about if we call you a midwifery student? And I'll think of some ideas to start you off."

"Thanks! So we can do it tomorrow night?"

"Let's plan to."

GABRIELA HUGGED her father. "I guess we're going." He smiled, eyes shining at hers, and the expression warmed her. He thought she was the greatest. She said, "You're the best dad."

"You're the best kid. Young woman," he added and hugged her back. "Have fun with your mom. Let me take your pictures before you go, and then I'll take some more when you come home."

Gabriela liked the idea. Would she seem different when she returned?

Cullen took some photos of them in their winter gear, each wearing a mountaineering pack, and then they left. How differently Gabriela behaved since Ivy had come back. Less...childish. Most of the time. Erratic emotions were to be expected, but he saw her growing, and he liked the idea that she was interested in midwifery as well as ballet. He just hoped she'd never abandon her own gifts, her own hopes, her own dreams.

Ivy had told him a hundred times that Gabriela needed to feel sure in her identity.

When he considered the past, he saw that part of Gina's trouble might have been that she'd never felt that certainty. Her grandmother had been pretty controlling and of a completely different generation, and she hadn't been willing or able to give Gina the things Gina had wanted.

Closing the door, suddenly alone in the empty cabin, he offered up a wish for his child. That she know her true self and love that self.

Hello,

Here I am in the woods in my tent. I'm not going outside unless I absolutely have to pee. It's quiet. Whenever I hear anything, it's creepy. But I want to make that feeling of quiet when I dance. People who are really good, it's more than just good technique. When I see someone great, I fall apart inside and then when it's over I'm back together and I'm better. I want to do that to people.

This midwifery thing is kind of weird. It's like I want to know how to do it, but what I really want is to DANCE. God, I'm going to dance! I'm really good. I know I am. This is what I was born to do in life. I was *born* a dancer.

A woman. A woman *dancer*. That is me. But it would be cool to be a dancer who could also help deliver a baby if I had to. That would be a cool thing to know how to do. Mom gave me a special book for writing down thoughts about midwifery and writing down things I learn that I want to remember. I'll save my midwifery thoughts for that.

Now, as for Brad. Okay, I'm over him. I'm

glad we're just friends, especially since I might meet someone really cool this summer. Someone who *dances*.

Oh, god, I had a great idea. I'm going to go dance in the snow! Right now, in the dark, under the trees. See ya.

THE FOLLOWING AFTERNOON at four, Cullen, Ivy and Gabriela arrived at Rhonda Davy's house for a second prenatal appointment.

When Cullen saw the shack, he drew a slow breath. This place had a ways to go. But at least there was some junk lying around, things he could use to keep the wind out. He'd have to get creative with insulation. Fix the stove...

As they walked to the door, he paused to kick snow off mysterious shapes in the yard to see what lay beneath.

Ivy knocked on the door, and a woman who looked about twenty-four opened it. "Oh, hi."

They all went in.

"I brought my family. Gabriela said she'd watch your little ones again. Hi, Jessica." Ivy picked up the toddler. "Remember me?"

Gabriela scooped up the other one. "You look like a little chimney sweep, Justin."

Cullen hid a smile, thinking how Gabriela mimicked Ivy in some things and how she ran from any similarity to her in others.

"I wanted Cullen to take a look at your stove and water," Ivy was saying.

"Oh," Rhonda said. "Chad's going to get around to that stuff."

Chad was nowhere in sight; only the signs of his presence were there. Liquor bottles, for instance. Ivy was going to have to talk to him about his duty to his partner. It might do no good. On the other hand, she might be able to get through to him by pointing out that hey, this baby was his, and Rhonda was going to need some help. He had a responsibility to his family now.

"Great," she told Rhonda. "In the meantime, I need Cullen to start working on it because I can't in good conscience assist at a birth without making sure everything's as good as it can be for the baby and the mom. Agreed?"

Rhonda nodded.

Ivy glimpsed an ashtray nearby. They'd had this talk the week before. "Have you stopped smoking?" Obviously not. Chad chewed rather than smoked. Another habit with grim consequences—but at least not a source of secondhand smoke.

Rhonda shrugged.

"Look, you're hurting your baby when you smoke." She was hurting herself, too, but Rhonda had plainly said she really didn't care. "This is not an okay thing. I need an absolute promise that you're going to quit. For the baby and for you."

"I ran out of cigarettes today."

"Good. Don't buy any more."

Cullen was checking out the stove. Ivy knew he'd have questions about the water, too, but now was the time to talk about the baby, to build a good rapport with Rhonda. The shack was separated into two areas by a curtain. Behind the curtain was the area where Rhonda and Chad slept.

"Let's...go back there and see how you're doing."

"Oh, Chad's back there."

Sleeping? Ivy schooled her features. "I think you should wake him up."

"I'll try." She went behind the curtain, and Ivy heard her say, "Chad, you have to get up. The midwife's here."

Ivy couldn't make out his reply and moved away, to give them privacy. "What are you playing with, Jessica?"

IT WAS A SILENT RIDE HOME until Gabriela said, "I think Chad should get a job."

Cullen headed the car out of the unplowed hollow. "It's possible he can't."

"Well, he should at least do some work around the house instead of getting drunk all the time."

Ivy held her silence for a while. "Sometimes people need help to get over bad habits." Chad had not been receptive to that idea. In fact, he'd basically ignored her suggestions except to say, "Yeah, I'm gonna give her a hand."

I can't stand this. How can I help these people?

She'd learned early as a midwife that the best way she could affect a family dynamic was by providing a good experience during pregnancy, birth and postpartum. But men like Chad were a real problem—as were women like Rhonda, who chose them. Except…

Ivy turned in her seat to look at Gabriela.

"Tara once told me a fairy tale about a dragon who'd been thrown out a window by the midwife right after he was born. He looked like a snake, you see. He grew up to be a dragon and married a succession of women and devoured every one. But then, a woman, even knowing he'd eaten his other brides, asked to marry him."

"Good grief," Gabriela commented.

"She convinced him to remove his skin one layer at a time. Every time she asked, he said no one had ever asked him to do that before. Finally, when he'd peeled off all his skin, she could see how damaged he was, and she scrubbed him clean and healed him, and he stood up and was a handsome and good man."

Gabriela did not seem to react.

Cullen said, "That's beautiful."

Ivy thought of Matthew. If any woman was capable of convincing him to peel off his skin, it was Shelby. She'd have to remember to tell Shelby that story.

That's why I ordered the dragon sweatshirt!

The thought filled her with hope.

Gabriela kept her thoughts to herself. *I would not want to peel the skin off some drunk.*

But she remembered what her mother had told her. That she was no better or worse than anyone else.

She supposed that applied to Chad, too.

In the back seat of the Saab, she rolled her eyes. And considered what she would've been like if someone had thrown her out the window when she was born.

CHAPTER TWELVE

"DADDY'S MISSING." It was Zeya. Cullen had come home early the day after New Year's to find Ivy and Gabriela out, probably visiting Devon or Rhonda or another woman who had phoned Ivy for an appointment.

"Where's George?"

"Day off. Matthew was watching him, and when Daddy took a nap, Matthew went to his and Shelby's room. Daddy woke up and wandered off."

Cullen considered saying he wasn't going to look, thereby increasing the odds that his father wouldn't be found. He rejected the idea. "Is he walking or driving?"

"Walking, and it's snowing. Matthew's gone looking for him. Will you come and help?"

"Yes." His father would be found by the time he reached Coalgood, but why not go? "See you soon."

MATTHEW WAS WALKING down the riverbank beside the bridge. Cullen pulled the Camaro to the roadside and jogged after him through the new snow, following his and their father's descent down the bank. Matthew was already halfway down, the judge nowhere in sight.

Cullen reached his brother and saw the other set of footprints on the shore, heading downstream and under the bridge.

Matthew said, "I'll find him. Go home, Cully."

"He's strong. If he starts arguing, it'll be better if there are two of us."

"I can handle it."

Cullen followed his slow progress. There was little shore to walk on down here, just the icy river.

They saw the judge. Farther downstream, he had stepped onto the river ice.

"Daddy!" Cullen yelled.

The judge did not turn.

Cullen wanted to run, to stop him, but Matthew was in his way, taking such slow steps.

The judge started across the river.

Cullen dodged around his brother, then slipped down ahead of him to river level. "Daddy!"

The ice cracked beneath the judge. His expression surprised, he plunged into the frigid water.

Cullen ran to the place where he'd fallen, Matthew behind him, skirting the shore, crowding him until Cullen fell. He picked himself up and stepped out onto the ice.

"Help!" the judge shouted.

"I'm coming. Stay still." Cullen flattened his body on the ice, reaching for his father's thin arms in the flimsy fabric of his shirt. *No coat, Daddy?*

He felt hands on his ankles, his brother holding him.

"Let me go farther, Matthew."

No reply.

Matthew was holding him back, out of reach of his father.

Cullen kicked free and the ice beneath his chest caved in, the water creeping into his coat. He was going through. "Grab me, Daddy!"

The icy water froze him.

The judge's next cry for help was inarticulate. The current pulled him, and Cullen tried to grab him, but the current was sucking at him, too. *I'm dying. We're both going to die here.* An ice monster, the cold, was sucking him down, cracking the ice. His father went under, and Cullen tried to grab him, losing his own purchase. Only holes in the water. Ice and nothing. *Daddy!*

"Cullen, keep still! I'm going to get you." Matthew yanked off his sheepskin-lined leather bomber jacket. He stretched out on the ice, held one sleeve of his coat and flung the other toward Cullen.

Cullen's mouth was open in a scream unspoken. *Daddy!*

His icy hands clutched the leather. It hurt.

"I'm going to move back, and more of this ice is going to break. Don't let go," Matthew warned.

Cullen held on to the jacket. *You killed him. You wouldn't let me reach him.*

Tears stung his eyes and froze on this cheeks.

The ice cracked. He was going under, going the way of the river. The leather jacket pulled him up. Ice cut him. *Daddy!*

The shore. He stumbled through snow, his legs crumpling, useless.

Beyond cold. Couldn't think.

Matthew hugging him, pushing him, dragging him up the bank. Searching his pockets for keys.

Shivering, Cullen tried to look to the river.

We have to get Daddy.

Crying, he saw Matthew's eyes, wet, too. *I have to go back to find him.* He tried. Matthew was hugging him, holding his arms down.

"He's gone. He wanted to die, Cullen. He asked me never to prevent it, and he asked you that, too. I could do it, and you couldn't. We know the one he loved best. Someday ask who loved *him* more."

Cullen was shivering too hard to find a word, let alone utter it.

Matthew had the keys to the Camaro. He shoved Cullen into the passenger side, came around and got behind the wheel.

Cullen couldn't think. Everything was too sharp. Cold. No, nothing.

The judge sliding under.

Coalgood.

Matthew was bringing him up to the house. Into the foyer.

"Matthew, don't drip on the—" Mitzi's silence was sudden and absolute. "Where's Daddy? Where's Daddy?"

"In the river. I'm sorry." Matthew was peeling Cullen's clothes off, dropping them on the way to the living room. "More logs on the fire. We have to warm him slowly. Get him a blanket."

His mother moved. "Zeya!"

BLANKETS COVERED HIM.

He shivered uncontrollably and could not even drink the hot tea his sister held to his mouth. *Everyone, go out.* He had to talk to Matthew.

Matthew, holding him back by his ankles.

Matthew, keeping him from the judge.

In any case, the judge might have gone down.

Together, we could have reached him.

They could both have died.

"What happened?" Shelby had come in.

Mother left the room.

Zeya said it. "Daddy's gone." She had been crying.

Cullen's chest was tight, and his heart... *Daddy!* Daddy slipping under, like in a dream where he was helpless to do anything.

Had Matthew wanted to goad him, to say he'd been the stronger of the two of them, letting the judge die? It hadn't felt that way.

What would have happened if I hadn't come?

Matthew walking so slowly along the bank.

"What happened?" Shelby repeated.

Matthew had answered that question for Mitzi. He answered it for his wife. "He tried to cross the river, and the ice cracked under him. Cullen tried to reach him, and the ice broke under him, too."

At this point, Cullen wondered, should he say that

Matthew had held him back, tried to prevent him from reaching the judge?

The front door opened, and he heard Ivy's and Gabriela's voices.

They must have gotten the message from Ivy's answering service.

Warmer now.

Her arms surrounded him. "Has anyone taken his temperature?"

"No. I didn't think of it," Matthew said.

"Let's get him upstairs to a bathtub. And bring me a thermometer."

GRANDPA WAS DEAD.

People were talking with the sheriff about how to get the body out of the river and the fact that it probably wouldn't come up until spring, far downstream.

Grandma had said she hoped they never found him.

All the words repeated themselves in Gabriela's mind.

Uncle Matthew had rescued her dad.

But no Grandpa anymore, saying weird things and pushing people down stairs. She knew she should be sad, but she wasn't. Not exactly.

She left the kitchen, where she'd gone to get away from everyone, and returned to the living room. The police were just leaving, and her dad was sitting on the couch with her mom. He'd put on some clothes of Uncle Tom's. Scout wandered into the hall before Gabriela could go into the living room.

"Gabriela." She beckoned. "Come here." Gabriela followed her into the dining room, where Scout shut the doors and asked, "Where's Grandpa?"

Gabriela sat down in one of the chairs that Lily always lined up against the wall. "In the river. He's dead."

"My mother says people bury dead people in the ground. Or sometimes they burn them."

"It's called cremation. They can't feel anything because they're dead."

"When will Grandpa get out of the river?"

"They don't know. His body should float up to the surface sometime, like in the spring."

"Will he be buried then?"

"I don't know. It's up to Grandma. He might never come up. Then he'd sort of be buried in the river."

Scout said, "I like that. He can live with the fishes."

Gabriela tried to imagine what bodies looked like after they'd been in the water a long time. Horrible, she bet. She hoped she never saw a dead body.

"Gabriela." It was her mother, calling for her in the hall.

"We're in here."

Before Gabriela could open the doors to the dining room, Scout said, "You know what we talked about? Don't tell."

"Okay."

THE JUDGE WAS DEAD.

Driving home, Ivy concentrated on the road, yet the thought returned again and again. The judge was dead, and with him the secret of whatever had happened after she hit her head.

But no, that secret was gone the moment she was injured, the same as all the secrets of her past. She would never know what had made Gina Naggy tick. If this had been some other kind of memory disorder she would've had the option of therapy to discover what had happened to her. She could have learned about her childhood, about how her mother's death had made her feel. Maybe these things could have told her how she'd come to betray Cullen.

But her fall down the staircase had ended those possibilities.

Maybe it was the judge who had done that.

I want it back. I want to know who I was, and I'll never know. It'll always be like reading a history book about the life of Julius Caesar. Historians can say what he did, but they can never say who he was.

No one would ever know who Gina had been.

Cullen could tell her some things but not enough to complete the picture.

I can't stand it. I can't stand it. I want my memory back.

"CULLEN."

Cullen broke his stare at the shadows on the wall. He'd thought she'd gone to sleep. He rolled over and rested his head against her.

Odd, how he'd cried so easily at the river.

Now he was numb. Numb except for when he'd made love to Ivy.

He thought, *He hurt my wife or let her be hurt.* It was worse than what Matthew had done.

But the father...his father was gone.

He spoke against Ivy's skin. "He asked me to let him die. Before he got so sick, he said he could wander off, and I could lead him into a mine shaft or the river. He asked Matthew the same thing. I thought about it—but I wouldn't have done it. When I lay down on the ice, Matthew grabbed my ankles and wouldn't let me reach him. So I kicked away. The ice broke, and I went in, and he went under. It was like a dream where something needs to be done and you can't do it."

Ivy absorbed it. He'd never told her what the judge had asked.

"When he talked to me about it, I kept wondering why he didn't end his own life instead of asking his children to do it."

Ivy tried to suppress her own desires of regaining her memory. She longed to tell Cullen, *The judge was a coward.*

But she found herself whispering, "I wonder if doctors could do something, something to help me regain my memory." But she knew the answer, the hopeless answer. She sighed. "No. I know they can't."

"Are you sure?"

"Yes. I'm sorry I brought it up." She hugged him. He'd lost his father.

In the darkness, in the quiet of his breath, Ivy heard

something outside. Footsteps in the snow? Someone knocked at the door.

"Devon." She jumped out of bed.

SHE WAKENED GABRIELA, and her daughter blinked, half-asleep, only waking as a child wakes. "Devon's baby is coming." Rowdy, Devon's boyfriend who had knocked at the door, had returned to the Workmans' place.

Gabriela opened her eyes wider. The baby was going to be born. "Can I come?"

"Of course."

Cullen was behind them in the doorway. "What about me? They might want photos."

"Come along, and I'll try to read how they feel about your being there."

IVY SCRUBBED in the Workmans' kitchen, demonstrating sterile technique to Gabriela and asking her to scrub, as well. Behind her, Devon told Cullen that he could take photos if he wanted. She didn't care either way. Rowdy said, "We can probably buy a few."

In the bedroom, Ivy listened to the baby's heart, timed contractions and checked how far along Devon's labor was. Four centimeters dilated.

"Why don't you get up and walk around, Devon?"

Devon assumed a method of standing up during each contraction, then resting between contractions either on the couch in the living room or on her bed

Gabriela stayed in the background but performed each task her mother set out for her.

Devon was walking the hall between the living room and the bedroom when her water broke. Seeing the huge gush of water, Gabriela felt her own heart pounding. She'd heard Tara and Francesca talking about "birth energy." Was this it, this feeling that everything in the whole house was alive?

While Emma mopped up the water, Devon returned to the bedroom. Gabriela followed her, alone, and Devon said, "I don't think I can do this. I don't think I can have this baby at home."

What should she say? What would her mother want her to say?

"You're doing great."

Another contraction shook through Devon as Ivy came in, followed by the others.

Devon said, "Everyone go out except you—" she pointed at Gabriela, then at Ivy "—and you."

Ivy gave the others a look that said, *You heard her.* Emma, Cullen and Rowdy filed out of the bedroom.

Devon settled on the bed to rest between contractions. She made no apology and gave no explanation for telling the others to leave. Neither Ivy nor Gabriela expected one.

"I want to listen to the baby's heart during the next contraction, and between contractions I'm going to check you again." When she examined Devon, the baby's head was crowning. "Devon, the baby's going to be born very soon. Can you pant like this?" She demonstrated.

Devon panted through the next contraction.

"Can the others come back in?" Ivy asked when it was through.

"Yes."

"Still want pictures?" Gabriela asked. She sure wouldn't.

"Right after."

"Now, here—you can feel your baby's head, Devon." Ivy guided the young hand over the velvety softness. The baby's scalp was healthy and pink, her heart tones just what they should be.

Gabriela went out to the living room. "Come quick."

When she returned to the bedroom, her mother asked, "Gabriela, do you want to touch the baby?"

That thing pushing out of Devon was the baby. Tentatively, Gabriela reached forward and touched the velvety head.

"Rowdy?"

He touched the baby, too.

"You can push now, Devon, slow and steady. That's right. Rowdy, put your hands here." The head was born, no cord around the neck. The rest of the body followed easily with the next contraction, slithering into waiting hands. Rowdy's. *Cullen caught Gabriela like this.* "Up onto Mom's stomach."

She felt Cullen somewhere behind her, and her eyes watered.

The emotion over her Gabriela's birth, the birth she would never remember, distracted her. She erased it to focus on Devon and her baby. To be a midwife. To be the woman she was at her best.

IVY WAS SUPPORTING DEVON as the placenta slid into a stainless-steel bowl in a rush of blood. Rowdy held his baby daughter, wrapped in a soft receiving blanket.

Moving around the room, keeping clear of Ivy, Cullen experienced the next moments through the viewfinder.

This is a life-or-death job you've got, Ivy.

No. More than a job.

You stay calm. I've never seen anyone more calm in a crisis.

Gabriela was touching the baby's foot. "She's so sweet."

Cullen remembered Gabriela's birth, that as she was born he'd remembered she was Matthew's child and yet sometimes he'd forgotten.

Grandmother Emma said, "Oh, Devon, she's just precious. You did so well."

The shutter clicked. It had caught Ivy, her woman's hand beneath the newborn's head.

He imagined his father pushing her down the stairs, then picking her up and putting her in the car to leave her somewhere.

His father was dead.

He lowered the camera very slowly.

CULLEN FOLLOWED IVY when she took Alison Angelina Workman to the kitchen to give the baby her first bath. He ran the water in the sink, tested it. She did, too.

He held the towel for the baby, and she put the wet newborn in his arms. She sang to her. "Oh, can ye sew cushions, and can ye sew sheets? And can ye sing balaloo when the bairn greets?"

Ivy dried Alison's soft little head. Cullen's hands looked so big next to the baby. *I wish I could remember him with Gabriela.* The anger at the stolen memories left her impotent. She stopped her song. "Let me take her back to Devon."

Tomorrow, she'd begin her postpartum visits, to make sure mother and baby were settling in as they should. There would be many visits.

She's so young.

But Ivy had learned long ago to support, rather than judge, a mother's choices. Whatever they were, they were the mom's.

As Ivy took the baby back to Devon and Rowdy, Emma joined Cullen in the kitchen. "How much will the photos be?" she asked. "We probably can't afford many, but I'd like a couple."

"I'll give you a set. No charge. Thanks for letting me be here. If you tell me what you want in the birth announcement, we can run a photo in the paper, too."

"Oh, thank you!"

It was 5:00 a.m. when he and Gabriela and Ivy went out to the car to head home.

Driving up the snowy road, Cullen listened to his wife and daughter.

"What did you think?" Ivy asked Gabriela.

"It was cool!"

Cullen's mind was stuck not on birth but on death and on the unchangeables, the things he could not say to his father now. What would he have done had his father been well when Cullen learned about Ivy's fall down the stairs? A crime had been committed.

You loved me. You called me your favorite.

Yet who had ever really stopped Matthew from tormenting him?

No one.

"We just can't do a thing with him." They'd said that all the time.

No one had suggested counseling.

No one had looked in the mirror.

Mirror, mirror, on the wall, who made my child act this way?

And his father had turned on Ivy, not Matthew. No, on Gina.

At the cabin, he said, "I'll be inside in a while."

Ivy asked, "Are you all right?"

"Sure." *The lies we all tell, that everything's fine when we're on the edge. It's called control.*

He walked in the snow through the trees and startled a deer. He often wished he could move like an animal, but that was denied humans, especially indoor humans. Where was the judge now? In the river, part of the river. Did he leave a soul behind to talk to his children?

Cullen thought not.

He kicked a tree. He kicked it again and again.

He did not cry.

WHEN HE RETURNED to the cabin two hours later, the phone was ringing. He picked it up. "Cullen, this is Shelby. I know it's early, but will you come over? Matthew went out in the middle of the night. He's down by the river and won't come back."

Cullen hadn't slept, but Shelby's words compelled him to go.

Instead of waking Ivy or Gabriela, he left them a note, then set out in the Camaro for the stretch of river near the bridge.

Matthew had walked.

Cullen found the footprints leading from Coalgood.

He followed them down the bank and thought for a moment that he would find Matthew and his father, alive. His father would not go out on the ice; he'd come home with Matthew and Cullen.

The footprints led over the path he and Matthew had walked, and he saw Shelby's footprints, too. She must have followed him down here when she discovered him missing.

Cullen saw his brother ahead. He wore the leather jacket that he'd used to save Cullen's life. He wore a blue stocking cap.

There was something different about him, something vulnerable, and Cullen tried to imagine what Matthew must have been like when he was small. He couldn't. But he could imagine his own mother dying when he was twelve, and it was a child's worst nightmare.

Matthew stood by the river looking at the ice, now

crusted over the water again, and Cullen saw that he must have been walking around to keep warm.

"Hi, Matthew."

Matthew looked at him.

His brother had saved Cullen's life at the risk of his own.

Would thanking him now make any difference in what Matthew was feeling? What *was* he feeling?

Cullen said, "Will you come home?"

Matthew seemed thoughtful. "You know, I should've asked him if he loved me, and maybe he would have said it."

"He loved you. He never protected me from you. He never blamed you for sleeping with Gina. He couldn't. You were his son, and he loved you."

"I don't think so. I wasn't what he wanted. I never *acted* the way he wanted. You were affectionate, and he could be affectionate to you. He never liked me. I was never who he wanted me to be. He never loved me. I think I see that, now."

Cullen didn't know what to say. "Your wife wants you to come home. She loves you."

Matthew blinked. "Where is she?"

"At Coalgood. She called me and asked me to bring you home. I think she wants to show you her love. Daddy must have been screwed up. I don't understand the things he did."

Matthew peered up the bank.

"Let's go home," Cullen repeated. They climbed the bank together. "You saved my life the other day. Thank you."

Matthew didn't answer.

When they reached Coalgood, Shelby opened the door and reached for Matthew, hugging him. "Come upstairs," she said.

Matthew held her as they climbed the stairs, and she was supporting him.

THE MEMORIAL SERVICE was held at a church in Guyandotte. Ivy didn't want to attend but knew she must, to support Cullen's family in their grief. She and Gabriela filed into a pew with Cullen beside Tom and Zeya; Scout was with a baby-sitter.

Another judge delivered the eulogy, praising Sam Till's integrity on the bench, his dedication as a family man. Every eye in the family's row was dry.

Outside, afterward, Cullen asked Matthew, "How are you?"

Zeya joined them. "The hypocrisy quotient is pretty high. What do you say we go acknowledge the judge's death our own way, just the three of us."

Cullen looked at Matthew and knew his brother was thinking the same thing. That they'd both seen the judge slip beneath the ice in the river.

But Cullen said, "What do you have in mind?"

"Let's write him letters and cut a hole in the ice and send them down the river."

Cullen considered. "I'm game."

"Me, too," Matthew agreed.

They set the launch date for the letters for that evening, and they all went to Coalgood.

Dear Daddy,
    Why didn't you love me?

Dear Daddy,
    I'm going to miss you so much. You were
the best dad.

Dear Daddy,
    You hurt my wife, or maybe you didn't hurt
her but just didn't help her when she was hurt.
I wish I knew what you did, and I resent finding
out so late that you're not the person I thought
you were.
    I wish I didn't love you. I wish I didn't at all.

TWO WEEKS AFTER his father's death, Cullen came
home from work to find Gabriela practicing ballet and
Ivy searching every corner of the house.

"What are you looking for?"

"Someone must have kept a journal. Gina or her
grandmother."

"Neither of you took much interest in writing,
though you read midwifery books."

"Maybe there's something. There has to be something."

Helpless, he let her search. The search had a frantic
quality at odds with his usually calm Ivy. "Why is it
so important to find it?" He crouched beside her as
she peered into some cabinets in the back corner of
the kitchen. He knew what was in every cabinet in
the house.

"I have to know who I was. I have to know what they did to me."

"What who did to you?"

"My grandmother. My mother before she died. I have to know why I slept with a married man and betrayed you."

Ivy seemed unaware of Gabriela's presence in the house, but Cullen was not. He glanced toward the door of the dance room. It was open, and music was still playing.

"Remember Gabriela's here," he said softly.

Frantic, Ivy hardly heard him. No journals. No books. Her grandmother's herbal and midwifery notes Ivy had already seen. Nothing personal in there. Did she have no feelings to record? Had she sublimated her feelings to that degree?

Cullen said, "Let's go up in the loft. Come on."

His eyes said she wouldn't find anything, no diaries, nothing to give her a clue to her past, to the person she'd really been.

Upstairs, they lay on the bed.

"I need to know who I was. I need some memory to tell me why I did the things I did."

"There's more I can tell you. I can tell you about every encounter I remember with you."

"But it'll be through *your* eyes. I want it through my eyes. And it will never happen." Tears came in a shaky flood, admitting the death of self. "I'm gone. I'm gone forever."

"You were born in that hospital in Boulder, all right?"

"It's not true. You've said yourself that I have the same gestures as her, some of the same speech patterns. I've never felt so weak in my life." She laughed through her tears. "In my memory."

"You know, what analysts do is put you in touch with your feelings, not necessarily your memory. You might be able to know the feelings of being Gina."

Ivy froze, breath suspended. He was right, of course.

"You have to be careful, though."

"Why?"

"You might not like what you discover."

She frowned. "It would take a damned good therapist. I don't know if I could find one in Guyandotte." And she had clients, a practice. What kind of impact would this have on them?

But I have to know.

"You're creative. Maybe you should do some reading, order some good books through the mail. You could make a quilt that's about your feelings. Don't *think* about it. Just try to feel."

She and Shelby and Gabriela hadn't finished their quilt. *I need to get Shelby working on it again.*

Her thoughts backtracked to Cullen's idea for accessing her emotional memory to try to get in touch with who Gina had been. She liked it. And she would give it a try. "I'm going to do that, Cullen. The quilt. And the books. I'll ask Tara if she knows of any. She's done a lot of therapy type things."

Cullen remembered Tara's incredible vibrance and

vitality. He doubted Tara had it all worked out, and he liked Ivy the way she was. But if she needed to find Gina, he needed to let her.

Even if he didn't like the result.

CHAPTER THIRTEEN

THE NEXT TIME SHELBY came over to work on the quilt, Gabriela was gone, working privately with Tracy Kennedy, and Cullen was photographing a wedding.

While the two women sat in the living room stitching squares, Ivy asked how Matthew was.

"Different. Really depressed. Fortunately, all he has to do on the Atlanta project at this point is occasional consulting."

"You know, I thought of a folk story I wanted to tell you, but first I wanted to tell you something else. It's about the day you lost the baby."

Shelby waited.

"He loves you so much. I saw that."

Shelby nodded.

"And when he was beating up Cullen, Gabriela was watching, and he called her 'your daughter.' He could have hurt Cullen by speaking the truth then. But I don't think he'd ever hurt Gabriela."

"I know. He says Cullen's a good father. It may be hard to believe, but he loves Cullen. You know, he was expected to take care of both him and Zeya a good bit when he was a teenager. I think that's part of his resentment toward Cullen."

"I can understand that. He'd just lost his own mother, and he was expected to mother someone else." Ivy paused. "So let me tell you this story." And she told Shelby the story of the dragon who ate his brides.

When she was through, Shelby smiled. "That's really nice. Very true, too. I think some of Matthew's skins are coming off now. I love that dragon."

Ivy hoped Shelby and Matthew were trying to conceive again.

She wanted a real friendship with Shelby, not just a situation where she helped her friend and behaved as though she herself never needed help. "So, I've started this quilt and I'm reading these books." She began to tell Shelby about her self-therapy. "It's strange. I'm getting so agitated and impatient. It's like something's wrong, like there's something attacking me and I can't see it. I've got three clients now, all due later in the year, and that's all I can handle until I work this out. But I really need to know who I was."

"You might not like it, Gina." Shelby caught herself and laughed. "Ivy."

"Well, Tara subscribes to the wounded-child theory, that we all behave the way we do because of the way our parents and caregivers treated us."

"I agree with her. But you know, Ivy, your life seems pretty happy, and you're not engaging in Gina's old *behavior*. Maybe you should let it rest."

"I would if I could. But I am *obsessed* by it. I dream I'm looking for people—my grandmother, my mother and Gina. I dream I'm going to where they are, and whenever I get there I learn they've all died. I'm *obsessed* by it, ever since the judge died.''

''Why since then?''

It needed to be said. To Shelby, because of what he'd done on Christmas Eve.

''Cullen and I think he may have pushed me down the stairs. And I lost a baby, too.''

Shelby's eyes changed. She whispered, ''I want to kill him, and he's already dead.''

''I feel that way, too.''

''Matthew needs my sympathy. Cullen needs yours. And *I hate him.* It doesn't help to tell myself he was sick. The price was too high. And he did the same thing to you.''

''He told Cullen that I fell. But he never sought medical care for me. He must have driven me some-where—God knows where—and left me.''

''I wish I'd been there to push him under the ice. Matthew let him die, and I was glad. I was only sorry for him that he had to do it. And sorry that he saw it as an act of love toward his father instead of revenge for what the judge had done to me.''

Ivy didn't argue with Shelby's feelings. They were feelings, and you couldn't argue with them. She hesitated. ''Has Matthew told anyone besides you?''

''No, and he doesn't intend to. He says Cullen would have fallen through the ice trying to go farther out, to reach the judge.''

Cullen had kicked away, and he *had* fallen through. Matthew's assessment could be correct.

"You know, there's a house for sale around the island from Coalgood. Matthew and I looked at it the other day. I asked him if he was serious about moving, and he said he wouldn't mind. He said he always sees Coalgood now as the house the judge wanted to give Cullen."

Ivy squeezed her eyes shut. How hard for Matthew. Cullen didn't even want Coalgood. He'd invested himself in the cabin, for Gabriela and for Gina.

Why had he loved Gina?

Ivy wished she could discover what had been lovable about Gina, what worth he'd found in taking credit for her unplanned pregnancy. That was a question she could put to him and had, but his answers never quite satisfied her. "There was something about you. I liked the way you felt about the baby. I liked the things you spent your time doing—gardening, growing herbs, midwifery."

When Shelby went home, Ivy turned to her own quilt. The nervousness came back. So far, she'd sewn some kind of road. But now she cut out a figure to appliqué to the sheet she was using as backing. A small blond figure.

Lost, so lost.

I hate me. I hate me.

A scream built inside her.

Cullen came in. She glanced up. "Ivy, are you all right?"

She shuddered.

He looked at her quilt and sat beside her to hug

her. She tried looking in his eyes and could not see him as a helpful human.

She backed away, tried to back away from the feelings.

She folded up the quilt.

"Do you think you were sexually abused?" he asked quietly.

"I don't know. I don't think so. I like making love with you."

"How does the quilt make you feel?"

"Deserted. I don't want to talk about it." She stood, trying to remember what day it was. Saturday.

Any appointments? No.

"I think I'll go for a walk."

"Want company?"

It was growing dark. She wanted to walk alone in the darkness and feel those emotions, those simple fears—that a bear might attack her, that something might get her. Because at the moment, it was all she could feel.

Cullen embraced her and helped her dress warmly. In those moments, she was Gina to him. There had been something broken about Gina, something that had made her do the things she'd done, and he wanted to help her heal. Wanted to heal the woman who'd gotten pregnant at twenty by his married brother.

"How long will you be?"

"I don't know. I just want to walk. Don't worry."

He would. He would worry until she returned, but he had to accept her need for solitude. Her need to search inside herself for who she'd been and who she was.

HE WENT TO PICK UP Gabriela at the ballet studio.

Tracy said, "I'm so glad you're going to look at dance schools in New York. Even if it's just for the summer."

Gabriela was excited about the trip to New York. They were going the following weekend.

His mind still on Ivy, he hardly responded to Tracy.

On the way home, Gabriela chatted about ballet and an audition that summer at whichever school she chose.

He listened as best he could, but when they reached the cabin and went inside, he saw that Ivy's coat and hat were still gone. "Your mom's out for a walk. I think I'll go find her."

He took a flashlight and a thermos of warm tea and told himself she'd be all right.

SHE WAS—physically anyhow. "Thanks for the tea. I'm cold."

"See anything interesting?"

"A deer. I followed its trail for a while. Tara says deer can lead you to magical places. So I followed it."

"What did you find?"

She didn't answer. She just shivered and drank some more tea.

"Want to see a professional?"

She shook her head. "I like going forth alone. Or with you."

He embraced her. "I'm always here."

ZEYA WAS GETTING MARRIED again, and Mitzi was taking her to buy a wedding dress. Ivy went along and saw Mitzi smiling over Zeya's choices, frowning at others, giving advice. Ivy was on the outside. Not a sister, not a daughter.

She woke slowly, and Cullen hugged her from behind, snuggled her close in safety. She could feel that he wanted to make love, but she didn't. In fact, she thought she couldn't bear it.

She shivered, trying to stop thinking.

"Why did you finish your workout early?" he asked.

"I couldn't concentrate."

"Ivy, I have some misgivings about what you're doing."

"Me, too."

"What did you feel working on the quilt?"

"Loss. It hurts."

"Do you know what you lost?"

"I think," she admitted, "it's who. Not what." And the tears came, tears for the mother who had died when she was five.

CULLEN AND GABRIELA accompanied her to her next prenatal with Rhonda Davy. Rhonda was five months pregnant. Her baby should arrive before Gabriela went away to study ballet for the summer.

Ivy noticed some change in Chad. When she came for prenatal visits, he at least feigned interest in the baby and caring for Rhonda. Ivy told herself repeatedly, *It is not my job to heal him or to send him away.* She'd never seen evidence that he abused any of the children. She'd never seen him play with them, either. But he was the baby's father.

She'd spoken to Mata Iyer about the situation, and Mata had said, "It's hard to know what to do. Sometimes a hands-off approach seems as useful as anything."

Ivy had begun teaching Gabriela to assess the baby's lie; Gabriela practiced the skill on Rhonda while the children stood near, watching.

When they returned home, the phone was ringing, and Ivy picked it up. It was Tara.

"Guess what?"

"What."

"Alex sold his house and the Victorian to an *obstetrician.*"

Ivy sank into a chair at the kitchen table. "Tell me everything."

"Well, Mom's stopped her home-birth practice, and I'm going up there in the fall. I've agreed to stay at Maternity House until then."

"How does Mom feel about your coming to Precipice?"

"She keeps telling me not to do it, but I've told her it's a free country, and nothing's to stop me from renting a trailer in Precipice. Living with her would probably drive me nuts anyway."

Ivy carefully withheld comment. Tara's voice grounded her, the same way the presence of her family did.

She told Tara about the quilt and the search for her identity.

"Are you doing okay?" Tara asked. "Do you need me? If you do, I'll tell them I have to go. I can give them two weeks later on."

"I think I'm fine. I've found the crux of it—losing my mother."

"Maybe you should put her and your grandmother in your quilt. Start rebuilding your past from the roots up. Use it as a way to celebrate your survival...your strength.'

Ivy drew a deep breath. "Tara—I love you."

THEY LEFT FRIDAY for New York; they were going to spend four days there. In Charleston, Gabriela had bought a dance magazine with reviews of the shows they were going to see. One was classical—Stravinsky's *Firebird*—the other was a performance by the Joffrey Ballet.

She'd also brought a book about ballet schools that profiled the two schools they'd be visiting. Neither of them had boarding options, but they were going to visit an aunt of Cullen's in the city who had expressed interest in Gabriela's staying with her for the summer.

Once they landed, Cullen got a taxi to take them to their hotel. The first ballet was Saturday night, the second a Sunday matinee performance.

In their two-room suite that night, after Gabriela

had gone to sleep on the foldout sofa and while Cullen was down the hall getting ice, Ivy went into their bedroom and took out the quilt to work on it. Using her recollections of photographs of her mother, she began an image of a woman giving birth to a child, to her.

With every stitch, she knew Tara's suggestion had been the right one. Cullen recorded memories with his camera. She would trace her life with this quilt. Not just the grief and sorrow but goodness, too.

When Cullen returned, he sat with her, watching her quilt and finally picking up a needle and thread to quilt with her. "Do you think you've found Gina?" he asked.

She nodded. "Not the Gina I hoped to find. And I guess I'll never completely understand why she—I— did the things she did, what drove her. But I realize I'm going to have to accept the Gina I've found."

THEY WALKED THE STREETS of Manhattan, saw ballets, visited ballet schools and met his aunt.

When they returned home, Gabriela had selected her dance school, and they'd made arrangements for her to stay with Cullen's aunt for the summer—if she was selected in the audition. Auditions for the summer program would be held the week after they returned home in major cities around the country. They would have to spend a week in Atlanta while she went to audition classes.

The following week, Cullen and Ivy drove her to

Atlanta, where they would stay in a historic hotel and visit historic sites when Gabriela wasn't in classes.

THE AUDITION CLASS was huge. Gabriela had never been in a room with so many other dancers, except during the audition for *Nutcracker,* and this felt like an even bigger deal. A girl about her age named Amy said, "There's a whole room full of us. They'll probably choose, like, three."

Gabriela had been warned of that, but seeing how many other dancers wanted to participate in the summer program was different from just hearing about it.

After class each day, she stayed behind practicing while her parents watched and talked together, until someone came to close up the school for the night.

The audition came at last.

Gabriela tried to quiet the butterflies in her stomach. She hadn't felt this nervous since she was Clara in *The Nutcracker* in Charleston. What if she totally flubbed the audition? What if the technique she'd learned from Tracy in Guyandotte wasn't good enough?

The ballet master was Russian, and he'd been picking on Gabriela at every single audition class. It was easy to see he thought she was the worst student in the class, the least likely to make it into the school.

What if she failed in front of her mom and dad? *I'll die. I'll die. I'll never go to ballet class again.*

A thought comforted her. If she wasn't good enough to be a ballet dancer, she could still be a midwife.

But I want to be a dancer. And I'm going to be.
She went out to show what she could do.

AS GABRIELA FINISHED the exercises, everyone in the room applauded. *Is it my imagination,* Ivy wondered, *or are people clapping more loudly for her?* Many of the children had been excellent, but Gabriela... *She's so lovely when she moves.*

They would receive the news by mail, but Ivy had a strong feeling that Gabriela had done well. If only the ballet master's face was easier to read...

Afterward, as the three of them went out to the car together to drive home, Cullen asked his daughter, "How do you think you did?"

Gabriela bit her lip. "I'm not sure. I tried to remember everything he said, but some things were hard."

"In any case, we're proud of you," Ivy told her. "That was a hard thing to do, and you looked it right in the face and did it."

IN THE FOLLOWING WEEKS, Gabriela resumed accompanying Ivy to prenatal appointments. She lived to find out if anything had come in the mail that day.

Ivy resumed work on the quilt, incorporating both facts of her heritage and new, blossoming moments of her life. She included Tara and Francesca as well as Cullen and Gabriela, the Rockies as well as the Appalachians. She felt herself—and Gina—beginning to heal. And Cullen sat beside her and helped with his man's fingers, appliquéing the cabin, their home, to the fabric.

Ivy, Shelby and Gabriela had finished piecing the other quilt and had put it on a frame when Shelby announced, "So. I'm pregnant again."

It was March, and Gabriela immediately asked, "If I get to go to New York, will I be back for the birth?"

"When are you due, Shelby?"

"Late October."

Gabriela gave a thumbs-up.

Later, when Ivy walked her out to the car, Shelby revealed, "Matthew's started talking to someone, a therapist. A guy in Charleston."

"Great!"

"I'm pretty happy about it." Shelby hugged her. "And you're doing okay?"

Ivy nodded. "Everything's wonderful. I'm putting in a garden."

"How's your own quilt coming?"

"Better than I could have dreamed. I'm beginning to know myself. I didn't know how badly I needed to."

Shelby smiled into her eyes. "I'm sure I'll like it."

The remark brought Ivy some peace. Gina, with her pain and her problems, was part of her. And thanks to Cullen and Gabriela, she'd become whole.

GABRIELA HAD NO TROUBLE keeping the names of the herbs straight in her mind. As she and her mother walked in the woods collecting them, she tried to absorb everything Ivy said about when certain herbs should be picked.

Later today, they were going to Rhonda's. Gabriela's dad had helped Rhonda and Chad with their water problems, and he'd fixed their stove. The kids seemed a little cleaner lately. Her dad had taken some photos of them with their mom and given them to Rhonda.

She heard a camera shutter, and Ivy turned around. "What are you doing here?"

Smiling, Cullen pushed through the weeds. "An appointment canceled, and I thought I'd come home and find my family."

"We're about done." Ivy lifted her face for his kiss. "Gabriela and I need to take these home and hang them to dry."

"I'll carry those, Gabriela," he offered, reaching for the sack brimming with cut herbs.

"Can I go home and start practicing, Mom?" *Darn. If only that letter would come. I'm going crazy.*

"Sure. Go on. Your dad can help me."

As she left, running over the grass, Cullen said, "It's going to be a long summer without her."

"You're telling me."

"But a good chance for you and me to spend more time together."

"Yes."

"Matthew came by the studio today."

Ivy knew this was significant. "What did he have to say? Anything?"

"Yes. He said he was sorry for sleeping with my wife."

Ivy consulted his face. She knew this remained a sore subject for Cullen—and probably always would.

She was right. His eyes had taken on a cold look, the unforgiving look. "I asked him if you two used birth control. He said you used some natural method. Which was what you did with me."

The baby could have been Matthew's. Or Cullen's.

"I'm sorry." How long would she have to apologize for this? When would he forgive?

She took a shallow breath. "I have some news for you."

"Yes?"

"I'd planned to tell you at a happier moment."

He waited, facing her in the tall weeds beneath the trees.

Come on, Cullen. Please. Forgive and forget. "I'm pregnant."

His mouth opened and shut. His eyes changed slightly, softening some.

He took her hand to walk home.

"Can you forgive me, Cullen? Really forgive me?"

"I'm working on it. In some ways, it was easier before your quilt. Now…you've become more Gina to me, as well." *And you're part of me, and I can't help it.*

"Is there anything, anything in the world, that I can do to make up for it?"

"Ivy, you know there's not. You can't make up for

it. But I love you, which you know, and you love me, and we should both try not to forget that."

"What if—" She stopped him on the trail they were following. "What if we got married again? Renewed our vows? We could do it alone or with your family. Do you think it would help?"

He considered. She'd healed some of Gina's wounds. And he and Matthew had settled some of their differences. Matthew and Shelby were having a child of their own. He and Ivy were having a child.

"How about…" he suggested uncertainly, "a double ceremony?"

"With Matthew and Shelby? Will Zeya and Tom feel left out?"

"I think Zeya will understand what's going on."

"I'd love that, Cullen. Shelby is a sister to me the way Tara is."

"Let's wait a little while," he cautioned. "I need to sort some things out."

Ivy understood and felt some misgivings. He was saying he wanted to forgive her completely but didn't know how.

"WHEN SHOULD WE TELL Gabriela?" he asked her that night.

"I'm not sure. Soon." Ivy frowned. "She'll need time to accept the idea. Who knows what she'll feel about the baby? She was deprived of me for crucial years of her life, and she'll have to see me care for a younger sibling and be there all the time for that child."

"She'll get used to it. I couldn't love her more than I do."

Cullen realized how hard he sounded and knew that his bitterness toward Matthew was tied to the child Ivy now carried.

I've got to get rid of those feelings.

He closed his eyes. "You're right about Gabriela. I vote on telling her sooner rather than later."

"Let's wait at least a week or so. It's very early yet."

She could lose the baby. He didn't even want to think about that. Anger washed through him, anger at himself.

Why couldn't he just feel love for his family, including the new baby inside Ivy? Why couldn't he be the one to pull them all together? *I have to get to that point. I have to get rid of this anger somehow.*

He told Ivy, "A week or so sounds fine."

THE FOLLOWING SUNDAY, while Ivy and Shelby and Gabriela worked on their quilt, Cullen hiked by himself back into the woods, enjoying the spring, feeling the onset of summer with its bugs and humidity. The bugs were already bad, but he wanted to return to a place where he'd seen a fox the other day.

He wanted to be alone to think about what Ivy had said.

To think about the nature of true forgiveness.

Thoughts of Matthew and Gina had faded entirely for a while. But Matthew had brought them back, and the notion that the child she'd been carrying could just as well have been his brother's, the fact that the possibility was very real, might drive him mad.

It occurred to him sometimes that his father had known, too—and that he'd pushed Gina down the stairs because of it.

By now, he'd seen enough of Ivy's emotional memory through the quilt that he could sympathize with what Gina must have suffered.

But it doesn't lessen her blame.

I married her. I agreed to become her child's father.

And she had betrayed him.

All he could come up with was the fact that he had a choice. He could hold on to this and let it make them both unhappy. Or he could rid himself of it.

But how to do that?

With a symbol?

What would symbolize Gina's betrayal?

He gazed down at his camera, and he knew.

CHAPTER FOURTEEN

HE'D SELECTED the wedding photo at random, barely glancing at it before tucking it in his shirt pocket to take to the river, the river where his father had died. Now he stood by the water, watching the tadpoles and the fish swimming in a slow eddy, and removed the photograph from his pocket.

He looked at it and saw his own young face, his love for Gina, and her smile back at him, a smile he'd interpreted in different ways—as trusting, as loving, even as manufactured for onlookers. He still couldn't guess what she'd really felt at that moment, but he couldn't quite believe she'd married him planning to continue sleeping with Matthew.

Their hands were joined, and he knew what he'd felt. He was going to marry the woman he most loved, the woman he most desired. They were going to have the baby at home....

He swallowed.

He'd planned to drop the photo in the river, to throw out the old marriage, the bad marriage, with its betrayal and pain.

He could not.

It was the same marriage he had today.

And he loved it.

He placed the photo back in his pocket and walked up the bank to go home.

GABRIELA FELT HER MOUTH falling open. Of course. Her mother and father *could* have another baby. It just never crossed her mind that they would. Her mind leaped to Rhonda's children, to Scout, to all the children who had annoyed her at one time or another. "Am I going to have to take care of it?"

Her mother laughed. "Of course not. It's not your baby."

"Phew." Gabriela released a sigh and looked somewhere between the two of them. She didn't even want to *think* about her parents doing what was required to make a baby.

Her mother was watching her in a penetrating way. "How do you feel?"

Well, you could have consulted me. But it didn't seem like the kind of thing parents did. She shrugged. "It's your headache."

Her dad said, "But we're a family. You're going to have a sister or brother."

Gabriela tried to imagine it. A baby in the house, and her mother would nurse it. She had the most interesting idea. What if *she* could help at the birth? "Can I help when the baby's being born?"

"All you want. I think I might try to arrange for Tara to come out here if she can, or for us to go there."

"The baby should be born here." Gabriela glanced around the living room. "All the babies in our family are born in this cabin. We don't want her—or him—to be born in Colorado.''

Ivy smiled, relieved by her reaction. ''Okay. If everything looks like it's going well, maybe we'll do it like we did with you. But you have to keep in mind I'm not twenty years old anymore.''

A thought needled Gabriela. What if the baby was a girl and grew up to want to be a midwife? Would her mother love the baby more? Especially now that she was going away to school...

Her father sat beside her on the couch and put his arm around her shoulders to hug her. ''Gabby. We're not going to love you any less. No one could replace you.''

She felt silly then. What was she, six? ''I'm not jealous.''

Her mother said, ''It's okay if you are. Or pissed off or anything else. Just know how much we love you.''

Gabriela smiled. ''I think I do.''

Her dad had stopped hugging her and taken her mother's hand. ''So the other thing...'' And he told her about the renewing of their vows.

GABRIELA'S LETTER CAME the next day.

Ivy stopped at Cullen's studio on the way to pick up Gabriela after school. ''It's here.''

''Did you hold it up to the light?''

She laughed. ''Of course. But I couldn't read anything. I guess Gabriela will have to tell us. Want to come with me?''

He shook his head. "Better not. In case she didn't get in."

"Good thought." Ivy kissed him. "If it's good news, we'll come by and tell you."

WHEN HER MOTHER HANDED her the envelope in the car, Gabriela trembled. "It's no big deal," she said. "If I didn't make it, I can still do other things. Maybe I can get into another summer program or something."

"We're proud of you in any case." Ivy waited a moment to see if Gabriela would open the envelope.

A second later, she did. Her face lit up, and she couldn't prevent a small shriek. "They gave me a scholarship!"

She started to cry, and Ivy hugged her tight.

CULLEN, IVY, MATTHEW and Shelby set the renewal of vows for May Day, and Shelby and Ivy shopped together for their dresses, with Gabriela along to give her frank opinion. They'd decided to have the ceremony at the state park. They'd say their vows to each other with Tom standing in as minister. They were already married after all.

On May Day, the whole family gathered in the park. Cullen remembered the last time he'd been there with his father, when snow was on the ground.

As they prepared to begin, Gabriela straightened her mother's ivory cotton skirt and chemise, then the flowers on her head. "I want to tell you something," she said. "Not that it really matters. I just thought you might like to know."

"What, Gabriela?"

Her mother's smile was so beautiful. *Should I bring it up? Well, why not?* "Tracy's getting married."

Ivy carefully concealed her flicker of annoyance at the mention of the name and concentrated on the news. She was truly happy for Tracy. It couldn't be easy to find the person you wanted to marry in such a small town. "That's great. I'm so pleased."

"He sells real estate, I think, or something boring like that."

Ivy laughed. "Obviously, she doesn't think so."

She glanced toward the area on the grass where Shelby and Matthew were holding hands, gazing into each other's eyes, and then she saw Cullen, waiting for her.

"Okay." She kissed her daughter. "Here we go."

"DO YOU, IVY, TAKE CULLEN to be your husband, to have and to hold, for richer for poorer, for better for worse, in sickness and in health, as long as you both shall live?"

Her eyes met his, giving a promise that she would always remember, and that her heart had remembered from long ago. "I do."

As Cullen repeated his vows, his eyes were on hers, and she knew he'd finally forgiven her, that the past was behind them and they were ready to move forward together. And she heard the healing and commitment in Matthew's and Shelby's voices, too, as they repeated their vows to each other.

As each couple kissed, Mitzi, Gabriela, Zeya and Scout cheered, and Ivy and Shelby turned, as planned, and scattered handfuls of flower petals all over the family.

Mitzi embraced each of the brides in turn, and for the first time Ivy thought she saw real warmth in her mother-in-law's eyes. She said softly, "I'm so glad you came back. Cullen and Gabriela needed you so much."

"Thank you." Ivy hugged her. "And I'm glad to be home."

Her purse, which Gabriela was holding, emitted a series of beeps.

Everyone turned toward the sound of the pager, and Ivy said, "Sorry," and hurriedly checked it.

The answering service.

"I'll bet you anything," she told her daughter, "that Miss Rhonda is in labor."

IVY HAD A FEELING this would be a long labor and hoped it wouldn't be. Rhonda's previous labors had been long, she was uncomfortable with physical exams and she'd been a victim of sexual abuse; she'd told Ivy that. One of her other children had been delivered by paramedics, the other in the emergency room.

The message had been left with the answering service by Chad. He'd said Rhonda had started having cramps early that morning, before it was light.

Since Rhonda had no phone, Ivy changed into the spare clothes she always kept in the car and Cullen drove her to the house, promising to return with Gabriela after they'd both changed their clothes.

Ivy found Rhonda pacing the front room. She wore a green cotton sundress. Chad was holding one of the children and yelling at the other one to be quiet, Mom was having a baby.

Ivy picked up Justin and held him as she asked Rhonda, "How are you feeling?"

"I feel like I'm halfway there. It's getting intense."

Halfway? Ivy watched the next contraction, timed it. "Justin, let me put you down so I can see how your mommy's doing, and then I'll hold you again, all right?"

IT WAS 9:00 p.m. Progress through the first stage had been slow, and Gabriela had swept the little dwelling, played with the two children and gotten them both to sleep.

In the curtained-off bedroom, Rhonda repeated, "I really don't want to be touched." No one was trying to touch her.

If Rhonda and Chad had been a different kind of couple, Ivy might have suggested they kiss and cuddle in the privacy of the bedroom. She said, "Well, I'm sure Chad won't try to touch you if you go for a walk with him. And if you need someone's hand to hold, he'll be there."

Her eyes distrustful—of her surroundings, of Chad, of Ivy—Rhonda slowly climbed off the bed. "Okay."

Ivy was glad to see Chad help her on with her sweater and kneel down to tie her shoes. Rhonda actually reached out and stroked his hair, then cast another glance at Ivy.

They all left the bedroom, and in the middle of the living room, Rhonda had another contraction. She looked exhausted, and though Rhonda had kept her liquids up, she hadn't been able to sleep. "When you get back," Ivy said, "if you've had a little more progress, we might try rupturing the membranes."

Rhonda nodded, and the couple went out.

Cullen rose from where he'd been sitting with Gabriela and approached Ivy. "How's the midwife holding out?"

"All right." In reality, she was feeling some of the exhaustion of early pregnancy. "You know, I think I'll nap until they come back. When you hear them, will you wake me?"

"Sure."

BY THREE IN THE MORNING, Rhonda was ready to push. She sat back in her bed with Chad holding her, while Ivy supported the baby's head, making sure it wasn't born so quickly that Rhonda would tear.

When the head was born, Ivy discovered the cord around the baby's neck, explained the situation to Rhonda and asked her to pant. "Rhonda, I'm going to loosen the cord and try to slip it over his shoulder. I can keep it loose enough for him to be born safely, and then we'll unwrap it." A few moments later, she said, "Okay, Rhonda, you can push now. You're doing great."

As the baby was born, Ivy guided it into a sort of somersault, to keep his head close against Rhonda and not tighten the cord. Gabriela watched its wet pink body come into the world as she'd watched Devon's baby being born. *How could I ever have thought birth was gross?* she wondered. It was totally amazing! "He's so cute."

Her mother unwound the cord and said, "Oh, look at you, you sweet little boy." Gently, Ivy placed the baby on Rhonda's stomach.

Chad twisted around to see the baby's face. "Look at him. Oh, wow!"

Rhonda touched her new son. "He's beautiful. Dylan. Dylan Jason Davy."

"You did so well, Rhonda," Ivy said, watching carefully for vaginal bleeding, for signs the placenta was coming.

Cullen asked, "Would you like some photos?"

"We can't buy 'em." Rhonda didn't lift her head.

"I give them away to new moms and dads."

"Thanks," Chad said, posing beside Rhonda with a big grin. "Thanks a lot."

ON THE WAY HOME, Ivy said, "So now I have a resident photographer."

"I think every couple should get the chance to have photos of their newborn and whatever photos of the birth they want."

Ivy briefly covered his gearshift hand and smiled tiredly at the man to whom she'd renewed her vows.

In the back seat, Gabriela said, "That was the cutest baby I ever saw."

Her dad said, "Oh, I've seen one I think was cuter."

"Mom?"

"Yes?"

"Do you think by the time our baby is born, I could catch it?"

"I think that's very possible. Barring any big problems, you can certainly help."

Gabriela shivered with excitement. In her heart, she knew how it would be, and she couldn't wait.

AFTER GABRIELA HAD GONE to bed, Ivy and Cullen made quiet love up in the loft. Later, holding her, Cullen said, "Renewing our vows was a good idea. You know, I went to the river to throw out one of our old wedding photos, like I was going to throw out the first years of our marriage, and I couldn't do it. I have no regrets, Ivy. Not one. I loved you then, and I love you now."

These words, more than anything yet, brought her a feeling of peace with herself. With her past, with her present, with her future as his wife and Gabriela's mother and the mother of the baby inside her.

"That makes two of us," she said. "With no regrets."

CHAPTER FIFTEEN

GABRIELA'S THIRTEENTH birthday fell two weeks before she left for New York. She would stay with her great-aunt Chloe, her grandmother's sister, and early in July her parents would come stay in the city for a week to spend time with her.

They'd decided to have her birthday party at home, and Tara drove up from Texas; Francesca wasn't able to come with so many clients due. After dinner, they all sat in the sunroom listening to the sound of insects outside, and Gabriela opened her presents, choosing Tara's first. Before unwrapping the purple tissue paper, Gabriela read the handmade card that said, "To the coolest girl I know. Love, Tara." She opened the package and drew out a hand-painted T-shirt bearing the legend "Mountain Midwifery" and pictures of many of the herbs she'd picked with her mother. "Look—nettles! And a raspberry bush!"

Tara said, "You can advertise your mom's business and tell people about midwifery if you want. It's big, so you can wear it over your dance clothes or to bed or whatever."

"I love it!" She did, too. She helped her mom so much she was part of Mountain Midwifery anyhow.

The next package, from her parents, contained

some CDs she wanted. Then her dad gave her a framed picture of him and her mom. The last package was from her mom, and it was pretty heavy.

Her mother sat beside her on the wood-frame couch in the sunroom as Gabriela untied the ribbons on the yellow tissue-paper package. Her mother had tucked dried flowers into the ribbon, and Gabriela couldn't help smiling at her. Her mom was so special.

She removed the tissue paper carefully and opened the box. "Oh, wow!" On top were new copies of *Spiritual Midwifery* and *Heart and Hands*. Beneath was her great-grandmother's midwifery book, with handwritten notes on different types of deliveries.

She grabbed her mom and hugged her. "I love you. This is the best present ever."

LATE THAT NIGHT, after her family members from Coalgood had stopped by with more gifts for Gabriela, Tara and Ivy sat curled up in the sunroom to talk.

"So, how's Mom doing with the new landlord?"

"He's given her notice that after December, when her lease expires, he'll be renting the Victorian to skiers on a weekly basis."

"*What?* That beautiful house? He's out of his mind."

"Mom says he wants the money. It's making her sick, you can tell. For the time being, she's even stopped arguing with me about my coming back there."

That had been a real sticking point between the two

of them. Francesca was for law and order; Tara believed in a woman's right to have her babies wherever and with whatever attendant she wished. And Francesca had voiced to Ivy her concern that Tara's arrival in Precipice could hurt her own reputation; Tara was a well-trained and experienced midwife, but she wasn't licensed to attend births in Colorado. Only certified nurse-midwives were.

"Well, can you really find a place to live? Will *she* be able to find another place to live?"

"She's looking already, but it's too early. And she can't afford to buy a house in Precipice. Who can?"

"No kidding." Ivy changed the subject tentatively. "So, I don't suppose you've met any interesting men in Sagrado?"

Tara laughed and shook her head. "You think I *want* a man?"

"Still hurting over Danny?"

"It doesn't hurt anymore."

"Even that he and Solange are having a baby?"

Tara made a face. "That has a tendency to evoke disgust in me, I have to admit. But I mostly get angry. No, I don't feel hurt."

Ivy wondered if Tara had ever given in to her feelings of hurt about Danny. She'd never shown them to Ivy. "I think the move to Precipice might be a good thing for you."

"Sure, I can meet someone rich and drive a Hummer and build my own birth clinic."

Ivy giggled at the picture Tara painted, and Tara laughed, too.

"Not," she concluded.

"We'll see," Ivy teased. "Or maybe it'll be the landlord-OB/GYN."

"Never."

"What if he's like Michel Odent?" Ivy named the French physician who'd long been an advocate for natural births and water births.

Tara kissed the air. "Well, *that* would change everything. But it's hardly what I expect from the greedy low-life scum who's kicking Mom out of her home."

AT THE FIRST boarding call, which included children traveling alone, Ivy and Cullen hugged Gabriela and walked with her to the airline representative who would be responsible for her until Aunt Chloe met her at the airport in New York.

After introducing Gabriela to the attendant and exchanging the paperwork, Ivy hugged her once more. "I love you. You can call us any time you want, any hour of the day or night."

Gabriela's smile said she was unlikely to call them at all.

Her dad hugged her next. "I'll miss you."

"I'll miss you, too. Both of you."

It was time to part. Gabriela carried her tote bag slung over her shoulder. She looked older and more self-assured than thirteen.

When she'd disappeared from sight, Ivy said, "We should watch the plane take off."

"Yes."

As they stood beside a window, arms around each other, and watched the plane finally move away from the gate, Ivy said, "You know, I never think of her as Matthew's and my child. Never. I sometimes completely forget that she's not your biological child."

Sometimes, rarely, Cullen forgot, too. He said, "I couldn't love her more. She's wonderful." He turned Ivy to face him. "And speaking of people I couldn't love more..."

"I hurt you, Cullen. I'll never forget that fact."

"But I forgive you." His eyes were on hers. "Completely and forever."

They turned to the window and watched the plane lift into the sky, carrying Gabriela to her dreams.

EPILOGUE

October

"SHELBY, YOU'RE DOING beautifully."

Ivy held Shelby's eyes through the next contraction while Matthew supported his wife as she sat on a beanbag chair and leaned back against him. Gabriela knelt beside her mother, and a camera shutter clicked.

"Gabriela, put your hands here." Ivy showed her how to push gently against the baby's head to slow the delivery. "Shelby, you can push. Try to do it in a long breath. Push with your breath. We want the head to come out slow and easy."

Between contractions, Ivy placed hot compresses on Shelby's perineum.

When the baby's head was born, Gabriela checked to make certain the cord wasn't around the neck. The baby's head rotated toward Shelby's right thigh, and as the shoulders came through, the infant opened its mouth in a yawn or a silent cry. There was the click of a camera.

The infant had been born into Gabriela's arms, and she carefully brought his slippery body up onto Shelby's stomach. She felt a sense of holiness. After a summer spent dancing, this was a different world, and she felt it tugging her in, pulling at her. *Oh, God, beautiful baby, beautiful birth.*

"A boy," Matthew said. "Look at him, Shelby."

A peacefulness settled on the two parents and their child, and Gabriela half leaned against her mother while Cullen photographed the new family and Ivy twisted around to see the baby's face again.

Behind his wife and daughter, Cullen lowered the camera and met his brother's eyes, and they were open and warm and filled with love for those around him.

READER SERVICE

The best romantic fiction direct to your door

Our guarantee to you...

The Reader Service involves you in no obligation to purchase, and is truly a service to you!

There are many extra benefits including a free monthly Newsletter with author interviews, book previews and much more.

Your books are sent direct to your door on 14 days no obligation home approval.

We offer free postage and packing for subscribers in the UK—we guarantee you won't find any hidden extras.

Plus, we have a dedicated Customer Care team on hand to answer all your queries on
(UK) 0181 288 2888
(Ireland) 01 278 2062.
There is also a 24 hour message facility on this number.

Historical Romance™

From Medieval pageantry
to the Restoration
and glittering Regency Seasons

1066 - 1920
all the ages of romance

Four new titles available every month

Available from

READER SERVICE

The best romantic fiction direct to your door

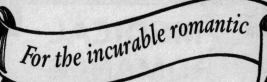

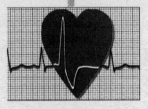

GIRL *in the* MIRROR
MARY ALICE MONROE

Charlotte Godowski and Charlotte Godfrey
are two sides to the same woman—a woman
who can trust no one with her secret. But
when fate forces Charlotte to deal with the
truth about her past, about the man she loves,
about her self—she discovers that only love
has the power to transform a scarred soul.

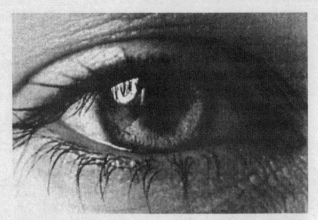

SWEET REVENGE

NORA ROBERTS

Adrianne led a remarkable double life. Daughter of a Hollywood beauty and an Arab playboy, the paparazzi knew her as a frivolous socialite darting from exclusive party to glittering charity ball. But no one knew her as The Shadow, a jewel thief with a secret ambition to carry out the ultimate robbery—a plan to even the score.

The Shadow was intent on justice.

MIRA®

**Available in October
from The Reader Service™**